Acclaim for Vannetta Chapman

"... a fun read for both mystery and Amish fiction readers."

—*RT Book Reviews*, 3-star review
on *Murder Tightly Knit*

"[Chapman] adeptly fleshes out her characters and weaves in facts about the Amish faith without overwhelming the narrative. Readers of inspirational fiction and fans of Beverly Lewis will delight in this gentle mystery."

—*Library Journal*, for *Murder Tightly Knit*

"Readers will enjoy figuring out the murder mystery while also growing close to the characters as they fall in love, learn more about one another, and grow deeper in their faith."

—*Booklist*, for *Murder Tightly Knit*

"Vannetta Chapman keeps the action suspenseful, and the who-done-it mostly unpredictable as her Amish and English characters work together to solve the mystery. Out of even such dreadful circumstances come moments of grace: between Amber and her Amish employee Hannah and between Amber and Tate, who had each given up on love."

—*BookPage.com*, for *Murder Simply Brewed*

"Vannetta Chapman has crafted a tightly woven tale in the best tradition of the cozy mystery ... Chapman's light touch and thoughtful representation of the Amish culture make *Murder Simply Brewed* a delightful read for an evening by a warm fire, a cup of tea in hand."

—Kelly Irvin, author of *The Beekeeper's Son* and the Bliss Creek Amish series

"*Murder Simply Brewed* combines all the coziness of an Amish home with the twists and turns of a great suspense. With a little romance thrown it, you can't go wrong! Vannetta Chapman has crafted a charming story that shows things aren't always as they first appear."

—Beth Shriver, bestselling author of the Touch of Grace trilogy

Other Books by Vannetta Chapman

The Amish Village Mystery Series

Murder Simply Brewed
Murder Tightly Knit
Murder Freshly Baked

The Shipshewana Amish Mystery Series

Falling to Pieces
A Perfect Square
Material Witness

Stories

Where Healing Blooms included in *An Amish Garden*
An Unexpected Blessing included in *An Amish Cradle*
Mischief in the Autumn Air included in *An Amish Harvest*
Love in Store included in *An Amish Market*

A Perfect Square

A Shipshewana Amish Mystery

VANNETTA CHAPMAN

ZONDERVAN

A Perfect Square
Copyright © 2012 by Vannetta Chapman

This title is also available as a Zondervan ebook.
Visit www.zondervan.com/ebooks.

This title is also available in a Zondervan audio edition.
Visit www.zondervan.fm.

Requests for information should be addressed to:
Zondervan, *Grand Rapids, Michigan* 49530

ISBN 978-0-7852-1713-8 (repack)

Library of Congress Cataloging-in-Publication Data

Chapman, Vannetta.
    A perfect square : a Shipshewana Amish mystery/ Vannetta Chapman.
      p. cm.—(Shipshewana Amish mystery ; bk. 2)
    ISBN 978-0-310-33044-8 (softcover)
    1. Amish—Fiction. 2. Murder—Investigation—Fiction. 3. Shipshewana
(Ind.)—Fiction. I. Title.
PS3603.H3744P47 2012
813'.6—dc23   2011048414

Cover design: Anderson Design Group
Cover images: Flash Parker / gettyimages®

Printed in the United States of America

---

18 19 20 21 22 23 /LSC/ 21 20 19 18 17 16 15 14 13 12 11 10 9 8 7 6 5 4 3 2 1

To my father-in-law,
George Robert Chapman

While this novel is set against the real backdrop of Shipshewana, Indiana, the characters are fictional. There is no intended resemblance between the characters in this book and any real members of the Amish and Mennonite communities. As with any work of fiction, I've taken license in some areas of research as a means of creating the necessary circumstances for my characters. My research was thorough; however, it would be impossible to be completely accurate in details and descriptions, since each and every community differs. Therefore, any inaccuracies in the Amish and Mennonite lifestyles portrayed in this book are completely due to fictional license.

Glossary

ack — Oh

aenti — aunt

boppli — baby

bopplin — babies

bruder — brother

daadi — grandfather, informal

daed — father

danki — thank you

dat — dad

Dietsch — Pennsylvania Dutch

dochder — daughter

dochdern — daughters

eck — corner

Englischer — non-Amish person

fraa — wife

freind — friend

freinden — friends

gelassenheit — calmness, composure, placidity

gern gschehne — you're welcome

Gotte's wille — God's will

grandkinner — grandchildren

grossdaddi — grandfather

grossdochdern — granddaughters

grossmammi — grandmother

gudemariye — good morning

gut — good

in lieb — in love

kaffi — coffee

kapp — prayer covering

kind — child

kinner — children

mamm — mom

mammi — grandmother, informal

naerfich — nervous

narrisch — crazy

onkel — uncle

Ordnung — set of rules for Amish living

rumspringa — running around; time before an Amish young person has officially joined the church, provides a bridge between childhood and adulthood

schweschder — sister

was iss letz — what's wrong

wunderbaar — wonderful

ya — yes

Chapter 1

"LESS THAN TWO WEEKS UNTIL THE WEDDING." Deborah Yoder glanced once at Esther, then focused again on the dirt lane, her horse Cinnamon, and guiding the buggy down the rutted path.

On both sides of them, fields of fall corn rose, golden and plump, ready for harvest. They shaded the lane so that the mid-morning sun broke through in a slatted fashion, as if it were winking at them.

Joshua and Leah spoke in hushed tones from the backseat, caught up in some game that children play. It never failed to amaze Deborah how they managed to find amusement in the smallest things. Yesterday it had been twisting stalks of corn shucks into absurd figures.

When Esther didn't comment, Deborah looked at her friend again. Esther's hands clutched the casserole bowl firmly, but she managed a radiant smile.

"*Ya.* Less than two weeks. One part of me wishes it were tomorrow. That I could wake up and we would be living our life together, as man and wife."

"And the other part?"

"The other part agrees with Tobias. There's still much to do

1

before he moves into my home. We're not ready, and as much as I'd like to wish the days away, I know it's all a part of the season and something I won't want to forget. Less than two weeks. I should be grateful for each day, as Tobias reminds me."

Deborah smiled as she began circling the small pond at the far end of Tobias and his cousin Reuben's place—actually it was their *grossdaddi*'s place, but they'd been farming it for the last several years. "Tobias has become quite industrious since he asked you to marry him. He's always been a hard worker, but in the last few months it's as if he's a man on a mission. He wants everything to be perfect."

"I know. He's working even more hours at the feed store, and he still needs to help with the harvest." Esther's hands worried over the top of the casserole dish. "That's why I wanted to bring them dinner. I'm not sure they eat well with Reuben's cooking."

Deborah laughed out loud, causing both children to pop up and hang over the front seat. "I've no doubt they'll be glad you made the chicken and potatoes. They don't strike me as *wunderbaar* cooks. Reuben burned the *kaffi* the last few times I stopped by. I wouldn't fuss over them too much though. I think the women in their family bring them dinners fairly often."

"I spoke with Tobias' mother Saturday when I saw her in town. No one was coming by tonight so—" Esther reached out and clutched Deborah's arm. "Could you stop the buggy? Just for a moment?"

Following her friend's gaze, Deborah immediately spied the tall bunches of wildflowers growing on the pond's southwestern side.

Black-eyed Susans swayed among autumn goldenrods, dipping and rising beside the blue water of the small pond in the late October morning. Nearly buried in switchgrass that was close to three-feet tall, Deborah was surprised they were able to see the cluster of wildflowers at all. If they hadn't been riding in the buggy, they would have missed the beautiful sight, which looked to Deborah like colors from a patchwork quilt.

Esther's fingers tightened their grasp on her arm. "Can we stop?"

"We don't have to be at Daisy's Quilt Shop for another hour. Let's pick a few."

"Callie will love them," Esther agreed.

"And when they're dried, you can keep the seeds for your garden." Deborah pulled the buggy to the side, noticing that Cinnamon was acting a bit nervous, tossing her head and dancing to the right of the road. "Whoa, girl."

"Will she be okay?" Esther asked, even as she pulled small quilting scissors out of her sewing bag.

"I'm sure. I'll stay here. You go and gather the flowers."

"Later I'll regret using sewing scissors for gardening."

"Callie will have cleaning solution, and you'll only snip a few. You use those for thread, not cloth. It will be fine."

"I want to go, *Mamm*." Leah's sweet little face peeped forward from the backseat toward her mother, Esther. She had recently turned three and had come out of her shell quite a bit over the last few months—perhaps because her mother was no longer so sad. Perhaps because her mother was *in lieb*.

Deborah's little Joshua wasn't far behind her.

"Josh go," he said, struggling to crawl out of the buggy.

Deborah studied her son. He'd recently turned eighteen months old, and some days she worried that he'd be the last baby she'd ever hold in her arms. "You? I thought you'd stay with me and Cinnamon."

"Josh go," he repeated stubbornly. He continued to reach past her, knocking the wool cap loose from his head in his attempt to climb out of the buggy and follow Leah. He was at the stage where he imitated Leah or Mary or his twin brothers every chance he got.

With a sigh, Deborah set him on the ground and tugged once on his cap before he darted away. Joshua smiled up at her, cap askew, pointed at the mare, and declared, "Ceemon."

The horse shook her head again, rattling the harness.

"I'll look after Cinnamon," Deborah said as she followed them around the buggy and stood with her hand on the mare. "You two go with Esther, but stay close to her and come back as soon as she says. We're going to see Miss Callie this morning."

Esther allowed each child to clasp one of her hands as they walked toward the flowers by the water's edge.

Deborah kept one eye on them as they wound their way through the tall grass, but another part of her mind was focusing on the mare. She ran one hand down her neck, whispering and stroking, attempting to calm her. Still, Cinnamon shook her harness and tried to pull away. Deborah ran a hand down the length of the mare's leg, wondering if perhaps she had something lodged in one of her hooves. She'd seemed fine trotting down the lane.

"Easy, girl. What's wrong?" Patting the mare's neck, Deborah found that the horse was actually trembling. Sweat slicked her coat though the morning was cool.

Deborah's own heart rate kicked up a notch as she responded to the mare's anxiety.

Maybe she had missed something. Perhaps there was a snake nearby or an animal carcass in the weeds. Deborah was scanning the surrounding area looking for the cause of Cinnamon's anxiety when she noticed where the dry grass was stamped down to the north. It looked as if someone had traveled the opposite direction of Esther and the children, though still heading toward the water, sometime earlier. The path that had been beaten down was wider than footsteps—smaller than a buggy.

Like something had been dragged.

The path extended well past the area where Deborah had stopped with the buggy . . .

She glanced back to where Esther still stooped among the flowers and the children played.

Yes, the path led to the opposite end of the pond. Deborah was surprised she hadn't noticed it earlier, but she'd been focused on the flowers. It was hard to imagine that Tobias and Reuben had taken the time to come out here, unless they'd been fishing. But Tobias had been so busy working double shifts at the feed store and on the farm, which had left Reuben pulling extra weight in the fields.

She focused again on the scene, tried to find the piece she was missing.

Esther and the children stood beside the water, snipping flower stems.

A slight breeze stirred the water.

Geese crossed the blue autumn sky, heading north, their cry piercing the morning, then fading, leaving it quiet but not peaceful.

Cinnamon tossed her head one more time, nearly pulling the harness out of Deborah's hand, when the morning's silence was broken by Esther's scream.

Callie Harper clomped down the stairs from her apartment to her quilt shop, tugging at her long, plain, dark green dress with one hand and readjusting the tie to her apron with the other. Oh, how Rick would laugh to see her now. There were a lot of things her husband would be amused to know about her new life. There wasn't a day since he'd died that she didn't miss him, didn't wish he could share things with her. This though ... oh, he would laugh about the dress.

She wanted to reach up and scratch under the *kapp* on her head, but it had taken so long to corral her shoulder-length dark hair underneath the white bonnet, she didn't want to displace any of it.

When she turned the corner into the shop's main room, her yellow Labrador, Max, let out a whine and placed his head on his paws.

Lydia, the seventeen-year-old girl who worked for her full time now and was currently helping her stock, dissolved into a torrent of giggles.

"Why are you laughing?" Callie spun in a circle. "Don't I look exactly like you?"

"No." Lydia collapsed onto the stool behind the counter. "You do not look like me at all."

"But I pinned the dress right."

"*Ya.*"

"And I put the apron on correctly, though I don't know how you manage to tie it in the back just so. I had the hardest time with that."

"The tie is fine."

"It's the *kapp*, isn't it? My hair isn't long like yours, but it still didn't want to stay in." She moved to a mirror that ran along the top of a fabric display. As she suspected, her dark hair had begun to escape from various corners of the white *kapp*. She looked nothing like the neat Amish women who were her friends.

She looked like what she was: an imposter.

"I don't think the *kapp* or the clothing is the problem." Lydia propped her chin on her hand and studied her employer. "It's not our clothes that make us Amish. It's obvious you're only pretending—an *Englischer* in plain clothing."

"Fix me." Callie's hands flapped at her side. "I have to sneak into Mrs. Knepp's store. To do that, I need to look plain."

"Why?"

"Because."

"I like how you normally dress. Why can't you look *Englisch*?"

"She's suspicious of all *Englischers*."

"Mrs. Knepp is suspicious of everyone—Amish or *Englisch*." Lydia hopped off the stool and joined Callie in front of the narrow mirror.

"You look a bit like her. Mrs. Knepp is exactly your size, only much older."

"She's ancient and her eyesight is poor. If I wear this, maybe she won't recognize me." Callie squinted her eyes at the mirror. "No doubt she does a better job taming her hair."

Carefully pulling the hairpins away one by one, Lydia removed the *kapp*, freeing her boss's dark curls.

"Now I look like a prairie girl," Callie said.

"*Ya*. You should change before a delivery happens by. And we wouldn't want Trent McCallister to happen in and snap a picture of you in this dress, then splash it across the front page of the *Shipshewana Gazette*."

Both girls turned to look at the framed photo of Callie, Deborah, and Max. The words "Burglar Apprehended" were printed in large letters under their names. Max padded over and pushed his head between their legs, as if he understood what they were staring at.

"Those were the days, right boy?" Callie reached down and rubbed the Labrador between his ears, pausing to adjust his orange-colored bandana. She might as well change back into her clothes. She preferred to match Max's wardrobe to hers—though she knew it was silly. Alongside her green dress, his orange bandana looked like something out of her fall window display. They didn't clash exactly, but it wasn't the look she aimed for when she picked out their wardrobe. She had a nice brown jumper that would be perfect. "I'm not worried about Trent. I'm worried about Mrs. Knepp. She hates me, and I don't know why."

"You can't please everyone. That's what my *grossmammi* says."

"We're losing customers because of her." Callie walked to the counter and straightened the stack of flyers announcing her weekly sales. "I don't mind competition, but this is growing nasty. We could work with each other instead of against each other. Her store is different than mine. We could be referring customers to each other if she weren't so stubborn."

"You said last month's profit was better than ever. The best since you reopened the store five months ago."

"True, but—"

The door to the shop burst open and Trent McCallister nearly fell through it. Wearing jeans and a long-sleeved Harley T-shirt, with a souped-up Nikon digital camera slung around his neck, he looked as if he belonged on the cover of a magazine rather than in Shipshewana, Indiana. Shoulder-length sandy hair was pulled back in a ponytail, and wire-rimmed glasses completed his West Coast look.

His eyes widened at Callie's outfit, but he didn't comment on it. "I'm headed out to Tobias' place. A call came in ten minutes ago over the police scanner."

"Tobias?" Callie moved forward. When she did, Max moved with her, on alert, as if he'd been called to hunt.

"Is Tobias all right?" Lydia asked.

"I don't know, but ..."

"Is there anything we can do?" Callie began fumbling with the tie on the back of her apron.

"Callie." Trent stepped closer and put his hand on her arm, waiting until she was still and looking directly at him. "Deborah and Esther are there."

"They're at Tobias'?" Callie reached for something to sit on, nearly stumbling. "But they're all right."

"I don't know."

"They have to be. Tell me there's nothing wrong with Deborah or the children." Her hand covered her mouth, as if to stop the words that were tumbling out. "Esther and Leah, they're fine—"

"I'm not sure. Callie ..." Again his hazel eyes sought hers. "All I know is that someone called in a fatality."

Chapter 2

DEBORAH LOOKED AT THE BODY of the dead girl floating face-down in the pond. She was fairly certain she didn't know her, but how could she be sure?

One part of her wanted to step back from the water's edge, look away, wait for the authorities to arrive and sort everything out.

Another part of her wanted to step forward and make sure she didn't know the teenager—the girl looked to be between six-teen and eighteen now that Deborah's shoes were almost in the water. She was thin in the way of girls before they'd had their first *boppli*, her white apron fanning away from her green dress—it was an attractive, harvest tone. The color of the dress alone indi-cated that probably she wasn't married, as in most districts when women married they began dressing in more somber colors.

Still, she couldn't be sure until the officers came and turned her over. Deborah had met eccentric older Amish women who stubbornly preferred bright colors for their dresses—it wasn't exactly a crime. One of the officers might turn over the body to reveal a ninety-year-old woman who had been pulling flowers and slipped to her death.

However, if she'd slipped and drowned, it wouldn't account for the back of her *kapp*, which appeared to be matted with hair and blood.

Nausea squeezed Deborah's stomach and her breakfast inched its way up the back of her throat.

Pulse hammering, she took one step closer so that her black shoe sank into the mud with the same weight that her heart dropped. The hair that had worked its way out of the prayer *kapp*—the hair swirling around in the pond water even as fish darted back and forth near the girl—was not gray and wiry.

No, this was a young teenage girl.

The hands floating by her sides showed no signs of age either.

Scrambling away from the water, Deborah glanced back toward Esther and the children. They sat near the buggy, which Deborah had moved farther down the lane, waiting for the Shipshewana police to arrive.

Reuben Fisher remained with Deborah. He stood off to the side a bit, shoulders pulled back and feet planted firmly, as if he expected a big storm to appear on the far side of his fields. At five-foot-eight, he was only two inches taller than she was, but he was much more solid. Farming was his life. It showed in the thick muscles of his forearms and neck.

Most days, Reuben spent twelve to fourteen hours working in the fields, and if he was kept inside because of weather, he found work in the barn that he and Tobias had reframed into two separate spaces—a living area and a work room. Plus there was the small woodwork shop he'd begun in the last year. The man didn't abide being idle.

This morning, the look on his face remained unreadable—mouth frozen in a scowl, eyes locked on the horizon. Thirty-five years old, his long sideburns were the same brown as the hair that touched the collar of his shirt. But since he'd never been married, he sported no beard.

For one fleeting second though, when he'd come running to the pond with her, Deborah thought perhaps she'd seen recognition in his light brown eyes. Then any remembering had left his expression, like the shades she pulled down over her windows in the house to block out the dark night.

When she'd asked if he'd known the girl, Reuben had shaken his head once, stuffed his hands in the pockets of his work pants, and stared out over the waters of the pond. He hadn't moved in the thirty minutes since.

"Did they say how long it would take to get here?" she asked.

Reuben shook his head slightly, but he didn't break his silence.

"Did you speak to Officer Gavin?"

Again the headshake.

Deborah had known Reuben all her life. He'd never been the talkative type, but even for him this silence seemed a bit ominous.

She was about to step toward him, reach out to touch his shoulder, and question him further when a Shipshewana patrol car bumped down the lane. Esther, Leah, and Joshua popped up and began waving their arms. The patrol car pulled even with Deborah's buggy and slowed to a stop before the officer rolled down his window and began talking to Esther.

As Deborah watched the scene play out, she noticed that Reuben never turned. If anything, the look on his face hardened.

Before she could puzzle it out, Officer Stan Taylor opened the door to the patrol car, stood and placed his hands across the roof of the vehicle. After he'd carefully assessed the situation, he looked toward them, looked back at her buggy, and then down at the ground. Taking off his officer's cap, he resettled it on his head, then continued alongside the path of trampled grass—walking in the high weeds as if he didn't want to contaminate any evidence that she, Esther, both *kinner*, or the horse hadn't already managed to destroy.

Taylor fit easily into the small Amish community of Shipshewana. In fact, if Deborah remembered correctly, he'd been born there. Old enough to be a grandfather himself, each year Deborah expected him to retire, but he didn't. As captain of their six-man department, he seemed to enjoy watching over Shipshewana and tending to what little needs their small community had.

Needs like dead girls in a pond.

The brown color of Taylor's eyes reminded Deborah of the Black-eyed Susans waving by her side. They were the same shade of brown, framed by bushy white eyebrows like the flowers' petals, and they were every bit as gentle as the blooms. A protruding stomach told Deborah that Officer Taylor wasn't having much luck with the diet his wife had put him on. He still moved easily down the path though, losing no time plodding toward her.

As he neared, Deborah saw his concern. She wouldn't have been surprised if he'd pulled her into a hug. Instead, he put his hand on the end of his pistol, which remained holstered in his belt.

"Are you all right, Deborah?"

"*Ya, ya,* I'm fine." She couldn't stop herself from sending a worried look Reuben's way. "I didn't actually find the girl; Esther did."

"I spoke with her a minute. She seems shaken, but okay." Taylor dropped into a crouch and studied the body floating a few feet away. "Reuben, any idea what happened here?"

The big man turned now, and Deborah had the oddest sensation that he'd been preparing himself for this moment, which was a ridiculous idea unless he had something to hide. Of all the people she knew, Reuben was the most forthcoming. He worked and he worked. There was little else in his life, and she couldn't remember a time when there had been.

Of course he visited with his family on Sundays, but other than that he didn't even like leaving the farm.

"No," Reuben said.

Taylor stood and backed away from the girl. Deborah

understood enough about murder scenes to realize he didn't want to disturb any evidence. Pulling out his pad and pen, he turned to her. "You found her first?"

Deborah knew Taylor was testing her story, since she'd just told him who found the body. She shook her head and repeated what she'd said a moment earlier. "No, Esther did. We were driving up with a casserole, and we'd stopped to pick some flowers. Esther and the children walked over here while I waited with the buggy."

"You had no indication that something was wrong?"

Deborah smoothed out her apron, looked back at the children. "Actually Cinnamon was acting a bit *naerfich*. I thought there might be a snake nearby."

"All right. So Esther had been here with the kids—"

"Maybe five minutes when I heard her scream."

"And what happened next?"

Deborah felt Reuben studying her as closely as Taylor was. She closed her eyes and allowed her mind to replay the scene, as if she were seeing the way a quilt would piece together. She knew the first time she told this story would be the most accurate, as each retelling of a story tended to stray further from the truth.

She'd heard Callie say so, based on the Agatha Christie books she read, but didn't Deborah know it from experience with her own children?

Pulling in a deep breath, she pushed on. "I ran down the path, thinking one of the *kinner* might be hurt. But Leah was clutching Esther's hand, and Esther was the one who had screamed. Joshua had plopped down on his bottom in the grass."

Her pulse began to accelerate as she allowed her mind to drift back over the scene. Even though she was standing by the girl's body now, telling of its discovery seemed somehow more urgent.

Why was that?

"And then?" Taylor didn't step closer. His voice was calm, focused, recording the facts that would begin to lead them down the path to the discovery of this girl's fate.

"Esther had one hand over her mouth, the other hand holding Leah's. When I arrived by the water, she pointed toward the pond, so I followed her gaze. I thought maybe she'd found a dead animal or … or, I don't know what. I never thought it would be a person … a girl."

Spiders tiptoed down her spine as she voiced the thought she'd been holding back. "What if she's someone we know?"

"We'll find out soon enough," Taylor said, his voice grim. "So are these Esther's footprints?"

He pointed to the imprints in the mud leading down to the body.

"No." Deborah felt the heat creep up her face. "I stepped a bit closer to see if I might know her. I'm sorry if I messed up your crime scene."

"Don't worry about it. You had a natural reaction to be concerned about the girl. Looks to me like the grass was trampled down on this side by Esther and the kids, but we'll have the crime techs check their shoe sizes to confirm that. I noticed a wider path going around the other side—"

"*Ya.* Looks as if someone had dragged something through the weeds."

Taylor paused, his eyes assessing her solemnly. "You didn't walk that way at all?"

"No. I stayed here, on this side."

"Should be able to collect some forensic evidence then. I suspect whoever dropped her off at this site—or killed her here—did so from the pond's other side and she floated this way."

"Floated?" Deborah reached for the strings of her prayer *kapp*, ran her fingers down the length of them.

"We're on the south side," Taylor said. "Wind's been from the north for several days."

He studied the scene a moment longer, then looked back down at his pad. "County should be here in a few minutes. Let's finish up with your initial statement. After you determined it was a person, what did you do?"

Deborah tugged on her prayer *kapp* and looked back toward Joshua. He was running in circles around Esther, playing with a long reed of grass. Soon he'd be finding something to put in his mouth he shouldn't. "I insisted they come away, come back from the water and the flowers. I didn't want the children to realize what they were seeing and grow upset. I pulled Esther and the children down the path toward the buggy and then moved the buggy a little farther down the lane."

Deborah peeked around Taylor's uniformed shoulders to catch another glimpse of the group still waiting on her.

"Why did you move the buggy, Deborah?"

"What?"

"The buggy? It was originally parked there, right?" He pointed to a spot approximately a hundred feet from where Esther and the children now waited. The same spot he had stopped to examine earlier. "Why did you move it farther away? The children couldn't see the body from where you were parked at first, so why did you move it?"

Deborah smiled, remembering what Callie had told her about an investigator's attention to detail. "Cinnamon was nervous, spooked from the moment we stopped. Once Esther and the *kinner* came back to the buggy, the mare seemed even more agitated. You might think it sounds *narrisch*, but I believe she smelled death in the air. I wanted to move her so she would calm."

Taylor rubbed a finger across his white, bushy eyebrow as he considered her reasoning. After a moment he seemed to accept it and wrote an additional notation on his pad.

"And then?"

"Esther stayed with the children and the buggy—where she is right now, and I ran to Reuben's house. He took his buggy to the phone shack and called you."

Turning his attention toward Reuben, Taylor mumbled, "All right. That's all for the moment, but I still need to take a full statement from Esther. And I'll want you to stay around in case I have any more questions."

"The children—"

"I asked the dispatcher to send someone out to your house when Reuben mentioned you were here. Jonas should be here soon."

As if his words had the power to produce the people she loved, a buggy and a truck pulled down the lane.

Deborah turned and hurried toward them, already feeling Jonas' arms around her, his dark eyes assuring her all would be fine. But something caused her to glance back.

When she did, what she saw surprised her nearly as much as the floating corpse.

Reuben had turned, ready to face Taylor's questioning, and for a fleeting moment, Deborah saw a look on his face. It was one she was familiar with. One she had felt often enough when she'd miscut a bolt of cloth or spoken too harshly to one of the children.

Reuben's look, though, was tinged with such pain, colored with such heartache, that Deborah's hand went instinctively to her throat.

It might have been only for one brief second when his thoughts were unguarded, might have been something that Officer Stan Taylor missed as he looked down at his pad to begin a new page of notes, but Deborah clearly saw how Reuben's expression was temporarily consumed by regret.

Chapter 3

SAMUEL WATCHED the *Englischers* from his hiding spot in the woods. He'd known the moment the taller woman started around the south side of the pond that she'd find Katie's body. If he were honest with himself, he'd prayed for it. The thought of her spending one more hour in the water would have split his heart right in two—if there was anything left of his heart to split.

He clutched his hat so tightly he could feel the brim breaking under his fingers.

Didn't matter.

Nothing mattered now.

Crawling forward on his belly, he inched toward the top of the slope he was lying against so he could peer more closely at the group of people gathering around the pond. There were the two women who had arrived an hour before, their *kinner*, Reuben, and the *Englischers*. One of the *Englischers* was the local police officer—Samuel knew that because of the automobile he'd arrived in as well as the uniform the man was wearing. Another seemed to be from the local newspaper. The large magnet on the door of his truck read "*Shipshewana Gazette*." The truck itself looked as though it had seen better days, even to Samuel, who wasn't so familiar with *Englisch* automobiles.

This man held something up and pointed it toward Katie, but it wasn't until the sunshine of the fall day reflected off the lens that Samuel realized it was a camera, understood that the man was taking pictures of her, photographing her body.

Samuel backed quickly down the hill and tried to stand, but he tripped over his pack of things and fell on top of Katie's duffle. Crawling on his hands and knees in the opposite direction—any direction away from the scene at the pond—he forgot to quiet his movements. Sweat slicked his palms, causing leaves to stick to them as he lunged onward like a child. And he might have continued that way, crawling clear out of LaGrange County and leaving their small bundle of things behind, if his stomach hadn't stopped him near the creek.

After no more than five—maybe six—feet of crawling, Samuel gasped, clutched one arm across his middle, and began retching. He hadn't eaten, but the little bit of water he'd had a few hours earlier found its way up. Mostly it was dry heaving—his body looking for something to expunge and finding very little.

His heart looking for a way to reject the final travesty of what he'd seen.

After two minutes he was done, though sweat now beaded along his forehead, and he'd lost his hat somewhere along the way.

Wiping the back of his arm across his mouth, he collapsed into a sitting position while searching for and finding his hat. Tears again coursed down his cheeks, through the beard that was less than a week old.

He scratched at the stubble, and then he was lost, drifting back to three weeks ago, when Katie had reached up and touched his cheek that was still smooth, teased him about how quickly his beard would come in . . .

"Within a month of our wedding, you'll need a comb to keep it proper." *Her palm lingered on his cheek, her brown eyes sparkling with laughter. When she did pull her hand away, it was to twine her*

fingers with his and tug him toward the barns. "You promised you would help me name the pups today."

"Pups don't need naming, Katie. They're only hounds."

"You sound like my dat. I want to name them even if we are selling them soon. Seems the kind thing to do—assigning a name to something that you have to feed and care for."

"Next you'll be naming the cattle." Now he was teasing her, though he didn't mind following her into the barn. He'd worked all day in her father's fields, and passing a half hour in the barn, looking at her pretty face, seemed a fair price to pay for naming a few hound dogs.

Though she wore one of her old dark gray work dresses, she'd starched the white apron that covered it. Her light brown hair was pulled back properly and covered with a white prayer kapp, *but nothing could hide the prettiness of her face. Katie was one of the most beautiful girls Samuel had ever seen, though that wasn't why he'd lost his heart to her. It was her kindness, the way she had of caring for every little thing—even hounds that would soon be gone.*

"'Course I wouldn't name cattle. Cows don't crawl up in your lap or lick your hand."

"Gut thing," Samuel muttered.

Katie stepped closer as they moved into the shelter of the barn. "When we have our own place, I'd like to have a pup. They're gut *for warning of snakes and also in case someone approaches who shouldn't be about."*

"And what stranger would be approaching here? Your family lives so far out, visitors are rarer than snow in September." Samuel tried to hold the criticism from his voice, but wasn't quite successful. He didn't realize he might have sounded a bit harsh until she turned to gaze at him with an expression that was now solemn. "I didn't mean to judge, Katie."

Glancing to the right then to the left as they walked down the length of the barn, Katie pulled Samuel into the last stall. The dog and her pups lay in a shaft of light in a corner on top of a pile of hay, but Katie ignored them, her attention focused completely on him.

"Does it bother you so much, Samuel? Be honest with me. Do you regret working for my father?"

"How could I regret it, when I wouldn't have grown so close to you otherwise?"

"It was Gotte's wille, *ya?"*

"Ya, I believe it was."

"But now— "

"Now, I wonder if perhaps we should stay here after we marry, or— "

"Or move off on our own. Move north to Shipshewana, where you can work in the RV factories." She crossed over to the pups, selected the smallest, and picked it up, cuddling it closely.

"It's what I've said before. Here the work is endless, and I'm not sure we'll ever make enough to get ahead. Look at how your father struggles. There hasn't even been time to begin building our own house, though he promised."

"I know he did. And he meant to, but the summer crops— "

"I understand his reasons, Katie. I understand." Samuel was running his hand up and down his jawline, trying to puzzle out all the emotions and conflicting thoughts running through his mind, when Katie stepped close to him, cupping her hand over his.

"It'll grow in nice and thick, Samuel. I can tell. Might not even take a month. Then you'll be needing a comb."

Chapter 4

REUBEN WATCHED DEBORAH WALK AWAY. Watched her walk toward Jonas, Esther, and her *Englisch* friends Trent and Callie.

Jonas wrapped his arms around her; then Esther and the children joined in the circle. Almost immediately, Callie Harper was pulled into their midst, and though Trent McCallister stood on the outside, soon he, too, was shaking hands with Jonas, tousling the *bopplin*'s hair, and lightly touching Deborah's and Esther's arms.

Good people, every one of them. Rueben hadn't been much help when Deborah was trying to clear the *Englisch* woman's name in the murder investigation last summer. Seemed ironic now. One thing he could bet the crops in his east field on—if Deborah Yoder said a person was honest and true, it was a fact.

Pulling in a deep breath, he forced his attention to the officer who stood waiting.

Didn't allow himself to stare into the water.

Wouldn't let himself look at Katie.

Though part of him needed to.

"Are there any corrections you'd like to make to Deborah's statement?"

"No."

"Do you know who the girl in the water is, Mr. Fisher?"

He didn't answer that one. Reuben knew who Captain Stan Taylor was. In a town as small as Shipshewana, you came to know everyone's name fairly quickly, and they'd both lived there as long as either could remember. After a long silence, Officer Taylor hitched up his pants and sighed before moving on to the next question. Reuben had seen Taylor around town plenty of times. Never had cause to speak to him before. Never had cause to like or dislike him.

"Any idea how she came to be in your pond?" Taylor asked.

Reuben shook his head.

Another police vehicle pulled in behind the truck that had brought Trent and Callie.

Reuben's jaw began to ache from clenching it.

Taylor snapped his notepad shut. "We're not making any progress with my questions. How about you tell me what you do know."

Until that moment, Reuben had avoided looking directly at the *Englischer*, but now he sensed the challenge in the man's words. He forced himself not to move, not to react physically in any way. That was easy enough after years of practicing *gelassenheit*. But of course this wasn't a normal situation, and he didn't feel anything close to calm or composed.

Was the girl's death *Gotte's wille*?

Hard to imagine.

Didn't mean he'd be willing to work with the *Englischer* though.

"Well?" Officer Taylor asked. "Do you have anything to add?"

Reuben met his gaze, not attempting to hide his contempt. "No."

Taylor stepped closer, close enough that Reuben could smell the man's sweat. He remembered then this officer had once worked in the *Englisch* prisons, had been a supervisor of sorts there. Tobias had told him all about it. Taylor had herded people in concrete jails at the county facility on the outskirts of town. He'd heard it was only for women, and only minor offenses at that, but the thought still turned his stomach. In other words, he was as foreign to Reuben as the scene unfolding before him right this minute.

"A dead girl shows up in your pond, less than a mile from your front door, and you don't see or hear a thing? I might believe that of a woman working in the home or garden, or a man who is a bit slovenly or absentminded." Taylor stepped back as the other officer approached, though he didn't stop speaking. "But from the looks of your farm, Mr. Fisher, you're aware of everything that happens in every field. I don't quite believe that someone killed and dumped this girl and you didn't see a thing."

Taylor turned and walked away, toward the other officer, leaving Reuben by the pond with Katie.

For the first time in many years, Reuben no longer felt distanced from other people—separate, as though he were watching from the outside.

No, standing beside the water, unable to turn and look at the girl who still hadn't been fetched, who couldn't yet be properly buried, he felt completely involved in life—involved in a way that stirred an ache all the way to the marrow in his bones. An ache that spoke to the regret for the things he'd done in the last forty-eight hours, the decisions he'd made.

Decisions that couldn't be changed.

Not now.

Though he was large, though he felt the strength he'd always known running through his muscles, Reuben was sure that his heart had been shattered in two.

Chapter 5

CALLIE FLEW STRAIGHT INTO DEB'S ARMS.

It didn't occur to her until later that her best friend might have wanted some time alone with Jonas. No. Callie's single thought had been that she needed to be sure Deborah was all right, that she wasn't hurt, that the call—the fatality—hadn't involved her.

When Trent had driven up, she'd spotted Esther's tall form immediately. With relief, she'd seen both of the younger children—Joshua and Leah. But when she hadn't seen Deborah, her heart had stopped in her chest.

"Someone called in a fatality." Trent's words had echoed 'round and 'round through her head as they traveled from town.

Max stood in the small space behind the single bench seat inside Trent's truck, his head resting over the back of the seat between her and Trent.

At one point on the ride over, Trent had tried to console her with *we don't know*'s but she'd waved him off, pulled her feet up underneath her dress, and wrapped her arms around her knees. Some part of her realized she looked ridiculous still wearing the Amish clothing, but she didn't care.

She needed to see Deborah.

She needed to know her friend wasn't hurt.

Deborah couldn't be dead.

With the weight of a bolt of cloth, it hit her—Deborah was the closest thing Callie had to family.

She couldn't bear the thought of losing her too. She'd only recently begun to heal from all the trauma in her life. First the death of her husband, not even two years ago. They'd had no children, but there had been the one miscarriage. She'd felt so alone, so deserted when Rick had died. Then she'd received the letter informing her Aunt Daisy had passed away. She hadn't intended to move to Shipshewana. Deborah would say God had plans for her—perfect plans. All of that had led to Callie becoming the shop owner of Daisy's Quilt Shop—and, yes, she could see how it had *all worked for the good*, as Deborah was fond to quote. This, though—this couldn't be good.

Jonas was ahead of them in his buggy. He'd pulled up beside Esther and the children. Callie jumped out of Trent's truck before it came to a complete stop. Even from a distance, she could see the anxious expression on the face of Deborah's husband.

Jonas tossed the reins of the horse on a nearby bush, not looking where they landed. His face pale around his beard, he strode toward Esther and scooped up Joshua, who'd run toward him.

"Callie, maybe you should give them some time." Trent reached out for her arm. She heard his words, knew he might be right, but she could no more have stayed away than they could have held back the sunrise that morning if they'd all stood against the eastern horizon and pushed.

Running toward the group, Max at her heels, Callie saw Jonas glance up and then south, around the curve of the pond, where Esther was pointing.

Finally, finally Callie saw a splash of color from Deborah's dark gray dress, then her white *kapp*, then the bit of her blondish-brown hair that had escaped from her *kapp*.

Finally she saw Deborah standing and talking to Officer Taylor and Reuben.

Callie skidded to a stop so fast Max loped past her, then turned around and gave her a quizzical look.

Trent caught up and placed a hand at the small of her back. "What is it?"

Bending over, Callie pressed one hand to her side, rubbing at the stitch that had appeared. She hadn't run that far, but perhaps she'd forgotten to breathe. Perhaps her fear had stolen her breath. Or perhaps she'd finally realized the value of friendship — on this bright fall morning, standing beside Reuben's pond.

In that moment Callie realized Deborah's friendship was more dear to her than she would have guessed — Deborah's and Esther's and Melinda's.

She'd known it when they'd all faced danger before.

And she knew it again now.

Perhaps some lessons had to be learned anew each day.

"Callie? What's wrong?" Then Trent must have caught sight of Deborah and Taylor and Reuben, because he began rubbing her back in small circles. "She's all right. Deep breaths. I believe you might be having a panic attack."

"I thought it was ..." She waved toward the south end of the pond. "I thought the dead person ..."

"I know. I know what you thought." Trent's voice was calm, solid, ever the newspaper man, but under that she heard her friend — and maybe, possibly, something more. Where Trent was concerned, she still hadn't decided. "Are you okay, gorgeous?"

Pulling in a deep breath, Callie stood straighter, adjusted her long dress, and smiled — though it felt shaky and unnatural.

"Yeah, I'm fine."

"Let's go see Jonas then and find out what this is all about." Then Trent raised his Nikon camera and clicked a shot.

Deborah reached her family and *freinden* mere moments after she saw Callie and Trent arrive.

"How are you?" Jonas asked, running his hand up and down her arm.

"Are we free to go?" Esther looked worried, but steadier than before, holding on to Leah's hand.

"Tell me you were never in danger!" Callie cried, throwing her arms around Deborah's neck.

Joshua reached for Deborah too, pulling at her dress with his chubby hands and saying over and over, "*Mamm, Mamm, Mamm*," in a sing-song voice. That he was completely unaware of what was going on brought her some measure of peace.

Trent stood back, taking it all in and trying to calm Max, who looked as if he wanted to leap into the middle of their get-together. Deborah did notice that his camera was slung around his neck, and he kept looking over at the murder scene.

Murder scene.

Was she really involved in another murder?

Perhaps it was an accident.

But the injury at the back of the girl's head ... Had there really been blood seeping through her *kapp*?

How could this happen?

She lived in a town of six hundred residents. There'd probably only been three murders there in the last twenty years: Esther's husband, which no one in her community considered a murder; Stakehorn's homicide, which they'd stumbled into while attempting to sell their quilts; and now this. Surely it was a coincidence that they had happened to stop and ended up finding the girl.

"Well? Can you go home?" Jonas pulled Joshua away and set him down on the ground. Immediately her son ran to Max and began patting the dog around his harvest-orange bandana—a color that most certainly did not match Callie's dress.

Callie's dress. It was Amish. Deborah opened her mouth to ask, but stopped when Callie held up her hand.

"Don't ask," Callie said. "I see your question, and don't ask. It can wait. Tell us what Taylor said. Can you answer Esther's question? Can you leave?"

"Leah's tired, and I'd like to be at home." Esther pushed at a wisp of hair that had escaped her *kapp*. "Not to mention I think the casserole I made for Tobias is ruined by now. A silly thing for me to think about, I know."

"I'm afraid we have to stay," Deborah said. At Esther's look of dismay, she added, "The *kinner* can go, of course. Jonas, would you mind?"

"Not at all. I can take them home."

"Could you take Leah by one of my *schweschdern*'s?" Esther straightened her daughter's dress, kissing her on the cheek as she did. "If it's not too much trouble."

"Your *schweschder* Miriam is the closest. I'll take her by there on the way home."

"Thank you, Jonas."

"But how long do you have to stay? Why do you have to stay? Haven't you already talked to Taylor?" Callie moved her arms up and down as the questions spurted out of her like hot grease popping out of a pan.

Deborah smiled her first genuine smile in what felt like days.

"What? What did I say?" Callie asked.

"I think it's the dress," Trent whispered, then scooted around the group and began snapping pictures of the crime scene.

"Oh. I forgot. Yes, well. I'll explain this—" Callie smoothed down the apron over her dress, grateful Lydia had at least removed the *kapp*. "I'll tell you about it later. What happened, Deborah? Who died?"

Deborah felt Jonas and Callie grow still and quiet, turn toward her, and wait for her answer. She found herself seeking Esther's gaze.

Who had died?

No, Esther didn't know either.

They hadn't had a chance to talk about it. Hadn't had a moment alone since Esther's scream and Deborah's run to find Reuben. But she knew in that moment that Esther had no idea who the girl was either.

"We don't know," she said, shaking her head. "I don't think anyone knows. We'd stopped to pick flowers—"

"What if we hadn't?" Esther asked. "How long might she have stayed there, undiscovered?"

"Not so long, I expect. Animals would have found her, and Reuben would have noticed that." Jonas picked Joshua up again as the boy ran back to him and tugged at his father's pants leg. "Is she Amish or *Englisch*?"

"She's wearing Amish clothing, though I don't suppose that means she is plain." Deborah again took in Callie's clothing, wondering absently what her friend had been up to while at the same time it occurred to her there would probably be several reasons why someone might want to appear to be Amish.

"So if you spoke to Officer Taylor, why do you have to stay?"

"County personnel are coming," Deborah explained. "We'll have to give our statement again, and Officer Taylor hasn't had a chance to actually question Esther at all. I think he didn't want to go into detail with her in front of the *kinner*."

"County personnel?" Esther frowned as she motioned Leah away from Max. "You don't mean—"

But she didn't have to say Shane Black's name. Before she could finish her question, they all heard two more cars bumping down the lane and watched them pull into the now-crowded area surrounding the pond.

Deborah would probably never feel completely comfortable with the county sheriff, who was tall, lanky, with dark, piercing eyes. But he'd saved her life. He'd been there for her and Callie

29

when they needed him most. For that Deborah was willing to overlook the fact that some in their Amish community were ill at ease around him, including herself and Esther.

Shane Black might not do things the way they wanted them done. He was patient to the point of resembling a bulldog more than a man at times, but he did it for the good of their community—the community of Shipshewana, both Amish and *Englisch*.

It could be for this situation, for the girl still waiting in the pond, that Shane was precisely the person they needed.

Chapter 6

SHANE WAS FRIENDLY ENOUGH as he greeted everyone, though he was quick and to the point, no doubt wanting to get down to business. It seemed to Deborah that his gaze lingered a moment on Callie, but she might have imagined that.

She had thought after the brush with death they'd experienced together, Callie and Shane might have a blossoming romance going on, but even after growing up beside *Englischers*, she still couldn't claim to completely understand their ways.

Stakehorn's murder had been solved in June. Whenever Shane's name was brought up, Callie still became flustered, but as far as she knew, Callie and Shane hadn't shared even one buggy ride since that time.

"You ladies found the deceased?" Shane asked.

"I didn't," Callie squeaked.

"Why are you in that dress?"

"Why is everyone worried about my clothing? Maybe I like Amish clothes. Maybe it's the new fall fashion." Callie crossed her arms around her middle and pulled in her bottom lip.

Shane placed both hands on his hips, scanned the site again, as if he were expecting another body to pop up, then focused on Callie. "I thought maybe you'd fallen in the water and Deborah had loaned you something to wear, but apparently not."

31

Callie stepped forward.

Deborah recognized her posture and the expression on her face—she was ready to start an argument, and that would most certainly not help the situation right now. She needn't have worried though, Shane had already dismissed her with a wave of his hand and moved on. "So who exactly—"

"It was Esther and myself," Deborah said, "and the children. But Taylor said they could go home with Jonas now."

Shane ran a thumb along his bottom jaw, and Deborah knew—she was certain beyond the smallest doubt—he was considering how to get a statement out of Leah and Joshua.

"*Ya*, I'm taking them home now. I wasn't even here, Shane. Haven't seen anything other than my *fraa*, and I'd like to see her again before the day wears on too long." Jonas nodded at the officer as he shifted Joshua to his other arm and reached down for Leah's hand. "I know you'll finish as quickly as you can."

Then he was gone, walking toward his buggy, not waiting for permission or any sort of confirmation. Deborah wanted to run after her husband and throw her arms around his neck. Thank him for bulldozing past Shane Black. She could tolerate standing here and answering his questions another hour or two, as long as their children were home and away from this scene of death.

Shane mumbled something under his breath as Jonas walked away but made no move to stop him. Instead he turned and shouted at Trent, who was still snapping photos for the newspaper. "Take it easy, McCallister. Don't step on my crime scene."

"I'll stay back the standard distance." Trent gave the *Englisch* thumbs-up sign as he began to circle the site.

"And don't take any identifying photos of the deceased," Black barked. "We want to notify her family before they read about it in the *Gazette*."

"She's facedown in the pond, officer. They won't identify her from my photos."

32

Shane ran his hand up and around the back of his neck. "All right, ladies. Take me through what happened from the moment you arrived."

Callie's hands came up, palms out. "I wasn't even here. I heard there was a fatality—"

"How did you hear?" Shane asked.

"Trent has a scanner." Callie's eyes were as wide as a doe's, her voice now sweet and charming.

Deborah wanted to laugh … the Amish clothing did make it hard to look at her without smiling. Her shaggy hair was so incongruous with the plain clothes, and besides, this was Callie, her closest *Englisch* friend.

"So you ran over when you heard about a fatality."

"No. Well, yes. But it's not like I have a fascination with death or murder investigations. I'm not creepy or obsessed or anything." Callie patted Max, who whined softly as he pressed against her side. "Trent mentioned Deborah's and Esther's names. I was worried. They're like family to me."

She linked arms with the two women.

Deborah had the image that they were forming a wall—a wall of friendship against whatever was coming toward them. She couldn't imagine what it was, but she had a feeling it might be more than the investigation regarding the body floating behind them.

Shane began his line of questioning, asking the same questions Taylor had asked her earlier. Esther repeated the exact same answers Deborah had given before, which was a bit surprising. Deborah knew enough about police and questioning to understand that if you had two witnesses, you usually had two different stories. It was human nature, rather like wearing two different types of glasses.

Human perception colored how one understood what they saw. Listening to Esther's answers closely, Deborah noted they were identical to hers in nearly every way.

The single difference being the one thing Esther had noticed about the girl, the one thing Deborah hadn't seen.

"You're sure about this?" Shane asked.

"*Ya*. I was bending down to cut the flowers. Why, do you think it's important? It might have been nothing."

"Describe it to me again. Anything you can remember."

"I don't remember it, not really. I was too frightened, worried about hurrying the children away."

"Then close your eyes and describe the moment before you thought of the children."

Esther hesitated, but finally shut her eyes and began recounting what had happened two hours earlier. "I had moved closer to the water's edge to reach some of the autumn goldenrods. I thought how lovely they would look on Tobias' table, how I wanted to take some to Callie as well, how the seeds would dry just so. I thought to plant them in my garden where the ground stays damp from the drip irrigation system my *bruders* set up last year."

A northern wind rattled the trees around them, and Esther's hand automatically reached for her *kapp*, steadying it on her head. But she didn't open her eyes. "As I bent to cut the flowers, I saw something in the water, something sparkling. It wasn't blue like the water was blue. It was darker. It caught the light, reflected it for a moment."

Shane looked to Deborah for confirmation, but she only shrugged then shook her head no. She'd seen nothing when she arrived except the body. Perhaps she'd been too surprised or too worried over calming Esther and the children. Her first thought had been that there was a snake in the grass, so she'd been too frightened to notice anything in the water.

Then, when she'd seen the body, she'd been focused on trying to determine the girl's identity. She hadn't seen anything else in the water.

"What else, Esther?" Shane's voice was gentle, smooth, like the molasses Deborah poured over the children's morning biscuits.

"Then I heard Leah giggle and Joshua say something. I turned toward them—"

"Right or left?"

Eyes still closed, Esther's right hand came out. "To my right, to check on them, and that was when I saw the body."

Esther opened her eyes, looked from Callie to Deborah to Shane. "That's it. That's all I remember. Do you think it's important?"

"It could be. You did well, Esther. One more question. You're sure you saw the shiny object first, to the left of the body?"

"Yes." Esther smoothed her apron with her right hand. Callie's arm remained firmly linked with Esther's left, as if she was afraid the woman would run away.

"Isn't it a little odd that you didn't notice the body as soon as you walked up?" Shane glanced down to where Taylor was still speaking with Reuben. "Doesn't look like it's far from the water's edge."

"Obviously you haven't been around Esther when she has her mind on flowers," Callie muttered.

Shane shot her a look to quiet her, even pointed his finger at her as if he were a teacher and she were a pupil. Deborah again felt the urge to laugh. She finally recognized the emotion for what it was: shock. There was nothing funny about this tragic scene.

A growing number of crime techs were invading Reuben's property.

The corpse still floated in the water.

And what had been a pleasant fall day now seemed to speak to her of winter.

Callie tilted her head and frowned at Shane. "I'm just saying, she's a bit focused when it comes to flowers."

"Callie's right," Deborah agreed. "Esther probably wouldn't

have noticed a buggy in the water. Plus, as you walk around the pond in that direction, the reeds grow taller and hide anything near the edge."

"Unless you walk very close to the water, which she did when she was cutting the flowers."

Esther said nothing to defend herself.

They all knew from experience that she'd answer Shane's questions, but she would say no more than required.

Shane looked past them, studied the scene, but didn't agree or disagree with what they were saying.

Finally, he turned and pierced Esther with those dark eyes that she'd been up against before.

It was obvious to Deborah from the way they were facing off that neither had forgotten the inquiry into Seth's death over two years ago. When Esther's husband had died, she'd wanted to bury him, to let him rest, but Shane had insisted on a complete investigation. Everything about Esther's body language—from her ramrod-straight back to the tilt of her chin to the look of bitter resolve in her eyes—said that she hadn't forgiven him for prolonging her pain.

Deborah had hoped they'd put it behind them with the events of the summer. Now here they were again, on the property of Esther's fiancé. And once again, they were facing another investigation.

Unless the girl had died of natural causes.

"Esther, humor me for a minute. I want to be sure I understand your statement correctly. You were cutting flowers, then you saw something shiny, something reflective in the water."

"*Ya.*"

"Then you heard the children."

"Right."

"And you saw the girl and thought what?"

"I saw her floating, facedown. I saw that she was dead."

"You didn't for a minute think she might be alive? It never crossed your mind that she might need your help?"

Deborah had feared the question was coming. Actually she'd dreaded Esther's reaction more than Shane's question. It was natural enough perhaps, if you'd not been around the dead before, but Shane Black should have known better.

Instead of being angered, Esther drew herself up to her full five-foot-ten height, looked at Shane as if he were a child, and said simply, "No."

"No?"

"I believe you heard me, Shane."

"That's it? No. You did not think to help her."

"As far as I know, I haven't the power to raise the dead."

"But ..." His hand went again to the back of his neck, rubbing at the muscles. "A person's natural reaction is to jump in and help."

"Your natural reaction might be. Perhaps you haven't sat with the dead as often as I have. Perhaps you haven't held them in your arms as I have. Perhaps our experiences have been different."

Then she pulled her arm out of Callie's grasp. The one indication of how emotional she'd become was the color blossoming on her cheeks. She turned and walked down the lane toward the approaching buggy, toward the man Deborah had watched her fall *in lieb* with over the last four months. She walked toward Tobias until he saw her and slowed the buggy. Then she gathered up the hem of her dress and ran.

Esther turned away from the *Englischer*, away from her group of *freinden*, and walked down the lane toward the man she loved.

The man she loved.

A year ago, she didn't think she'd ever love again.

A year ago, Esther Zook thought love had died beside her barn in the middle of the night when Leah was a *boppli*.

She had thought her heart had died with it.

Yes, she'd walked through her days, kept up appearances, done her duty for her precious little girl—but her heart, the part inside of her that once sang when the sun rose and used to pound faster when she worked in her flower gardens, that part of her had not known hope for quite some time.

Then, four months ago, Tobias Fisher had strolled over to her table at Sunday luncheon and asked if he could sit down in the empty chair.

In that moment, everything in her life had changed yet again. And she had not been prepared at all. She'd thought to turn him away. But something in his smile, in his gentle ways, in the eyes that looked at her—not with pity but with kindness and hope—something about Tobias had touched Esther's heart and awakened it.

"Esther, *was iss letz?*" Tobias stopped the buggy in the middle of the lane and jumped out of it, caught her as she ran the final few steps to him, and pulled her into his arms. "You're trembling. Don't speak yet. Just be still a moment. Whatever it is, don't worry. There's no need to worry. We're together now. We'll stand together."

His hands on her back, rubbing in small circles, eased the knotted muscles that had begun to ache. Esther felt the tension lessen for the first time in hours. She wanted to sink to the ground there in the dirt lane and pretend the scene unfolding around the pond was nothing more than another one of the bad dreams that had plagued her for so many years.

"Can you climb into the buggy?"

"There's no need. I can walk."

"I want to talk to you though. Away from—" Tobias waved a hand at the people tromping around his pond. "Away from everything and everyone. It will give us a bit of privacy."

"*Ya.* All right." She allowed him to help her into the buggy, allowed its smells to comfort her. It was an older model, without the new built-in heaters or the fancy leather seats. Something about the age and dependability of the old carriage soothed her nerves. Or perhaps it was only the memories she connected to it.

They'd ridden to a dozen picnics in Tobias' buggy. Gone to church and socials and family gatherings—all things Esther would have done before, but she would have done them out of duty and with a heavy heart. The times with Tobias had been happy, with Leah laughing between them. They'd even visited the different living quilt gardens around the Shipshewana area. The fact that Leah now played and smiled like the other children eased Esther's soul more than Tobias could know.

Or perhaps he did.

Perhaps he understood exactly the things that caused her to worry.

"I heard the *Englischers* were here, and that there'd been a death. Is it true?" At her nod, Tobias picked up the reins and murmured to the horse. "I see Rueben from here, so I know he's fine. Not that I'd ever believe anyone could better my cousin. He's bigger than the work horses."

"It's a girl, Tobias. A girl who is dead, and I found her."

"You found her? I don't understand." Tobias guided the horse to the side of the lane, a few feet away from the other buggies and vehicles, secured the reins, and turned her toward him. "Tell me everything that happened since you arrived. And why were you here to begin with?"

So she told him about the casserole and the flowers. Described seeing the shiny object, then spying the body.

"A girl, huh?"

"*Ya*, but she didn't look familiar to me."

"There have been no strange girls about this property." Tobias' jaw clenched, a look Esther had rarely seen before. "You know our families. Are you sure she's not related?"

"She's young—looks to be between fifteen and eighteen. I don't believe you or Reuben have any girls that age in your family."

"No. Our nieces and cousins are younger, and they wouldn't have been out here on a school day, and certainly not alone."

"Plus her dress was different than ours, Tobias."

"She wasn't Amish?"

"No, that's not what I mean."

Tobias listened as she worked through the details she hadn't shared with Shane Black.

"It was hard to see with the girl still in the water, but it looked like her dress was different than those we wear here in Shipshe. It wasn't the material so much as it was a peculiarity about the design or pattern."

"You told Black?"

"What would I tell him? That her dress didn't look right? He'll have his ways of confirming who she is, believe me." Esther heard the bitterness creep into her voice, like frost tiptoeing up on a fall morning, but she couldn't stop it.

"I know of your troubles with Black." Tobias pulled her hands into his own, massaged her fingers until her trembling stopped. "Look at me, sweet Esther. Look at me, dear."

When she finally did, he smiled.

How could he smile when her heart ached so for what was happening only feet away and for what had happened only a few years before?

"I don't know what tragedy befell the poor girl in the water. And I don't know why you've once again been thrown into the path of Shane Black. But I do know one thing."

Esther looked down at their hands. She didn't want to hear the words he was about to say. She was afraid if she didn't accept them, it would drive a wedge between them, and she needed Tobias in her life.

Their wedding was less than two weeks away.

"Look at me, Esther."

He waited until she did, then he continued softly, gently. "Do you think it's by chance that you are the one who found her body?"

"It was the flowers." Her head began shaking, side to side as if she had no control of it, as if the wind had picked up and was shaking the buggy. "I wanted to bring you something nice—a casserole and then the flowers. You know how you two keep that old barn you live in. It's clean but . . ."

"And it was a kind thing for you to do, but Esther look out in front of the buggy, look toward the barn." To the right of the buggy, across the road and away from the pond waving in the gentle breeze were more flowers. "They grow near the creek as well, and also around the edge of the field where the birds have seeded them."

"I don't understand," she whispered.

"It was *Gotte's wille* that you look up and see the ones by the pond's edge. That you find the girl this morning. I don't know how she died or why she died, but now her body will have its proper burial as it should. One day her parents will thank you for that."

Esther wiped at the tears spilling down her cheeks. "I don't want to be involved with this. I don't want to answer Shane Black's questions."

"Often we don't want to do what God throws us in the midst of, but I'll be there with you." Tobias squeezed her hands one more time. "Now let's go and see if I can help my cousin before his famous temper lands him in jail."

Chapter 7

Callie's last view of the crime scene was from the front of Melinda's buggy. As they rumbled down the lane, she leaned back against the leather seat and turned to study the woman she was growing to think of as her younger sister. Smaller, with glasses and honey-brown hair that peeked out from her *kapp*, Melinda's size was in direct contrast to her emotional strength. The mother of three children, one of whom was handicapped, Melinda was probably the strongest person Callie knew.

"Thank you for coming to fetch me."

"*Gern gschehne.*"

"How did you know I needed a ride?"

"Jonas mentioned to Esther's *schweschder* that you arrived with Trent. She told my *bruder*, while he was at my *mamm*'s house, who told me when I stopped by. I figured Trent wouldn't be ready to leave anytime soon."

"The Amish grapevine."

"Something like that."

"Trent was still taking pictures. Honestly, how many photos can you take of a dead girl? It's a bit morbid." Callie glanced back at her dog, who was now sitting in the buggy's backseat, trying to look out the small window. "I wouldn't leave if it weren't for Max. I believe he's getting hungry."

"Of course you wouldn't." Melinda reached across and patted Callie's hand before covering her mouth to trap the giggle that threatened to escape.

"What can you possibly find funny at a time like this?"

"I'm sorry. It's just that I've never thought of you as plain before."

"Seriously? The clothes? You're going to focus on the clothes when it looks as if Shane might handcuff Reuben at any moment?"

"Oh, come now, Callie. You don't actually think Shane will arrest Reuben, do you?"

"From what I could tell—not that I was eavesdropping—they were able to establish an approximate time of death to within twenty-four hours. Tobias has a strong alibi, which Shane was able to immediately confirm."

"Tobias had been working and sleeping at the feed store."

"Yes, and there were plenty of witnesses to support that, but Reuben—"

Melinda maneuvered her buggy onto the two-lane road and allowed the horse to pick up speed as they headed back toward town. "Reuben rarely leaves the farm."

"I don't know what I think, but Shane was not happy about the way Reuben refused to answer questions."

"It's Reuben's way. You know that from Stakehorn's murder earlier this year."

Callie cornered herself in the buggy and studied Melinda. It might be Melinda's size that brought out Callie's protective instincts. Of the three closest friends she'd made since coming to Shipshe—Deborah, Esther, and Melinda—Melinda was the one who seemed to need looking out for, but in reality, there was a lot of courage and grace in the little person sitting next to her. Callie had learned that firsthand in the last five months.

43

Watching Melinda with her children, especially with her son Aaron, had convinced Callie that here was a woman who would fight whatever battles necessary for her family or friends. Or as Callie's Aunt Daisy would have said, "Tough stuff comes in small packages."

"Now *you're* laughing," Melinda said. "Or at least smiling."

"Just remembering something Aunt Daisy used to say. I'll tell you later. Back to Reuben. What did you mean about Stakehorn's murder and Reuben keeping his mouth closed?"

"Well, I thought it was you who had tried to talk to him, but I suppose it could have been Deborah." Melinda pulled up on the reins as a Mustang convertible sped past them on the road. Max barked at the car once, then settled down on the seat. "It isn't that Reuben held anything back during the investigation, though I'll admit he's not comfortable speaking with *Englischers*."

She threw Callie a glance, her gaze traveling from the hem of Callie's long dress to the top of her dark brown hair, a smile splitting her face. "No offense," she added. "He wouldn't be rude or anything. Reuben's not comfortable when he's off the farm, and he certainly doesn't know how to act outside of plain company."

"Is he more like the Old Order Amish? I've read a little about them. They're stricter, right?"

"*Ya*, but I'm not sure that describes Reuben well. He fits in with our beliefs here in Shipshe. It isn't that he thinks the *kinner* shouldn't have bicycles or that phone shacks are bad for the community. It's more like he personally belongs to an earlier generation. My *mamm* would say that he was born old."

Callie ran her hand through her hair. She knew what that felt like. Some days she was sure she woke up years older than when she'd gone to sleep. When she watched television, she felt like she might very well be in the wrong decade, as she was often confused, lost, or plain repulsed by what she saw. Other days she still felt like a child. So it wasn't that she always felt old exactly, only out of sync at times. "But he would speak up if he knew something, right?"

"I don't know," Melinda confessed, her face growing more serious. "The older people, they believe we should handle things within our community. That's what we have bishops for."

"But there are laws," Callie said.

"*Ya*, you're right."

"Certainly Reuben would see that too, especially for something like a homicide or, worst case, murder."

"Such things aren't always cut and dried though. Remember what happened to Esther's husband? The *Englisch* laws said that the boys who caused his death committed murder, but the Amish bishops considered it an accident. Our laws handled it differently." Melinda slowed as the front of Daisy's Quilt Shop came into view.

"Esther told me that was why she tangled so much with Shane," Callie agreed. "She explained that it's the Amish way to forgive. But this is different, Melinda. This is murder."

"Maybe . . ."

"You don't think she fell, hit her head, and landed in the pond, do you?"

Melinda glanced sideways. "I didn't notice any boulders or large rocks nearby, but you and Deborah are the detectives of the group."

They both grew silent as Melinda pulled the buggy to a stop in the parking lot of the quilt shop.

Callie looked up and felt a little thrill at seeing her aunt's name on the marquee: Daisy's Quilt Shop. Three small words that provided a connection to the family she no longer had. And yes, there was also the personal pride she had in the tidy little shop. She wasn't afraid to admit that any longer. She'd worked hard the last five months.

Neat raspberry-colored awnings shaded sparkling, clean windows. Two ladies stood on well-swept sidewalks admiring her pretty fall displays. Autumn flowers bloomed in the beds lining the property.

"Looks *gut*," Melinda said, following Callie's thoughts.

"*Ya.* A lot better than the first time I saw it." Callie leaned over and hugged Melinda. "Do you have a minute to come in for tea?"

"No. The boys will be home soon, and I wanted to sew a bit before then. We're working on that new diamond pattern."

"Bring it by when you have a chance, would you? I'm dying to see how it's coming along."

Melinda's eyes sparkled as she snagged Callie's hand before she stepped away from the buggy. "Do me a favor?"

"Of course."

"Go up to your apartment and change before anyone else sees you. It's unsettling enough having a possible murder in the area. No one needs the added discomfort of seeing you in plain clothes."

Max barked once.

Callie shook her head but couldn't help smiling as she moved toward the shop. Melinda's ribbing helped ease some of her tension. That and a few hours on the job would put everything right. Surely it would, because back at the pond, she'd had the uncomfortable feeling they were all in for another long ride.

In fact, she'd had the distinct thought, standing beside Esther, that this time could be worse than the last.

But how was that even possible?

Before she could dwell on the possibilities, she opened the door to the shop, Max bounded inside, and Callie lost herself in the warmth of her fabric and buttons and quilt kits.

Then the afternoon activities took over, including changing clothes as Melinda had suggested. During the course of those chores, Callie did what she'd often done as a child: She pushed what was troubling her to the back of her mind.

Reuben watched the scene unfolding outside his barn window, and it was as if it were one of the *Englisch* motion pictures he'd heard his nephews describing. It was as if all that had happened since Deborah had driven her buggy onto his land earlier that morning, discovered the girl's body, and run screaming for his help—as if all of that had happened to someone else.

No chance of that. It had happened and was happening . . . to him.

Reuben closed his right fist and worked it into the palm of his left hand. Though he wasn't old, arthritis had already begun. He massaged his knuckles, kneaded the tendons like his sisters kneaded bread.

He was a big man, accustomed to long days of hard work. It was work he enjoyed. When his muscles ached from long hours in the field, he felt as if he'd done what he should for the day. When his back was sore from hauling feed or cleaning out stalls, he knew he'd completed his half of some contract established long ago.

Each evening he looked out across his *grossdaddi*'s land and asked himself if he had done his best. If he could honestly answer yes, then he was pleased with that day's work. His *dat* and his *grossdaddi* had always taught him that his best—and only his best—was good enough.

Now, watching the sun set over the unharvested fields, Reuben had the uncomfortable feeling that somewhere, somehow, he'd broken the contract. He'd betrayed both his parents and his grandparents.

But where?

How?

Which step had been the one that had ultimately been the wrong step?

How could he have dealt differently with the girl?

What would have been a better way?

As he watched Shane Black walk toward his door, watched a

47

house key swing back and forth from the officer's hand, he knew that the next few moments would be the hardest.

The next few moments, another life could hang in the balance.

Reuben closed his eyes and did what he often did. He prayed for wisdom, that he might choose the correct path this time. He prayed for strength, that he might be able to endure what lay ahead. And he prayed for mercy, God's mercy, as man's mercy meant nothing to him—he neither expected nor wanted it.

Then he took one last swallow of cold, bitter *kaffi*.

Something told him it might be the last homebrewed *kaffi* he would have for quite some time.

Shane didn't bother to knock on the door. He did stop to argue with Tobias.

Reuben turned away, not wanting his memory of this last sunset to be scarred.

"I have a legal right to question him again, Tobias. Now you can be present or you can leave, but you will move out of my way."

Shane stepped through the door, still holding the key. Apparently Tobias hadn't noticed it yet. He was still trying to prevent the lawman from entering their house.

"Don't think because we're a bit unfamiliar with your ways, that you can come in here and—"

"It's all right, Tobias." Reuben met Shane's gaze without flinching. He wasn't sure why the key had been in the pond, but when they brought the machinery and the nets, he'd suspected they would find something. There were only three questions to be answered now.

What else had they found?

How much did Shane know?

How much would he guess?

There was no use shying away from it.

"Esther mentioned she saw something shiny in the water, Reuben. When she was first cutting flowers, it's what drew her eyes to the body." Shane stepped forward, placed the key on the wooden table that stood between them. "Apparently the girl had this clutched in her hand, or she might have been wearing it around her neck. Sometime between when Esther spied the body and when our crime techs arrived, the key sank to the bottom. It took us a while to dredge it up. Look familiar to you?"

"Don't answer that, Reuben. You don't have to answer any of his questions." Tobias now moved forward to the end of the table, his shadow casting a straight line across the room as the evening's last light fell through the window. "That key could have been in the pond for years."

"Yeah, I suppose it could have. The string would have rotted though. I suspect Reuben knows that."

Reuben joined them at the table, put his hand on Tobias as if he could keep him out of the middle of this, as if he could move him back out of the house where he wouldn't have to hear what was coming. "Say what you intend to say, Mr. Black."

"I want to know what this key was doing in the bottom of your pond? Why did the girl have it in her possession?"

Reuben didn't answer.

He'd decided when they'd first shown up this morning that if his answer would require him to lie, he'd remain silent. A nod could be interpreted any number of ways, but an outright lie he would avoid. It was a fine line, but the best he could do under the circumstances.

"We've already tried the key, Reuben. We know it unlocks your grandfather's house. Was she staying there?"

"You had no right!" Tobias practically exploded. "The pond, yes. But you had no right to go into my *grossdaddi*'s house." His face turned red in the light of the setting sun, and Reuben had to look down, look away.

The pain on Tobias' face was nearly more than he could stomach.

"We had every right. When Judge Stearns cleared a search

warrant for the area surrounding the body, it included the entire murder site—"

"You don't know it's a murder. The girl could have fallen. She could have slipped. She could have even jumped in and drowned herself." Tobias' hands went up and out in frustration, finally settled on his head and yanked at hair that was already an unruly mess. He pulled with both hands, causing it to stand out like the horns of the old bull in the back pasture. It was a habit he'd had since they were boys.

Reuben wanted to reach over and calm him, but instead he waited.

As much as it hurt him, he waited.

Shane stood up straighter, pushed his hands into his pockets. "Drowned in water she could have stood up in? Not likely. Then there's that nasty head injury. We've established an approximate time of death. As I said before, your alibi is good and the folks at the feed store have backed you up, but Reuben has yet to answer my questions."

"I hear no questions—only accusations."

"Did you drag her around the pond, Reuben?"

"Why would he drag anything? He can easily carry a hundred-pound sack of feed."

Shane sighed and ran his hand up and around his neck. "Tell me what happened. Reuben, I've known you for years. You can trust me to do the right thing, but you have to tell me what happened here, and regardless, I have to collect the evidence."

Reuben remained silent, and Tobias continued to rant.

"So you have the right to tramp all over our place?"

"Yes, I do, and he will have to start answering my questions." Shane jerked a thumb toward Reuben. "I'll search your grandfather's place, your barns, this place—I see you've fixed it up quite nicely. Is there some reason you didn't want to live in the house? Something you were hiding there?"

"That's ridiculous." Tobias shook his head and clutched the back of the chair in front of him.

"I will have my answers, whether they come from you or Reuben or the evidence. I want to know why that girl had the key to that house. I want to know if she was living there, and if so, why." Shane's voice never rose in volume, but it became colder with each word, like a winter storm blowing across the fields.

Reuben felt it and steeled himself against the fight to come. From the worry lines creasing his cousin's face, he knew Tobias felt it too.

Tobias turned and walked to the wall of the barn. He stood facing it, his hands in his pants' pockets, his head bowed.

"Reuben, I don't want to arrest you for murder, but you have to give me a reason not to. You have to give me something. At least start by answering my questions." Shane leaned forward, both hands on the table. "Why was this girl here? What happened to her? And how did she come to have the key to your grandfather's house?"

"Maybe she stole it." The words tore out of Tobias like lightning ripping across a clear blue sky. He stalked back across the room, stopped inches shy of the table, and stood staring down at the key. "Maybe she stole it. We didn't even know she was staying there. I give you my word that I've never seen that girl before today, before I saw her on the stretcher. She could have been a runaway. Reuben's in the field all day, and I've been busy at my job in town and over at Esther's."

"All right. I suppose that's possible." Shane looked at Reuben, locked gazes with him. "Is that your take on it? We have a forensics team in the house now. We won't find any of your DNA in there? Any of your fingerprints on anything of hers that might be in there? No evidence that you've been in there?"

"It's our *grossdaddi*'s house. Of course you'll find evidence, but it will be very old." Tobias shook his head. "We haven't been in that house in several years. Our *schweschdern* come over and give it a good cleaning every spring, but it's too big for two bachelors to live in. That's why we chose to live in the barn instead."

"All right. DNA does degrade over time—heat, sunlight, and moisture will all affect any traces that have been left in the house since it's been closed up." Shane paused, scrubbed his hand over his face. "But if what you say is true, I shouldn't find any signs that either of you have been there recently."

"No. We haven't." Tobias slapped his hand on the table, satisfied they'd reached some compromise. "And then you'll go?"

"I didn't say that, and you have to stop answering for Reuben. He's not mute. I know that. He has to answer for himself. I have to receive a statement from him or—"

Two knocks sounded on the door to the barn, and Andrew Gavin stepped through. Reuben felt his pulse kick up a notch, felt sweat begin to trickle down the small of his back, but he forced his expression to remain neutral.

"Black." Gavin pulled off a ball cap he was wearing as he stepped into the room. "Evening, Tobias, Reuben."

Tobias and Shane mumbled hellos.

Reuben remained perfectly still.

"Getting here a little late, aren't you?" Shane's voice held a bit of a scolding, like Reuben's father's when he was working on training a pup.

"Actually I wasn't on duty tonight, but Captain Taylor called me in. I was fishing out on the lake when I received the message."

Closer to Tobias' age, Andrew Gavin was different from most Amish and *Englisch* men that Reuben had encountered. His short haircut, jeans, and T-shirt left no doubt that he was an *Englischer*, but he was extremely quiet most of the time, which made him seem more like the Amish to Reuben. He also kept himself somewhat apart, and Reuben wondered about that. Perhaps it was because of the things he had seen while he'd fought in their war—serving overseas in Afghanistan, or maybe because once he'd lived overseas he saw things in Shipshewana differently.

Regardless, Andrew Gavin didn't seem to fit completely into the *Englisch* side of things. In fact, in a lot of ways, Gavin reminded Reuben of a younger version of himself. In other words, he was built like a bull: solid. Some folks would say stocky, but he was really six feet of muscle.

The fact that he'd served in the *Englisch* military would have normally put a wedge between any friendship, but he was impossible not to like. Quiet and unobtrusive, Gavin had always been respectful of their plain ways. He was also a good customer for Reuben's burgeoning woodwork business. Over the last year they'd moved from being acquaintances to something more— something that included a deep respect for each other's work.

"Is there a reason you're in here . . . right now?" Shane glanced at his watch. "We were in the middle of something."

"Right. The Captain asked that I tell you they're ready to move the body to the morgue."

"Got it."

Gavin turned to go, then stopped as if he'd forgotten something. When he turned back toward them, Reuben wanted to shout out, to stop him, but he didn't know how without pulling the entire barn down on top of them all.

"By the way, Reuben, I wanted to say I'm sorry for your loss."

Reuben nodded once in thanks, hoping Gavin would move on to his work. He nearly did too. He was practically out the door, when Shane called him back.

"What did you mean by that?"

"By what?"

"That you were sorry for Reuben's loss."

Gavin looked from Shane to Reuben and back again. "Only that she was his friend and now she's dead. I wanted to offer my condolences."

Silence filled the barn as Shane let Gavin's words sink into the night. Reuben still hadn't moved, his muscles growing rigid from standing there in one spot for so long, from anticipating what would happen next.

"I'm curious. Why would you say the deceased was his friend?"

Once again Gavin glanced from Reuben to Shane. This time his military training took over though. He clasped his hands behind his back, posture perfect, and limited his response to the bare facts. "Because when I was here last Saturday, I saw them coming out of the main house together."

Chapter 8

SAMUEL COULD ACTUALLY SEE better once darkness fell.

The *Englischers* had set up large lights around the pond, mounted on poles and the tops of their vehicles. Harsh and unnatural, they cast everything in a ghoulish brightness. Giant shadows leapt across the water as the *Englischers* moved west to east, working the net—throwing it into the water, allowing it to sink, then dragging it toward the other end. It wasn't a fishing net, that much was certain. He wondered what they hoped to find in the deep water among the fish and turtles of the pond, which was surrounded by the wildflowers Katie had found so lovely.

Katie's body remained in the ambulance.

He'd watched them place it into a dark bag, zip the bag closed, then place it on a wheeled stretcher.

As if they could take her in the ambulance to their hospital and make her well.

As if they could fix all that had gone wrong.

As if they could turn the clock back . . .

"It seems real, now that we have the official papers." Katie *clutched the envelope with their legal papers allowing them to marry in her hands, scooted closer to him in the open air buggy.*

"It is real." Samuel hunched over the reins as he drove the buggy slowly away from town, back toward her father's farm.

"Can you believe it though? Less than a week and we'll be man and wife. It's what I've dreamed of for a long time, Samuel. Since the first day you came to work for my dat."

Samuel did smile then, there was no helping it. "You're telling me you knew over a year ago that we would fall in lieb?"

"I didn't know for certain, but I knew that you were a gut man. I could tell by the way you shook hands and the way you set to work. A woman notices these things."

A scowl replaced the smile as Samuel thought of his younger self. He'd been so sure he could work hard and make progress on Timothy's farm in one year. But like most things in his life, it seemed that God or fate had been dead set against him. When the rains had come, they'd nearly flooded the crops. The southern fields had needed replanting, and the harvest had been late. The work was too much for two men, but Timothy refused to hire additional workers, refused to even ask for help from among the local brethren.

Things were different here than they had been in Pennsylvania. Perhaps he'd been wrong to move here alone, but the memories back home had been painful after his daed's death. Then his mamm had remarried, and Samuel knew he needed to leave. He'd thought starting over would set things right. Meeting Katie had offered him his first glimmer of hope.

Where was his hope now?

A year later he was doing the same chores Timothy had assigned him when he'd first come. The man refused to trust him with more responsibility. He felt as if he were treated like a boy just out of eighth grade rather than a man.

Nineteen years old and he was still living in the little room back behind the barn. Next week would bring few changes. He'd be allowed to sleep in the house, with Katie, but their room would be small with very little privacy. The other rooms were all brimming with Katie's five younger sisters.

Seeing an Englisch rest area ahead on the road, he pulled the buggy over into it.

"Is there a problem with the mare?" Katie asked, concern coloring her voice.

"No, it's not that." Samuel secured the horse, helped Katie out of the buggy, and commenced pacing.

"What is it? You're not having second thoughts are you?"

"I would never have second thoughts about marrying you. How could you think that? Are you going to question my every move?" His anger spiked, and he felt the desire to punch something, anything. The weeks had slipped past like a noose settling around his neck. He had to think of a way to fix this, and he could only think of one. Pulling in a deep breath, he pushed the anger down, forced a smile on his face. "Katie, darling, do you love me?"

"You know I do. Samuel, what's wrong?"

"And do you trust me?" He sat beside her at a picnic table, pulled her hands into his, and rubbed his thumbs over her fingers, which had grown cold.

"Of course I trust you."

"I want us to go north, to marry there. I want to work in the RV factories near Shipshe."

"But— "

"Hear me out. I have a delivery to make for your dat tomorrow. Tell your mamm you want to ride along. Tell her you want to visit your aenti for a couple of days. Doesn't she live in Middlebury?"

"Ya, but— "

"We'll see your aenti but you won't stay there. That will give us time to marry. I've asked some friends, and we can do it with these papers." He touched the envelope that she still clutched, the one they had signed for in town. It was to be used at their wedding, in Goshen, next week. It was to be used with the bishop.

57

"An Amish wedding?"

"No. You're not listening!" Samuel stood again and resumed pacing.

"You want us to marry outside the church?"

"God will understand. Katie, there is no other way that I can see. Your father is a hard man—"

"My father is a *gut* man."

"He is that." Samuel stopped in front of her, rubbed at the headache pulsing in his temples. "But he sees the old ways and no other. He doesn't remember what it's like to be our age. He doesn't remember how it feels to be young, to be starting a family. He clings so hard to the old that he won't even accept the changes the bishop allows. It's why your life is so hard. Why your mamm *struggles* so with the work and your schweschdern."

"He loves us," Katie whispered.

Samuel waited ten seconds, then twenty. Waited until she raised her gaze to his. "Ya, I know he does. I love you too, and I believe you love me."

When she nodded, he continued. "Go north with me. We'll marry there, among the Englischers. I have Mennonite freinden in the factories who will help us to get started. Amish folk as well—there's a man my mamm knows. He'll let us stay with him for a few days. We won't be alone, and it will actually help your family to have two less mouths to feed."

"How will dat work the fields alone?"

"He'll be forced to accept the community's help. It's what he should have done long ago."

She looked away for a moment, across the trees that surrounded the parking area. "There is a community where we would go?"

"Amish and Mennonite. You know this. It's not as if we're going to Chicago. I give you my word. They're gut people. I've met them before when I delivered things for your dat."

Katie nodded once, and though tears escaped from both eyes, she glanced at him and smiled slightly. With that smile, Samuel released the breath he didn't realize he'd been holding. "We'll send word to your parents within the week, so they won't worry."

"All right, Samuel. I don't believe you'd suggest this if you hadn't thought it through carefully."

"We'll leave tomorrow?"

"Ya, tomorrow." She brought his hands to her lips and kissed them once, then stood and pulled him back toward the buggy.

Chapter 9

DEBORAH CHECKED THE PINS holding up Martha's long brown hair as her daughter lined up the lunch pails on the counter. She'd done a good job of fastening on her *kapp* but needed help with the back, where it was difficult for her to see or reach. "There. It'll hold nicely now."

"*Danki.* How did you ever learn to do it yourself?"

"Practice. And it helps when your arms grow a bit. Did you remember to add the raisin cookies we had left over from last night?"

"I did. I even gave the boys an extra one each. Have you noticed how they're hungry all the time?"

"*Ya.* That was good thinking on your part."

"Maybe something's wrong with them, *Mamm.* Joseph and Jacob had seconds at dinner. Last year they grumbled about stew, but this year they ate more than I did, and I'm four years older than they are."

Deborah smiled at her ten-year-old as she heard the boys clambering at the backdoor.

"Boys are different," she said.

"Is that why they like being dirty?"

Turning to look at her twins, Deborah closed her eyes for a moment. Maybe when she opened them again, the boys would be clean. Clean, like they'd been when she'd sent them out with Jonas an hour ago.

Opening her eyes, she shook her head, and Joseph and Jacob froze—each with one hand on the back of a chair.

"What did we do—"

"This time?"

"You're filthy," Deborah answered.

"Huh?" The word came out from both of them at the exact same moment, in the exact same pitch, with equal innocence.

"Look down."

They did and seemed to realize for the first time that their pants were covered in hay and mud, their hands were filthy, and yes ... as they felt in their hair, it, too, had managed to get hay in it.

"Get as much of that mud and hay off as possible and then head upstairs."

"But we're hungry." Joseph smiled so that his freckles popped across the bridge of his nose.

"And we did all of our chores." Jacob was her serious child. He appealed to reason every time. He was also a hair taller than his twin brother, but who knew if that would last until November. They'd turned six a month ago and seemed to be growing faster than the crops Jonas had begun to harvest.

"Ask *Dat*," Joseph added.

"That they did," Jonas agreed, coming in the backdoor and washing his hands at the sink in the mudroom. "I believe the problem came with the game of chase after their chores."

"It wasn't chase exactly," Joseph said, looking down at his hands—covered front and back with dirt—as if they'd betrayed him.

Jacob reached over and pushed his brother's hands down and out of sight, then stuck his own in his pockets. "We were keeping a box of turtles in the back of the last stall."

"Turtles?" Deborah reached for her *kaffi*.

"*Ya*. We were afraid they might not do well in the creek. What with the cold weather and all." Joseph nudged Jacob.

"But somehow they escaped from the box, and when I opened the stall, they scampered out of the stall too."

"I was feeding the pigs, like *Dat* asked." Joseph smiled again, freckles spreading.

"Turtles move faster than you'd think. Don't know why they'd head to the pigpen."

"Seems like the smell would keep them away."

Both boys fell silent, either considering the pickle they were in or contemplating the wonders of turtles. Deborah honestly couldn't have guessed—with those two it was an even chance either way.

"I'm sure the turtles appreciate your care, but you can't go to school dirty. Now pick off that hay, head upstairs to change your clothes, and clean up. Tonight you'll have to soak and hang those dirty clothes yourself." Deborah turned back to the stove and poured Jonas a mug of *kaffi*.

His fingers brushed hers as he accepted it, reminding her of the moments they'd shared before the day's work had begun. The memory stirred a warmth deep within her, helped her to keep some perspective regarding the two imps standing in front of her.

"But we were going to build the turtles a better box tonight." Joseph shifted from one foot to another.

"I even had planned a ramp that would allow them to get more exercise."

"Don't argue with your *mamm*." Jonas sat down at the table and began heaping food on his plate.

"What about breakfast?" Joseph asked.

"I'll put some muffins in your lunch pail. You can eat them as we walk to school." Martha turned and began wrapping muffins in dishcloths. "And if I help with the clothes, maybe you can do both tonight."

"Thanks," Jacob and Joseph said in unison. Their worried looks vanished completely as they turned and hurried from the room, nearly running over Mary who was carrying a clean cloth diaper and leading Joshua.

"Martha, that was nice of you." Jonas salted his food and helped Mary into her seat at the same time.

"They're just kids," Martha said in a voice that sounded ten years older than it should have. "I remember going without breakfast once or twice when I had trouble getting up in time for chores."

Martha tucked the muffins into the already-full lunch pails, then reached down for her baby brother, who had plopped onto the middle of the kitchen floor. "He's wet, *Mamm*. Do you want me to change him?"

"I'll take care of that. You're not so grown you don't need your own breakfast." Deborah smiled at Jonas and nearly laughed out loud when he winked at her over the kids' heads. Five children were a handful, but they made for interesting mornings.

She'd picked up Joshua, taken the clean diaper from Mary, and was heading back into the nursery to change him when a knock sounded at the front door.

"I've got it." With her left hand, she moved Joshua so she was carrying him in the front—facing out, like a bolt of cloth. She knew from experience not to carry him on her hip when the boy had a wet diaper. Potty training would come in the spring, and though she wasn't looking forward to it, certain things would be easier, like early mornings.

Joshua twisted in her arms to look at her and began giggling when she met his gaze.

"You're going to be like your *bruders*. Aren't you? Hmm? That's why you're laughing at me."

She was so busy talking to her son that she didn't glance out the glass of the front door as she reached for the handle and pulled it open. It wasn't unusual to have visitors so early, what with the various farming activities Jonas attended to. It never occurred to her to check to see who it was.

Later the moment would crystallize in her mind, for it seemed—even more than when she saw the girl in the pond—this moment changed their lives.

What had happened the day before had been at Reuben's house. It hadn't seemed quite real, as she'd explained to Jonas the night before when they snuggled on the couch.

This morning, she opened the door, smiled down at Joshua, and listened to the sounds of the girls and Jonas at the table behind her as beams of fall sunlight shone through the windows—and everything changed.

This morning the tragedy on her doorstep spilled into her home, shattering the sweet, warm nest she and Jonas had made.

Esther stood there, or a shadow of Esther, reminding Deborah of one of those paper dolls the girls cut out from their books. She looked as if the sun would not continue rising on the day. Pale and rumpled, her hair barely covered by her *kapp* and clinging to Esther's hand, stood Leah.

"Deborah." Esther's voice trembled. She stopped and pressed her fingers against her lips, as if to regain control of herself.

"Esther, *was iss letz*? Come in. Come inside."

Deborah pulled her friend into the sitting room. "Martha, come and get the baby, please. Mary, would you take Leah to the table and offer her some breakfast?"

Esther nodded when Leah looked up at her for permission.

When they'd crossed the few steps to the sitting room and sat on the couch, Esther covered her face with both hands and began to sob, her shoulders shaking as the last thread of her composure snapped.

Deborah's body flooded with alarm.

She'd never seen Esther show such emotion before. Maybe recently she'd begun to allow herself to show some happiness, a smile here and there, even a laugh occasionally. But she'd never actually expressed strong joy or grief—not even when her husband, Seth, had died.

Deborah moved closer to her on the couch, placed an arm around her shoulders, and began to rub up and down. She prayed silently for a moment, prayed for a way to calm her best friend. "Would you like some *kaffi* or some tea?"

"No. No." Esther wiped at her face with her sleeve, and Deborah handed her the clean cloth diaper she'd been carrying. "I'm sorry. It's just that I've been so upset. I wanted to wait until the children were at school, only I couldn't. I needed to see you, to talk to you."

"Of course you did, and I'm glad that you came over. But what's wrong? Is it Tobias?"

"Yes. No. I'm not sure."

Deborah accepted the hot mug of tea Jonas handed her and pushed it into Esther's hands. "Drink this. It will calm you."

"Where is Tobias now?" Jonas sat down on the chair across from them, braced his forearms against his knees, and looked straight at Esther. Perhaps it was his no-nonsense voice that brought Esther around. He'd always been kind to her, always helped during planting and harvest, though she had plenty of brothers and brothers-in-law who had picked up on chores when Seth had died.

Sometimes, though, it was a relief to have friends step in. Deborah was guessing that was why she'd turned to friends now.

"He's in town, with Reuben. And Reuben's in jail." The words out, Esther's hands began to shake. She tried to raise the mug to her lips, but seemed to realize she would spill its contents.

"Let me help you, Esther. I believe you might be in shock."

Deborah glanced over at Jonas, worried that this latest blow might be more than Esther could handle. She'd always been the strong one, but this turn of events, on the doorstep of what was to be a new life—

"How did you hear Reuben had been arrested?" Jonas asked.

"Tobias called down to the feed store before first light, since he couldn't make his shift. They sent the delivery boy out to t-t-tell me."

"All right. And what exactly did he say?" Jonas' voice was smooth, like the horse brush gliding over Cinnamon.

As Esther began telling them what had happened since sunrise, she drank more of the tea, and her shaking eased.

"Martha, bring me one of the muffins for Esther."

"Yes, *Mamm.*"

"He said that Shane Black—" Esther closed her eyes, then began again. "That Black arrested Reuben last night. That the girl in the pond—the dead girl—had been living in the house."

"Their *grossdaddi*'s house? No one's lived there for years."

"*Ya.* I know."

"This makes no sense." Jonas stood and crossed his arms. "Black can be insensitive, but he always does what's within *Englisch* laws. He must have had a reason for arresting Reuben, though he also must be wrong. Maybe he received some incorrect information. Maybe it's all a misunderstanding."

Esther pushed away the muffin Deborah offered and stared down into what remained of her tea. "Tobias told the boy at the shop Black had accused Reuben of having intimate relations with the girl. Black suggested that Reuben fought with her, shoved her maybe, causing her to fall—"

"Which would explain the injury to the back of her head," Deborah murmured.

"Reuben couldn't have done that though." Esther looked up, her face completely drained of color. "He would never have carried on with a girl we didn't even know, never have carried on in an improper way. And Reuben isn't a violent man. Can you imagine him shoving anyone? Hurting anyone? But Reuben didn't say a word to defend himself. He allowed them to handcuff him and then was driven away in their vehicle."

"What evidence did Shane have?" Deborah asked.

"I'm not sure."

"He must have had something." Jonas didn't pace, but the muscles in his neck tightened.

Esther pulled in a deep breath, her eyes again brimming with tears as she looked up at them both. "He only said that he had enough evidence to hold him ... hold him until the forensics team had completed their work."

"And then?"

"And then he could be charged with manslaughter."

Callie snapped on Max's leash, though she could have sworn his brown eyes looked a bit reproachful when she did.

"I trust you not to run off, Max. You've never run off. It's just a habit from when I lived in the city."

Max's tail thumped on the hardwood floors of the hall. She reached forward and adjusted the deep purple bandana he wore. "Obviously I'm taking this bandana thing too far, but that color does look nice on you. And it matches the fall flowers in my skirt."

Max cocked his head.

"A cat would never put up with this, and we both know I'm not having a baby anytime soon. There's a bigger chance of a snowball falling out of the October sky than there is of me having a baby." Opening the door to the shop, she peered up at the blue morning sky, just to be sure she hadn't tempted God into making a fool of her, then walked Max the short distance to the side yard.

"The good Lord knows there's not even a man in my life, which is why I'm having my morning conversation with a dog—no insult intended."

Max didn't look offended. At this point, he was more focused on the activity going on in his yard than he was on the words coming out of his mistress' mouth. Callie didn't blame him. She enjoyed prattling on sometimes, especially when she was in a good mood, and for some reason she'd awakened in a very good one—despite all that had happened the day before.

Something told her today was going to be special.

Though it was a tad cool, her tan sweater provided the right amount of warmth. As Max took care of his business, she puttered around her little garden admiring the corner bed, breathing in the scent of herbs, flowers, and fall leaves. Esther had been helping her restore things to order. When she'd moved in earlier this year, the garden had been one of the last things she'd tackled—weeds had nearly overtaken the broken pots and little brick path.

This morning she could appreciate all the evenings of work she'd spent weeding and deadheading plants. Finally the small area had taken on the beauty it must have had when her Aunt Daisy had been alive.

Regret reached out and squeezed Callie's heart, stealing some of the loveliness from the fall morning. Why hadn't she visited her aunt more while she was alive? Aunt Daisy had been her last living relative, and she'd been too busy with her job as a pharmaceutical rep to even fly up on the holidays.

Max barked at a squirrel, bringing her back to the present. She turned to call him back to her side and nearly tripped over an old, all-but-rotten birdhouse. Buried among the chrysanthemums, somehow she had missed it in her early gardening forays, or perhaps she'd been too busy to see it.

Now she squatted down and righted the tiny house. Fastened to the top was a miniature bird, but that wasn't what caught her attention. Over the hole, where an actual bird might enter, were words. All Callie could make out was a capital letter *A*, so she used her thumb and forefinger to rub at the caked-on dirt.

Tiny musical notes, stenciled in black, trailed away from the words, down the side of the house. "Amazing grace . . . How sweet the sound."

And suddenly Callie was four again, sitting on her mother's lap on Daisy's front porch. It must have been before her aunt had moved to live above the shop, because Callie clearly remembered a yard overshadowed with large trees and a stone wall that separated Aunt Daisy's property from her neighbor's. The wall wasn't tall, and Callie had decided to climb on top of it, though her mother had warned her not to. Standing up, she had been able to see far, able to see the neighbor's house. When she'd begun to walk, her Sunday shoes had slipped on the stones, and she'd tumbled into the grass.

Daddy had been there almost before she'd settled into the grass, checking her and proclaiming her okay. But she'd wanted mother. And so her momma had rocked her and sung "Amazing Grace" as Callie's tears turned to hiccups and then disappeared completely.

Max barked once, jarring Callie back to the present once again.

She righted the birdhouse, dusted off her hands, and turned toward the front of the shop.

An elderly man stood at her gate, waving at her with his cane.

Max looked to her for permission.

"No, Max. Heel."

The dog came to her then and walked calmly by her side.

"I'm sorry, sir. We're not open for another hour."

The man was quite old. Callie would have guessed that he was maybe in his eighties—his skin weathered and worn thin like the pages of a well-read book. Though his head was bald, he sported a long white beard. Dark brown eyes appraised her and the dog in one quick swoop.

"You're her all right."

"Excuse me?"

"You're the one. I know, because you have the dog and you wear matching clothes—like in the paper."

"Can I help you, sir?" He didn't look Amish exactly. No hat, for one thing. She thought he might be Mennonite, but didn't the Mennonite also wear hats?

His gaze jumped around—taking in Max, the shop, her, then back to Max. The man didn't wear a jacket of any type, only dark pants, a long-sleeved shirt, and the typical suspenders. And the cane he gripped in his hands.

"Sir, can I call someone for you?"

"No. I don't need anyone else. I need you."

"Me?"

He whacked the cane against the fence, causing Max to emit a low growl.

"Are you deaf? Maybe if you moved closer you'd be able to understand me. Surely you're not afraid of an old man."

"Why don't you lower your cane?" Callie aimed for pleasant but firm.

The old guy looked at the smoothly carved cane, stared at it as if he was seeing it for the first time. His hand touched the wood. Trembling fingers ran up and down the smooth surface. It seemed to calm him a bit when he reached the top, when his fingers found and paused over some engraving that she couldn't make out.

"Are you going to ask me inside or not?"

"As I explained, the shop doesn't open for another hour."

"Not interested in quilts. Have plenty of those." He began to turn in a circle. "Sharon sewed the prettiest quilts you have ever seen. My daughter-in-law tries, but she can't put the squares together quite right. Sharon always quilted a perfect square."

He stopped in his circle, looked over at Callie, and shook his head. Max padded over to the fence and stopped next to it. The old man reached out over the short fence, his hand still shaking, and ran his fingers through Max's coat.

Callie realized then that something was wrong. The look of confusion, the way the old man seemed clear one moment, then foggy the next, his disorientation. Suddenly the training she'd left in Texas kicked into gear. "Why don't we go inside for a minute? Maybe I can call someone to help you."

"I told you already. I want *you* to help me. I want you to find my *dochder*." His voice rose in pitch, and he gripped his cane with renewed vigor.

"All right. I was about to make some tea, and Max hasn't had his breakfast yet. Perhaps you'd join us while you tell me about your daughter."

The man thumped his cane against the ground and considered her offer. "Isn't proper for a man to go into a woman's home with her alone, but seeing as this is your business it might be allowed."

"And we do have Max as a chaperone." Callie passed through the gate and did her best to guide him across the parking lot. Where had he walked from? There was no horse and buggy or car on the street or in the lot. Once inside, while he was eating, she'd call Andrew Gavin.

The thought of Andrew calmed the anxiousness in her stomach. He'd know what to do.

Perhaps someone had lost their grandfather.

Chapter 10

ESTHER LOOKED DOWN at Deborah's hands on top of her own. She needed to calm herself. She needed to rein in her emotions.

Leah's voice pierced through her heartache. She was in the kitchen, saying something to Mary. Esther heard her soft laugh and wanted to drop her head into her arms and weep again.

Leah laughing ... finally.

Now—like the last time—it was all about to be ripped away. Life wasn't fair.

"I'll ready my buggy, drop Joshua off at your *schwesder*'s place, then head into town." Jonas' voice was calm and steady.

"*Ya*, and I'll drive Esther's buggy. She doesn't need to be driving. Esther, would you like Jonas to take Leah as well?"

"Take Leah?" Esther wiped her tears away with the sleeve of her dress. "Take her where?"

"To Miriam's again—she's the closest from here."

"I don't think ... I'd like her to stay with me." Esther glanced from Jonas to Deborah, then down to the mug of tea Deborah had pressed back into her hands.

"It's growing cold, but it will still help. If you want Leah to come with us, then I'll take Joshua as well."

"Who are we going to see?"

"I'd say your first stop is by Bishop Elam's. No doubt he'll already have heard, but he might have some important words of advice for us." Jonas ran his hand over and through his hair. "And the man's prayers wouldn't hurt either."

"Then Adalyn Landt's." Deborah squeezed her arm lightly.

Esther had started to feel a glimmer of hope. At the mention of Adalyn's name, however, despair crept back in. "I don't think so. I've been up since four, remember? Running this through every possible angle. Surely Adalyn heard about the girl. I think all of Shipshe heard about what was going on at Reuben's farm. If she'd wanted to help, she would have shown up. I imagine that Adalyn has had quite enough of our special cases."

Deborah smiled and pulled Esther to her feet as Jonas moved to the backdoor. "I guess you've been too busy with wedding plans to know everything that is going on in Shipshe."

"What do you mean?"

"Adalyn was in South Bend yesterday. Shopping for those fancy bags of hers. She didn't get back until late last night. Somehow, even though it was after nine, she heard about the girl and drove all the way out here, wanting to know if she should go on to Reuben's house. We told her not to, and now I'm sorry for that. As far as we knew, no arrests had been made." Deborah stopped, turned, and enfolded her friend in a hug. "Maybe if we'd sent her on, all of this could have been avoided. I'm sure it's only a misunderstanding."

"You couldn't have known. But you think she will want to help?"

"*Ya.*" Deborah smiled as she tugged her toward the kitchen. "I believe her exact words were that another tangle with Black would make her day."

"Make her day?"

"That's what she said."

"Sometimes I don't understand *Englischers* at all."

"The point being that she looked forward to helping you. I think she views Shane as an equal adversary, someone worth competing against—rather like our buggy races."

"This isn't a game though, Deborah. This could be Reuben's life." Despair settled over Esther like a heavy quilt as her dreams for the next couple weeks—dreams for her future—wavered.

"She knows that." Deborah slipped lunch pails into each of her *kinner*'s hands and hurried them toward the backdoor. Then she turned and grasped Esther's cold fingers in her own. "She knows that, but she believes in showing no fear. We know fear isn't of the Lord, and we're fortunate to have someone on our side who believes the same, someone who can navigate the *Englisch* legal system."

Deborah's four school-aged children kissed her as they left and said good-bye to Esther. Both women watched as the little group trudged out the door and down the lane—Jacob and Joseph running a few steps ahead; Martha moving slower and holding hands with Mary.

The walk to the one-room schoolhouse would take them fifteen minutes. The schoolhouse had been built on a piece of land owned by Jonas' cousin, and it housed approximately thirty-five students. At the rate they were growing, another schoolhouse would need to be built next summer and the group split. If she and Tobias had decided to live on his *grossdaddi*'s farm, Leah would have attended the same school as Deborah's children. If—

"Tell me what's really bothering you." Deborah focused on rinsing their two cups as she spoke. "I've known you since we were *kinner*, and I've never seen you so upset. It is more than Reuben being taken into custody, isn't it?"

"I don't know how to explain." Esther turned so her back was at the sink and she could watch Leah play with Joshua on the floor at the far side of the kitchen.

"Try."

"I've grown to love Reuben. He's become like a *bruder* to me."

"Of course."

"But—"

"But?" Deborah turned and leaned against the cabinet as well. They stood side by side, the material of their dresses barely touching.

It was so familiar, so ordinary, that Esther found herself able to let the words slip out, the words and worries that had been circling in her mind and shredding her heart for the last three hours.

"I never thought I'd meet another, Deborah. Never expected to love again." She paused, searching for a way to express all that had happened so quickly. "I've known Tobias for years."

"But your heart wasn't ready."

"My heart wasn't ready. *Ya*, perhaps you're right. And then he sat down beside me, asked if I was going to eat my apple strudel." Esther shook her head, as her fingers found and traced the ties of her prayer *kapp*. "He's the most gentle, loving man, and somehow I think Seth would approve."

"Of course he would. Seth would want you to be happy. He'd want Leah to have a *dat* in her life."

Esther nodded, tears once again stinging her eyes, causing her throat to tighten. "In the last few months, I've come to realize that Tobias and Reuben are more than cousins though. They're more like twins. I think you can understand that better than most people—having Jacob and Joseph."

"*Ya*, my boys are like one sometimes. They finish each other's sentences and carry each other's burdens, even at their young age."

Esther nodded. "That's exactly how it is with Tobias and Reuben. If Reuben were convicted of this, I don't know how Tobias would bear it. And now, I don't think . . ." Her voice shook, and she pressed her lips together to stop the sob from escaping. She'd begun though, and the need to express her deepest fear won over the agony of verbalizing it. "I don't know if he'll be able to go on with the wedding."

Deborah turned toward her, touched her face, and forced her to meet her gaze. "You don't think he'd call it off, do you?"

"I don't know. Don't you see? On the one hand, he might call it off, because he needs to be there for Reuben. On the other hand, he might go on with it, but his heart wouldn't be with us anymore — with me and Leah. Which would be worse?"

"But his obligation to Reuben doesn't stretch that far."

"It's more than that, more than a feeling of responsibility. I've seen them, how they are together . . . like your boys. It will be as if Tobias is being accused as well. If Reuben has to stand trial, then Tobias will be there with him. And if Reuben is made to stay in the *Englisch* jail, if he is convicted of this terrible thing . . ."

Esther's right arm began to tremble, and she clutched it to her side with her left hand. "I think it will be better to postpone our wedding. And I don't want to sound selfish, but I want to ask, *Why me?* One girl has died, and Reuben's future lies in the balance, and I'm worried about a wedding. It is selfish, but there you have it. It's as if a big hand has come down and wiped away our happiness. As if I was allowed to see future happiness, but I'm not going to be allowed to have it."

"Oh, Esther. Honey. The hand of God is not like that."

"Are you sure? How can you know?"

Instead of answering, Deborah pulled her into an embrace. Esther allowed it, but she was still left with the image that had haunted her since the delivery boy had arrived so early to shatter her day . . . the image of a giant hand about to reach down and wipe away her future, an image of darkness and fear.

Callie flipped the switch to ON, sending water through the little coffeemaker. She didn't use it to make coffee. Too many of her customers preferred tea. When she first arrived in Shipshe, she was a Starbucks drinker herself, and she still liked a nice strong cup first thing in the morning. But Deborah was winning her over to the pleasures of a nice hot cup of tea.

Or perhaps it was the Indiana weather.

The front windows of her shop rattled lightly with the fall wind, reminding her she would soon experience her first Indiana winter. Her childhood memories of visiting her aunt all took place around the milder months. Mother used to proclaim that the Indiana winters were why they lived in the south and that Daisy could come and see them if she wanted to. But her aunt never had.

Each year Callie had received a Christmas postcard from her aunt instead. One even had the quilt shop on the front, covered in snow. Callie shivered at the thought. In Houston, a cold front had been anytime the temperature plummeted below sixty.

Walking back toward her unexpected guest, Callie noted the sun was making its way through the front display windows. She wasn't having a problem coping with an Indiana fall—the dazzling display of colors had lived up to her expectations and more.

"I have several types of teas here and a few pastries. The hot water will be ready in a minute." She set the tray down on the table in the back sitting area. "Now Mr.—"

"Bontrager. Name's Bontrager."

"Mr. Bontrager, what would you like to drink?"

"That dog of yours looks hungry. Most Amish people keep their animals outside." He reached up and combed his fingers through his solid white beard, reminding Callie again of the snow that was to come.

When Bontrager had stepped into the shop, he'd reached up as if to remove his hat, then looked around in confusion. His hand had rubbed across his shiny bald head instead. He'd finally shrugged and followed Max toward the chairs in the back area. "We don't abide animals in the house."

"Yes, I realize that, but Max sort of guards the shop for me. And as you can see, I'm not Amish."

"Does he eat?"

"He does."

Bontrager picked up a shortbread cookie and threw it at Max, who caught it midair. He also swallowed it whole, not pausing for such niceties as chewing. The dog licked his chops once, wagged his tail, and waited for more.

Smiling as if he'd seen a circus bear perform a trick, Bontrager picked up a pastry.

"Actually, I prefer to feed him dog food. Sweets aren't terribly good for him."

"He looks hungry to me."

"Well, he probably is. I usually feed him as soon as we come in from his morning yard time."

Bontrager leaned forward and looked under the table, then around the side of it. "Don't see any food. Did he eat it already?"

"No, he didn't. Mr. Bontrager—"

"Say, did you have some water to go with this tea? I prefer apple cinnamon myself." He'd picked up the basket of tea bags and begun pawing through it, his concern for Max apparently forgotten.

Callie closed her eyes and mumbled a brief prayer for patience. She hadn't been much of a praying person before coming to Shipshe, just as she hadn't been much of a tea drinker. Funny how a place, how the people in a place, could influence you.

Deborah, Esther, and Melinda, with their quiet ways, had made an impression on her—sometimes more than she realized. Perhaps that was why she'd found herself walking through the doors of the local Presbyterian church the last several Sundays, a first in many years and one she knew would have made her Aunt Daisy smile.

Bontrager placed the basket back on the table and gazed around the room.

"Place looks about the same. I believe even the flooring is unchanged." He thumped his cane against the hardwood floor. "Ever thought of updating?"

Attempting to keep up with the turns and twists in the old man's conversation was like trying to have a sensible talk with Deborah's youngest. With Joshua, she never quite understood his one-word commands, and he bounced from one need to another before she could answer the previous one. Which reminded Callie, she hadn't called Gavin yet.

Someone had to be looking for the old guy.

"Hold that question. I believe our hot water is ready." Callie rushed back to the kitchen, called Gavin on her cell phone, and said, "Get over here." Then she poured two mugs of hot water and carried it back out to where Bontrager and Max were still waiting.

"So you've been here before?" She set the mug in front of him, even plucked a package of apple cinnamon tea from the basket, but Bontrager didn't appear interested.

Callie moved to the chair beside him, opened the bag for him, and dipped it into the steaming water. Clutching the hot mug appeared to calm him a bit, though it was still too hot to drink. He inhaled deeply, seeming to enjoy the scent of the apple cinnamon tea, and closed his eyes.

When he looked at her again, his eyes had taken on a faraway look. In fact, as he gazed around the store, she was sure he wasn't seeing what she was seeing at all.

"*Ya*, course I've been here before. You know I stop in regularly. Come in to the Quilt and Shop every time we come to town. It's not easy on a man, what with the roads impassable so much of the time. But I made a promise to Sharon when we moved here."

His hand began to shake as he raised the mug and took a small sip. "It's been hard on her, leaving her family and all. Maybe I shouldn't have asked her to come west. Maybe I should have waited until there was more of a town, a bigger district. I didn't know though. Didn't know women counted on such things."

Tears welled up in the old man's eyes, turning their blue to a shimmery lake. When he looked at her, a single tear slipped down his weathered cheek, though he didn't seem to notice. It caught in the wrinkles of his cheeks, then worked its way down. "She couldn't come today. I thought I'd stop in just the same. Stop at the general store and the post office. See if there was any news from the family."

"Mr. Bontrager, who is your family? Can you tell me their names?"

"Normally I pick up the supplies at the general store, and Sharon, she comes over here and picks out a little material." He pronounced it *mater-ee-ail*. "Women-folk don't call it that."

"Cloth?" Callie asked gently.

He looked at her sharply, his gaze clearing for a moment. "*Ya*. The last time she came in, she picked out a little bit of cloth for the baby." His hand shook more, causing the tea to slop and spill over the side of the cup. He leaned forward, set it down on the saucer.

Then he reached for his cane and ran his hand up and down the wood. She noticed that the engraving wasn't letters but rather a cross, a hammer, and a nail — three items in a row but touching at the corners, forming a ring that circled the cane. It seemed to calm him, center him in some way. When he spoke again, Callie had the sense that he was back in the present time and place, but the feeling remained that something wasn't quite right.

"The baby is why I'm here."

Callie glanced toward the front room, out the windows. *Where was Gavin?*

"I'm afraid I don't understand, Mr. Bontrager."

"Need you to find my *dochder*. Are you daft?"

"If your daughter's missing, you should see the police."

"Too late. It's too late for that. Might be old, but I'm not senile."

The word senile set off an alarm in Callie's mind. He probably wasn't *senile*, but he might have Alzheimer's or another form of dementia. If he'd been walking all night and missed his meds or become dehydrated, his condition was no doubt worse.

"Mr. Bontrager, is there someone I can call for you?"

"You already asked me that. There's no need. Besides I heard you call someone. They'll be here soon enough, and they'll take me back to that place. Before they do, you need to listen to me. You and that dog. You're both good at solving things, right?"

"I'm not sure why you think that."

"Saw your picture in the paper." He raised his cane, nearly knocking over the basket of tea, and pointed it at the framed picture of her and Max, the one taken after they'd caught Stakehorn's murderer.

"That was an unusual situation. We don't normally go looking for trouble."

"Most of us don't, *dochder*. But trouble sometimes has a way of coming to us. Find my girl—find Bethany." Bontrager reached out a hand lined with age. It was mostly bone, skin, and veins. Trembling, he grasped her arm. "Please, find my *dochder*. I need to see her one more time."

There was a light tap on the shop's door, followed by a jingle of the bell. Gavin had finally arrived. Bontrager let go of Callie's arm, reached for another cookie, and tossed it to Max.

81

Chapter 11

DEBORAH WAS ON THE WAY DOWN Main Street, headed toward the bishop's when she saw the police cruiser parked at Callie's shop. "Should we stop?"

"*Ya*. Reuben's not going anywhere. Let's see if Callie needs our help."

She pulled the buggy into the parking lot of the quilt shop and shot a glance at Esther. She couldn't imagine what else had gone wrong, why Callie would be standing with Max while talking to Andrew Gavin and two Amish men.

Esther reached for Leah while Deborah secured Cinnamon and helped Joshua out.

"Why is the officer talking to Miss Callie, *Mamm*? And whose *grossdaddi* is that?" Leah slipped her hand into Esther's as they hurried toward the front of the shop.

"Thank you again for watching after my *dat*." A portly, middle-aged Amish man helped his father into an older buggy. He nodded once at Deborah and Esther, then climbed into the buggy himself.

"Mr. Bontrager, are you sure ..." Callie hesitated, speaking to the younger of the two Amish men, then pushed on. "It's just that he seemed so sure about a missing daughter."

Deborah couldn't see the expression on the old man's face from where she stood, but it was quite clear to her that the younger man was struggling between anger and exhaustion. As with most Amish men she knew, he remained quiet until he was sure he'd won over the anger. When he did finally answer Callie, his words were a bit sharp, but even-toned.

"And wouldn't I know if I had a *schweschder* missing? I can assure you, it was his mind wandering. Next time he could show up and tell you that he has the keys to the great farm on the hill." He picked up his hat and resettled it on his head. "But there is no great farm, and there's no missing *dochder*. It's the sickness."

He glanced at Callie once. "Thank you again for calling Officer Gavin."

A bit of the anger seeped into his voice, winning over his attempt to master it. "They should keep a closer eye on him. Shouldn't be allowing old men to wander around in the dark of night. Anything could have happened to him." He pulled a handkerchief from his coat pocket, mopped at the sweat running down his face, then carefully folded it and returned it to his pocket. Without looking back at them he muttered, "*Gut* day to you."

A snap of his wrist set his mare to a trot.

Callie, Gavin, Deborah, Esther, and the little ones were left standing in the parking lot, staring after the buggy as it made its way down Main Street. Finally they remembered to say hello to one another.

"Callie, who was that man?" Deborah shook her head, unable to imagine how her friend had managed to find mischief so early in the day.

"I don't know exactly, but he showed up in my garden this morning, and then ... well, come inside for tea, and I'll tell you the whole story."

"I'll leave you to explain your latest escapade," Gavin muttered with a smile—a smile that Deborah thought was very sweet.

Why was Callie turning down dates with Gavin? He'd called her again last week; Callie had admitted as much to her. He was such a nice young man. "I need to complete some paperwork before I go off shift."

"Thanks for coming so quickly. I wasn't sure what to do." Callie tucked her hair behind her ears then reached down to pat Max.

"You did the right thing. They didn't even realize he was gone at the *Grossdaddi* House. According to the night supervisor, Bontrager was there when they checked on him at three this morning, but apparently the old guy is quite skilled at sneaking away." Gavin turned and had made it halfway to his police cruiser, when Esther called out after him.

"Officer Gavin, how is Reuben?"

"Reuben?" Callie turned to Deborah. "Why is she asking Gavin about Reuben?"

"I'll explain in a minute."

Gavin stopped and it seemed he would answer her from the distance of six feet, but he walked back across the pavement, stopping next to them. "He's all right. No one else is in the jail right now, so it's pretty quiet."

"In jail? Reuben is in jail?"

"Callie, stay calm. We're here to work this out. We were on our way to see the bishop and then Adalyn. I'm sure it's a misunderstanding." Deborah placed her hand on Callie's arm to settle her down.

"It's not a misunderstanding," Gavin said. "But you don't need to worry about him. He's in no danger in the jail."

"That's good to know, but it's not exactly what I was asking. What I meant is, how long—" Esther moistened her lips, then pushed on. "How long do you think he'll be there?"

Deborah saw Gavin's eyes fill with compassion, saw him glance away, then force himself to look back at Esther, and she knew then, knew fully and completely, that they were in for a long fight.

"Shane plans to file charges."

"File charges?" Callie's voice rose so high Max growled. "For what?"

"For murder. Shane doesn't like it either—believe me—but he can't ignore the evidence, and he has enough to hold Reuben until the judge hears the initial arraignment."

"Like what?" Callie moved toward Gavin, but he shook his head.

"You know I can't tell you—"

"Well, what did he find, Andrew? Reuben's fingerprints around the girl's neck? Oh, wait. She'd been whacked in back of the head ..."

"Callie—"

"Did he find a hammer hidden in the woodshed?"

"Callie."

"You know Reuben couldn't have done this!" Callie actually stamped her foot.

Deborah stepped forward and put her arm around Esther lest she collapse right there on Callie's pavement. Though they'd known Reuben had been arrested and had talked about it at the house, to hear it coming out of Gavin's mouth made it seem more real, more serious. "Adalyn will be there soon—" Deborah said, trying to comfort Esther.

"It's good that Adalyn will help, but it won't change the nature of the charge," Gavin continued.

Esther's entire body had gone rigid, like ice had settled over her, and it worried Deborah more than if she'd broken into sobs. She glanced at Callie for help.

But Callie was still trying to catch up, still looking from Deborah to Esther to Gavin, her head moving back and forth like a bird caught on a strong breeze.

"What is an initial arraignment, Andrew?" Deborah kept her voice steady, aiming for optimism. "What does that mean?"

"It's a formal reading of the charges. The defendant — Reuben — is informed of his right to retain counsel."

"Adalyn." Callie stepped closer to Deborah and Esther, finally seeming to grasp what was happening, and as she did, she joined them in this wave of trouble that was crashing toward them. "His counsel will be Adalyn."

"Yes, or he can choose someone with more criminal experience."

"Then what happens?" Deborah wanted it out, wanted the worst of it right now.

"The judge will decide whether to set bail, and if so, what amount. In this case, I wouldn't expect it. That's only my opinion though, and Shane would have my head if he even knew I was talking to you about a pending case."

"Why wouldn't the judge set bail?" Callie sounded calmer now, but still offended, as if it were all some giant mistake.

Deborah wasn't entirely clear on what bail meant, though she understood it had to do with money, and money wouldn't be a problem. Family and friends would provide whatever money Reuben needed.

"I can't say any more." Gavin's radio squawked once, and he reached to answer it. When he'd clipped it back to his belt, he turned again to Esther. "I'm sorry I don't have better news. The judge wasn't scheduled to be here again until Friday, but she's coming in early for the initial arraignment. She'll be here Thursday morning."

"Thank you, Andrew." Callie looked as if she wanted to say more, even reached out to stop him, but then drew her hand back. Instead she herded the children into the shop, Max trotting along beside them, while Deborah helped Esther.

What was it that Shane Black had learned? What terrible evidence had he found that would convince a judge that Reuben needed to stay in the *Englisch* jail? And did this mean Esther was right? Would Tobias want to postpone the wedding?

Reuben gazed down at his handcuffed hands. The confines of being arrested still surprised him, even after two days. He woke in the morning and expected to be able to walk out to the fields and do his day's work.

Being idle was difficult.

His arms were large, powerful.

He tugged on the chains once, then again, causing them to rattle. It seemed as though he should be able to break the thin bands of metal, but of course they didn't give at all.

The *Englischers* had done their job well.

"Reuben, are you listening to me?" Adalyn Landt leaned across the table. She was a big woman, reminding him some of his own *mamm*—gray hair pulled back in a bun, thick through the waist, tallish, and no nonsense about her. There the similarities ended though. Adalyn wore a dark blue business suit with a bit of orange trim, light makeup, and her mannerisms were all *Englisch*.

She tapped the folder that lay on the polished oak table.

Oak.

He rubbed his fingers across it. There were so many things he'd miss if matters continued down the path it seemed they would, the path that seemed to be *Gotte's wille*. Already his heart ached from all that would be torn from his life.

He touched the overly polished finish of the table and longed for the clean scents of his woodworking shop. It had been only two days, but he missed working with his wood, missed his family more—his *mamm* and *dat* and, of course, Tobias—missed the fields and the animals.

Missed his freedom.

But what was the alternative? He'd chased it round in his

mind like a hungry barn cat chasing a mouse through bales of hay. He saw no way out.

A girl was dead, and according to *Englisch* laws, it must be investigated.

According to Black, murder had been committed, and the guilty party must pay.

He looked up to meet Adalyn's waiting gaze. "Did you speak to Deborah?"

"She'll be here soon, but I don't see how Deborah can help your case."

He shrugged and stared down at his hands again, which he'd allowed to fall in his lap.

Instead of backing off, Adalyn walked around the table, pulled out the chair next to him, and sat. "Stop frowning at your hands, Reuben. Look out the window. Look at that large tree, how it rises against the sky. Look at the last of the fall leaves."

Resisting her suggestion was futile. Reuben raised his eyes and took in the autumn morning.

Her voice was urgent, low, and so close he could smell the peppermint candy she'd eaten before entering the room. "Now I can't guarantee that we can win this. However, I can promise that you won't see fall turn to winter—not one day of it—if you don't start talking to me and give me something, some reason to convince the judge that you aren't going to hurt anyone. *Englisch* trials are a long, slow process. I'd rather you do the waiting on the outside."

Reuben looked at her then, really looked at her. Let his gaze drill into the depths of her blue eyes, eyes that resembled the steel he'd seen on the rims of the *Englischers'* tires. This was a woman who would fight for him. The problem was that Reuben had spent his entire life avoiding fights, and yes—avoiding the *Englischers* as much as possible.

Now he was to trust her?

How could he begin to tell Adalyn Landt everything that had happened since Katie had shown up at his farm six days ago? How could he explain what he didn't understand himself?

He was saved from the attempt by a light tap on the door.

He saw Deborah's prayer *kapp* first, then she entered the room, turned toward them, and allowed a small smile to crease her worried face. Reuben let out an audible sigh.

"I'm glad you're here, Deborah. Maybe you can talk some sense into him."

"There are more problems?"

"He won't speak. He won't give me anything to use in his defense. We go in front of Judge Stearns in fifteen minutes, and I don't know what I'm going to tell her other than this man who looks like he could take on an ox single-handedly most assuredly didn't kill anyone, because he couldn't kill anyone, because he's Amish, and we all know Amish folk are the meek of the earth." Adalyn picked up her bag, which appeared to be made of a nicer leather than Reuben's finest harness and matched the piping on her dark blue suit, and pulled the strap over her shoulder.

She walked across the room as if she were ready to take on the Shipshewana officers outside. Reuben had no doubt that she could handle them on her own.

"I'm going to the ladies' room. There's a guard in the hall, so don't even try escaping with him." She stopped and gave Deborah a hug. "I'll buy you pie for a month if you persuade him to talk."

Then she was gone.

Reuben waited until the door had closed, waited until Deborah had walked across the room and taken the seat Adalyn had vacated. He waited until the silence had settled around them with the warmth of a quilt against a blizzard.

Deborah didn't speak first, but then he didn't expect her to. The quietness soothed him. If there was anything about the jail that pricked his soul, it was the constant noise. He supposed it was a small price to pay.

Raising his still-cuffed hands, he clumsily ran one over his face, then cleared his throat and began. "Guess you're wondering why I sent for you."

"Your *mamm* and *dat* are waiting outside. Tobias and Esther as well."

Reuben shook his head. "They'll be having a hard enough time with this. Don't want to cause them more pain than what has already been laid at their door." Tears stung his eyes, but he blinked them away.

"You've always been a *gut freind* to my family," he continued.

"And I always will be."

"I knew I could trust you to see that what I ask is done. Tobias is to proceed with the wedding next week. He might be tempted to postpone, but I want him to carry on as if I were there. I imagine it would be easier if they live at our place now, since it might be some time before I'm back home to work the fields and see to the animals. Suspect they'd rather live in the house than the barn, but that's up to the family to decide."

"Reuben, why are you speaking as if you won't be home for a while?"

He tried to answer her, tried to push out the words that had been filling his heart with dread. Inside it felt as if one of the rare earthquakes of central Indiana had hit. He actually reached out for the table in front of him, as if the ground had shifted and settled again.

But it hadn't.

It was his life that had changed, and it would never be the same.

"You mustn't act as if you're going to be here long. Adalyn is a fine lawyer—"

He stood suddenly, her words dying when his chair crashed to the floor. No tears came to his eyes though. He wouldn't cry for this thing he'd pay for. Best to bear a thing and be done with it. Best to keep the emotions at arms' length in this case.

"And I appreciate you sending her, but I'm thinking there isn't much she can do. Black laid out the evidence they have, and he explained the sentence for murder."

Pulling in a deep breath, he forced himself to look at her. "Will you tell them what I said?"

"*Ya*. Of course I will."

He turned his back to her then, stared out at the fall day, and refused to speak any more. Which was how Adalyn found them when she returned with the guard to escort him in to see the judge.

Chapter 12

CALLIE COULDN'T HAVE BEEN HAPPIER despite the circumstances.

A year and a half ago she'd been flying around the country, hurrying to sales meetings, and pushing to be the top pharmaceutical rep for the Houston firm that employed her. She had no real friends, an apartment she rarely visited, and a giant hole in her heart left from Rick's passing.

Looking around her circle of friends, she was still amazed at how much could change in so little time. Deborah, Melinda, and Esther were not the type of women she'd have associated with in her other life, but now it seemed as if she'd known them forever. She couldn't imagine going through a day without them.

Her life was very nearly perfect, except for the absence of Rick and the fact that someone dear to her was once again involved in a murder investigation.

And the mess of material in her lap.

"Are you sure this wouldn't be easier with a machine?" Callie looked down at her crooked row of stitches and considered ripping them out.

"Easier isn't always better," Melinda noted, her eyes crinkling into a smile as she quickly and neatly sewed a strip of blue fabric around a green quilt block.

"Say. I like what you're doing there. Maybe I should try that."

"She's sashing, and you're not quite ready for that step yet. Best to continue with piecing your square together." Deborah exchanged a smile with Esther.

"I don't know. Maybe I should start over. This looks terrible. My stitches aren't the same size, and they look more like a wave than a row. I think I'll pull them out—"

"Don't do it, Miss Callie." Martha, Deborah's ten-year-old daughter, set her own sewing aside and moved to stand beside her. "Imagine a straight line and keep sewing. If you continue to pull out those stitches every ten minutes, your quilt square is going to look like Swiss cheese."

The group of women burst into laughter. Callie wanted to stick her lip out and pout, but she was so relieved to see Esther laugh, even for a moment, that she didn't mind being the brunt of the joke. "This is terrible, and you know it. Mine will never look as good as your *mamm*'s."

"Each person's work looks different." Martha pulled her stool closer. "Your stitches look as good as mine when I started."

"And you were—"

Martha hesitated, but Deborah answered.

"She finished her first quilt when she was eight. It was a small one that we used for Joshua's bed."

"Eight? I was playing with Barbie dolls when I was eight."

"*Ya*, Amish children have a different life—it's true." Melinda reached under her glasses to rub her eyes. "But don't think it's not playing for our children as well."

Callie followed Esther's glance, over to Leah, who was using a large plastic needle to draw yarn back and forth through a wooden board that had holes drilled out of it. The board had been sanded, smoothed, and shellacked so the yarn wouldn't catch on the edges. Leah was making a design all to her liking, that much seemed obvious to Callie. The girl was humming softly as she sewed.

Esther turned back to the group, a wistful note in her voice. "I remember when we were *kinner*, nearly Martha's age. We used to pretend that we were grown-ups, making quilts for the kittens in the barn."

"I remember taking one to the barn and having to do extra laundry chores for a week." Deborah stood and rubbed at the small of her back. "I could not understand why quilts weren't for kittens."

"So you're telling me to keep sewing."

"Exactly," Martha said. "You'll improve, as I did. Try holding your needle this way."

"I want perfect stitches, and a perfect square like everyone else," Callie muttered.

"We don't all receive what we want, and best be glad for that." Martha sounded so much like Deborah that they all burst out laughing again, all except Esther, who set her quilting aside.

They'd chosen Friday and Monday afternoons for their quilting circle. On Fridays, the weekend shoppers hadn't arrived yet—and it wasn't a market day. On Mondays, the shop was closed, and by the afternoon, Callie was done restocking.

"How is your feud with Mrs. Knepp going, Callie?" Melinda never slowed in her stitching as she glanced up then back down again.

"I tried sending her a letter, but it was returned unopened."

"She's a bit mulish," Deborah admitted.

"A bit? I thought Texans were stubborn. This woman is more obstinate than a west Texas bull. The letter was an invitation to tea. I thought we could host a quilting sale together, maybe promote each other's business. So far nothing I've tried with her works."

"Perhaps you should let her be," Melinda suggested.

"Hard to do since hers is the only other quilt shop in town. It just seems that we'd do better business if we coordinated things occasionally."

"It didn't help when Trent included a picture of you in Amish clothing on the front page," Deborah teased. "Mrs. Knepp was ranting about it when I stopped in to say hello. She seemed personally offended."

"As if my being there was related to the story at all." Callie frowned as she focused on ripping out her stitches. "I asked Trent why he included the picture of me and Max hurrying toward the scene and he said we sell papers. People want to know what trouble we've managed to find."

"I doubt Shane was happy with the photo of the girl in the pond—even if there wasn't much of her shown." Melinda glanced around the group. "Trent must be pleased though. I heard they had to print extra copies of the paper, they sold so many."

"That man would photograph his own mother if it would sell papers." Callie set aside her sewing.

When Esther stood and began pacing slowly back and forth, her hands crumpling her apron, Callie decided it was time for tea and cookies.

Hurrying to the kitchen, she grabbed the tray of mugs and tea supplies, then turned and nearly bumped into Deborah.

"I'll help you carry those."

"Thanks. Do you think she'll be all right?"

"Esther will be fine. It's natural for her to worry. We're all worried, but God will take care of Reuben. Have faith, Callie."

Instead of asking the dozens of questions she had, Callie nodded and marched toward the sitting area at the back of the shop. Max looked up hopefully, so she gave Leah a dog treat and asked her to take it to him.

"Esther, tea?"

"*Ya.* I suppose so." She sat, then popped back up again.

Melinda carefully stored her own sewing needle, walked over to her, and planted herself firmly in the path of her pacing. When Esther moved to sidestep to the right, Melinda stepped with her, reaching out to rub both of her arms gently.

"It's going to be all right."

"I know it will."

"Come and talk about it."

"*Ya*, maybe that will help."

It took an entire cup of chamomile before Esther found the words, but then they began pouring like water from a stream that had been suddenly undammed. "Tobias agrees with what Reuben said, Deborah. He wishes to go on with the wedding. Says our life —" she glanced over to Leah, down at her lap, then back up again. "He says that we can show our faith in Reuben best by continuing on as usual."

A tear slipped down her cheek, and she brushed it away. "He really is a very *gut* man — they both are."

"Of course they are." Deborah reached over and squeezed her hand. "Yesterday was only the informal arraignment, Esther. We mustn't become discouraged."

"Explain to me again why the judge wouldn't grant bail?" Melinda reached for an oatmeal cookie, broke it in half, and handed a small piece to her one-year-old, Hannah.

"Adalyn said it was because he hadn't cooperated with the court. What do you think she meant by that, Callie?"

Looking around her, Callie took a few sips, wondering how to explain the *Englisch* legal system to her Amish friends. Even after what they'd been through a few months earlier with Stakehorn, this seemed new to them, perhaps because they'd never had a friend on the other side of the jail cell. The situation when Esther's first husband had died had been somewhat similar, but the boys responsible had never been charged.

"Didn't you say he refused to enter any kind of plea?"

"*Ya*. He still won't talk." Deborah shook her head.

"I looked that up on Google last night, since both Andrew and Shane refuse to discuss the case with me. The defendant has a right to silence. He can stand mute."

"Reuben appears mute," Melinda muttered.

"Apparently it's frowned upon."

"Adalyn was very upset," Esther admitted. "She even left her leather bag in the car, and I've never known her to forget it."

"If he had not insisted on remaining silent, the court would have entered a plea of not guilty. It looks better if the man on trial *says* he's not guilty," Callie continued. Everyone thought on that for a moment. "You said he's still refusing to give a statement?" Callie asked.

"*Ya*, I think that's what Adalyn was so bothered about."

"The court can't require him to testify against himself, but if he were cooperating—which the judge would prefer—he would seem more forthcoming."

Every face in the room remained turned toward her, waiting for more of an explanation. Callie looked toward the front of the shop, toward the windows, where she could see the back of the "Information Wanted" poster that Gavin had taped there yesterday. It contained an artist's rendering of a young Amish girl with beautiful brown eyes and golden hair, wearing a green-colored dress.

There was one in every shop window in town.

"For instance, Andrew said that Reuben knew the girl, but has he explained to anyone who she is?"

Now the women looked down at the quilting materials in the middle of their circle.

"Perhaps Officer Gavin was mistaken," Melinda finally offered.

"Doubtful. Andrew's trained in such things." Callie set her cup down on the table.

"If he saw them together, which is what Tobias heard Officer Gavin say, then maybe they do know each other, but not well." Esther nibbled around a cookie as she spoke. "But it doesn't seem possible that the girl was staying in the house."

Deborah never glanced up. "Tobias told Jonas that before they handcuffed Reuben, they did some sort of testing in the house. Do you know what that was?"

"Supposedly they found blood from the girl's head wound. Tobias was allowed back in the house the next day, but he didn't see anything."

Callie had forgotten there were so many things the Amish simply were not exposed to — like crime television. "Blood can be washed away to the point where you can't see it, but there are still trace particles there. When the police use luminol sprays, the spray exposes even small amounts of blood."

"How do you know these things?" Deborah asked. "Agatha Christie?"

"Television."

"Oh. Esther, how did Tobias not see her? What I mean is, does he think the girl was hiding, so he wouldn't see her?" Deborah blushed slightly as she asked the question.

"No. We talked it through some last night, and he admitted he hadn't even been back to his *grossdaddi*'s property in a week, and he hasn't been inside the house in a year or more. Otherwise Shane might have tried to arrest him as well. Tobias could be sharing that *Englisch* cell with Reuben." Esther paled as she spoke. Deborah picked up Esther's cup of tea and pushed it into her hands, but she ignored it. "Tobias was pulling double shifts at the feed store, so he had been staying with his parents for the past week. They live closer to town. Some nights he even slept on a pallet in the workroom."

"And he has witnesses to attest to that, I'm sure." Callie reached out and rubbed behind Max's ears when he padded next to her.

"*Ya*, lots of them. Apparently the girl arrived sometime after last Wednesday. Tuesday was the last day Tobias had been to the farm. He hadn't mentioned to me he was working extra hours. He didn't want me to worry. The money was to help with our setting up house."

"All right. This is good. Maybe we can solve this thing." Deborah sat forward, an optimistic look on her face.

"Solve this thing? Now you sound like old Mr. Bontrager. We're not sleuths. We're quilters. Well, you all are quilters; apparently I make cheese." Callie put an arm around Martha as the last words popped out of her mouth. "It's not our job to solve this crime."

"But it is our job to stand by *freinden*," Deborah pointed out. "For some reason Reuben won't defend himself."

"And to Shane and the judge, that looks like guilt." Melinda picked up her quilting and began sewing again. "But our men have times where they grow quiet. When that happens, it's no use trying to pull a word out of them."

"Reuben's not one to offer much up in the way of conversation anyway." Esther motioned to Leah to begin collecting her things.

"But to stay quiet when it means serving time in jail for murder?" Callie shook her head, dark hair bobbing side to side. "I can't imagine what would cause anyone to do that."

"Of course you can. We all can." Deborah reached for her purse and pulled out a small pad of paper and a pen. "There are reasons you'd do such a thing. It's only that the list is short. We'd all keep our mouths closed and suffer years for our children."

"But Reuben has no children." Esther was clearly considering Deborah's words.

"Let's start there. We don't need to find the girl's killer, Callie. You were right. We were lucky with Stakehorn's murder—"

"And technically we caught the wrong person," Callie cut Deborah off.

"True enough, though it still resulted in the correct arrest."

Callie rolled her eyes, feeling like a twelve-year-old, but also feeling better with the immature gesture.

Deborah pushed on. "All we need to do is find Reuben's reason for remaining silent."

As Deborah wrote her list, which was disappointingly brief, Callie wracked her brain trying to think of possibilities to add to it. But even as she focused on helping Deborah, on helping Reuben, her mind began wandering back to Tuesday morning, back to Mr. Bontrager and the daughter he claimed to have lost.

Chapter 13

FRIDAY EVENING, Samuel crept deep into the woods, far from Reuben's house. He'd wanted to stay, wanted to see if Reuben came back, but the police had made him nervous, so Samuel had left and wandered around the woods for days, confused and disoriented. Lost without his Katie. But he'd been careful to stay beneath the trees.

Now he dumped everything out of his pack and took stock.

He was cold and he was hungry and he didn't think he'd survive another night in the woods. Already he'd developed a hacking cough. The hunger pains that had increased as his supplies diminished had been replaced by a constant nausea. He'd taken to drinking water from the stream when the bottles he'd brought had run dry.

It was time to make a decision, starting with what he knew.

Katie was dead.

Reuben wasn't coming back any time soon.

The police had searched the entire property and started toward the fields, but before they'd gone as far as the woods, someone had shouted from the pond. Apparently they'd found whatever clue they had sought. Then there was a lot of activity and excitement for a time. When they'd begun searching the house, the house he'd shared with Katie, someone actually yelled out for the officer from the front door, though he couldn't make out the rest of the man's words.

The amount of equipment they'd used was staggering. What could they possibly have been looking for?

Whatever it was, they'd apparently found it.

He'd watched as they'd cuffed Reuben, then escorted him to the police cruiser.

Terrified they'd find him in the woods, Samuel had pulled his things together—including Katie's quilt, and he'd run.

He flipped on his flashlight and pawed through the contents of his pack: a county map, his pocketknife, the trash from what he'd been eating—which was mostly junk food he and Katie had bought together in town—both of his changes of clothes, and the envelope from the LaGrange justice of the peace . . .

Samuel's fingers lingered on the envelope, brushed across their names, but he pushed the memory away.

The map, he studied.

He'd need to stick to the smaller roads. Maybe he could pick up a ride once he'd traveled another ten miles. He'd have to find something to eat soon, and he needed to burn the bloodstained quilt.

As long as he continued to follow the creek south, he should be okay. Four miles, maybe five, then he could move out of the woods.

Making his way down to the water, he removed his shirt, then his undershirt. He dipped a corner of the cloth into the water and began scrubbing himself, cringing when the fabric met his skin. It would do no good to frighten people with his smell.

Once he was as presentable as he could make himself, Samuel changed into the cleaner set of clothes and bundled the dirty set, placing it into the bottom of the pack—on top of the trash.

The second set of clothes went above that, and the knife he slipped into his right pocket.

What to do with the envelope and papers?

He should burn them with the quilt. He knew he should.

Samuel started a small fire with kindling he collected from the forest, letting it build to a good blaze before pulling the knife out of his pocket and cutting the quilt into strips, which he fed to the flames. While the quilt burned, Samuel held the envelope and papers in his hand, trying to convince himself to throw them in the fire.

But instead he slipped them back into the bag and slung the bag over his shoulders. Then he reached down and picked up Katie's duffle. What was he to do with that? The heaviness of his burdens suddenly seemed too much. He didn't know how he could carry them.

One thing was certain.

He couldn't wait here in the woods forever.

Kicking dirt onto the last of the fire, Samuel clutched the duffle, cinched his bag over his shoulder, and began to walk.

With each step, it seemed he could feel the weight of the words printed on the top sheet. But for those words, would Katie still be alive?

Samuel tried to focus on the ground, on making as little noise as possible, and on staying near the creek as he made his way south, but his mind insisted on going back ...

"Nervous?" he asked, helping her out of the buggy.

"A little." She smoothed her apron over her blue dress, then reached for his hand as they walked up the steps of the LaGrange County Courthouse.

Instead of opening the door for her, he pulled her toward a bench that had been placed to the side, under the branches of a silver maple tree. Most of the leaves were gone, but the day was warm for late October. Katie looked up when a yellow warbler lighted near them, sang once, then flew away. When she glanced back at him, he thought his heart might burst right out of his chest.

He loved her more than he'd ever thought possible.

More than he had last night when they'd stopped to rest at her aenti's house. It had seemed the wise thing to do, and they hadn't exactly lied when they told her that their business required they press on earlier than they had originally planned. It was but a stretching of the truth and would keep Katie's family from worrying. By the time her mamm and dat realized Katie hadn't actually stayed there, that Samuel wasn't coming back when he was scheduled to, they would be married, and it would be too late for anyone to change their plans.

He'd wondered if he might have second thoughts as the moment grew closer, but the strength of his feelings for her surprised him. Was this what it was like to care for someone more than yourself? He found that he was more certain than ever that their plan was the right one.

In Shipshe he'd be able to find good work and provide for her like a husband should.

Still, he needed to allow Katie one more chance to change her mind.

"What is it, Samuel? Are you having second thoughts?" She smiled up at him then, her brown eyes looking fully into his, and he had to reach out and touch her face. He marveled that the brush of his hand could make her blush, but she did.

"I'm thinking a lot of things, Katie, but I'm not questioning the wisdom of what we're doing. I want to give you a chance to stop here, though. I'll take you back to your parents if that's what you want, no harm done."

Her eyes widened, but he pushed on.

"And though you know how I feel about continuing to work for your dat, I would do it. I'd do it because I care for you, and I wouldn't want to rush you into anything or deprive you of an Amish wedding with your family. That's one thing that weighs heavy on me now that we're about to— "

Katie put her fingers to his lips and pressed lightly.

"Stop."

"But—"

"No. Stop. I appreciate your concern, Samuel. And at first maybe I did agree because I saw how much it meant to you. But after we talked I began to watch how things were around my dat. You're right. He clings to the old ways even more than the Ordnung requires. Perhaps because he is afraid, or because he doesn't know how to move even with the changes that our bishop allows. I don't know. But I see the burden it has brought upon my mamm."

She looked up at the warbler, which had returned to a neighboring tree. "Not that I love him any less. I couldn't, but I also think we have to do what is right for us. It's gut and right for us to begin with our own life, together."

"And the Amish wedding?"

"I brought the one quilt that meant the most. It's in the buggy. You spoke with the Mennonite bishop?"

"Ya. He's probably waiting inside."

"Let's go see him then. Let's go be married, Samuel."

Chapter 14

SATURDAY MORNING Esther sat beside her mother, Sara, yards of cloth for her wedding dress, and for a dress for Leah, stretched between them.

"This dress will be nice for Sundays," Sara said, straightening the dark blue material before she pulled it through the treadle sewing machine. "I've always liked the way this color looks on you. Do you remember the dress you had for Christmas when you were fifteen?"

"*Ya*. We let it out three times before I would admit I'd outgrown it. I always loved that dress." Esther paused in her hemming of Leah's dress, fingered the soft cotton a moment before she looked up at her *mamm*. "Seems a long time ago. Hard to believe I'm more than double that age now. Thirty-one sounds old."

Sara cocked her head, paused in turning the wheel of the old-fashioned Singer machine. When she began again, she had to raise her voice a little to be heard over the whirr as the stitches were laid down in a perfect row, pulling the seam together neatly. "Suppose it does sound old to you, but trust me when I say it's not."

Esther shook her head and began stitching again, whipping the hem by hand.

Sara stopped sewing, went to the *kaffi* pot sitting on her stove, and refilled her cup. When she came back to the table, she sat with her back to the machine, facing her daughter instead. For Esther, looking at her mother was like looking in a mirror. Sara had the same dark hair—now tinged with gray—blue eyes, and thin frame. They differed only in height, which Esther had received from her father.

"Don't believe me?" Sara asked.

"I suppose it seems that way to you. After all I've been through the last few years though, I feel old."

"*Ya*. At your age, when the *kinner* are small yet, it can appear that way. I think in another year or so, you'll feel younger."

Esther glanced up, giving her a disbelieving look, but didn't bother to argue, didn't pause in her sewing.

"Do you remember when your *dat* first planted the orchard of dwarf apple trees in the southern pasture?"

"How could I forget? Every year we would wait for the harvest because we were allowed to eat the seconds. Every year I made myself sick eating too many." Esther smiled at the memory. The Red Delicious apples had given her plenty of stomachaches at the time, but she had never been able to resist eating just one more.

Age and maturity had finally taught her to stop at two.

"What you might not remember is that after we'd been harvesting for five years, we had a late spring snow, very late." Sara stared out her kitchen window. Though the orchard was not visible from the window, Esther knew she was seeing it. "The flowers had barely bloomed on the branches when the snow began to fall. Your father was certain it would ruin the year's fruit, and possibly damage every tree in the orchard. We were new to apple growing then and have since learned just how sturdy apple trees are, but at the time he worried. He wanted to take all of my bedsheets and cover them. Instead I convinced him to go down to the phone shack and call the man he'd bought the trees from who owned an orchard in Ohio."

107

She sipped the *kaffi* and smiled.

"I don't remember any of this," Esther admitted.

"You wouldn't. You were very young at the time, worried more about your lessons and what would happen at recess the next day."

"How many of the trees did he lose?"

"None. Just the blossoms." Sara shook her head, as she carried her cup to the sink. "It's not what he lost that I was thinking of though. The man from Ohio told him that the storm would make the trees stronger. He told your *dat* not to worry, not to fret over what he had no chance of controlling. The trees were young then. Now they're mature, and your father—both of us, truthfully—worry less about storms. We know the trees can handle whatever nature brings."

Esther stared at her for a few seconds, before finding her voice. "Would you be comparing me to an apple tree?"

Sara kissed her on the top of the head, making Esther feel for all the world like a small *kind* again. "No, *dochder*. I'm comparing you to your father."

As Esther finished Leah's dress and new apron, then helped her daughter try it on, the daughter whom she loved more dearly than the breath she pulled into her own lungs, she kept thinking of her mother's story. She kept thinking of the trees in the orchard. Esther had grown up there, and maybe they were the reason she loved to garden so.

After Seth's death, when little else could sooth her soul, when reading the Bible seemed to bring more questions than answers, Esther had been able to walk through her garden and find the closeness to her Lord that she needed.

When she'd knelt in the dirt she'd been able to pray.

When she'd trimmed away the flowers' dead buds, she'd finally been able to cry.

And when she'd seen the new blossoms of spring, she'd felt a tiny sprig of hope, and yes—she'd finally been able to thank God again for all he'd left her.

The land.

Her family.

Leah.

Still, Esther did feel old, and it was hard to believe she would feel younger as the years passed. She would admit she was like her father in many ways—that part of her mother's story she understood. And she even understood that hard times created strength in each person.

But younger as the years passed?

No, that was beyond her ability to imagine.

Just then, Tobias arrived to take Esther into town.

"You have your invitations?" Sara asked.

"Yes. They're all here in my bag."

"Why can't I go, *Mamm*?" Leah knelt in the dirt outside, drawing something with her finger and looking forlorn.

Before Esther could think of an answer, her father, Obe, was there, kneeling beside Leah. Esther had always considered him as something of a mountain of a man—nearing six-four or six-five and muscular in the way of men who worked the land. As he'd grown older, he'd retained the fitness he'd needed, but something had softened about him. She could see it as she watched him with Leah.

"Thought you were going to help me catch some fish for dinner?" Obe asked.

Leah didn't look up immediately, but she did dust her hands on her apron. "I'm not a *gut* fisher."

"You will be today. Your *onkel* Saul told me they were fairly jumping out of the creek."

"Fish don't jump, *Daadi*." Leah began to giggle.

"Well, now. We'll have to walk down to the creek and see. Perhaps we should take the little butterfly net you received for Christmas just in case any happen to jump onto the bank. We could catch them in the air." Obe reached out with his hand and pantomimed the act of catching and wrestling a small fish, finally subduing and putting it into his pocket.

Leah turned and threw her arms around her grandpa's neck. "I left my butterfly net in the family room. Come with me to get it."

"*Ya*, and maybe while we're in the house your *mammi* will give us a snack to eat at the creek."

Esther mouthed a thank-you as she climbed into the buggy. When her father winked at her and waved good-bye, she saw it—she saw the younger man her mother had spoken of. When she'd been growing up, he'd been weighed down with burdens. Where were those now? Had they disappeared? Or had he learned to lay them down?

"You're awfully quiet today." Tobias directed the mare onto the road.

"Thinking of something my *mamm* said earlier."

"Anything you want to share?"

Esther sighed. "I'm not sure I understand it completely, but it was about apple trees and how we grow younger as we get older."

Tobias' laughter echoed down the road as they began to make their stops, inviting friends and family to their wedding the following week.

The concern about Reuben remained with them throughout the trip, something Esther knew they'd both live with until his situation was resolved.

But the image of the trees—mature, strong, and fruitful—along with that of her father, carrying Leah back into the house to find a net for catching flying fish they might eat for their evening meal, gave her hope that God remained in control.

Callie had enjoyed a busy Saturday morning. It was past one when things had finally settled down enough to take Max for a quick trot around the garden. The weather was so nice she'd left him sleeping in the sun and had come inside to heat a bowl of soup for her lunch. She was cleaning up her dishes in the quilt shop's kitchen when the bell over the door rang again.

Callie was surprised to see not only Esther, but also Tobias. As far as she knew, Tobias had never been in the quilt shop before.

Immediately her mind went to Reuben, and she hoped they weren't in town because something else had cropped up with his case. Then she noticed the smile on Esther's face and she relaxed. This was definitely a good-news visit.

"It's so nice to see you both," Callie greeted them.

"Nice to see you as well. Tobias, you remember Callie."

"Hello." He tipped his hat, and Callie thought of Ollie from the old Laurel and Hardy re-runs she'd watched with Rick. Tobias was such a tall man, and a perfect match for Esther. Not just because of his height, but because it was plain he was completely smitten with her.

His hand hovered near her elbow, and a smile played on his lips as if he were about to reveal the world's best-kept secret.

"What brings you into town today?"

Esther stepped toward the counter, pulled an envelope from her bag, and placed it on the glass between them, her fingers lingering for a moment on the edges. Callie's name was written in beautiful handwriting across the front. "We wanted to invite you to our wedding next Thursday. It will be at my parents' home. I wrote directions for you on the back of the invitation."

Callie picked up the envelope, unsure whether she was supposed to read it now or wait.

"You can open it." Tobias stepped even closer to Esther. "She's been working on them for over a week—"

"Melinda helped."

"They both did a *wunderbaar* job. Look and see."

Callie popped open the envelope and slid out the card, which she couldn't read a word of. "It's in German."

"*Ya*, well the service is in German too, as all of our church services are."

"You can make out our names though." Tobias chuckled and pointed to their names on the card. "Names pretty much read the same whether in the new language or the old."

"Also you can tell the time. The service begins at eight thirty in the morning." Esther gazed up at Tobias as she spoke, and Callie inexplicably felt tears sting her eyes.

"That's wonderful. I think morning weddings are beautiful, though I've never been to one quite that early." Callie wondered if she'd ever stop being surprised by how different some things were between the Amish and *Englischers*. About the time she thought they were really more alike than different, she was confronted with something like an early morning wedding.

"Actually, our weddings last all day." Tobias chuckled when Callie looked from the card to him to Esther, then back down again. "She's not accustomed to our ways, I see."

"Callie learns fast, but this is her first wedding season."

"Did you say all day?"

"*Ya*. The service is approximately four hours ..." Tobias rubbed his chin thoughtfully.

"Followed by the meal, which will take another two." Esther pulled her bag up over her shoulder.

"And then the singing and supper," Tobias added. "We'll be handing out candy bars after supper so you won't want to leave early. Excellent chocolate."

"I think you'll enjoy the experience." Esther looked up at Tobias. "Not many *Englischers* have the opportunity to witness an Amish wedding. I hope you can come. Actually it would mean a lot to me—to me and Tobias—if you could be there."

Callie knew then she would go, even if it meant closing the shop for the day, though that probably wouldn't be necessary.

"Lydia is working full-time now, so I'm sure she can watch the shop for me. Unless she's going to be at the wedding too?"

"I hadn't thought to invite her, no." Esther shook her head. "Say, Callie. Would you mind if I used your restroom?"

"Of course not. You know where it is."

Callie was left standing at the counter, staring at Tobias. She probably hadn't talked to Tobias three times since she'd moved to Shipshe, and never alone. Like most Amish men she had met, he seemed content to stand in silence.

Her mind drifting back to Reuben, Callie felt like she needed to offer her sympathy. Perhaps while Esther was gone would be a good time. "Tobias, I don't know Reuben very well, but you know … after my run-in with the law a few months ago I can certainly sympathize."

Tobias nodded. After a few seconds, he removed his coat, folded it neatly in half, and set it on the counter. Then in a conspiratorial voice, he said, "Half of Shipshe was afraid the new shop owner might end up in the pokey for good. You gave us quite a scare. Not that anyone would think you were capable of murder — Esther and the girls certainly didn't think so."

He stood straight again and grinned.

"Tobias Fisher. Are you teasing me about being arrested?"

"You have to admit, it didn't look real *gut* being new in town and all."

"It certainly didn't. I was mortally embarrassed. Not to mention, I didn't even know Andrew Gavin or Shane Black." Callie's stomach flipped at the memory of sitting across the table from Shane inside the Shipshewana Police Department. He didn't intimidate her — not exactly. The man was infuriating on one hand and intriguing on the other. "I thought Gavin might be incompetent and Black … overzealous possibly."

"And what do you think now?" The joking suddenly gone, Tobias studied her carefully, waiting for her answer.

"Now I think they're good men who are intent on doing their job. But, Tobias, why won't Reuben speak to them? Why won't he tell them what he knows? It might help to gain his freedom, at least until his trial."

"Did it help you any when you talked to Black?"

"Well, no, not really, but—"

"Then why do you think it would help Reuben?"

"This is different."

"Perhaps it is. Perhaps it isn't. I have to trust that my cousin knows what he's doing."

Callie opened the cash register drawer, picked up a roll of pennies and cracked them open, emptying the contents as she spoke. "That's it? We trust him? Isn't there something we can do while we wait?"

"I'm doing what he told me: marry Esther and take care of the farm. Haven't heard that he left you any instructions." His gaze traveled to Callie's framed picture as Esther walked back into the room.

This was twice in the last week that someone had drawn her attention to Stakehorn's case—a case that she and Deborah hadn't actually solved. They'd survived it, but it wasn't actually fair to say they'd solved it.

Okay, maybe they'd helped to solve it.

Callie walked the happy couple out to their buggy. They'd climbed in by the time she thought to ask Tobias about Mr. Bontrager.

"*Ya*, Esther told me you met him, but I don't remember anything about a *dochder*."

"I asked my *mamm* as well, Callie. She did know Mr. Bontrager's wife, but not well. They attended church in the next district. She didn't know anything about a missing girl—said perhaps she'd met Mrs. Bontrager after the son was born."

"Sorry we can't be more help." Tobias flicked the reins and set the buggy in motion.

Waving, Callie waited until the buggy was out of sight, then retrieved Max and brought him back into the shop. She tried to focus on Reuben, tried to think of what she could possibly do to help with his case. But as she went to the stockroom and brought out a box of quilting kits to unpack, her mind kept going back to Mr. Bontrager and a daughter that he might have lost. If Mr. Bontrager's son didn't remember having a sister, then apparently the girl had been missing for over forty years.

Chapter 15

It took Deborah twenty-four hours to decide how best to proceed with helping Reuben. Saturday, after seeing to lunch for her family, she pulled out the list she had made in the quilt shop — the list of reasons Reuben might insist on keeping quiet.

Callie had been right.

There weren't many explanations for Reuben's silence, not when a brief explanation could gain his freedom.

Deborah sipped her warm tea, then tapped her pen against the paper. Had she missed anything?

"One: money." Did Reuben need money? Was this girl somehow blackmailing him for money? Did she somehow threaten his ability to keep the farm?

"Two: love." She took her pen and wrote beside this the word *Romantic* with a question mark. Had Reuben been in love with the young girl in the pond? Seemed unlikely.

"Three: love. For family or *freinden.*"

"Four: *Ordnung.*"

This last would be harder to explain to anyone outside their faith, but if Reuben felt it was the right thing to do to remain silent, the moral thing to do, then he would. Much as Esther had remained silent when Seth had died, though she had known almost immediately which boys were responsible. But then Esther hadn't been in danger of losing her own freedom. The *Ordnung* did not require this. Again Deborah put a question mark.

She couldn't think of any other reasons to add to the list, so she folded it and put it inside her handbag. Then she called Martha into the kitchen.

"Yes, *Mamm?*"

"I need to run errands in town. I'll be taking Mary and Joshua. Would you like to come with us?"

"'Course I would. What about the twins?"

"Went with your *dat* to pick up new pigs."

"New ones? What happened to the old ones?"

"Nothing happened to them. Your father thinks we need more this winter. Actually he thinks your *bruders* need more responsibility, so he's adding a few more animals."

"I wish he'd asked me about that first. I would not have picked pigs." Martha walked out of the room shaking her head, and Deborah found herself laughing even as her mind went back over the list.

Why was she so sure that Reuben was holding back something? Could be he was silent because he had nothing to say.

Then it came to her, as quickly as a bird lighting on a tree limb. She remembered the thing she'd pushed to the back of her mind. When she'd first gone to fetch Reuben, when they'd first discovered the dead girl, there had been the briefest of seconds when his eyes had grown wide, he had gone pale, and a deep sadness—like a shadow—had passed over his face. It had occurred so quickly, Deborah was surprised she'd caught it and remembered it at all.

There was no doubt at all that he'd known the girl.

His expression hadn't been one of shock or surprise like Deborah had felt. It was the look of someone who'd seen something precious ripped away.

In that split second, Deborah had seen Reuben's grief.

The question was—grief over what? The girl's death? The fact that she was found? What did the girl's death mean to Reuben?

"*M-Ma-Ma-Mamm.*" Joshua tugged on her dress, one arm wrapped firmly around her leg.

"I don't think she can hear you. You need to learn to be patient when *Mamm*'s concentrating on something else, at least that's what *Dat* says." Martha offered Joshua his favorite stuffed bear, but he turned away and buried his face in Deborah's dress.

"It's all right. I was just remembering something."

"Something important?" Martha helped Mary gather up her books and put them in a small backpack as they all made their way out the front door.

"Could be. I hope so."

"*Dat* says when you get that look on your face, we should try to wait or come back around later. He says you're puzzling things out."

"He does, does he?" Deborah reached over to straighten the prayer *kapp* worn by her eldest as they continued walking. The child was growing up too fast.

"*Ya.* He also says I act exactly like you at times."

"Hmm. I'm sure that was a compliment."

"I don't know. He said it after I'd poured hummingbird water into the pot on the stove that was for tea."

Deborah helped the children into the buggy Jonas had hitched up before he left for town. "Yes, I suppose I remember doing that once before." Deborah climbed into the buggy's front seat. "It's merely sugar and water though. I told your *dat* I was saving him the trouble of adding the sugar to his tea afterward."

She clucked to Cinnamon and turned the mare toward town. Deborah had three stops to make. Best hurry if she was to be back before dark.

Her first stop was Reuben's parents. They lived on the piece of land next to Tobias' parents—the fathers were brothers. Deborah had known the family all her life, though she'd spent more time with the women than the men.

"Why did we bring the apple crisp pie?" Mary held it in her lap as if it were a dozen eggs.

"Always nice to bring a gift, especially when a family is experiencing trouble."

"I like pie, but I don't want to have trouble to get it." Mary rubbed her hand under her chin, then looked to her *mamm*. "Is that a terrible thing to say?"

"Not at all, and I left a pie for us at home, cooling on the counter."

"*Gut*. Smelling this is making me awfully hungry."

"You ate lunch not an hour ago," Martha reminded her.

"I'm growing though—same as Jacob and Joseph."

Deborah pulled the buggy to a stop in front of the rambling farmhouse. "It's a warm day for October. I'd rather you children play on the porch while I speak with Reuben's parents. I shouldn't be long."

Martha took the younger children to the rockers at the corner of the porch as Deborah knocked on the door. Five minutes later she was sitting at the table with a cup of tea.

"So you never met the girl?" Deborah asked.

"Never even saw her. We'd been hoping Reuben would find a nice Amish girl, but he kept saying it wasn't *Gotte's* time yet." Abigail Fisher was nearly as round as she was tall, and it was plain from the redness of her eyes that she'd spent the last few days crying over her son's predicament.

"Abigail, excuse me for being so bold, but I'm trying to help Reuben—"

"I thought that woman was helping him, that lawyer."

"*Ya*. I'm sure she is. Adalyn Landt is a good lawyer, and she'll help Reuben every way the *Englisch* legal system allows her to, but there's something here that doesn't add up. It's puzzling me a bit. I don't understand why Reuben won't make a statement. Why he won't say what happened and how he knows the girl."

Tears tracked down Abigail's cheeks as she nodded her head. "I know. I don't understand either. Reuben's always been the stubborn one, but this doesn't make any sense. It's probably the reason people are saying the things they are—"

"Saying what things?"

But Abigail shook her head and refused to speak more on the subject.

She did walk Deborah out to the buggy and say hello to the children.

"Did you like our pie, Mrs. Fisher?"

"Yes, Mary. Thank you for that. Mr. Fisher will be very pleased, as I haven't done much baking this week."

Deborah climbed up into the buggy, then tried one more question. "Abigail, when was the last time you saw Reuben?"

"It's same as I told the police fellow, that Mr. Black. Reuben came by the house the Saturday before the body was found. Asking if his *dat* knew anywhere that was hiring for work."

"Work?" Deborah looked out across the fields and thought about what Tobias had told her about staying in town and covering double shifts. "But wasn't he having trouble keeping up at the farm, what with no help from Tobias?"

Abigail sighed, scrubbed at her cheeks again with the handkerchief. "Makes no sense, no more sense than anything else, anyway. Daniel told him the only places hiring wood craftsmen were the RV places up by the toll road."

"So he wasn't looking for work here in Shipshe?"

"I don't know, Deborah. I wish I could be more help. He seemed pleased with the answer, I do remember that, as he slapped his *dat* on the back and said the toll road would be fine, said it wasn't but a twenty-minute ride with a driver. When has Reuben ever hired a driver?"

"When indeed." Deborah nodded, then thought of one more thing. "This might seem personal, but it could help us. Has Reuben ever been *in lieb*?"

Abigail smiled, though there was no happiness in it. "Once. He cared about her for sure, but they were so young. Reuben was like a young bull then, unable to control his emotions at all. One minute he'd be in a tear, angry about something. I never knew what. The next moment he'd be like he is now—quiet, sweet, and solid."

"Reuben?"

"*Ya*. I know. It's hard to imagine."

"Why don't I remember this?"

"He's older than you are."

"Just a few years."

"Well. Some things you can't really know unless you're inside a family."

Deborah thought on that. "What happened to the girl?"

"Came down with the fever. She died the same year they were courting."

Deborah left then, steering the mare down the road, trying to fit the puzzle pieces together, but what she'd learned at the Fisher place had added more confusion to Reuben's case. As she drove into town, Deborah wondered if she should stop by Adalyn's office and tell her what she'd learned, but that was when the quilt shop came into view and she realized Callie was standing at the side of the road, waving to her frantically.

Callie had been trying to track down Deborah for the last hour. It wasn't easy to locate an Amish person. Well, it wasn't as hard as you might expect—considering they didn't have telephones. If you could reach one person, they seemed to know a piece of useful information, and then it was only a matter of following it to the end.

In this case, she'd reached Tobias' sister at the shop where she worked. Tobias' sister had just talked to her cousin, who herself had come in from the farm moments before and had seen Deborah's buggy there.

Callie guessed that Deborah was having a cup of tea with Abigail and would be heading into town next. Then it became a matter of waiting for her friend's buggy to pass by.

"Callie. What are you doing?" Deborah pulled into the quilt shop's parking lot, looking at her as if she were crazy.

"I need to talk to you. Are you sure you can't get a cell phone or a pager or maybe a walkie-talkie?"

Martha, Mary, and even Joshua crowded toward the front of the buggy, all shaking their heads no, though Martha asked: "What's a pager?"

"Can we go and see Max, *Mamm*?" Mary asked.

Joshua fairly bounced on the seat.

"We promise to stay clean," Mary added.

"I'll watch them," Martha offered. "And it will give Joshua a chance to run off some energy."

"Best let them go. We need to talk."

"Well, all right. But I still have two more errands and can't stay long."

"You're going to want to hear this. Or rather see it."

Callie practically yanked Deborah into the shop.

Deborah looked surprised to see that several customers were shopping in the buttons and trinkets aisle. "You left customers so you could stand at the side of the road?"

"Lydia's here, and I needed to catch you." Callie made sure Lydia was at the register, then tugged Deborah into the small kitchen. "Esther and Tobias were by earlier. Tobias left this here by mistake."

She shoved a long, black woolen coat into Deborah's hands, then collapsed on the room's single stool and immediately began chewing on her thumb nail.

"So they were here—"

"To invite me to their wedding."

"And he left—"

"That coat!" Callie stood and began pacing the tiny room.

Deborah took her place on the stool. "All right. You've officially lost me."

"I saw him put it on the counter when Esther went to the restroom, but then I forgot about it. I got busy with Max and restocking." Callie paced as she spoke, her arms crossed and her fingers drumming a frantic rhythm on her arm. "Lydia came in later and spotted the coat. She gave it to me, but I don't think she looked in the pockets. I'm sure she didn't."

Stopping midstride, Callie turned to face Deborah. "I wasn't sure whose it was, but I'm sure it had to have been left today. I always clean up at night when I close the shop. The only man who came in today was Tobias, so when I saw it, saw that it was a man's coat, I was sure it was his, but I checked to see if there was any identification in it."

Deborah waited, but didn't say anything.

"Look in the pocket," Callie prodded.

Unfolding the coat, Deborah reached into the right pocket. It was empty.

"Other one." Callie moved closer, until their heads were nearly touching, bowed over the coat.

Deborah put her hand into the other pocket and pulled out a cell phone. Sleek and black, it was obviously brand new, without a scratch on it. She held it in the palm of her hand as if it had the power to strike out and bite her should she close her fingers around it.

"This belongs to Tobias?" Deborah's voice was a whisper.

"I don't know."

Deborah turned the coat over, studied the collar, ran her finger along a tear in the seam. "What would be the odds that two coats would have a tear in the same exact spot?"

"Slim. Why?"

"Because Reuben's coat had a tear here. I noticed it at the last church meeting. The meeting was at our house, and I took his coat from him when he came in. I noticed the tear then and offered to mend it for him. I took care of it the next day and returned it to him. I'm sure these are my stitches."

Callie allowed that to sink in for a moment.

"All right. Let's think about this. Tobias was wearing Reuben's coat . . ." Deborah stopped, clearly stumped.

"Probably didn't realize it. Probably picked it up the night everyone was in their house. They're nowhere near the same size, but Amish coats all look the same to me."

Deborah placed the phone on the kitchen counter. "Could be. That could be what happened. So you don't think Tobias realized it was in his pocket all this time? That was six days ago. I put my hands in my pockets every time I put my coat on."

"Women do, but men don't. I know because I watch people as I sit at the counter or while I'm looking out the front of the shop. Men hardly ever place their hands in their pockets."

"We could ask Tobias," Deborah whispered.

"Or Reuben."

The choice hung between them for a moment, until Callie stated the obvious. "Once we ask either one of them, then our choices are limited. Tobias will insist we return it to Reuben. If we try to return it to Reuben, it will be turned over to the authorities."

"To Shane."

Callie's throat went dry at the thought of going to Shane with a piece of evidence. Why did he affect her that way? It wasn't like he'd arrest her. "Correct."

"This doesn't belong to us though." Deborah stood, backed away from the phone. "It belongs to Reuben. I suppose. Who else would it belong to?"

She looked at Callie then, and Callie knew the moment dawning fell over her, because her face turned the same shade of white that Callie had felt when the thought had first occurred to her. She knew then that white was more than a color: It was a cold, pale shade of understanding that seems to take all of your hope away.

"Oh, Callie. You don't think this belonged to the girl?"

"Who else?"

"Then how would Reuben have come by it?"

"I don't know. But if we give it back to him now, it becomes state evidence. We'll never know what's in it or if it could help Reuben's case."

"And if we keep it?"

"Then we're withholding evidence."

Chapter 16

ESTHER WOULD HAVE LIKED TO GO with Tobias to see Reuben.

"Next time," Tobias promised. "We need to talk farming, and I promise it will bore you. Didn't you say you'd like to shop at the General Store?"

"*Ya*, but——"

"Then go and enjoy your time alone. I'll stop by the police station, visit with Reuben, and meet you back here in an hour."

"Will you give him my love, and tell him that Leah ..." A sob caught in her throat and she had to look away. She'd told herself she would not cry today, that today would be a joyful day. With the last of their invitations given out, they were to go back and share dinner with her parents, then prepare for worship tomorrow. Their last service together as two separate individuals rather than man and wife.

"I will tell him that you both remember him in your prayers, that you and little Leah count the days until you see him again." Tobias put a finger under her chin and turned her face gently until she looked up into his eyes. "He knows. He knows that you and Leah whisper his name each evening as you kneel and unburden your hearts. But I will tell him."

Esther forced herself to nod, all the time wondering how this man could know her so well. How could he read past the mask she worked so hard to present, the one that assured everyone all was fine when inside she felt as if her world might crumble?

"Now go and purchase your things. Take your time and enjoy the few moments alone. It's uncommon in a mother's life, or so I hear. Perhaps soon we will have another *boppli* on the way and then quiet moments will become even more rare."

Esther's blush grew in proportion to Tobias' smile.

That he could tease as he set off to see his cousin in the Shipshewana Municipal Jail was a comfort to her, but then Tobias' faith ran deep. It was one of the things that drew her to him. They had spoken at length about this, especially after Deborah had walked out of the meeting with Reuben stating that they were to go on with the marriage. Tobias had nodded and said he had expected his cousin to issue such a decree.

What she didn't know is why he thought Reuben would see him now when he'd refused to see him before the hearing. But then, men didn't always make sense to her. She was turning it over in her mind, when she pushed through the front door of the General Store. She nearly bumped into Mrs. Drisban, who was standing at a card carousel a few feet inside the door.

"Hello," Esther said.

The woman returned her greeting, but with a frown and a nod, not offering even a single word.

Esther shrugged, then moved past her to the kitchen aisle. She was hoping to find some new shelf paper, since they had decided to move into Tobias' *grossdaddi*'s house. She was both excited and nervous about leaving her own home, but she understood that it made the most sense. They had talked about it at length with both their parents, and this was the best plan. This way, Seth's brother and his young wife could move into the home she'd shared with Seth when he was alive. And someone had to be at the larger farm, since no one knew how long it would be before Reuben would be free to work there again.

Esther chose a blue shelf liner with white flowers that could easily be wiped clean. Turning toward the checkout counter, she was surprised when she nearly tripped over Mrs. Drisban, who had moved closer and was still frowning at her.

The woman barely topped five feet. Probably sixty years old, she dressed in what Callie had called sweat suits, though hers usually sported words on the front. Today's shirt said *What Happens at Grandma's House Stays at Grandma's House.* The words were bordered by a marquee like the one over the Blue Gate Restaurant.

"Is there something I can do for you, Mrs. Drisban?"

"There might be something I can do for you, Esther Zook. You've always been a good girl, and I think it's my duty to speak my mind right now, so I'm going to do it."

"Excuse me?"

"Is it true you're about to marry Tobias Fisher?"

Esther's lunch began to tumble around in her stomach. "Yes, ma'am. Tobias and I are marrying next week."

"Well, what are you thinking? You with that sweet little girl, and you're going to marry the cousin of a murderer? For all you know, he could have been there when Reuben killed that Amish girl. Has that occurred to you?"

Esther stepped back, feeling as if she'd been slapped.

Mrs. Drisban moved forward. "I want you to take this pamphlet. Don't just stand there! Take it. It'll explain the Bible to you. Talks about good parenting. Has Bible verses and everything."

Esther opened her mouth to speak, but nothing came out. She suddenly felt incredibly warm. There was a roaring in her ears, but unfortunately not loud enough to block Mrs. Drisban's parting remarks. "I would think you'd put the needs of your daughter first, even if you didn't care about your own safety. I declare, you Amish people can be so simpleminded at times."

Then Mrs. Drisban turned and swept out of the store, leaving Esther standing there, holding the Bible pamphlet in one hand and her new shelf paper in the other: blue with white flowers.

"I don't have to agree to see him, do I?" Reuben didn't bother to look through the bars at Andrew Gavin, and he most certainly didn't stand up from his bunk.

"No, you don't have to, but if you want my opinion you should."

"Didn't ask for it, so I don't suppose I want it." Reuben regretted the way the words came out, but truth was he'd rather be left alone. He stared at the closed Bible on the cot beside him, then glanced up at Gavin. "You're still here."

"I am."

"Is there a reason?"

"There is."

"Want to share it?"

"I do."

Reuben sighed and ran his hand over his face—smooth, shaven, unmarried. Hadn't bothered him before, but in the last week, he'd begun questioning his choices, begun questioning a lot of things.

"Spit it out then, since you're apparently not going to leave until you have your say."

Gavin stood perfectly straight, the way he always did. Even the times he'd come to pick up the wooden furniture he'd ordered, he'd held himself that way—rather like the bishop at the front of the church. As if he needed to stand perfectly erect in order for others to see him clearly. There was also usually a quietness about him. He wasn't like many of the *Englischers* who felt like they needed to speak to fill up the silence. Perhaps that was why they'd struck up a friendship of sorts.

"I see a lot of people come through here. Many never have a visitor. You keep turning people away. That man out there is like your brother, and I don't understand what it would hurt to give him five minutes of your time."

"That's just it. You don't understand. Probably because you're not on this side of the bars now, are you?" Reuben allowed some of the anger he'd been so carefully controlling to slip out, like steam escaping from a kettle. It was not the Amish way, he knew, but the anger had been building for days and wouldn't be denied.

"No, I'm not. And I don't plan to be." Gavin's voice remained perfectly steady and even toned. "We're not talking about me though, and at the moment we're not even talking about you. We're talking about Tobias."

"And what would you know about him?" Reuben was off the cot now, halfway between the cot and the bars, his voice rising. "He's not your kin. You haven't lived with him, watched him pass life by only to see him finally get a chance at the one thing you haven't had. What could you possibly know about my cousin that I don't?"

"I know he's out there torn in two because you won't give him fifteen minutes. I know he's about to get married, apparently because you told him not to postpone it—"

"That would be none of your business."

"Someone has to tell you when you're messing up, and you won't allow anyone else near you. So why don't you man-up, walk out into the visitation room, and face your cousin. Consider it your wedding present to him."

Reuben had made it across the small cell and was now clutching the bars, staring into Andrew's eyes. Andrew hadn't backed up, not even one step. And though he was armed and there were cameras watching their every move, Reuben suddenly realized those weren't the reasons the young officer hadn't backed down. The reason was the same reason his sisters had stopped by and

Tobias was waiting even now—somehow Andrew had grown to care for him over the last year.

Somehow Andrew believed in his innocence.

Ten minutes later Reuben found himself sitting across a metal table from Tobias, his hands cuffed in front of him.

Tobias had gone through a rundown of the final harvest and how the few animals they kept were doing, and was now reciting who he and Esther had seen this morning to invite to the wedding.

"Look, I don't mean to interrupt, and any other time I might be interested in these details." Reuben took his hands from his lap and dropped them on the table with a clang that caused Tobias to jump. "But we have about ten minutes left here, and I don't really think you stopped by to tell me these things."

"No. I suppose I didn't." Tobias ran his hand over the top of his head, and Reuben knew he felt odd without his hat or wool cap on top of it. "Actually I came to ask you to break your silence, to ask you to give a statement to the officer. I know you didn't have anything to do with that girl's death—"

"And how do you know that?"

"I know you didn't, and there's no use being contrary with me. I've lived with you too long. So whatever is wedged into that head of yours, whatever reason you're doing this, I've come to ask you to reconsider."

Reuben sat back in the metal chair and stared at his cousin.

"I suppose you've thought it through, as you do most things. Never knew you to rush into any decision. But I've done a lot of thinking myself since Esther stumbled on the girl's corpse. However you knew her—and I don't know how; I'd love to hear that part someday when you're back home and ready to tell me—I reckon you were as surprised as Esther was to see her floating there."

Tobias looked up at the television monitor in the corner of the room, licked his lips, and pushed on. "Figure that must have caused you no small amount of pain, especially seeing as you did allow her to stay on our place and she was part of the fellowship."

"You think her death would matter less if she were an *Englischer*?" Reuben's voice was a low growl.

"Didn't say that, did I? Truth is, I'm trying to work through why you'd be willing to give up your freedom for a girl you didn't kill." He paused, and Reuben knew he was waiting for him to agree or deny, but he didn't. "Best I can come up with is that you're protecting someone."

Reuben thought of the letter he'd received a month ago, the one he'd responded to and then destroyed. He could tell Tobias about it, but what good would it do? Tobias would then be keeping information from Shane as well. Tobias would then also be *obstructing justice.*

"Can't imagine who you'd be protecting or why you'd protect a killer, but that's not my place to know either."

"So what is your place, Tobias? Why are you here?" Reuben leaned forward until their faces were a mere inch apart.

The officer in the corner of the room cleared his throat, shook his head no, and Reuben sat back.

"I'm here to remind you of your duty to family, Reuben. You do remember your family, right? You remember your *mamm* and your *daed* and the commandment to honor them? If you could see your parents right now, if you would agree to see them right now, you would understand that you've broken that commandment along with a few others."

Reuben stood, his chair screeching as he pushed it back. "So you came to lecture me about the Scripture."

"I came to ask you to reconsider, if not for yourself, then for your family."

Reuben looked out the small window that was in the visitor's room. When he did, he could see a few branches of a tree outside the Shipshewana City Hall, which housed the Shipshewana

Municipal Jail. He was reminded then of Adalyn Landt's words, when she'd warned him that he might miss fall turning to winter.

But he'd missed a lot more in his life than the changing of a season.

He knew that now.

"Most folks think they'll have all their lives, Tobias. Think they'll have another chance. Think *If I don't do this today, I can do it tomorrow. If I don't ask her this Sunday, I'll ask her next.*" A fist closed around Reuben's heart, and he wondered what a heart attack felt like, wondered if he even cared anymore. "We think, *If I don't marry this season, I can do it next.*"

Reuben shook his head, stepped around the chair, and pushed it back toward the table with the toe of his county-issued shoe. "Doesn't work that way. You marry Esther, be a *gut dat* to Leah. Those are things you will never regret."

Then, before Tobias could answer, Reuben told the officer he wanted to be taken back to his cell.

Chapter 17

Callie helped load the children into the buggy, then waved as Deborah drove away. They'd decided on a plan of action.

Hopefully it would work.

Hopefully it was legal.

Holding Max's leash, which was clipped to his collar, she walked him into the shop. Lydia was helping two out-of-towners check out, and they stopped to admire Max.

"How old is he?" The woman waited before petting Max, waited until Callie nodded her assent. The couple appeared to be in their late forties. By the looks of them, they were probably empty nesters, traveling from somewhere to Chicago. They wore designer clothes, and the woman's auburn hair was cut in the latest fashion. Her nails were also perfectly manicured.

"I'm not completely sure. I inherited him from my aunt."

"Your aunt?" She straightened and pulled her purse over her shoulder.

"I expect that would be the sweet lady who used to run this shop." The man had light streaks of gray running through his short-cut hair. He looked as if he ran in marathons and worked out in a gym twice a week. Callie mentally slapped herself for making stereotypes. "Her name was Daisy?"

"Correct. The shop's named after her. Daisy passed on earlier this year. When I inherited the shop, I also inherited Max."

"I'm sorry for your loss," the woman said sincerely, before turning and glancing around. "I noticed changes in the store. You've kept the main things the same—still looks vintage and authentic. I don't like to walk into a quilt shop and feel like I've stepped into a chain store. I can do that in Chicago."

"We've been dropping in to Shipshe to shop for years. Every time we cross the state on our way back to the city. I'm Robert Jarrell, by the way, and this is my wife, Nancy."

"Pleased to meet you." Callie shook their hands. "I'm Callie Harper, the new owner of Daisy's Quilt Shop." Her heart danced a two-step when she spoke the words. She'd accepted for several months that she was staying in Shipshewana, but it wasn't very often she acknowledged it out loud.

"As I said, you've done an excellent job of balancing change and preserving what made this place uniquely Daisy's." Nancy turned and walked toward the quilt display.

"Thank you," Callie murmured.

"My wife works for the Chicago Museum of Arts, the textile collection," Robert explained. "She's used to giving her opinion."

"I don't remember ever seeing Amish quilts offered via the Internet." Nancy glanced from the computer terminal to the display of quilts. "These are quite beautiful."

"Some local women sew them. We auctioned a few on eBay." Callie laughed at the look of surprise on Nancy's face. "That was the general reaction. These women have special circumstances though, and I wanted them to fetch as high a price as possible. Their bishop allowed it, on a trial basis, but after the initial three sold we had a meeting. Now we sell exclusively through my shop's online site."

"And how are they doing?" Robert asked.

"Well. I drive a hard bargain." Callie hesitated, then continued.

"I've only lived in Shipshe since June, but these women have become close friends. I feel like it's my job to get the best price I can for their work. Of course, they could sell them at the local auction, but we think by offering them on the Internet and showing them in the shop, we can appeal to a wider range of buyers."

"I've looked at a lot of quilts, but their stitching is exquisite, and the way they piece together their patterns . . . well, let's say it shows a sophistication and artistry that I don't see very often." Nancy smiled and turned toward her, reaching into her handbag as she did. "I've been thinking about putting together an Amish quilt exhibit."

"How would that work?"

"I have benefactors who would pay to have the ladies come to Chicago and place their quilts on exhibit. We have a limited area for displaying textiles, and I run more than one exhibit at a time. I wouldn't need more than say . . . a dozen." Nancy handed Callie a business card.

Callie thought about the stack of quilts — finished and waiting to be sold — at Deborah's house. "I'm not sure they'd be comfortable traveling to Chicago. And they'd have to speak with their bishop."

"Of course," Nancy said. "Talk to them, and I'll check with my director."

As they walked toward the door, Nancy added, "They wouldn't *have* to travel to Chicago, you know. That's not a deal breaker. You could travel with the quilts, but it would be nice if the artists could attend the opening night, or if at least one of them could."

"Nancy's exhibits do quite well for her artists. They often raise the value of artists' works significantly, largely because of the publicity they receive." Robert reached down and gave Max one final pat.

As they drove away in their new, small, hybrid vehicle, Callie stared down at the card in her hand. What was that all about?

When she'd walked inside with Max, her mind had been totally focused on Deborah and Reuben and what to do with this unclaimed cell phone in her pocket. And then she'd stumbled on what—a real mother lode for Melinda, Esther, and Deborah. Not to mention the commission she'd make for herself.

"Might be able to buy you that new doghouse after all, Max." But she wasn't envisioning a new doghouse as she walked down Main toward Adalyn's office. Instead she was thinking of Melinda's middle child, Aaron, and the new wheelchair he'd purchased when school began this year. Aaron suffered from chicken breast disease, an inherited muscular disorder. Among the Amish, it affected the chest, making the breastbone more prominent. The disease also stalls the growth of muscles, making it impossible for him to walk. While he was doing remarkably well at the moment, he would undoubtedly face increasingly high medical bills in the future. It would be nice for Melinda and her husband, Noah, to have a little money put back against those needs.

Then there were Reuben's legal fees. Adalyn couldn't work for free all of the time.

Suddenly Callie remembered the pastor of the church she'd been visiting saying that God works in unusual ways. It would seem there was something to that idea. Now if only the cell phone could provide some connection to Reuben and point to his innocence.

Her stop at Adalyn's office was a waste of time. Adalyn was out, this time with a client over in Nappanee.

"I'll leave her a message to call you as soon as she has a moment," Adalyn's receptionist told Callie.

"Thanks. I appreciate it."

"No problem, Callie. Good-bye, Max!"

Since she was already out and Lydia was watching the store, Callie decided to run some errands. She thought about stopping by Mrs. Knepp's quilt shop. The woman had placed an ad in the

Gazette vowing to match any sale in Callie's store. It was as if Knepp was trying to provoke her.

Callie looked down at Max and changed her mind.

Knepp hated dogs. The old woman had a cat that slept in the window, and this wasn't your normal sweet tabby. Last time Callie had walked by to check out the window displays at Quilts and Needles, the cat had stood, stretched, then hunched its back like a Halloween cat and hissed. Max had gone berserk and started barking so loudly Callie had needed both arms to drag him away.

Best to walk on over to the *Gazette*. Maybe Trent would have some idea how she could find information about the phone—or he might report on it in tomorrow's paper. She'd have to handle this just right.

Unfortunately, Trent wasn't the first person Callie saw when she walked into the newspaper office. The smell of newsprint hit her as soon as she opened the front door. The paper's top editions were framed and hanging on the south wall, including the one that featured herself, Deborah, and Max.

Her celebrity status, however, did nothing to soften the attitude of Trent's receptionist, Mrs. Caldwell. Callie had a sneaking suspicion that Caldwell had harbored a secret love for Stakehorn, the paper's previous editor, and somehow blamed Callie for his murder.

As if to prove her hunch, Caldwell glanced over and glared at her.

Baron Hearn was handing a check to Caldwell. Hearn was tall and lanky, had black hair cut short, and dark eyes to match. Though he was smiling cordially, Callie had no doubt he was laughing at her, since she and Baron Hearn did not have a good history.

"Well, if it isn't Miss Harper." Hearn stuck his checkbook in his back pocket. "Girl, you manage to involve yourself with every murder for a hundred miles, not that we had many of those before you showed up."

"Dogs are not allowed in this establishment. I'll thank you to take that mutt right back outside." Mrs. Caldwell pointed to the front door as if Callie were too daft to understand where outside might be.

"Good afternoon to both of you. Actually we're not staying, Mrs. Caldwell. I was wondering if Trent was in this afternoon."

"And I'd be happy to answer, once you take that dog outside."

This time Caldwell stood before jamming her finger in the direction of the front door. Max looked from the door back to the receptionist, as if he were missing something, then let out a small whine.

"But I—"

"Out."

"Can't we—"

"I said *out*!"

Baron was actually holding his side, he was laughing so hard, and Mrs. Caldwell's face was turning quite red. Callie decided maybe she should step outside and call Trent instead.

"Come, Max." Turning and starting out of the room, determined to ignore Baron's laughter and Caldwell's whispers—"that Callie Harper tries my patience more than flies on a summer day"—she walked to the front door, and even had her hand on the knob, when she heard steps between the press room and the front office.

"Leaving so soon, Callie?" Trent caught up with her in a few long strides. Nodding to Baron and Mrs. Caldwell, he opened the door and followed her out into the October sunshine.

"I was going to call you from outside. Your bodyguard insisted that Max wait here."

Trent grinned as he walked her over to a bench positioned under the plate glass window. In spite of her irritation with him over his handling of the murder scene, she couldn't help smiling in return. He had such a boyish way about him.

"You have to admit. She does look out for the place."

"If you're trying to scare people away."

"How are you, Max? Huh, boy?" Trent used both hands to scratch behind Max's ears and was rewarded with a sloppy kiss.

Callie had the passing thought that dogs get all the fun, then wondered where such an idea came from.

"So, why did you really come by?" Trent returned his attention to Callie.

"I found this." Callie pulled the cell phone out of the pocket of her jacket. "And I wondered if you could help me with it."

"Help you?"

"Say I wanted to know something about it. Like who owns it, how to get past the password protection—"

"Okay. I get the idea." Trent took the phone from her. "I'm pretty sure I don't want to ask where you got this."

"It could be important, Trent." Callie tucked her hair behind her ears as she studied the shoppers strolling down Main Street in the brisk fall afternoon and wondered what secrets the small phone might hold. "Is there anything you can tell me about it? Can you get past the password—"

He opened it, turned it on, pushed a few buttons, then smiled. "Personally, I'd start by listening to the message."

Chapter 18

"HOW DID YOU DO THAT?"

"Wasn't so hard. Most people use something easy to remember, like four zeros or, in this case, one, two, three, four."

Callie reached over and put her hand on Trent's arm, leaving it there until he raised his eyes from the phone and looked at her. "Don't touch that button—yet."

"Having second thoughts?"

"Yes. No." Her throat suddenly felt incredibly dry, as if she'd been battling a high fever. "Maybe."

"You sound like a woman."

"Listen. Tobias came by the shop earlier this morning—"

"Tobias into quilting now?"

"He was with Esther. They were bringing me a wedding invitation."

"Don't those Amish weddings last, like, all day?"

"Pay attention." She swatted his arm, then reached down and stroked Max's fur as she worked out the progression of events. "He left his coat, but I didn't realize it until later. When I saw it on the counter, I wasn't sure whose it was, so I looked in the pocket. And that was when I found the phone. The only man who'd been in the shop up to that point today was Tobias."

Trent looked into Callie's eyes then and—for a moment—all of his teasing fell away. Possibly, just possibly, he even forgot he was an editor of a small-town newspaper looking for the next front-page story. He reached out and tucked Callie's hair behind her ear, sending a delicious shiver from her face—where his hand brushed—all the way down to her toes.

Callie closed her eyes, melted into the moment, and wondered what it would feel like to kiss Trent McCallister. But she quickly shook any romantic notions from her mind. She needed to focus. She needed to think of Deborah, Reuben, and the phone they'd just broken into.

"You don't think this belongs to Tobias. You think it has something to do with Reuben, something to do with the murder."

"According to Deborah, Tobias would never own a phone. She's also certain it's not his coat that was left at my shop. It's Reuben's. She knows because there's a torn seam along the collar. She mended it, so she's positive it's Reuben's coat—"

"So why was Tobias wearing it?"

"Deborah said that the night of Reuben's arrest, Shane was questioning Reuben and Tobias at their house—or rather the barn where they've been living."

"I remember."

Callie's gaze snapped up, met his. Trent the Reporter was on duty. Trent, the guy who would photograph anything, who had often managed to splash her own photograph on the front page of the *Gazette*, was staring back at her.

"I suppose in the heat of the moment, when they arrested Reuben, he grabbed the wrong coat."

Trent shook his head. "What's more likely to have happened is that Shane arrested Reuben, put him in the cruiser, then went back inside to get Reuben's coat for him."

"And picked up the wrong one."

They both stared at the phone still in Trent's hand.

"So why would Reuben have a phone?" Trent finally asked.

"Maybe he was keeping it for someone, like the girl staying at his place."

"There's still only one way to find out, and that's to listen to the message. I can also take it inside and run a check on the serial number, try to find where it was purchased, research the call history, maybe even run the GPS tracker—"

"You can do all those things?"

"I was an investigative reporter before I was an editor—oh wait, come to think of it, now I'm both." Trent smiled and Callie began to have second thoughts—maybe she didn't want to get messed up with Trent and his nefarious ways.

"Okay, the next question is *should* you do that, should *we* do it? What if this is considered tampering with evidence? Isn't that a felony or something? I tried to stop by Adalyn's and ask, but she's out of the office until tomorrow." Callie crossed her arms, hugged them around herself. "I've been arrested by Shipshewana's finest, and I don't have any desire to go back into their interrogation room, thank you."

Trent rubbed his thumb over the blank phone display. "Be reasonable. You can't know it is evidence unless you listen to it. If what we find seems to indicate anything about the girl's body, anything that will help to identify who she is, then you take it to Black. Whether it helps Reuben's case or hurts it."

"And you won't report what we find?"

"I didn't say that." Trent gave her a crooked smile. "You have to leave me something here, gorgeous. Even if it's just a few crumbs, or in this case—even if it's just a few lines of copy."

Callie snatched the phone out of his hand, held it close to her heart. "I can listen to a message by myself."

"All right. And do you know how to trace the registration number from the SIM card?"

"I didn't know SIM cards had registration numbers." Callie

felt herself frowning, pouting actually, like a child, but she made no effort to stop it.

"Every subscriber identification module is registered, and of course, all new phones have GPS as well, which constantly tracks the whereabouts of the phone and, presumably, the person it's with. We could possibly access those logs, but if you don't need me ..."

Glowering at Trent, Callie pulled Max's leash more tightly and stood. "You don't have to be so arrogant."

"It's not arrogance if it's true."

And to think she had been considering kissing him not five minutes ago. "Come on, Max."

With a slight woof, Max hopped to his feet and trotted by her side. Dogs were loyal and true, and they didn't try to benefit from every single situation that came their way.

"I'll run the article by you before I print it."

She stopped but didn't turn. Trent was at her side in a second, smiling down at her. "Understand I'm not saying that I'm going to let you edit it."

And she absolutely refused to smile at the eagerness on his face. At times he did remind her of Max—not the loyalty part, but the enthusiasm.

He wrapped his hand around hers, around the one still clutching the phone. "We'll work out a compromise as far as whatever information I find and what I put in the article. Face it, Callie— we need each other on this one. I need a follow-up piece on the front page, and you need some help with the technology. Let's work together."

She didn't want to look into his hazel eyes, at the blond hair flopping over his forehead. She sure didn't want to be amused by him or admit that she needed him, but at the same time he was right. So she slipped the phone into his hand and muttered, "Call me." Then she tried to ignore the knowledge that he was watching her as she continued walking down the street.

Callie's attraction toward Trent McCallister—which she did not understand at all—didn't matter at the moment. What mattered was helping Deborah and Esther, which meant helping Reuben. Not that she wanted to be drawn into another murder, but it was beginning to feel as if she didn't have much choice.

A few minutes later Callie was home. She pulled the mail from her box and sorted it while standing in front of the recycle bin and next to her in-box tray. She'd learned that trick years ago. Junk mail went straight where it belonged. Bills went into the in-box tray. Efficiency simplified life.

Sadly she didn't have to worry about a third stack since she rarely—correction, never—received personal mail.

The thought had no sooner crossed her mind than she saw a small personal-sized envelope made out in wobbly handwriting to Ms. Callie Harper. She set it on the counter and continued sorting.

Why did companies insist on sending so many advertisements? If she wanted to order something, she'd look online. Oops—except for this one from L.L.Bean. She did love to look through their clothing line—a guilty pleasure that she rarely indulged. She'd keep it and see what her profits were from this month. Setting it on the counter beside the hand-addressed letter, she sorted through the last two pieces of mail. Both were credit card applications she hadn't requested and went straight into the shredder.

But the letter, now that was a mystery.

She slit the top of the envelope with her letter opener, then poured hot water over a chamomile tea bag. Lately she'd been experimenting with the different flavors she stocked for her customers.

"Let's go, Max. We'll read this one sitting down." Making sure the sign on the door said *closed*, since it was after six, Callie wound her way over toward the chair near the front windows. On the horizon she could see clouds pressing toward town, clouds that hadn't been there a short while ago when she'd made her way home from her meeting with Trent, who still hadn't called with any information.

She sat in the big overstuffed chair near the plateglass windows and watched the wind throw leaves down the street. "Looks like it's going to get cold."

Max whined and placed his head across her feet.

"I agree, boy. Now let's see who would send me a letter."

Ms. Harper. Have you started looking for my dochder *yet? I'm currently in* gut *health, but can't be sure how much longer I'll be on this earth. My age is eighty-nine.* Gotte *could call me home any day. I know you can find her.*
Ira Bontrager

Callie stared at the letter far longer than it took to read its contents. The handwriting was shaky, like that of many of her older customers who wrote out checks or signed her guest book. But the words he'd written were remarkably clear, indicating none of the confusion she'd seen in him when he was at her place a few days ago.

How many days had it been? Tuesday she'd found the old guy on her doorstep, it was Monday when Esther had found the dead girl in Reuben's pond. Hard to believe how life could change in less than a week. Before then their lives had been traveling along fairly smoothly.

Callie folded the sheet of paper and placed it back in the envelope.

There were times she felt much less alone here than she ever had while living in Houston. When the shop was open and people were stopping in, Callie felt a part of the community, even though she'd lived in Shipshewana less than six months. Through the mess with Stakehorn few people had really seemed to believe she could be guilty of murder, and most had been vocally pleased that she'd permanently taken over her aunt's shop.

But when the shop closed and everyone went home to their families, Callie sometimes did feel alone. Occasionally it seemed she'd traded her life in Houston for an identical life in Shipshewana, only planted in different soil.

Perhaps that was her own fault.

Trent had asked her out twice, and both times she'd made excuses and said no. She'd wanted to say yes. She'd wondered what it would be like to spend time alone with him. The entire situation reminded her of her junior year in high school, when she'd had a crush on a guy in her homeroom class, but never had the courage to let him know.

Trent seemed to understand there was an attraction between them. Callie admitted it to herself occasionally, so why did she always back off when the opportunity to investigate those feelings arose? She'd caught herself comparing him to Rick, but she also compared Andrew and Shane to Rick as well. She supposed all widows did that. There was a physical attraction between her and Trent, but in other areas they seemed like complete opposites.

Was physical attraction enough to make a relationship worth pursuing?

If you had to think about even pursuing a relationship, was it worth chasing down? She'd always thought a relationship was butterflies in your stomach and something that you couldn't live without, not something you put on your calendar—like a dental appointment.

As Callie checked the automatic lighting outside the shop to be sure it had turned on and straightened a few items up and down the aisles, she admitted the problem was probably within herself. She wasn't sure that she was ready to move into another relationship.

Maybe she was.

When Trent touched her arm or looked into her eyes she thought she could be.

Sometimes she'd even wondered what it would feel like to see Andrew Gavin on a personal level. He seemed to understand what she was thinking and feeling, and he wasn't always interested in what he could gain from a situation.

But then she'd feel herself pulling back, which was why she'd turned Gavin down when he asked her out to the movies, to the concert over in South Bend, and to the police barbeque. One part of her really wanted to go, but the other part . . . the other part was scared.

"Come on, boy. Let's go home." Max barked once, then bounded up the stairs to their apartment.

Callie stopped at the mirror at the top of the stairs to study her reflection. Her hair was a bit of a mess, had been since she'd started growing it out. Her eyes still took up too much of her face, but the chocolate-colored sweater she wore accented them well.

All of that was cosmetic though.

What she saw in the mirror was the same thing she saw between the lines of Ira Bontrager's letter: a reflection of herself, a reflection of her loneliness.

She couldn't find the old guy's daughter. She had no illusions about that. Even if the girl had existed, which Callie somehow doubted, the police would have found her if it was possible. Surely he had notified the police if he'd actually lost a daughter. What more could she do than the officials? Maybe she could somehow ease the loneliness that she'd sensed in him.

For whatever reason, the man's son wasn't able to help him, maybe he wasn't even able to spend time with him.

So beginning tomorrow, Callie would.

Chapter 19

SAMUEL THANKED THE TRUCKER for the ride as he let himself out of the eighteen-wheeler. He'd purposely avoided smaller vehicles. Didn't want to end up thumbing a ride from anyone he knew.

There was no way he was ready to face friends — today would be difficult enough.

He carried his one bag over his shoulder. He'd left Katie's bag on the doorsteps of a less prosperous-looking Amish home on the outskirts of Middlebury. Hopefully someone there would be able to use the clothes. It had hurt him to leave them, but he told himself that Katie would have been glad to know they were helping make someone else's life easier.

As soon as the farm came into sight, a sweat broke out across his forehead. He'd stopped in a gas station last night and shaved off the beard. Not that it was very thick yet — despite what Katie had predicted.

The memory was a sharp ache in his side, like the cut of a knife.

He raised his hand to his cheek, as if to remind himself that it was real, that it had all actually happened. But the envelope in the bottom of his pack proved the last week hadn't been just another nightmare.

As he walked toward the farm, toward Katie's parents, he rehearsed again the story he planned to tell them. Lying didn't come easily, but he couldn't think of another alternative. And it was wrong. He knew that. It certainly wasn't the Amish way to lie, but in this case not lying would hurt Katie's family more, would be an even bigger sin. Samuel had worked through his options, and he didn't see that he had any other recourse available.

Working on Timothy's farm was the last thing he wanted to do. He'd left just over a week ago, unable to stomach the thought of spending another season under Timothy's backward ways.

Now what?

A lifetime making atonement for his and Katie's mistakes? The old anger burned in him, but he tapped it down. One thing he knew—none of this was her fault.

Katie's error had cost her life. And what had her mistake been? Trusting him.

The knowledge of that nearly drove him to his knees.

He paused, caught his breath as Timothy's silos came into view while the afternoon light slanted across the fields.

His sins, they were much worse. He should have protected Katie, should have been a better husband. For that he was prepared to pay with years.

Placing one foot in front of the other, he continued slowly walking down the lane that led to Timothy's house. They wouldn't be home from church yet, so there was no need for him to worry about being seen. It would give him time to think. Time to be sure he had his story straight.

As he neared the old farmhouse, he didn't see the rambling structure where he'd first met Katie or the fields where he'd worked over a year hoping to earn her father's respect. Instead his mind went back once more, and he saw their eldest daughter, saw her how she'd looked the morning after their wedding night ...

Samuel turned from his place at the window where he'd been watching the sun rise over the countryside bordering the LaGrange Inn. Pink and purple clouds fanned out above the hills that rolled one after another as the sun broke through the morning mist.

Just one thing was prettier than that sight.

Samuel heard her stirring in the king-sized bed across the room. He walked over, sat beside Katie, and combed his fingers through her golden hair—he'd never imagined that she had so much of it. When she'd taken off her kapp *and removed the pins last night, it had fallen nearly to her thighs. Thick, the color of wheat, and with a slight curl to it, he thought he would be happy to stare at it for days.*

Then she'd taken his hand, and he forgot about her hair.

"Gudemariye," she said sleepily.

"Gudemariye to you, sweet Katie." Samuel leaned forward, kissed her softly on the lips. "How did you sleep?"

"Wunderbaar, when I slept at all." A blush stained her cheeks, but she laughed at the memory and reached for his hand. "Do we travel on to Shipshewana today?"

"First there are some things I'd like to take care of."

"Like?"

"Like feeding you breakfast."

"That shouldn't take long." When she reached forward and ran her hand down his cheek Samuel felt his heart begin to thump faster. He'd rather stay here, in this room, and forget the list he'd been making by the window. But the list wouldn't wait. It was important as the man of the family to take care of his wife. It was important to start their marriage out as well as possible.

"We need to return your father's horse and wagon."

"I don't understand." A frown creased her forehead, and Samuel's patience began to ebb.

"It's not right to keep what belongs to him, Katie. He'll be needing it, and we can get by without one at first."

"How will you send it back?"

His hand came down hard upon the nightstand, causing the lamp to rattle and Katie to jump. Samuel stood, walked to the window, and forced himself to take several calming breaths. It was only the pressure of starting over. She didn't mean to question his every move. Turning back toward her, he started again.

"I met a man at the feed store yesterday who has a load he needs to take to Goshen. He said he could catch a ride back and was happy to pay me for the use of the horse and wagon. We can use the money."

"Won't father wonder why his horse is coming back, without us?"

"I've thought of that, and I prepared a note." Samuel walked over to the small table in the corner of the room. He picked up the sheet of paper and brought it back to Katie. As he handed it to her, he began explaining even before she could have read to the end. "I know this is hard for you, and I know that you don't like lying to your dat—"

"Do you really think we can't tell him the truth now?" When she raised her eyes to his, it felt like a razor was being drawn across his heart.

The razor opened a crevice and doubt began to creep in.

What if they were doing the wrong thing?

What if they were wrong about marrying this way, about moving away from people who could help them?

What if he couldn't find work in Shipshe? How would he support them then?

Samuel stomped back to the window. "If you don't trust me, then how are we supposed to build a marriage? If you're questioning me at every turn, I can't see how I'm supposed to hold up. It's not easy figuring our way, you know."

He didn't hear her cross the room, but he did feel her arms reach around his waist. She pressed her face to his back and spoke softly, her words like a slow spring rain to a newly planted field. "I didn't mean to question you, Samuel. I only meant to ask if this is the way it must be. If it is, then we will do it, and we'll do it together."

Turning to look in her eyes, he didn't see the condemnation he *expected to find.* "*Lying is hard, and I realize it's wrong,*" *she continued.* "*But it's better than having them worry. You're right about that.*"

"*And it's only for a few days.*" *He took her hand in his, drew her back to the bed.* "*Don't you see? We're buying ourselves a few days so that we can reach Shipshe without them calling the police or contacting the local bishop. Once we're settled, once our marriage is a few days old, and once we have a place to stay and I have a job——*"

"*You will have a job. Of that I'm certain. You're a* gut *worker. My* dat *often said that about you.*"

"*Then we'll send the note with the man and the buggy?*"

Katie picked up the single sheet of paper, and they read it silently, slowly, one last time.

Mr. Lapp,

Katie has run off to the city. She's run off to the *Englischers*. I suppose she's run off because of her *rumspringa*. I'm sending back your horse and buggy and traveling on to find her. I'll send word when I know something. Don't worry. I'll bring her back.

Samuel

"*Send the note. What else do we need to do?*" *Katie stood and began gathering her few things, placing them into her duffel bag.*

"*I want to go to the store in town and purchase a phone.*"

"*A phone?*" *Katie caught herself and put her fingers to her lips, then giggled.* "*I sound like a parrot I heard once. He was in the* Englisch *store in downtown Goshen. The one that sells pets. He repeated the last phrase you'd say.*"

Samuel smiled as he pulled his own things together.

"*And who will we be calling with this phone?*"

As he explained, Katie combed and braided her hair, then pinned her prayer kapp *carefully into place. Samuel wanted nothing more than to take it off her, pull the pins out, unbraid her hair, and forget all their errands.*

The sun was rising though, the smell of kaffi *was drifting up the stairs, and they had more miles to put between them and Goshen. They were now a few short hours from their new life together. For that Samuel was grateful.*

As he walked toward the dining room with Katie, his heart swelled with hope, just as it had the day before when the justice of the peace had declared them man and wife. The Mennonite preacher had said a prayer over them afterwards, had offered his name and phone number.

Samuel still had it on a piece of paper in his pocket.

But they wouldn't be staying.

Their future was to the north, in Shipshewana.

Chapter 20

DEBORAH WAS HELPING ESTHER in Tobias' *grossdaddi*'s house on Monday morning. Shane had finally allowed them to remove the crime scene tape and begin cleaning it.

"This woodwork is beautiful." Deborah ran her hand over a cabinet face.

"Tobias told me that their *grossdaddi* made all the cabinetry himself."

"It's still in very *gut* condition."

They had already wiped down all the cabinetry and placed the new shelf paper in the drawers and on the lower shelves. "Do you want it on the upper shelves as well?"

"I know no one can see them, but I like the idea of it being there. Is that silly?"

"Not at all, and you bought plenty. Might as well use it."

"Exactly, plus it's easier to clean a shelf that has been lined." Esther pulled a table chair over to the kitchen counters and stood on it. The extra two feet allowed her to reach the top shelf, given her height. "If you'll cut the lengths, I'll lay them down."

"Fair enough. We should be done in here before Leah and Joshua wake from their naps."

"I can't believe they still rest in the mornings."

"Well, you may not be so lucky with your next *boppli*. The twins were not sleepers. I think they took naps until they were six months old. After that, I was lucky to have the evening hours to myself."

"You're the second person to mention another baby to me in the last week." Esther accepted the long strip of blue paper and stretched to place it on the top shelf. "How do I know I'll have more babies though? Maybe after all this time I won't be able to."

"Not likely that your body has forgotten how."

"I suppose. It seems so odd though. It's been me and Leah for so long now that I don't know what to think about the idea. When Tobias mentioned it the other day, I felt all disoriented, but at the same time excited." Esther put her hands on her hips and studied the cabinets. "Looks *gut*."

Climbing down, she smiled at Deborah. "I suppose it will all work out."

"Of course it will. It's like I tell Mary. God will bring babies when he's ready for them and not before." Deborah pulled Esther into a hug.

"*Danki*. You're a *gut* friend. How about we go and see what needs to be done to the sitting room?"

They walked into the room, walked in front of the large window that looked out over the yard and the dirt road leading off the property, when they both saw it, or rather, them.

Esther drew in a sharp breath and pulled herself up straighter.

"What do you suppose it's about?" Deborah whispered.

"I don't know, but it can't be good if there're three cars of them."

They walked outside and reached the patrol cars the same time as Tobias, who had come in from the fields. Taylor, Gavin, Black—they were all there, and more.

"Tobias, Esther, Deborah." Taylor was the one to step forward and hand a folded sheet of paper to Tobias. "This gives us the right to search the premises again. It's been approved by Judge Stearns."

"I don't understand." Tobias quickly scanned the document. "What is it exactly that you're looking for?"

Shane had been speaking to Gavin and several other officers who now fanned out—some moving toward the pond, others going in the direction of the barns.

"What is this about?" Esther asked.

Taylor cleared his throat. "Officer Black is going to need to ask you some questions, Tobias. You have a right to have an attorney present."

"I don't have an attorney. I didn't know that I needed one."

Shane stepped forward. "Are you waiving your right to legal counsel?"

Tobias stared down at the paper again, began reading from the top.

"Why are you here, Shane?" Deborah slipped her arm around Esther. The way she had begun shaking, there was a possibility this new blow might be too much. Certainly there was a limited amount of shock a body could take.

Instead of answering, Shane showed them an eight-by-ten photo he was holding. It was a picture of a teenage *Englisch* girl. She had long auburn hair, a smattering of freckles across the tops of her cheeks, and the sweet smile she sported revealed a mouth full of braces.

"Do you know her? Have any of you seen her?"

"No," Deborah said.

Esther shook her head, her gaze flying to Tobias.

"I have never seen this girl. Now why are your men on my land?"

"Because she's missing, Tobias. She's been missing for two weeks, and we have reason to believe that Reuben had something to do with it."

Tobias' face flushed blood red. "You don't mean that."

"I do mean it, and we will search this property."

"To find what?"

"To look for her body, man. What do you think?" Shane stepped closer then, and his next words pulled the breath out of Deborah's lungs. "And if we find her, it's going to be harder for you to explain away. One girl you might not have noticed. One girl you might have an alibi for. But two? That's not very likely. Two you'd have a harder time explaining. Two, he'd probably need an accomplice, someone who helped or knew what was going on or at least covered for him."

"I am a peaceful man." Tobias was within an inch of Shane's face now. "But if you say one more word to me, if you make one more false accusation, I will take my fist, and I will put it—"

"Tobias!" Esther's scream split the morning. She pulled herself away, out of Deborah's grasp, and threw herself into Tobias' arms. "Come with me. Come inside. Let Shane's men look for what they must. Then they'll go. They will find nothing, and then they will go."

She linked her hand with his and pulled him toward the house, and though his face had turned a deep red, he went.

Deborah followed them as Shane turned back toward the pond.

Why would they think Tobias or Reuben had anything to do with this missing girl?

How could they think such a thing? Certainly Tobias had nothing to do with the first one, and now . . . now there was a second? It seemed once doubt had been cast on a person's character, then it was too easy to make the next connection.

She thought of the conversation that Esther had suffered through with Mrs. Drisban in the General Store. The one where the woman had given her a Christian pamphlet—as if Amish folk weren't Christians. On telling her about it, Esther's cheeks had paled, and she'd pulled the pamphlet out of her bag like it was a hideous thing.

Deborah had been curious though.

Drisban and Shane had known Reuben, Esther, and Tobias all their lives. How could they doubt them so? Was it that they believed they'd changed? Or was it that they believed all men were capable of such evil?

It wasn't like Shane Black to jump to conclusions without some evidence — the blood he had found in the house didn't prove anything in Deborah's opinion. Yes, there were questions. Yes, Reuben should answer them if he could, but still he was not guilty. What else had Shane found? Tobias said they'd searched the woods with dogs before the arraignment. Why?

Something else was at work here, and Deborah was ready to find out what it was.

Since the shop was closed on Mondays, Callie used the day to place stock orders, catch up on paperwork, and run errands. Today's errands were going to take her by the *Grossdaddi* House on the edge of town. First, though, she stopped at The *Kaffi* Shop.

"I thought Amish people kept their parents at home with them."

"Most do," Margie agreed, handing Callie a to-go cup of coffee with a shot of espresso, all topped off with whipped cream. Margie's bright red hair was cut in a short 'do that looked great, and Callie wondered for a minute about her decision to grow her own hair out. "I think with Mr. Bontrager the problems were twofold. The son sold his farm and bought a place here in town above the CPA office where he works."

"How does an Amish person work in a CPA office. I mean —" Callie stopped, not sure how to continue.

"I know what you mean. It's the schooling thing, but many

times they do have a talent for professions that traditionally require more education. For instance, the younger Bontrager—I don't remember his name now—was always very good with numbers. He had a real gift. No doubt he would have gone to one of the big schools with a scholarship if he'd been an *Englischer*."

"But because he's Amish he didn't."

"Right. He tried a few different jobs and finally answered an ad at the CPA office, just as an errand boy at first. He was older even then—too old to be an errand boy." Margie swiped a dish towel across the already clean counter.

"So what happened?" Callie sipped her coffee and reached into her to-go bag to pinch off a corner of her cranberry muffin.

"Didn't take long for the owner to realize his gift for numbers. They kept promoting him, until now he handles almost as much work as the CPA."

"But he's not a CPA."

"No. He makes a good living though, and he seems satisfied with that. Married late and they had no children. But living in town, there wasn't really a good place for his father to live once he couldn't stay alone. The *Grossdaddi* House seemed like the best place when you add in the complication of Mr. Bontrager's dementia."

"How do you know so much about everyone?" Callie smiled and folded her to-go sack shut. "It's not as if you're a gossip. Yet, you seem to know everyone's history."

"It's a small town, Callie. Live here long enough, and you'll know as much as I do." Margie walked around the counter and squatted down, gave Max a good rub behind the ears. Then she stood and pushed a box of cookies into Callie's hands. "These are oatmeal raisin. The old folks like them. Mind taking them out there for me?"

"Not at all."

"And next time you come by, you can tell me what this is all about."

"I'd love to. In fact, I might have some more questions for you. Want to grab a bite to eat next Monday evening?"

"It's a date. Hubby has a late meeting, so I was on my own anyway."

Callie felt more optimistic as she climbed into her car than she had in the past week. Finally, it seemed, things were starting to come together.

Chapter 21

CALLIE MIGHT HAVE DRIVEN past the *Grossdaddi* House if she hadn't received instructions from Margie—single story, farm-like, with a barn, on the southwest edge of town, just past the local medical clinic.

It did not look like the retirement villages in Texas. For one thing, there was the barn, which apparently had animals in it. As Callie pulled her car into the parking lot beside the house, she saw an older gentleman lead a horse out of its stall, tether it to a fence, and begin to brush it.

Interesting.

Secondly, there was a large garden area between the barn and the house. There wasn't much growing in it now, except for fall flowers, and yet there were still three older women turning over the sod with a hoe and what could have been a nurse sitting next to someone on a bench.

Callie clipped Max's leash to him, then picked up the box of cookies. Before they started toward the building, she cautioned Max to behave. "Where there's a barn, there are bound to be barn cats."

Max looked at her with what she was sure was hope in his

eyes. "Your idea of play and their idea of play are different, Maxie. Remember what happened to the last kitten you found? You treed it, and I had to climb up in the branches to free it. I'm not going to let you forget that little incident."

Callie stopped at the front door, checked to be sure there was no sign prohibiting pets, then walked inside.

Rather than having a reception area with a bell to ring, she stepped into a front hall like you would find in most homes. There was, however, a small old woman in a prayer *kapp*, sitting in the middle of a bench, knitting.

"Hello," Callie said. "I was hoping to visit someone I think is living here."

The woman looked over the top of her half-glasses, but didn't pause in her knitting. Her hands were moving awfully fast. Callie watched in awe. Max whined lightly as the ball of green yarn took a spin with each flick of her wrists.

"My name is Erin Troyer." She knitted even as she spoke. "I had a dog once. Most people think Amish don't have dogs, but that isn't true. We have them, and we love them, but we treat them like animals rather than children."

Max lowered himself to the floor, his head now on his front paws.

"I see that one thinks he's part human."

"I suppose he does. Max stays with me at the quilt shop. He's a big help, since I live there alone."

Erin paused for a fraction of a second to look Callie up and down, then knitted even faster, as if she needed to make up for her lost time. "You must be talking about Daisy's shop."

"Yes, ma'am."

"I'd heard someone took it over. Daisy was as fine an *Englisch* woman as I ever met. Always real kind and helpful."

"Thank you." Callie's throat tightened at the mention of her aunt. As usual, she found herself wishing she'd known Daisy better. This time though, that feeling was mitigated by a sense of pride. She'd heard similar sentiments so many times since moving to Shipshe from such a variety of people, that now it felt like brushing up against a familiar quilt.

There was a comfort to it.

"I sit here mornings, helping folks who come in. Afternoons, one of the younger gals from the local schools takes over. Now who would you like to visit? I know most of our regulars, and I've never seen you before."

"No, ma'am. I want to see Ira Bontrager. I think he lives here."

The woman continued knitting, though she slowed gradually until she reached the end of the row she was working on. When she did, she pushed the needles into the ball of yarn and scooted over on the bench. Callie recognized it as an invitation and sat down.

Max settled himself between them on the floor.

"Yes, Ira lives here, has since the sickness worsened. Today he's having a good day. We're all a little protective of him though. Do you mind my asking why a young girl from Texas would stop by to see an old Amish man?"

Callie was a bit taken aback that the old lady knew so much about her. Was she a receptionist or a guard? Then Erin looked her full in the face and waited, the folds around her blue eyes wrinkled with age but the gaze not wavering. When she did, Callie realized that this wasn't a nursing home resident doing a part-time job.

This was one friend looking out for another.

"Ira stopped by my shop the other morning—nearly scared me to death appearing before I'd even had my morning coffee, insisting that I listen to him."

"That would have been on Tuesday when the nurses discovered he was gone. There was quite a ruckus."

"Yes. Yes, you're right." Callie hesitated, unsure how much to reveal. "He stayed a while, told me a story. I fixed him some tea and called Andrew Gavin to help me find his kin. Andrew found his son."

"So why are you here today?" Erin's voice was softening, and Callie knew she was almost in. Of course, she realized she didn't need Erin's permission to walk down the hall and find Ira. She could barrel her way past the ninety-pound lady, but something told her it would be a good thing to have Erin on her side.

"Saturday I received a letter from Ira. He asked for my help with something."

Erin waited, nodded, but didn't interrupt.

"So Max and I, we thought we would come and visit."

Reaching out, Erin patted her hand. Though Erin's hand was mostly bones and blue veins, it was incredibly soft on top of Callie's, reminding her of the few times she'd held Melinda's baby.

Those times had scared her senseless, as she had no experience with infants. This was a bit frightening too. She suddenly realized how fragile the person sitting next to her was—the fragileness of the line between life and death.

"As I mentioned, today's better than most for Ira. He's in the barn. I'd take you to him, but I'm not supposed to leave my post unless someone else is here. You can't access the barn or garden areas from the front parking area, since some of our residents tend to wander off. Instead follow this hall until you come to the first left. Then go on down that hall and it will lead you outside to where they're working."

"Is it all right if I take Max through the house?"

Erin was already knitting again, but she spared a glance to Max, who cocked his head as if waiting for her permission.

"Smart one, that mutt is. Look at him waiting on my answer." She leaned forward, put her eyes close to his, and Callie wondered how well she could see, wondered how she was able to knit the yarn at all. "You may go down the hall, but don't frighten the residents. Go quietly."

Max stood and shook himself, but he didn't make a squeak.

"Thank you, Ms. Troyer. Maybe I'll see you again."

"That would be *gut*. Ira doesn't get many visitors."

Callie started to leave when she remembered she was still carrying the box of cookies. She took them back and set them on the bench beside Erin Troyer, who made Callie promise she'd thank Margie for the residents. Then Callie made her way to the barn, one suspicion confirmed: Ira didn't have many visitors, so he must be lonely.

If he was lonely, perhaps he'd made up the story about a lost daughter. There was something in the way Erin had hesitated when Callie had said Ira wanted her help with something—in fact she hadn't seemed surprised and she hadn't questioned her about it.

Was that odd?

Or was it the Amish way of staying out of other folk's business?

Or had Erin heard the same stories?

Before Callie could puzzle it out, she reached the barn. Both doors were open, though the day was cloudy and threatening rain. The man she'd seen brushing the horse still stood outside. Now he was leading the horse slowly around the enclosure.

She walked into the barn, and Max yanked on his leash.

"Heel, Max."

He stepped back to her side, but with a whine. She saw immediately why—two cats sat at saucers with milk in them. When they saw Max, one hissed, but the other continued lapping at the milk.

"Let him go. Don't expect he'd catch anything more than a swipe on the end of his nose."

Callie pivoted around and saw Ira Bontrager standing in the door's shadow, holding the handles of a wheelbarrow. She had to stifle a giggle, he looked so much like a figure out of a history book. Tall, thin, with his white beard reaching nearly to the waist of his pants and his suspenders pulled up over his dark blue work shirt. Today he also wore a wool stocking cap.

"Hello, Mr. Bontrager. Max and I thought we'd stop by for a visit."

"You can call me Ira. Visit a man while he's mucking out a stall, you ought to call him by his first name."

"Do they make you work for your room around here?" Callie smiled, unsure whether she should offer to shake his hand or give him a hug.

"Nah. They think it's good therapy, as if I didn't do enough of this when I had my own farm. Now I get to do it on someone else's place." Ira motioned her toward a stall. "Truthfully I don't mind though. Beats sitting inside where all those women are knitting."

"We met Erin when we arrived." Callie and Max followed Ira into the enclosed area. It was small but warmer, with the sun shining through the high windows that ran the length of the barn. The smells were earthy and strong.

"*Ya.* She's one of the better ones. Some are real hens." Ira proceeded to stick a long-handled tool into a pile of wood shavings.

"Is that a pitch fork?"

He shook his head but didn't bother to look at her. "I thought I read you were from Texas. Don't you have a lot of horses in Texas?"

"Yes. We do." Callie moved to the corner of the stall, looped Max's leash under the corner of an upended wooden crate and sat on the ground beside it. Max stretched the length of his leash, investigating. "Can't say I've been around them much. I lived in the city mostly, since I've been grown."

She looked around the stall and added, "When I was a child, we lived on military bases. They had mounted divisions, cavalry, and I remember watching them practice with the horses. Don't know that I ever saw anyone clean out a stall."

"This is an apple picker." Ira waved it at her with a gleam in his eyes. "And these are wood shavings. Guess you can see it's not hay. An apple picker works best for separating out the horse's droppings and removing the soiled shavings."

He plunged it into the pile of shavings, releasing more of the pungent odor, and shook it a tad so that the clean shavings fell to the stall's floor. What remained on top he dropped into the wheelbarrow. "Wanna try?"

"Umm. Maybe I should watch this time." At the rate he was moving, Callie figured it would be lunch before he finished with this one stall. She hoped no horse needed back in there soon.

"Guess you received my letter."

"I did."

"So you'll help me?" He didn't look at her, kept working the apple picker into the wood shavings.

"I won't lie to you, Ira. Can't really see what I can do to find a girl that went missing so many years ago—"

"It was 1965. I know it was 1965." He jabbed the apple picker in more forcefully and lifted it, though his arms were trembling. When he turned to look at her, his gaze never wavered. "Suppose I know how many years ago it was. Might forget where I am sometimes, but I don't forget the year those funnels from hell came tearing out of the sky, the year my *dochder* went missing."

Callie had thought she could come and pay a visit to an old man, maybe brighten his day a little. She thought she might be able to ease his pain a bit. Would dragging his memories back to something that had happened so long ago help? Was there any chance at all that this woman could still be alive?

This was a fool's errand, and Callie was a sucker to think she might do any good.

"Thirty-nine twisters. That's what those newspaper men said when it was all over." His work took on a slow, methodical rhythm as his voice recited the facts. "Across the central plains they came—Iowa, Illinois, Wisconsin, Michigan, and of course here in Indiana, leaving two hundred and sixty people dead."

He took a handkerchief out of his pocket, wiped his brow. Callie couldn't tell if it was from the labor or from the remembering.

"Would you like me to get you a glass of water, Ira?"

He waved the request away, resumed cleaning the stall. "Palm Sunday. Terrible day for such a thing to happen. Day of the Lord's triumphal entry. *Hmph.*"

He shook his head, was silent for several minutes. Finally he stopped working and leaned on his apple picker. Max padded over to him and licked his fingers. When he did, Ira reached down and ran his hand gently over the top of the dog's head. Then he leaned the picker up against the side of the stall and sat down on the crate beside Callie.

"Haven't spoken of that day all these many years. A thing that terrible. You try to move past it. You tell yourself it's best forgotten and maybe it was. Maybe it was."

"How old was your daughter?"

He didn't answer immediately. When he did, his voice sounded distant and wavered like the trees in the wind.

"She is three, just a wee thing. She is but three years old." Tears began to travel down the grooves and crannies of his cheeks made by the many years and dozens of wrinkles. "Rainbows. So many rainbows around the lake."

Callie thought not to ask him. She started, then stopped herself, then started again. The problem was that at some point since entering the stall, she had started believing his story. And if she believed his story, than she had to ask. If she was going to help— and it still seemed a harebrained thing to believe she could—then there were two things she had to ask.

"Why do you think she's still alive?"

"Never found a body. All the others, eventually a body showed up—under the rubble, or sometimes miles away, but it did appear. Might be days later, but they found something." He rubbed at the tears on his face. "Sharon, she kept saying to wait one more day. That maybe Bethany would show up. Maybe she'd wandered off with the wrong family and they'd bring her back. We'd had a late meal at church that day, and there was a lot of confusion."

He pulled in a deep breath, rubbed Max's ears when the dog leaned against him. "But days stretched into weeks, and finally I accepted no one was going to be bringing Beth home."

"And you never had a funeral?"

He shook his head. "Sharon won't hear of it. She can't bear to hear Bethany's name spoken, but she keeps a little box of things for her, just in case. I know it's not right—that something in my wife was broken by those storms, but I don't know what to do. So I keep farming best I can. Helps to have my son, Caleb, around the place. Have you met my son, Caleb?"

"Yes. I met him the other day."

Ira stood, shuffled over to the wheelbarrow and pushed it out of the stall.

Callie gathered Max and his leash and hurried to catch up with Ira.

"But after all these years, what makes you think Bethany's still alive, and that I can find her? Any number of things could have happened to her since then. Why look for her now after all this time?"

Ira's constant drift between the past and the present wasn't lost on Callie. She understood he was struggling with dementia and knew that condition was influencing what he remembered as well as how he perceived things.

When he turned to answer her though, his eyes were as clear and cognizant as Shane's—though why Callie thought of him at that moment she had no idea.

"Why you?" Ira drew himself up straight. "Because you're the only one who will listen to an old man's ramblings. Why now? Because my heart tells me now is the time. Because I have a pain that won't stop hurting, won't stop until I see her again."

As he turned and walked out of the barn, Callie realized whether she wanted to or not, she was about to start searching for one Bethany Bontrager, lost since 1965.

Chapter 22

REUBEN HAD HEARD THAT PRISON was immensely tedious, that the hours stretched endlessly on, and that men cracked and spilled their secrets for no other reason than to be relieved of the boredom.

So far he'd yet to have an uninterrupted day.

"Lawyer's here to see you, Mr. Fisher." The pip-squeak of a girl who announced this did not look like she could be old enough to be out of the *Englisch* school system.

Reuben thought about arguing with her, then decided it wasn't worth his effort. Easier to see Adalyn Landt then send her on her way. Probably quicker too. He rose from his bunk, allowed the young officer to cuff his hands, and walked down to the room set aside for attorney-prisoner meetings.

This was a different place than where he'd met Tobias. Smaller—nearly the size of Reuben's cell, it was also quieter, and no one else was in the room with them.

Reuben looked up at the camera mounted in the corner of the ceiling as he walked through the doorway.

"They'll record our images, but they can't listen to what we say."

Reuben shifted his feet uncomfortably.

"I understand you don't like being photographed, Reuben, but by now you know that you're being monitored constantly. It's one of those rights you lost when you became a resident of Shipshewana Municipal Jail, and it will be worse when they transfer you to the county jail next Monday."

"Is that what I'm paying you for now? To bring me *gut* news?"

"Your family is paying me to craft a defense." Adalyn placed a large leather bag on the table between them. This one was a light tan color, and Reuben found himself wondering how many bags Adalyn owned. "Something we need to start working on today."

Reuben sat in the chair across from her as she took out a tablet and pen.

She looked up to find him staring at her bag.

"Twelve hundred dollars. That's what this one cost. Is that what you were wondering?"

"That's a disgusting display of materialism, even for an *Englischer*."

"Do you think so, Reuben?" Adalyn sat heavily on the chair, and the look that crossed her face reminded him again of his mother. It occurred to him that he should be careful angering this one. She looked as if she'd fought her share of battles.

"It's not your place to be judging me though. Is it?" She twirled the pen once, twice, then three times. "I don't usually justify my purchases to my clients, but in this case perhaps it will help us to move forward. The reason that I buy Louis Vuitton ..." She tapped the *LV* monogram on the front of the bag. "The reason is because I appreciate the highest quality in craftsmanship. Louis lived in France in the eighteen hundreds. He became an apprentice to a *layetier*. Are you familiar with that word?"

"*Ya*. It means one who makes luggage or trunks."

"By hand. Louis Vuitton crafted his merchandise by hand and sold it in small boutiques, and Louis Vuitton merchandise is still made by hand today. That quality makes this brand one of the most valuable in the world."

Adalyn again set her pen into a spin. She watched it as silence filled the room, then her hand came down and stopped it midspin. "In my job sometimes I have to go lower than I'd like, get a bit dirtier than I'd prefer. Sometimes I have to hear things I'd rather not hear and look at things that I'd rather not see . . ." Her hand went to the bag, brushed the logo. "It helps to know that quality does matter, and that hard work is rewarded. Though of course this is just a bag, and you're correct—twelve hundred dollars is a ridiculous price."

She smiled and picked up her pen.

Reuben realized with a rush of emotion that he and this middle-aged, overweight, commercially minded *Englisch* woman had something in common after all. Though looking at them you couldn't find two more different individuals, they both appreciated doing things right.

And isn't that what had landed him here? His thoughts went again to the letter he'd received from Emma, to the promise he'd made her, and how it had somehow led him to be in this place. How many from the community would even remember Emma? Yet it seemed God had brought her back into his life for a reason.

"The one thing I wanted was to be a *gut* farmer. Not just *gut*, but one of the best."

Reuben stared down at his hands, hands that he now knew were capable of both good and bad. "I suppose you'd think it was for the profit it would bring, but money is only useful to a point. The land was a burden to my parents. They'd grown too old to farm it. Folks like to think Amish people work until they step into their graves, but it isn't true. No, they step aside and hand it to the next generation. My folks moved in with my *schweschder* and the place that had been farmed by my *grossdaddi* passed to me—to me and Tobias."

Adalyn had taken a few notes. She stopped now and looked him in the eye. "When was the last time you saw the girl?"

Reuben shook his head, stared down at his hands.

"Why was she staying in the house?"

He clenched his teeth together.

"How long had you known her? Who made the tracks in the woods?" She waited, then added, "They know it wasn't you. The shoe size is different. Black is going to claim you had an accomplice."

When Reuben didn't answer, Adalyn set the pen down, perpendicular to the pad. "Reuben, the judge will require you to answer these questions. Not Monday. Monday is when the prosecution will prove the murder charges are valid. They'll present what evidence they have and possibly call witnesses."

Reuben looked up then.

"From what Tobias and Esther have told me, I suspect they'll call Gavin. He seems to be the one person to have seen you in the girl's company. But it's possible that someone else saw you as well. I am not allowed to call witnesses. The reason I'm asking you these questions is that I'd like to start building our argument to those charges."

Reuben shook his head, finally cleared his throat, and said, "I can't tell you anything about that girl."

"Can't or won't?" Adalyn waited one, then two minutes.

When he didn't answer, she cleared her throat, pulled out a picture, and set it on the table. It was of Katie's duffel bag. He had been wondering what had happened to it. Why take a dead girl's clothes? When he'd gone back into the house, all he'd found was the cell phone.

"Someone brought it into the police station in Middlebury. How did this bag end up in Middlebury? They know it belonged to the girl. It has her prints on it. I suspect it has your prints on it too. But you didn't take it to Middlebury, since you were already incarcerated. So the person you're covering for took it there. Why would he do that? And when did you handle the girl's things?"

Had he picked it up? Maybe. Maybe when he'd helped them carry their things into the house.

If she thought she could make him uncomfortable by waiting him out, she'd never been to an Amish church service. He wondered how she'd respond to three hours of sitting on backless wooden benches.

There was a light tap on the door behind him. Adalyn motioned for one more minute.

"I need to tell you something else. I don't want to, because I think the prosecution is grandstanding, but as your attorney, I believe it's my job to make you aware of any developments in your case. The police department and the county detectives went out to your farm again this morning."

Reuben had been staring at a yellow stain in the linoleum, but something in Adalyn's voice caused him to glance up at her.

"They're looking for another girl."

"I don't understand."

"A girl from the South Bend area has gone missing. At first they thought she'd run away, but then the boyfriend showed up. Turned out he'd been on a camping trip with his family—he has plenty of witnesses. They issued an alert immediately. A judge granted a release of her cell phone records and the police were able to trace her final calls. They were made here in Shipshewana."

"I still don't see what this has to do with me."

"Her last call was placed two days before the girl's body showed up at your place."

All of the blood flowed out from Reuben's head, like the time he'd been hit with a baseball as a boy, the moment before he'd passed out. He could still hear Adalyn's voice, but it was as if it were coming from a great distance.

"In my opinion, there's absolutely no proof connecting this girl's disappearance to you, but the judge allowed a search warrant on circumstantial evidence and the slim chance that the girl might still be hidden on your place."

The door behind him opened, and Reuben didn't have to turn

around. He knew who had walked in, could smell the leather jacket Shane Black wore before he walked up beside the table.

Black dropped the picture of a young girl onto the table. She looked to be a bit younger than Katie and had long red hair. A smattering of freckles lined the tops of her cheeks, and her smile revealed the metal braces so many of the *Englisch* teenagers wore.

"What about it Reuben? Want to tell us where she is?" Shane's voice was low and rumbling like a coming storm.

Esther couldn't believe Deborah had talked her into going to the quilting circle.

"What else are you going to do? Stay there and stare a hole through the police officers?" Deborah glanced back at Joshua and Leah. "Can you wipe his nose? I'm sure it isn't catching. I know you don't need a sick *dochder*."

"Probably allergies from being in that dusty house." Esther reached over the buggy seat and swiped at Joshua's nose with her handkerchief, though Joshua did his best to avoid her. "If I had stayed at the house perhaps I could have watched over Tobias. You were standing right there. Did you not notice how he went after Shane?" She turned around and clutched the half-finished quilt in her lap.

"What does *went after* mean, *Mamm*?" Leah continued playing with her doll as she waited for her answer.

"Their ears miss nothing," Esther muttered.

"What am I supposed to miss?"

Deborah glanced at her and smiled, which eased a bit of the tension in Esther's shoulders—not all but some.

"Tobias will handle himself. When we left he was splitting wood with a vengeance."

"What does *vengeance* mean?" Leah play-walked her doll across the top of the buggy seat.

"Can I send her to school early?" Esther asked. "Surely they won't notice if I drop her off a few years before it's time."

"I like school. I play school with Mary and Martha." Leah's head popped between the seats, and Esther kissed her on the forehead.

"Sit back beside Joshua. Wipe his nose if it runs any more."

"Eww." Leah took the handkerchief and sat back, followed by a squeal, a commotion, and giggling. Esther didn't have the energy to look and see what caused the ruckus.

"Time spent playing with Max will do them both good. Always wears them out, and they sleep better in the evening." Deborah pulled into the parking lot of the quilt shop as Melinda was stepping out of her buggy.

"Oh, she brought Hannah with her." Esther's mood began to lift at the sight of the baby.

"My girls should be here somewhere as well. I'd asked her to pick them up from their *grossmammi*'s. They were to walk there after school." Deborah stepped out of the buggy after Esther.

Esther hugged Melinda, then reached for the baby. She felt a small spot of happiness for the first time in hours. Though she hadn't admitted it to anyone, all the talk of babies had reawakened her dreams of having a big family, dreams she'd let die when she'd buried Seth two years ago. Now that it seemed they were in reach again, everything was falling apart at the seams.

Melinda looked at her quietly from behind her wire-rimmed glasses, saying nothing but seeming to take in everything.

Surrounded by their children, they made their way into the quilt shop.

"Perfect timing, gals. I just returned from running errands, and I have tons to gab about." Callie peeked around the corner of the kitchen where she was putting up supplies and running a pot of hot water for tea.

"*Ya*, so do we."

"Max looks gorgeous today, Miss Callie." Mary reached down

and straightened Max's purple scarf. "Does he mind wearing a girl's color?"

"I thought dogs were color-blind," Deborah confessed.

"No. I googled that one night when I was bored. They see color, but it appears paler to them. They do, however, have excellent night vision."

"So he can see the color of his scarf?" Mary's eyes widened.

"Possibly, but I don't think he pays it much mind. Mostly he's happy to receive his treat, which he doesn't get until after I tie on his scarf each morning."

"Nice trick."

Esther listened to the prattle, but focused on baby Hannah. The child was nearly a year old now, but still smelled of powder and sweetness. Not quite awake from the walk inside, she snuggled against Esther's chest and popped two fingers into her mouth.

"I worry she's going to suck those fingers until she's twelve," Melinda said, as she hustled children and toys to the back of the store.

"Doubtful," Deborah reasoned. "I've yet to see a teenager with her fingers in her mouth."

"We worry about our children, just the same." Melinda spread an old quilt across the floor and pulled a few toys out of the bag. Joshua immediately reached for the wooden blocks and began banging one against the floor.

"Anyone want to take Max out to the garden for his afternoon romp?"

"I'll do it!" Mary squealed.

"And I'll watch her," Martha added.

"I don't always need watching, Martha. *Mamm*, tell her I can walk Max by myself."

"What will you do if he sees a bird and runs off down Main Street?" Deborah asked.

Mary scrunched up her eyes and glanced out the front window

at a passing car. With a sigh she handed the leash to Martha. "Maybe you should walk him to the gate, then I'll take over."

Martha, Mary, and Leah were at the door when Joshua spied them and went running in their direction. "Do we have to take him with us?" Mary asked.

"How would you feel?" Martha asked.

It sounded to Esther as if Mary said, "I can't win today."

Hannah was content to remain in Esther's lap. Everyone except Esther pulled out their quilts and began stitching while Deborah explained what had happened at the farm that morning.

"Were they still there when you left?" Melinda asked.

"*Ya*. It's terrible. They even had the canine unit out." Deborah shook her head as she pieced a blue triangle to a black one. Esther watched the familiar pattern fall into place and wondered why life couldn't be as simple. Quilting made sense to her, had since she was a small girl learning the craft at her mother's side.

Life though—for many years now life had been a puzzle.

It seemed as if Esther were caught in the impossible task of trying to piece together an unworkable pattern. No matter how much she focused, how hard she bent to her task, the pieces would not fit together. Oh, at times she might think she'd made progress, but in reality she'd made none at all. Like a quilt that couldn't be finished.

Melinda rethreaded her needle. "I heard the girl was from South Bend."

"I don't understand Shane Black at all." Callie poked her needle through her material too roughly. "Why would he jump to the conclusion that Reuben had something to do with a girl missing from a different town?"

"Think about it, Callie. Maybe he didn't have any choice. Maybe if a girl goes missing in the same area where a body has been found, they have to check it out." Deborah didn't look up as she spoke. "I'm not saying it's right, but maybe that's the way the *Englisch* system works. Suspicion by geographic proximity."

Callie glanced up and immediately pricked herself with the needle. Sticking her finger in her mouth, she grimaced. "Are you sure you don't watch *CSI*?"

"C-S-who?"

"Never mind."

"Esther, you've nothing to say on this?" Melinda pushed back from the quilt stand and reached for her tea.

"What is there to say? A week ago all was well. Then I stumbled on a dead body, my soon-to-be-cousin was arrested for murder, I learned we're to live somewhere else, and now there may be another body buried on the land. As soon as I speak, something else will happen. Best I hold Hannah and keep my peace."

Esther was painfully aware the others were all staring at her, so she kept her eyes on Hannah's perfectly arched eyebrows, tiny nose, and two fingers still firmly stuck in her mouth.

"I believe she's in shock," Deborah murmured.

"Who could blame her?"

"Shane should be ashamed of himself." Callie reached for the Band-Aids she kept in her sewing supplies and slapped one on her finger, then resumed sewing the pieces of her lap quilt together again—each stitch larger than the last. "I have a mind to find him and talk to him. He might think that he can push you around because you're Amish women, but that doesn't make you stupid, and it doesn't mean you don't have rights. He needs to watch who he's messing with."

She snipped off her last stitch and glared at Deborah and Esther. "What else were they doing other than searching with the dogs?"

Deborah glanced uneasily at Esther. "Might as well tell her."

"They were going through the house and the barn, dredging the pond again, and searching the silo—"

"He can't do that!"

"But he can, Callie. He had the official papers signed by the court. Officer Taylor was there and showed us the forms."

Callie stuck her needle inside her fabric and stood, now thoroughly agitated. "Did he even look anywhere else? Doesn't he have other suspects? I bet they don't have a single stitch of proof Reuben knew that girl from Cedar Bend—"

Esther looked up when Melinda and Deborah began to giggle.

"I can't imagine anything funny." Callie placed her hands on her hips. "Honestly, this is very serious. You need to learn to stand up for yourselves—"

"No, Callie. It's not about the officers." Deborah pointed to Callie's sweater, which now had the quilt top sewn to it in giant, loopy, uneven stitches.

"Well, good grief!" Callie flopped into her chair. "I can't concentrate is all." She took up her scissors and began snipping.

"Not that way. Let me show you." Esther moved over, still carrying Hannah. "When you remove stitches, it's best to use a seam ripper so you don't mistakenly cut the fabric."

She popped the first stitch with the small red tool, then handed it to Callie so she could do the rest.

"I'm betting you never sewed anything to your apron," Callie muttered.

"Actually, I sewed one of Seth's socks to my nightgown when we were first married." Esther smiled at the memory, surprised to find there was no pain in the remembering. "This was before I was pregnant with Leah, and I was determined to finish the sewing before bed, but Seth ... Seth had other ideas."

Esther felt the heat rise in her cheeks. "I was trying to hurry, and I darned it right to my gown."

The room grew quiet, each woman lost in their own thoughts, Esther lost in another place and another time. She placed Hannah on the quilt, on her back since she'd fallen asleep. They all resumed their sewing, and when Callie had removed the rest of her stitches, she turned to Esther. "Deborah is always saying that God has a perfect plan for each of us, that he has a hope and a future planned out for us. Do you believe that?"

Esther pulled in a deep breath, found that the sewing had soothed her nerves, as it always did. She didn't answer Callie's question immediately, searching her heart first — searching through the heartaches and fears and doubts. "It's what I've been taught since I was a *kind*. What we've all been taught."

"*Ya*, our training has been *gut*," Melinda murmured.

"I do believe the Lord's Word," Esther continued. "But when my heart hurts, as it does today, I have to wonder if his plan doesn't include a bit more refining and learning than I would have chosen. I have to wonder if there couldn't have been an easier way. I wonder why."

Esther wouldn't have spoken such truth to anyone else, probably not to her own *mamm*, but somehow, here in this circle of friends, in this circle of sewing, it seemed all right to give voice to the hurts that ached like a tooth gone bad.

The thing that helped, the thing she would have liked to thank them for, was that they did not argue with her.

Then the door opened and the children were tumbling into the room, full of life and energy and smiles and hope.

It wasn't until they were leaving that Deborah asked Callie what her news was. "When we arrived, you said you had something to talk to us about."

"Oh, yes." Callie tucked her hair behind her ears. She seemed to hesitate, glanced around the room and finally stared down at the dog. When she looked up a smile played across her lips. "I went to see that old man I told you all about."

"The one who was confused?" Melinda turned and looked back, her eyebrows popped up over her glasses in surprise.

"Yes. His name is Ira. His story about his daughter is actually quite interesting. It's all tied into a terrible tragedy, something about tornadoes that struck here in Shipshe."

"That would be the Palm Sunday Tornadoes." Deborah pulled Joshua's cap more firmly down over his ears. "It was a terrible time, Callie, but interesting history. You can go to the library or the visitors' center and read the details — there's even a display."

Stepping closer to Callie, she added, "But stay focused on helping Reuben. One mystery at a time is enough."

Callie hugged each of them as they passed through the door of the shop. Esther waited until last. She thought of how it had been her habit to stand back when the time for parting came, how she dreaded when everyone embraced because she couldn't stand to have her isolation breached.

It was too late for that though.

The bubble she'd built around herself after Seth's death had been popped, and it seemed there was no going back. She felt Callie's arms around her, breathed in the scent of her floral perfume — light but enough to make Esther smile. If Esther knew her flowers, and she did, there was a bit of daisy in the fragrance.

Englischers had such interesting ways.

Spring flowers in the fall.

Still, it was a nice reminder that spring would come again.

Chapter 23

DEBORAH ARRIVED HOME in plenty of time to make dinner—at least she would have, if it hadn't been for her children.

She left the buggy parked near the front of the barn.

"Martha, would you run in and tell your *dat* we're home? I need him to unhitch Cinnamon for me, as I believe Joshua's had a bit of an accident."

"It smells terrible, *Mamm*."

"Yes, well, I think he has a bit of diarrhea." Lifting him off the backseat of the buggy there was a big sucking sound, followed by Martha and Mary clambering over each other to see who could exit the buggy the fastest.

Martha stepped away as Joshua began to cry and rub at his eyes. "I knew it smelled bad, but when you picked him up you released something awful."

Deborah held him at arm's length, trying not to soil her dress.

"Martha, go and tell your *dat* the mare needs unhitching. Mary, I want you to go and find a rag and a pail and clean up the mess on the backseat."

"Why do I have to do it? I'm only a little kid, barely old enough to—"

"Would you rather clean up your *bruder*?" Deborah thrust Joshua toward her.

"No, *Mamm*. I'll fetch the bucket." Mary disappeared faster than a fresh-baked pie on a Sunday.

Martha was giggling as she walked away.

"Hurry, Martha. I'm going to need your help with dinner. I believe he's only teething, but let's take him in and take his temperature to be sure. Either way, we're in for a night."

"I'll run."

Deborah thought of stripping her youngest one's clothing off outside, but the weather had turned colder with the clouds, and soon it would be dark. As she hurried inside and set Joshua in the tub, tugging off his soiled clothes, then filling the sink with warm water and wetting a cloth, she thought of Esther's words earlier. God's plan did seem to include a bit more refining and learning than any of them would have chosen. Often she wondered why life took turns through rough weather.

Why couldn't things be easier?

Tonight certainly wasn't the best time for a sick *boppli*.

But when was a good time?

Then again, her problems were nothing compared to Esther's. The thought was a sobering one. She finished cleaning Joshua, then lifted him out of the tub, his cries now little whimpers. Pressing her lips to his forehead she was relieved to feel its coolness.

Perhaps he was merely teething, but she would insist everyone drink orange juice tonight nonetheless. A good dose of vitamin C to chase away the germs of winter.

If only every ill could be cured as easily.

Thirty minutes later, Martha had heated the stew left over from two days ago. Deborah took the fresh bread out of the oven — bread her mother had been kind enough to send along.

"*Grossmammi* makes the best bread," Mary said.

"That she does," Deborah agreed. She'd just placed it on the table along with a plate of fresh-cut fruit for dessert—it was as good as orange juice—when there was a loud commotion at the backdoor.

"What now?"

"It's not Joshua. I checked on him. He's been asleep since you rocked him." Martha followed her to the back porch, where the last of the day's light fell on her two sons.

"Jacob and Joseph. Dinner's ready. Whatever you're doing there, finish with it and come in."

"Sure thing, *Mamm*. We're just about done."

"Just about isn't what I asked."

She was turning away when she caught sight of something large and close to the ground, something with a snout.

Reversing directions, she pushed open the screen door and walked out onto the back porch.

"Can you tell me why there are two pigs here?"

"They're not just any pigs," Jacob explained.

"They're our new pigs." Joseph continued hammering a board onto the front of the crate—a crate that was beginning to look suspiciously like a doghouse.

"Why—" Deborah stopped, closed her eyes and counted to three. When she opened them, the pigs were still there, this time staring right up at her. "Why are they not in the barn?"

"Funny thing." Jacob rubbed at a bit of mud that was smeared across his right cheek. "These two don't take to the mud very well. Maybe that's why we got them so cheap."

"*Ya*. The man *Dat* bought the pigs from allowed as they were a bit peculiar."

"Boys. These pigs cannot live outside my backdoor."

Joseph stopped hammering, and Jacob stopped scratching. At the exact same moment in the exact same tone, they said: "Huh."

Then Joseph picked up another nail and went back to whacking it with the hammer, this time on top of the crate, and Jacob reached a hand up to scratch underneath his wool cap, where there was more mud, no doubt.

"No. No, no, no. Stop what you're doing this very minute." Deborah felt a meltdown coming. She didn't have them often, and she wasn't proud when she did. But one was headed toward her boys now. "I want this crate and these—these pigs off my back step and in the barn this very minute. Do you understand me?"

"But—"

"No buts. I want no argument. I want it done, and I want you back in this house in less time than it takes for me to fill the dinner glasses with water. I want you to be so fast that those pigs will think they're flying. Am I being perfectly clear? Doesn't matter to me if they're in the mud or beside the mud or across the creek from the mud. You can make them mud pies and serve it to them for breakfast, but I will not have them sleeping outside my backdoor."

Her voice had risen and she'd gained speed as she'd lectured them until she'd felt like the train that sometimes traveled past the market in Shipshewana.

The boys were staring at her now like she'd sprouted wings herself. Their eyes were wide, and they didn't seem to know whether they should continue listening or start moving the two pigs.

Fortunately for them, Jonas showed up. "Sounds as if your *mamm* wants the pigs moved."

"Yes, *Dat*."

Jacob opened the crate's door, and Joseph led the two pigs out. Deborah was able to see, now by the light of the kitchen's gas lamp since it was beginning to grow dark, that they'd used two of the lead ropes for the horses and tied them around the pigs like they were dogs.

While Joseph walked toward the barn leading the pigs, Jacob struggled with the crate, alternately pulling and pushing it.

Deborah watched, her pulse slowly returning to normal, the heat of her anger cooling.

Jonas didn't mention her temper. He smiled, kissed her lightly on the cheek, and said, "At least the bacon would have been close to the kitchen." Then he walked inside to clean up for dinner.

It wasn't until well after midnight, when she'd been up with Joshua twice and had finally tumbled back into bed only to toss and turn, that Jonas pulled her into his arms and asked her what was wrong.

"Probably just that I'm tired." She fought to keep the tears out of her voice.

"I'll get up with him next time. I can hear his cries as well as you can." He brushed the tears from her face with his thumbs and kissed her on the forehead. "You don't have to talk about it if you'd rather not, Deb, but I don't think it's the babe's teething or the boys' pigs that's causing you to cry."

She blubbered then, soaking his nightshirt. He didn't tell her to stop, didn't rush her through it. He also didn't ask any more questions. When she'd finally wrung herself dry, he rolled over onto his back, and she cuddled up beside him.

"I always found a good cry to be beneficial myself."

Slapping him across the stomach, she tried to smile in the darkness, but she felt too raw for that.

"Jonas Yoder, I'm betting you've never cried a day in your life."

"Not true. I cried when I was eight, when the doc had to cut a fish hook out of my hand. I cried when my *grossdaddi* died, and I cried when Martha was born. Those are only the times that come to mind."

"We were so young then."

"That we were. You're not worried about Joshua are you?"

"No. I can feel the swollen places on his gums. Poor guy is miserable, but the Tylenol is helping. He'll be fine once they break through."

189

"That's *gut*. Soon he'll be plowing the fields with me. He's going to be a strapping young man, just like his older *bruders*."

"I shouldn't have yelled at Jacob and Joseph so."

"Maybe you were a bit harsh with them, but who wants to hear pigs squeal while they're eating?"

Though the room was pitch dark, not even a sliver of a moon peeking in through the windows, Deborah could feel Jonas smiling. She could also feel the sadness descending over her like a blanket as she wondered whether she should share the reasons for her previous tears.

Jonas must have sensed her hesitation, because he turned toward her in the darkness.

"I love them so much, Jonas. The idea that anything might happen to them or anything might happen to you . . . I don't know how I would handle it."

"Is that what this is about?"

"Esther didn't expect to lose Seth, but she did. Melinda didn't expect to have a sick child, but look at Aaron." Tears filled her eyes, but she blinked them back. "And Reuben most certainly did not kill that girl. Still, he sits in a jail, maybe for the rest of his life. When I think of all the things that could happen to us—"

"Whoa there. You're losing me, love. What do all of these things have to do with us?"

"Don't you see? That's what each of those people thought, until it happened to them. That's what Reuben was probably saying two weeks ago." She began to shake, and Jonas once again put his arms around her, this time rubbing her back and pulling the blankets around them.

When she quit shaking, he spoke slowly, quietly. "Deborah, I know your faith is strong."

"Yeah, but so is theirs."

"So it's not a question of faith that you have."

"No. It's a question of why."

"Let me ask you a question instead. How much do you love Jacob and Joseph?"

"Jonas—"

"Answer the question."

"You know I love them more than myself. I would do anything for them."

"And yet you still forced them to move the pigs this afternoon, which actually crushed a little bit of their six-year-old hearts."

"Yes, to teach them."

"As God does with us."

Deborah shook her head in the darkness, but didn't speak.

"Esther's troubles and the boys' are nowhere near the same. But your love for the boys and God's love for Esther is similar."

"*Ya*, I suppose."

"Only similar, Deb. We must remember that, because we can't begin to imagine how much he loves us."

She drew in a shaky breath, considered for a moment what he said. "I know what you're saying is true, but Tuesday Esther said it seemed as if God's hand came down and wiped away her happiness. When I told her God wasn't like that, she asked me how I would know. Which started me to thinking, how would I know? And what, what ..." The tears started streaming down her face again, but she pushed her words through them, "What would my faith be like if I did know. If I had lost one of the children or you."

"Ah, finally." Jonas combed his fingers through her hair, kissing her temples as he did.

"Finally?"

"Finally we're to what is truly weighing on your heart."

"You never think of it?"

"Of course. I suppose everyone does. At every funeral and every birth." Deborah waited for him to say more, becoming aware of the winds picking up outside their window.

When she thought he wouldn't add anything else, he bent

over her in the darkness, found her mouth with his, and kissed her more gently than a sunrise spreading its light across the field on a fall morning.

"Always when I think of it, my answer is the same. If I only had one day with you, Deborah. If I only had one day with any one of our children, I would still count myself the most blessed of men. Would I hurt? Yes. Would I feel loss? Yes. But I'd rather have that one day, or one year, or a dozen, than to spend my life without any of you."

Chapter 24

CALLIE LOOKED OUT over the snow-covered mountain and understood instantly they were in trouble.

She glanced to her right and saw a sign with the familiar black diamond shape. Dread filled her stomach, and her pulse began to jump. She had skied green circle slopes and a few blue squares, but she'd never tried a black diamond, and she hadn't skied at all since right after college. Once she'd begun working as a pharmaceutical rep, there hadn't been time for vacations. She'd wondered when she was moving to Indiana if there were any ski resorts in the area. Apparently she'd found one.

But where was she?

This black diamond slope was steep and difficult. She glanced behind her again, trying to remember exactly what mountain she was on, and that was when she saw Deborah, Esther, and Melinda.

They, too, wore snow skis and had on ski jackets. Though they had goggles on to protect their eyes against the glare of the setting western sun, they still wore their prayer *kapps*. Callie wondered if the *kapps* would blow off when they started down the slope, but then she realized they had bigger problems. All three of her friends still wore their long dresses beneath their jackets.

This was going to be impossible.

They had to find a way off the mountain though, and quickly. The sun was beginning to drop, casting shadows from the woods that bordered both the eastern and western edge of the ski run. It would be dark soon. They didn't want to ski down in the dark.

Looking overhead Callie caught sight of the ski lifts—the last gondola was barely a dot in the distance. She turned and looked back down the trail again. Now the wind was picking up, throwing snow across the trail and into the trees.

Her three friends scooted forward on their skis, using their poles to carefully navigate through the snow. Callie tried to throw out her arms like her mother used to do in the car when she had to stop suddenly. Callie was certain someone was going to topple over the crest of the hill, and then there would be no stopping them. It was a straight shot down.

But how else would they get home?

Movement in the trees caught Callie's attention. She turned to look at the exact moment a man stepped out. He wasn't wearing skis or glasses, which is how she recognized Shane Black.

Her temper flared instantly. She could feel the heat of it even in the cold, but she couldn't remember why she was angry with him.

He motioned them toward the tree line, toward a trail that she could now see snaking off into the woods.

Callie shook her head, refusing to move, and looked back down at the black diamond slope.

Shane was walking toward them now, yelling something and gesturing toward the woods. Callie didn't want to go even though she knew it was the right choice, and she knew choosing the slope because he angered her was immature, even dangerous.

She examined the course in front of her, saw that the front half of her skis were hanging over the edge, hanging in the air. All she had to do was lean over.

Except she'd never skied a black diamond before.

Suddenly the horizon tilted. Callie was a child again, running in circles to make the world spin, and spin it did, crazily whirling in a blur of images as the abyss below her opened up, and she began to fall.

Shane pulled her back, his hands on her arms, steadying her and dragging her away from the edge.

Callie looked for Deborah, Esther, and Melinda, but they were already in the woods, standing there waiting with all of their children — nine in all. How would they make it back to the lodge with all the children? They couldn't possibly carry that many.

Then she saw Max. He barked at her, and Callie knew it was the right thing to go on the trail, to go with Shane.

Except his barking was off. As she skied toward the edge of the woods, skied closer to Max — though it seemed to take many long strides and her legs became terribly heavy — she realized his barking sounded more like a ring.

It was so funny that baby Joshua started clapping his hands.

Callie finally reached the group and bent down to scratch Max behind the ears, to assure him everything would be all right. She thought to quiet his ringing bark, but then she was on the edge of the slope again, and this time she was falling forward . . .

Callie nearly fell out of bed, catching herself with the blankets tangled around her legs and grasping for Max, who was barking at a fever pitch.

"It's all right, boy."

She reached for her alarm to shut it off, but tapping the top button repeatedly did not stop the noise. Peering at the numbers, she finally understood why. "Five a.m.? You must be kidding."

Then she thought of Deborah and Esther and Reuben sitting in the jail. She jerked her cell phone off the nightstand where she set it to charge each night without looking at the display.

"Hello?"

"Morning, gorgeous. We need to talk."

"Trent. It's five o'clock. That's still night. Call me back when the store opens."

"I have your information—about the cell phone."

Callie had crawled back under the covers dragging the phone with her, burrowing deep down so that even her head was beneath the quilt. When she heard his words though, she immediately popped back out. "What?"

"Took me longer than I thought it would. Had to ask for the help of some . . . outside sources."

Throwing back the covers, Callie reached for her robe. "So tell me. What did you find out?"

"I'll be there in five minutes."

Callie had just enough time to grab her robe and house shoes, run a comb through her hair and brush away her night breath—though she didn't understand why she should care about the last two. She hated to admit it, but she was still off-kilter by the dream, something about skiing and the girls and Shane Black. The whole thing was upsetting, and the idea that a dream could upset her was even more disturbing.

When Trent still wasn't there, she threw a coat on and hurried Max outside for a quick morning trip to the garden. They were on their way back in when Trent drove up in his old truck.

Callie glowered at him—for making her wait since Saturday, for pulling her out of bed early, for being male. But then he held up a to-go container with two cups of coffee and rattled a paper bag from The Kaffi Shop.

"Margie sent your usual."

Callie's glower softened, and she motioned Trent inside.

Callie sat behind the counter and Trent stood. He looked disgustingly fresh for a man who had been up all night, which was obvious from the fact that he hadn't shaved, his clothes were rumpled, and he was more hyper than Max on a bird hunt. How much coffee had he had?

"I was able to track the SIM card. The phone was purchased at a drugstore in LaGrange."

"You're sure?"

"Sure I'm sure."

"What else?" Callie sipped the coffee, feeling the first hit of caffeine.

"The message was from a man saying that a job was available. Sounded like he was at a factory. You can hear machinery in the background. I called the number, and it was a cell phone with a computerized message. The person never called me back. When I traced that number, it was another disposable, which makes me think it was another Amish person."

"Why would you think that?"

"They don't normally sign up for a monthly plan."

"That's not true, Trent. Quite a few Amish people conduct businesses, and the bishop has allowed them use of cell phones. In those cases, I'm sure they do have a monthly plan."

"All right, but if they're one of these kids who are sneaking around, then they buy it off the rack and maybe they add some minutes to it."

Callie bit into her muffin and nodded. Deborah had said the same thing to her. Often kids going through their *rumspringa* would have a cell phone their parents didn't know about. They'd bring them into town and charge them at their job or maybe at a restaurant or fast-food place while they were eating.

"So you think the other phone might have been a disposable, but you have no proof of that. What else?"

"Like I said, the guy never returned my call, and the disposable number isn't listed to anyone. All cell phones are listed."

"Mine's not. My business number is, but I prefer to have my cell phone number unlisted."

"It's not listed to the public, gorgeous. I have a different database."

She wasn't awake enough to digest his arrogance, not this early. "Trent, I don't believe you. That sounds like undercover stuff, and you're a reporter, not a cop."

"Believe what you want. We have to have our sources too, or we'd never find out enough to fill a paper. Anyway, the reason I'm telling you this is to explain why I brought in my source."

Callie pushed away the last half of her muffin, suddenly no longer hungry. "I should have never given you the phone. I still haven't heard back from Adalyn, but I'm sure we shouldn't be sharing possible evidence with every newsman in your iPhone."

"She works at the phone company, and now I owe her dinner in South Bend. Trust me. This information is good."

"Was dinner with you a reward or are you punishing the poor woman?" He was worse than arrogant when he was tired. He was also egotistical.

"Gorgeous, this one has been calling me for weeks, but let's try to stay focused on what she told me about the phone."

"I don't think I want to hear any more." Callie turned her back toward him and opened the cash register, checked to see if she would need any more bills or change in the drawer before she opened the shop for the day.

"She happened to be doing random audits last night and guess what she came across?"

"Ones look good. I'm a little low on fives."

"She came across our mystery phone's call. She thought it odd, because there'd only been one call made and one call received on the phone since it was purchased — both to the same place."

"And now I'm counting change."

"Don't you want to know where?"

Callie stopped counting and clapped her hands over her ears. Trent picked up a pen and wrote across the top sheet of her sales flyer in giant letters: *RV factory, north of Shipshe.* Then he turned and walked out of her shop.

Callie stared at the words for thirty seconds, then ran after him, her robe flying behind her like a cape in the predawn light.

"Give it back. You have to give me that phone back."

Trent was already opening the door of his truck.

"What if someone in that factory can clear Reuben? We have to take it to Gavin or Black or someone."

"You must be kidding. I'm not done. I can probably crack this case."

"Stop it! You're not the detective. You're the newsman. Now give it back." She walked around his truck and closed in on him.

Smiling just enough to make him look like something out of a Clint Eastwood movie, Trent reached into his jacket pocket and pulled out the phone, but he held it out of her reach.

Instead of grabbing for it, she stomped on his foot.

"Hey!" He jerked his foot up, and his hands came down.

Callie began prying his fingers away from the phone. "I want it back right now—or I'm going to report a theft."

"Fine." He dropped it into her hands as he rubbed his foot. "You don't have to become violent."

"And you don't have to be such a jerk." She turned and stormed back toward her shop. "You don't have to always put your headlines above our friends. The way we handle this could have an effect on the outcome of Reuben's trial. You do realize that, right?"

When Trent only shrugged, she shook her head, slipped the phone into the pocket of her robe and turned back toward her shop.

"You forgot to thank me," he called after her. "By the way, nice jammies."

But she barely heard him. She was trying to decide who she should call first—Gavin, Black, or her attorney.

Deborah woke the next day feeling tired, but clearer minded about what she needed to do.

She'd been thrown off her mission by that evil mischief-maker: *doubt*. Not to mention the days on the calendar were slipping by. Esther's wedding was in forty-eight hours. Deborah wanted to give her friend the gift of peace — the gift of knowing her life could go on in a normal fashion. The best way to do that was to prove Reuben's innocence.

Which meant returning to her list.

Fortunately Joshua seemed better after his rough night. She did stop the twins before they headed off to school. "I want to apologize to you about last night. It's true I don't want pigs living outside my backdoor, but I lost my temper a bit, and I'm sorry."

"That's all right, *Mamm*." Jacob tugged on his woolen cap. "We're going to ask our teacher about it today."

"*Ya*. Maybe we can train them back into a pigpen." Joseph gave her a crooked smile, looking so much like Jonas that it felt as if a hand were pressing on Deborah's heart. Some of her fear from the night before pushed on the corner of her mind, but she refused to acknowledge it, kissing both the boys instead, and reminding them to wear their jackets. "It's supposed to grow colder today. You'll need them."

Martha and Mary were already out the door and the boys ran to catch up, their lunch boxes banging at their sides.

"Just you and me, kid." Joshua smacked the cold teething ring she'd given him against the tray of his high chair. His nose was still running, but he seemed to feel better. Well enough that he wouldn't mind going to town, but first Deborah needed to clean up this kitchen and prepare dinner. She had a long day ahead, and she knew she'd be arriving home at the same time everyone else was hungry.

Before she left, she pulled out the list of possible motives for Reuben's silence and scanned it one more time.

"One: money."

"Two: love. Romantic."

"Three: love. For family or freinden."

"Four: *Ordnung*."

Taking her pen, she crossed out the second and third items. According to his mother, Reuben had said he'd find the right girl when it was time. She knew he wouldn't lie to Abigail. He might not introduce a new love to his family until he was sure the timing was good, but he wouldn't lie about her. And the girl was definitely not family.

Abigail had also shared that she'd been asked to look at the pictures, to try to identify the body, and she couldn't. How could Reuben possibly love a girl he didn't know? It didn't seem possible.

Which left two reasons for her to investigate.

No doubt Shane had already talked with these people, but had he asked the right questions? It frustrated Deborah sometimes how closed the Amish community could be. She understood why, knew that they were trying to "circle their wagons." She'd heard that expression from Callie, and it seemed like a good description. The idea of old covered wagons, pulled up in a circle to draw protection and comfort from one another made Deborah smile as she placed a sleeping Joshua in the backseat of her buggy.

"Have everything you need?" Jonas asked.

"I do."

He didn't mention last night, only leaned in and kissed her once, then walked off whistling. It was enough to let her know all was well.

And all would be well in their community also, in spite of their circled wagons. Sometimes though, they needed to let someone else in, between the wagons, someone who could help them. In this case, it seemed that person could be Shane Black. Was Shane their friend or their enemy in this instance? His dedication to his job could prove Reuben's innocence, but it could also convict him. Those two thoughts felt like a paradox in her head, but she realized they were both true. Shane would do his job — no matter what it meant, no matter who went to jail. But it was his dedication to his job that would lead to Reuben's freedom. She trusted that as surely as she trusted that Cinnamon would see her safely down the road.

Her first stop was at the bank.

Deborah and Jonas didn't do a lot of business there, since they tended to pay cash for most things. But she had been depositing the money from her quilt sales into an account, hoping she could build up enough to buy Jonas another workhorse. He never complained, but Deborah knew it would allow him to plant more crops in the spring if he had another. Planting more would mean more harvest — given good rain and a decent growing season.

The small account of quilt earnings had continued to increase.

She helped Joshua out of the buggy, setting the black hat usually reserved for Sundays firmly on his head. Then she reached into the buggy and pulled out a baby quilt she'd finished last summer.

There was a queue in the lobby. She waited in the line so she could talk to one of the tellers and tell them what she needed. When she reached the front of the line, the teller asked her to have a seat until her name was called. After she was seated, she allowed Joshua to walk around the room. Hopefully by allowing him to walk now, he'd use up his energy before they went behind the half wall where Mrs. Barnwell sat.

Mrs. Barnwell.

She was tough, but she understood Amish ways. In fact, she was sort of a bridge between the banking world and the Amish community.

"Deborah?" If anything, Mrs. Barnwell's gray hair was shorter than the last time Deborah had seen her. She peered at Deborah and Joshua over her reading glasses, then lowered them to her starched white blouse. A thin, small woman, she reminded

Deborah of the winter finches she'd had on her windowsill this morning. "Would you like to come back now?"

After they'd settled into chairs, Mrs. Barnwell repositioned her glasses and folded her hands. "What can I do for you today?"

"I was wondering if you could check my balance. I know the teller girls can do that, but we had discussed last time whether it would be best to leave the money where it is or put it into a certificate of deposit."

"And you were thinking you might need the money in the spring?"

"Possibly, yes."

Mrs. Barnwell wrote down her balance on a small square of paper and handed it across the desk to Deborah. "The rate of return is somewhat low for under ninety days. If you were able to leave it in for six months it's a little higher, but then the funds wouldn't be available until May."

"I see." Deborah's mind searched for a way to prolong the conversation. "Do you have anything in writing I could take home, perhaps to show to Jonas?"

"Absolutely." Mrs. Barnwell reached into her drawer and pulled out a pamphlet. "This lists the term for each CD and the amount of deposit required."

"*Danki*," Deborah said. Then she spotted the photograph on the bookshelf and remembered the quilt she was holding. "I had heard about your new grandbaby, and I wanted to bring this by."

"Deborah, you shouldn't have. I can't accept this."

"I always have extra quilts sewn up, which I enjoy giving as gifts." Deborah was determined to be truthful about this. "You've always been helpful to Jonas and me. I want you to have it for the *boppli*."

"Well, thank you. It's quite beautiful." Mrs. Barnwell's expression softened as she reached for the quilt. "You do exceptional work. I hope you know that."

"The Lord gives each of us a talent," Deborah said gently. "Yours is with numbers. Mine is with fabric."

"I suppose. There are days I wish I'd chosen something a bit more personal though — something like yours." Mrs. Barnwell stood and opened a cabinet. Deborah caught a glimpse of her coat and purse. She tucked the quilt inside. "Well, thank you so much for stopping by. If you have any questions about those CDs after you speak with Jonas, let me know."

"Actually I do have one more question."

Mrs. Barnwell had already started around her desk, on her way to walk Deborah out. Now she stopped, one hand touching her in-box tray. "Oh. Absolutely. What is it?"

"Perhaps you know that Esther Zook is like a *schweschder* to me. She and Melinda and I sew the quilts that are offered for sale in Daisy's Quilt Shop." Deborah reached over and picked up Joshua, who had been looking contentedly through a picture book. Suddenly she felt the need to hold him in her arms. "Esther is to be married to Tobias this week, and Tobias is — "

"Reuben's cousin. Yes, I know. I'm sorry to hear about his current situation. What that family's going through is a shame."

Deborah strained to hear any other meaning behind Mrs. Barnwell's words, but if there was anything else there, it eluded her. "I've been close to Reuben for years. His farm is near ours. Is it possible, what I mean is . . ."

She felt the heat crawl up her neck, even as Joshua turned in her lap and pushed his fingers into her mouth. She kissed him once and continued. "Is it possible that he was having any kind of financial difficulties?"

Mrs. Barnwell didn't answer right away. She sat down in the chair Joshua had been in, took off her glasses, and wiped them clean with the hem of her blouse. Putting them back on, she finally looked at Deborah. "I can't discuss another customer's finances with you. That's against regulations."

"I see. Of course, I understand."

She stood and made her way to the doorway of the cubicle. Mrs. Barnwell walked back around behind her desk.

"Deborah."

"*Ya?*" Deborah turned around. Mrs. Barnwell was flipping through a stack of envelopes on her desk.

"I have had this statement here for Tobias and Reuben for some time. They asked me to hold their quarterly statements rather than mail them. Heaven knows why. Since you see Tobias fairly often, could you let him know that it's ready? I thought one of them might stop by, but I haven't seen either one since September."

"*Ya.* Sure. I'd be happy to."

Deborah set Joshua on the ground, took his hand in hers, and walked him out to the buggy.

Mrs. Barnwell had found a way to tell her what she needed to know. Reuben had been nowhere near the bank in over six weeks, which meant he wasn't in financial straits. After she placed Joshua into the buggy, she took out her list and marked off the first item.

She looked longingly down the road at the quilt shop, but her last errand was in the opposite direction.

So she murmured to Cinnamon and set off to find Bishop Elam.

Chapter 25

SAMUEL ACCEPTED THE LUNCH from Katie's mother. "*Danki.*"

She nodded once and turned back to helping the younger children. He hadn't seen her cry since two days ago, since the afternoon they'd returned from church to find him sitting on the front porch. He'd told the story exactly like he'd rehearsed. How he'd gone after Katie, begged her to come back with him, but she'd refused.

Timothy had said nothing. He'd listened then walked off toward the barn.

Rachel, his wife, had sat down on the porch and wept.

That moment had been the hardest. He'd wanted to confess then and there, wanted to tell how she had looked as she'd died.

But if he'd done that, what would they have been left with?

No hope.

No help in the fields.

Nothing.

So instead, he'd told the story exactly like he'd rehearsed.

Since Sunday they'd all gone through the same routines they'd gone through any of the days before he'd left, before he'd convinced Katie to trust him, before she'd become his wife.

There was a difference though.

He worked harder now. Didn't stop for breaks when Rachel brought out something to drink. Didn't stop until it was too dark to see. And mornings he was up and working before Timothy was out of bed.

It wasn't much. He knew it wasn't enough, but he'd do what he could to atone for his sins.

He'd do it until he dropped from the weight of his guilt.

Now, pushing away from the lunch he hadn't eaten, he returned to the stack of wood that needed splitting. Raising the axe, he brought it down in one smooth motion, feeling some satisfaction as the blade met the log, as his muscles ached from the work he'd done since before sunrise.

He tried to focus on the task at hand, but the last week of her life continued to play, like an *Englisch* picture show caught in a loop, never ceasing, even in his sleep ...

"Why didn't we stop in town?" Katie asked as Samuel waved his thanks to the man who had given them a ride from LaGrange.

"Could have, but it would have just meant extra walking. I believe we can stay here."

"You know these people?" Katie peered down the lane, past the pond to the old farmhouse. "Fields look tended, but the house appears deserted."

"That's because the two cousins who live here stay in the barn."

"Are you playing with me, Samuel?"

"I'm not. They like the barn, say it's simpler, and it's fixed up real nice."

Katie's worried expression began to ease as they walked down the lane. With the October sun shining on them, the idea that they might have a place to stay was obviously easing her anxiety. He sometimes forgot how hard this must be on her, leaving not just her family but her things behind.

All they brought from home, they carried.

He had the backpack slung over his shoulder, and she had the small duffel bag of her things.

"So no one lives in the house?"

"No. Looked at it pretty close last time I was here. Reuben, the older cousin, offered to help me out if I ever wanted to go into the woodworking business. He showed me some of the cabinetry done in the house, and it's practically art. His grossdaddi *did it all himself."*

"How did you meet him? Reuben, I mean."

"My mamm *knew him. A long time ago. When I told her I was moving here, she gave me his name. One week I was in Shipshe delivering an order for your* dat, *so I looked him up."*

Samuel thought of his own dat *and how he'd died in the prime of his life. Thought of the man his mother had recently married, how cold and distant he was. Then he thought of Reuben.*

Samuel didn't need anyone telling him what to do, but he could use a place to stay for a day or two. "I came out and shared a meal with them. Seems Reuben knew my mamm *and* grossdaddi *very well. He's a big fellow, but kind."*

Katie stopped, staring toward the small pond.

"What is it?"

"The flowers, Samuel. Look at them."

"I see them." He laughed when she continued to stare at them. "Women and flowers. How is it that you're taken with such things?"

"The black-eyed Susans are nearly three feet tall. It looks as if they're stirring the goldenrods." Katie smiled up at him, the blue of the sky reflected in her eyes, causing his heart to beat a double rhythm. Would he ever grow used to the touch of her hand in his, the way she had of making him feel like he was capable of accomplishing anything, the adoration in her eyes?

"Want to take a closer peek?"

"Shouldn't we go and see your freind *first?"*

"He won't mind. Look, there's a path that leads around the edge. I'll bet they use it for fishing." He tugged her hand and pulled her toward the small pond, and it seemed in that moment, as October slipped toward November, that the world belonged to them.

They laughed and played beside the pond, almost as if they were children—even daring to dip their feet into its cold waters.

He didn't notice until they were drying off that the small phone he'd bought in Goshen had rung. The symbol indicating he had a message flashed red.

"Who was it?" Katie asked anxiously as he listened to the message.

"Don't worry so. It's a gut thing. The job in the factory is open. I'll call him back in a minute. First let's go and see Reuben."

Samuel had leaned forward and kissed her then, the sun shining on them as they sat among the flowers surrounding the edge of the pond.

Everything was turning out exactly like he'd hoped.

Chapter 26

Callie glared at Shane Black, anger surging through her veins. Suddenly she remembered bits and pieces of her dream from the night before, and she wanted to pick the phone up off the desk—where it sat between them—and chuck it at him. If she hit him hard enough, perhaps it would wipe that smirk off his face.

"Shane. Play nice," Adalyn was saying. "Perhaps Callie and Deborah should have brought it in as soon as they found it—"

"Perhaps? Perhaps?" His voice grew louder each time he repeated the word, as if that would make him more convincing. "Come on, Adalyn. A teen who watches *Monk* on television would know that this phone is evidence and needed to be turned in the minute it was found." He punched in the passcode.

"Not necessarily, and stop talking about me like I'm not here." Callie slapped her hand against his desk. A sheaf of papers on the corner slid off to the floor. Honestly, you'd think the man would be more organized. "As I explained to Adalyn earlier, at first we thought the phone might belong to Tobias, and then it wouldn't be evidence."

Shane collapsed into his chair causing it to squeak. He drilled her with his stare. "Tobias?"

She refused to squirm under those dark eyes. "It's possible. Some Amish folk do have phones for business purposes."

"All right." A smile played on Shane's lips, and Callie had the uncomfortable sensation that he was thinking about a fish snagged on a line. She was the fish. "So you find the coat, search it for identification, find the phone, think it might belong to Tobias. What happens then, Callie? You went out to his place and asked him? Or did you go to the feed store?"

Instead of answering his question, she tried to remember what her rights were. She hadn't been sworn in or anything. Not that she intended to lie, but she couldn't exactly tell the truth.

Fortunately, she was rescued by her lawyer. "Look, Shane. You have the phone. What else do you need from my client?"

"I'd like to follow the evidence trail. Where else has it been since it left Reuben's pocket?"

She and Adalyn had been over this scenario. After she went to Adalyn's office and learned that Adalyn never received her message—it had been buried under a heap of mail—they'd discussed what she did and did not have to say.

She did not have to offer information.

She did have to answer direct questions.

"I took it to Trent."

"McCallister?" Shane boomed.

Was he in danger of having a heart attack? His face was actually red and sweat was beading on his forehead. He'd been so calm during the Stakehorn case. What was with him today?

"Why would you take evidence to our town newspaper?"

"I didn't know who it belonged to, and I couldn't get past the passcode. I thought he might be able to help me."

Now the smirk was back. Maybe it was better than the yelling, but Callie wasn't sure. "Friends, huh? And was your friend able to help you?"

As he questioned her, she went through the entire last few

211

days—how she'd been stumped by the passcode, how Trent had listened to the phone message, how he was able to trace the SIM card registration number and the origin of the call. She left out the part about the fight with Trent outside her shop.

Shane's face grew redder with each detail, but there were no more explosions. Finally Adalyn picked up her black Louis Vuitton bag and touched Callie's arm. "I trust you're satisfied we've done everything possible to rectify this matter."

"You trust I'm satisfied?" Shane shot back.

"Did your coffeemaker explode today, Black? Maybe your dog chewed up your remote last night? Or did that clunker you drive around refuse to start?" This time it was Callie doing the talking, and Adalyn was quiet.

"What's your point, sweetheart?"

"My point is that I thought you'd be happy I brought you a piece of evidence you weren't able to uncover yourself."

"Versus hiding it from me?" Shane stepped closer, close enough that Callie could smell the starch from his shirt, along with the light scent of his aftershave. Callie felt a current running between them, an actual electrical charge, and it scared the boots off her. His smell brought back images of the black diamond ski slope, him grabbing her arm as she was about to fall, the urgency in his eyes, and how she'd followed him into the woods, to safety.

She closed her eyes for a second, trying to reconcile what she'd experienced in her dream—because she had experienced it— with the flesh and blood man standing in front of her. Her pulse accelerated and sweat gathered in her palms. When she blinked her eyes open, Shane's face was only inches from hers.

"Save it for date night, you two." Adalyn nudged Callie out of the office and toward the station's front door.

"Call me if you find anything else. As *soon* as you find anything else, and before you call the *Gazette*!" Shane's words cut off as the door slapped shut behind them.

The cold autumn breeze tugged at Callie's coat, clearing a dozen questions tumbling through her mind.

"Don't let him grate on you." Adalyn pulled out her car keys. "How about coffee and pie?"

"I'd love to, but I need to go and check on the shop. I've been leaving Lydia alone too much lately."

"Understandable. She's a good girl, but when you're a sole proprietor it's very much like being a single mom. You always feel as if you should be somewhere else."

"I hadn't thought of it that way, but you're right. Not to mention, Max misses me." Callie hesitated, knowing she should go, but needing some reassurance. "Do you think the phone will help or hurt Reuben's case?"

"It's hard to say." Adalyn glanced out at the cars and buggies making their way to and from town. "I've learned through the years that I can't determine the outcome of a case—be it civil or criminal. All I can do is my best to represent my client before the court in a favorable light, to make sure his or her rights are protected, and to guide him or her through the legal process. The rest is in higher hands."

Callie wondered if Adalyn meant the judge, the jury, or divine hands. She decided she didn't want to know. "According to Deborah, Reuben hasn't made your job very easy."

Adalyn shook her head, gray hair slipping a little from the bun at the back of her neck. "Like many Amish men, Reuben is reticent, but there's something more going on, and he's not willing to share it with me—even if it means he spends the rest of his life in prison. Based on that, I'd say any new evidence in this case has a fair chance of being a good thing."

"I wish Shane were on our side."

Adalyn stopped fidgeting with her keys, studied her a moment. "Shane's not on anyone's side. He's just doing his job, and he'll do it well."

Callie nodded, but felt unsatisfied with Adalyn's reply.

Reaching in her bag, Adalyn pulled out a business card. "My cell and home phone numbers are on this one—just in case you don't have them from the last time I represented you. In the future, if I don't return your call in an hour, try the other numbers."

Callie remained standing in the parking lot after Adalyn had driven away. She did need to return to the shop, but she had the niggling feeling that there was something more important she needed to do. Go see Ira again? It was past noon and he'd probably be resting.

Setting aside the uneasy feeling she had, Callie decided it best to wait until tomorrow morning to visit him. So she climbed into her car and drove the mile to her shop. Perhaps a few hours of stocking shelves and selling quilting supplies would help put her emotions back on track.

But it didn't, and then Lydia called Callie to the phone. It was the *Grossdaddi* House. Ira Bontrager had been kicked by a horse and was at the local medical center. He didn't appear to have any serious injuries, but he was upset and he was asking for her.

"You should go," Lydia said.

"I hate to leave you here alone. You covered the morning shift by yourself."

"I took a two-hour lunch break, remember? You asked me to go shopping in Mrs. Knepp's quilt shop and check out her aisle arrangements, but she caught me and insisted I leave. So I had some extra time on my hands."

"That's right. I still can't believe she kicked you out."

"She knew I was spying."

"Define *spying.*"

"She caught me with the camera you sent."

"So I wanted a few pictures. She won't allow me in the store anymore."

"Do you blame her? Maybe you should call a truce."

"A truce? But she's stealing my business! I tried working with her, but she won't accept my friendship. The world thinks Amish folk aren't competitive but let me say, the owner of Quilts and Needles is determined to be cutthroat competition!" Callie jabbed a needle into a pin cushion, then looked at Lydia and smiled sweetly. "Forget about Mrs. Knepp. I need to focus on Ira. Thank you for agreeing to stay until we close. All I need you to do is lock up."

"No problem."

"You're sure you don't mind?"

"I'm sure."

Callie pulled the young girl into a hug. "You're an angel. Could you take Max out for a walk before you leave?"

"Of course I will."

"Somehow I don't think they'll allow him in the medical center."

Callie was halfway to her car when Deborah pulled her buggy into the lot.

"You're leaving?" Deborah asked.

"Yes. I'm on my way to see Ira."

"Who is Ira?"

"Ira Bontrager, the old man I told you about who lost his daughter."

"Callie, you can't really be trying to help him find her." Deborah reached for Joshua, who had pulled a banana from the bag of groceries and was trying to put it into his mouth without peeling it.

"It's a long story, but he's been hurt and he's at the medical center. Now he's asking for me, so I'm going to see if I can help."

"Doesn't Ira's son live here in town?" Deborah peeled the banana and broke off a piece, then handed the smaller bite-sized chunk back to her son.

"Yes, but ... it's complicated. I wish we had time to talk. Are you headed home now?"

"I have an hour yet. I stopped by to see if you had time to run an errand with me?"

"Sure, as long as we hurry. I need to be at the medical center before visiting hours are over."

Callie hurried into her storage room and fetched the car seat she'd purchased at a garage sale. Within five minutes they'd buckled Joshua into the backseat of her car and were on their way.

"This will give us time to catch up," Deborah said, as they drove out of Shipshe. "Joshua's been feeling badly, but I gave him Tylenol and he seems better. He's cutting teeth."

Callie peered into her rearview mirror at Joshua, who was reaching for the banana Deborah was still holding. Some things in life could be solved with a bite of soft fruit. The thought flashed through her mind and brought her the first real peace of the day.

"I had to go and see Shane about the phone," Callie told Deborah.

"Oh dear. Does he think it's going to help Reuben?"

"Those weren't his exact words. He did holler a lot."

"Shane does that sometimes, especially when he's worried."

"He didn't arrest me, so yeah—let's call it *worry*. How was your day?"

"I tried to run down some leads, but they didn't pan out either."

Callie looked at Deborah, a smile slowly spreading across her face. "You've been sleuthing without me?"

"It was only to the bank and the bishop. Mrs. Barnwell at the bank was kind enough but it was a dead end. Bishop Elam ..." Deborah stared out the car window at the falling leaves.

"What is it? What did your bishop say?"

"That he'd seen Reuben in town the Saturday before the body was found, and Reuben asked to have a word with him. The bishop is a private man and would never tell another person's confidences, but he did share the nature of Reuben's concerns.

Reuben wanted to know whether the *Ordnung* would have him put the needs of a *freind* over the needs of family."

"And what was Bishop Elam's answer?"

"A wise one—that the *Ordnung* and the Lord would never ask you to make such a choice. That there would always remain a way to do both. He said Reuben wasn't satisfied with the answer."

"Imagine that," Callie muttered.

"*Ya*. It's not like Reuben to question answers from the bishop, though he's been known to be stubborn when he sets his mind to something, as you can tell from this situation."

Callie pulled into the parking lot of the RV factory. "And he asked this before the girl died?"

"*Ya*. Bishop Elam was sure of it."

"So unless she was in that pond for two days—and I doubt that—Reuben wasn't asking about covering up a murder." Callie lowered her voice as they walked into the door of the factory.

The receptionist didn't look surprised to see an *Englisch* woman with an Amish woman and her baby. She did seem a bit uncertain as to what to do with their "Information Wanted" poster. Finally she called the floor supervisor, who took them into his office.

"I've definitely never seen a girl who looks like this, but then we don't hire many Amish girls, as you can imagine." In his fifties and practically bald, the supervisor slid the poster back across the desk. "I'm a little curious as to why you all are here. I already explained all of this to Detective Black."

Callie and Deborah glanced at each other.

"He was here?" Callie asked.

"About an hour ago."

"Can you tell us what he said?" Callie wound a piece of her hair round and round her finger.

"Same things you did. Showed me the same poster. Asked the same questions. Say, I wish I could help, but I do have a business to run here. We have quite a few young Amish men on our floor and part of the reason I hire them is they don't give me any trouble. Hard enough to make a profit these days."

"We understand. *Danki* for your time." Deborah stood and moved toward the door.

Driving back to Shipshe, Callie and Deborah both tried to find something positive gained from their trip. "We were able to spend time together," Callie pointed out.

"*Ya.* Why don't you follow me to the house for dinner? Maybe we can think our way around this."

"No. I really feel I should go see Ira. Deborah, I want to know more about the Palm Sunday Tornadoes. I did some research on the Internet, but I would like a more detailed, more personal account. Do you know of anyone who could help me?"

"You're a bit determined about this."

"If anything it could ease Ira's mind . . ." But Callie was remembering the confidence in Ira's voice when he'd said he knew his daughter was still alive. How could he know that? He couldn't. Not after all these years.

"There's a display at the visitors' center that gives quite a bit of information."

"Yes, I remember you told me that before."

"And then there's the president of the historical society."

"Shipshe has a historical society?"

Deborah turned to hand Joshua a soft toy to play with, then reached into her purse and pulled out a receipt and a pen. She scribbled a name on the back of the receipt. "I don't know her phone number."

"I'll find it. Thank you so much."

"Remember, right now we need to stay focused on Reuben."

"I understand, but I don't know what else we can do. We seem to have hit a dead end."

"*Gotte* will give us direction, Callie. He always does." Deborah pulled Callie into a hug before climbing into her buggy with Joshua.

Then they drove off in different directions, the afternoon sun and the fall wind sending a shower of leaves down between them.

Chapter 27

"ADALYN'S HERE TO SEE YOU." Gavin's voice was quiet, revealing nothing. There'd been a type of truce between him and Reuben for the last few days, since Reuben had agreed to see Tobias. Since Tobias had stormed out of the jail.

Reuben glanced up from his bunk in surprise.

He hadn't been expecting to see Adalyn Landt again so soon.

What more was there to say about the upcoming hearing?

Why had she come?

Maybe Samuel had returned.

But the boy had run—for whatever reason, he had fled. No, he wouldn't be returning to Shipshewana unless he, too, had metal cuffs around his wrists. And how would he survive such a thing? Some days Reuben didn't think he could endure it another moment himself.

As Reuben allowed Gavin to place the handcuffs around his wrists, waited for the door of his cell roll open, and walked down the hall, he thought of how quickly one's routine could change. He should be in the field today. He could feel it in his bones. But something told him he wouldn't be sifting earth between his fingers for some time, and it wasn't a lack of faith.

It was a deep sorrow building in his soul.

Then he saw the sheet of paper—the photograph—Adalyn placed on the table. Pulled from her black leather bag—her Louis Vuitton bag. He saw it and understood why she'd come. Shane Black was putting all the pieces together, and soon even Reuben's silence wouldn't be able to hide the facts.

"It's an *Englisch* phone, *ya*. What about it?"

"We go before the judge in six days. By then Black will know every call that has been made to or from this phone. And he'll know where the person was standing when the calls were made."

"Black found it?"

"Actually Callie found it—in your coat pocket. Any idea how it wound up there?"

He tried to think back to the evening Samuel had come to him. It was a jumble of images and words, promises given long ago, and decisions made in haste. Reuben was accustomed to resolving things in his life deliberately, often over a period of days if not weeks.

That day, there'd been cause to move quickly.

"Not sure," he admitted.

"You're not sure."

"You heard me."

"That's not going to work on the witness stand."

"Thought you said I wouldn't have to testify."

"True. The state can't compel you to testify against yourself. But we had discussed that it might help your case if you did give your version of what happened that night."

Reuben scratched his face, trying to remember. Had he picked up the phone? He didn't remember doing that. He didn't know why he would have under the circumstances. He rarely even used the phone shacks as most things he needed to say could wait until he saw the person he needed to talk to face-to-face, so why would he have grabbed this phone?

Shaking his head, Reuben glanced up at Adalyn—weariness once again settling over him like a blanket. "Can't recall picking it up, but I'm also not accustomed to anyone else putting their hands in my pockets. If that's where it was found, then I must have put it there."

To his surprise, Adalyn shrugged and put the sheet of paper back into her leather bag. He might have been seeing things, but it seemed she offered a hint of a smile. Soon Reuben's own frown disappeared. He didn't know quite what the joke was, but she was tickled about something.

Soon they were both grinning.

It was probably the first moment they'd shared without tension.

"You might be aware that the police can lift fingerprints off a cell phone. In fact, that technology has progressed in recent years. They can now tell if the person whose fingerprints they find is a smoker or not or if they have recently ingested drugs."

Adalyn studied her hand, rubbing her right thumb against her index finger.

"All of those residues come through your dead cells and skin oils, and they land ..." she pushed a finger against the tabletop, leaving a smudge, "... in your fingerprint. Rather remarkable, the advances in forensic science."

Reuben grunted, not quite sure where she was going with her lecture.

Adalyn stood and pulled on her jacket. Only then did Reuben look up at the small window, notice the wind blowing the now bare tree branches outside. "Unfortunately this phone passed through a few hands before it landed on Shane's desk, so it's not likely to reveal much. Too many fingerprints make deciphering difficult."

She walked to the door, tapped on it. "They also can't see inside a man's head—yet."

Gavin opened the door and Adalyn turned to leave, but before she did, she stopped and faced Reuben again, drilling him with her steel-blue eyes. "The girl from Cedar Bend? She came to Shipshewana, but lost her phone here before boarding a train to Chicago. Ran off with an older guy who's in a rock band, and called home yesterday when she saw her face on the news. Seems you're not a suspect in that case anymore."

Then Adalyn left, leaving Reuben to stare at his own hands and think about fingerprints. What story would his tell if they could?

Callie walked into the hospital room and noticed at once how much smaller and older Ira looked in the bed with bandages wrapped around his head. Then he pushed himself into a sitting position and started talking.

"You didn't bring Max? I told them I wanted you to bring Max!" He thumped his hand against the blanket. Callie was relieved to see some energy and color in his wrinkled face. She was also thankful to see his cane was on the other side of the room, out of reach.

"I'll leave you two alone." The nurse smiled and made a quick escape.

"What are you doing here, Ira? Erin Troyer told me something about a horse and you being kicked."

"*Ya*. That horse is stubborn, and I should have never turned my back on it. I'm an old fool." Doubt clouded his features like a storm passing in front of the sun. "Sharon will understand though. Is my wife on her way? I imagine Caleb went to fetch her. I thought they might be here by now."

His hand plucked at the covers, and he looked around the room as if he could find a clue as to where he was, who he was, and what had happened to his world. Unsure what else to do, Callie pulled the single extra chair closer to his bed, reached out, and placed her hand over his. When she did, he stared down at it a moment, his lips trembling.

Then his eyes closed and he seemed to relax.

They remained that way for the space of a few heartbeats. Until a Carolina chickadee landed on the windowsill and started raising a ruckus. Callie didn't know many bird names, but she knew that one — the little guy with a black-and-white-striped face had been a constant visitor on her apartment patio in Houston as well.

"That would be the reason I was kicked to begin with," Ira confessed, without opening his eyes. "Turned to look and see what kind of bird was making so much noise. Turned and didn't keep my eye on that brute of a horse. He'd been a bit ornery all morning, and he kicked me right in the keister."

Ira's hand went to the bandage on his head. "Horse hurt my hip. Ground hurt my head. Landed in the dirt as if I were a sack of potatoes someone had thrown out in the lot for the pigs."

A smile tugged at the corner of his mouth.

Callie patted the top of his hand with hers, then pulled away, sitting back in the chair. "Well, I'm glad it's your keister he kicked and not your head. While you seem stubborn, I'm not sure how well you'd take that."

"Worried about me, were you?"

"Of course, Ira."

"Are you any closer to finding my girl?"

"I was planning to stop by the exhibit at the visitors' center after I leave here. See what information they have." Callie tugged at the hair that now curled well past her collar, thinking of Deborah's words of caution. "But Ira, I don't want to raise your hopes. It's not likely that Bethany even survived the tornados, and if she did — "

"She did. I know in my heart she did, and don't start asking me again how I know or why it is that I know now. Maybe it's a gift the Lord has given me here in my last days."

"Maybe so." Callie paused, then plunged on. "That doesn't mean he's given me the gift of second sight though. I'm not sure exactly how to find someone who has been missing for so long. Someone who probably wouldn't know they're missing."

"You found that editor's murderer."

"He was right here in town, and he was still looking for something."

"Well maybe my *dochder* is looking for me, in her heart. Maybe she is but she doesn't know it yet."

Callie nodded, because she knew that she should. She nodded and forced herself to wait, but she really wanted to go see what was at the visitors' center and speak to the president of the historical society.

After a few more minutes had passed, Ira began to nod off. Callie stood and tiptoed to the door. She was pulling it open when Ira called out from the bed.

"Don't forget, when you find her, tell her how much I love her and that I've missed her every day."

"If I find her, you can tell her." Callie stepped out into the hall and collided with Caleb Bontrager.

"If you find who?"

"Oh. I'm sorry. I didn't mean to walk into you." Callie looked down at the linoleum floor, then across the hall, and finally at the roundish man standing in front of her. He bore a strong resemblance to Ira, though he had a full head of dark hair and, of course, a dark beard.

"No harm done. Nice of you to stop in and see my *dat*."

"Yes. Well, I was relieved to see he's recovering nicely." Callie pasted on her best smile. "You have a nice evening, Mr. Bontrager."

She thought she'd made a clean escape, was a good two doors down the hall, when he called out.

"You won't find her. I don't even know that she exists. I have no memory of my *mamm* mentioning a girl."

Callie stopped and turned toward him, but didn't walk back down the hall.

"He talks about all manners of things when his mind clouds. Moves from today to years past. It's hard to follow, hard to know how best to answer."

Callie nodded, met Caleb's gaze and held it for a moment, then continued out of the building, out into the waning afternoon light.

A stop at the visitors' center turned up facts and a lot of information. But Callie also hit a dead end of sorts there.

Miss Morton, the president of the Shipshewana Historical Society, had been working the afternoon shift behind the counter and had been happy to help her. Callie had the sneaking suspicion someone had told Miss Morton that Callie was on her way over—Shipshe was a small town. Callie had to keep reminding herself of that. She wasn't in Houston anymore.

"No Amish people from Shipshewana lost their lives in the storms, though one Amish man was killed in the cleanup operation," Miss Morton told Callie.

"Are you sure?" Callie peered down at the historical account that Miss Morton had pulled out and set on the counter.

"Positive. I don't need to look at this book to tell you that. I've been president of the Historical Society long enough to know the history of the biggest catastrophe to ever strike this town." Miss Morton paused, tapped the book once with a sensibly manicured nail, no polish. "Now what is it you're looking for, exactly? Don't tell me that you've lived here six months and suddenly had a burning desire to know about the Palm Sunday twisters."

Callie thought of making up an excuse. She understood how crazy her quest would sound—as if she were searching for a letter that had been left out in the rain for years on end. Worse, she knew that if she spilled Ira's story, she risked losing more than Miss Morton as a good source of information; she risked losing what little respect she might have from someone she had already decided she'd truly like to learn more from. There was more than one story here, more than Ira's story. Now that she'd spent time in the center, she understood that Shipshewana's entire history was contained within its well-designed walls.

And not all of it was in the displays. Some of it was in Miss Morton's memories, in her knowledge of the town. So Callie took the risk and, instead of putting a bow on it, pulled in a deep breath and told the truth.

"It's not *what* I'm looking for, it's *who*." Then she told Ira's story, in a condensed version.

Miss Morton didn't scoff at her, didn't so much as blink.

When Callie had finished talking, Miss Morton pulled a slip of paper off her notepad and wrote down a name and number. "Call this man. Or go and see him. He teaches at Notre Dame, and he's had a Tuesday evening class every semester for the last twenty years. If there's anyone who can help you, it's Professor Reimer."

"But, well . . . Do you mean just show up?"

"You could wait until tomorrow, but didn't you say Mr. Bontrager is in the hospital and upset?"

"Yes."

"And didn't you say he suffers from dementia?"

"He does."

"Then I wouldn't waste any time. If there is a girl to be found, and she'd be nearing her fifties by now, you want him to remember her—at least during his good moments. Yes, it sounds like a bit of an emergency."

Callie stared at the small piece of paper covered in Miss Morton's neat handwriting.

"The campus is in South Bend, forty-five miles west from here. I imagine you used to commute farther than that."

Before heading to the campus, Callie stopped by her shop

and checked her phone messages. One was from Margie asking if Callie'd like to go see a movie. One was from Trent telling her he'd been visited by Shane—he sounded somewhat amused and not the least bit put out with her. The call made Callie realize that that would be Trent's way—doing his job one minute, cordial and friendly the next. The last message was from Nancy Jarrell saying she had the go-ahead for the Chicago quilt exhibit if Callie and the quilters were still interested.

None of the calls seemed important enough to return immediately. Instead, Callie changed clothes and prepared Max for a ride in the car. She didn't know if taking her Labrador to Notre Dame was an acceptable thing to do, but it felt like the right thing. Daddy had always raised her to think safety first. And as she'd told Shane Black during the last investigation, she had a handgun permit, but she hadn't brought her firearm to Indiana. No, it seemed God had given her Max for any protection she might need when wandering around alone in the dark. She clipped his leash to his collar, straightened his scarf, and locked the door to the shop behind them.

Before leaving town, Callie stopped by The Kaffi Shop for a sandwich and a hot drink. Kristen was filling in for Margie, which explained the movie invitation. While Callie was grabbing extra napkins from the self-serve counter, she spied Shane sitting in the back corner.

"Working late?" she asked him.

He didn't answer, only reached for his coffee and took a long drink, staring at her over the steam.

"Can't we pretend to be friends?" Callie didn't know why it mattered, but it did. "We always seem to end up on the opposite side of things."

She reached down for Max and found him pressed against her leg, his presence a warm comfort. When Shane still didn't answer, Callie shuffled from one foot to the other, feeling for all the world like a child called to the principal's office, which was ridiculous. Shane Black was not her principal. Her discomfort didn't seem to faze Shane at all, but when Max whined once, he finally shook his head and moved over in the booth.

Callie hesitated a moment, then sat down beside him.

"It's not that we're on opposite sides, Callie."

"Then what is it?"

"A week." Weariness mixed with anger in his voice, but weariness won. "It's been over a week since Deborah and Esther found her body, and I still haven't been able to notify her next of kin."

He glanced at her then—not through her, not past her, but at her, for the first time since she'd seen him in the booth. "Do you have any idea how that wears on me?"

Callie thought about that, thought about all the things she might say, all the things that might possibly make him feel better but would probably fall short. In the end she simply reached over and found his hand, which was sitting next to hers on the seat of the booth. He stared down at their hands, at her fingers entwined with his.

She might have imagined it, but it seemed like some of the tension went out of his shoulders. He rubbed his thumb over the back of her hand, then pulled away. Her heart dropped, a stone headed to the bottom of a very deep pond, but then he placed his arm across the back of the booth, his hand lightly touching her shoulder.

She didn't know what to think of that, but she was very glad she hadn't decided to have a frozen dinner at home.

Chapter 28

DEBORAH WAVED when she saw Callie being ushered toward their bench. She couldn't help smiling as her friend drew closer — the look of surprise on her face was comical. What had Callie expected, that an Amish wedding would be so different from an *Englisch* one?

Callie made her way down the bench, past several older women, until she reached the empty spot Deborah had saved. The area where they'd set up the benches looked out over harvested fields, now clean and ready for winter. Though it was early in the day, and cool for the first Thursday in November, the sun promised perfect weather for Esther and Tobias' wedding.

"Am I late? It looks as if all of Shipshewana made it here before me."

"There's at least ten minutes still before the singing begins, and I saved you a seat with us. I wanted you close in case you have any questions." Deborah smiled over the top of Joshua's head as he climbed onto her lap. "Did the professor you visit have any information on finding Mr. Bontrager's *dochder*?"

"No. It was a long shot, but he said he'd call if he found anything."

"Well, you did your best." Deborah patted her hand.

"Men and women sit separately?" Callie waved at Martha, who was seated next to Mary. The twins were seated at the end of the row. Everyone was dressed in their Sunday best.

"At church we do, and a wedding is another form of holy celebration for us. Jonas is a little farther back on the other side."

"Oh." Callie stared around her, still feeling at a loss. Finally she turned to Deborah and said, "I would have been here sooner, but I changed clothes three times. You wouldn't believe how hard it is to pick something to wear to an Amish wedding."

"What you chose is fine," Deborah said, reaching out to finger the tailored suit made of a beautiful pearl-gray wool.

"Lydia said any color is fine. She said the bride doesn't wear white."

"No. Our brides wear blue, and it's fine for others to wear it as well, as you can see." Deborah nodded to the women around her. The dresses created a virtual color wheel. Though they tended toward the darker side, there was no doubt that everyone had on their very finest—still clothes that could be worn on Sunday, still functional, but made special for the day by extra starch in the aprons, prayer *kapps* pinned with extra care, and eyes that sparkled.

Or maybe it only seemed that way to Deborah.

Perhaps she was reading her own excitement in what her friends wore and how they looked.

"All the men look so nice. Everyone in black jackets and black hats—I've never seen them so spiffed up."

"Is that what you call it in Texas?"

"Spiffed? Maybe. Of course in Texas, there would be cowboy hats on the top and cowboy boots on the bottom."

"Do you like my dress, Miss Callie?" Mary pulled on her white apron, which covered a dark green dress.

"It's very pretty, Mary." Then Callie added, "Maybe I should have borrowed Lydia's dress again and worn it. I thought it fit okay, and I'd blend in better—"

"I'm glad you didn't. I believe people are still talking about how you looked that day." Deborah smoothed her own dress, then turned toward the rear of the seating area as she noted the hush that fell over the crowd of nearly two hundred people.

She tried to see the wedding as Callie must see it. There were no flowers. Though some of the younger Amish girls now did put flowers on tables, Esther had decided to stay with the traditional ways. There was no formal wedding gown nor any music to greet the prospective bride and groom.

Then everyone in the church rose, in one accord, and began to sing. And Deborah knew it didn't matter that there were no instruments to accompany them. The sound of their voices—raised in harmony, joined in singing the songs of their parents and grandparents—was a more beautiful sound than any instrument could make.

As she glanced around at her children, at her friends and relatives, Deborah understood in her heart the absence of decorations as well. They were all the decorations that Esther and Tobias needed—the beautiful sight of so many loved ones gathered in one place, so many turned out in their finest to spend an entire day wishing them the very best, singing praises to the Lord on this—the first day of their married life—and praying for the birth of their marriage.

Not one often moved to tears, Deborah was surprised to find her eyes stinging as they began singing the second hymn. Twice in one week now she found herself crying. Why was that? Why on this day? On Esther's day?

As she accepted the handkerchief her mother-in-law passed back to her, Deborah stared down at it. The cloth still held the indention from where Ruth had held it as she passed it to her, passed it over her grandchildren. There was a bond between them as a congregation, as a family, that was stronger than anything could tear apart.

Now Esther would again have such a bond — with Tobias' family.

And Reuben?

She would have to trust Reuben into God's care.

So Deborah sang, and she cried a little more as she thanked God that Esther would have Tobias' hand to hold, like she herself had Jonas'. That Esther would have Tobias' strong presence by her side, like she herself had Jonas'. And that Leah would have Tobias to guide her through the years ahead, as her own children had Jonas.

Once again, God had taken care of his own.

Three hours later, Deborah placed a plate of food down in front of Callie.

"Aren't you eating?" Callie asked.

"I will as soon as I finish serving."

Then Deborah spun and hurried back toward the kitchen. They'd worked out a serving line of sorts, and the plates were practically flying out of the kitchen. The meal had taken the work of many hands, but one look at Esther's face, sitting with Tobias at the corner table, sitting at the *eck*, convinced Deborah it was worth the effort.

"Go and sit, Deborah. You look flushed. We have this." Esther's sister smiled and handed her two more plates. "One for you and one for Jonas. Now go. Sit and eat."

She found her place across from Callie and beside Jonas, surprised to find her stomach growling by the time the blessing had been given.

"So what did you think, Callie?" Jonas had a teasing note in his voice, but it didn't slow him from shoveling a forkful of roast chicken covered with bread stuffing into his mouth.

"I've never attended a wedding that long before," Callie admitted. "I've never been to any service that long—maybe a college lecture or two, some business meetings, but not church."

"Do you regret coming?" Deborah asked.

"Are you kidding? I wouldn't have missed it for all the free fabric in the world." Callie had been spreading butter on fresh bread, but she stopped, studying the newly married couple who were seated at the special table across the lawn. "I don't understand how the ceremony was so romantic, but it was. There were no rings, no vows, they didn't even kiss."

"But there was their love for each other," Deborah pointed out.

"And the blessing. Don't forget the blessing." Jonas salted the mashed potatoes and creamed celery on his plate. "What is more romantic than a new couple being blessed by the bishop as they head out into the world?"

"I suppose. I'm going to have to think about it. This is all so different from what I'm used to, from my own wedding." Callie set down her fork, though she'd yet to take a bite.

"So you had the typical *Englisch* wedding, *ya?*" Jonas grinned mischievously. "Long white veil, tall *Englisch* shoes, long skirt thing that little mice had to carry."

Deborah slapped him on the arm. "You know very well that's a fairy tale. There are no mice in *Englisch* weddings."

Callie picked up her fork again. "He's correct on all other counts though. I did have the long veil and the tall shoes, and I even have photos to prove it. I can show them to you—" As soon as she closed her mouth around the food, Callie's eyes grew wide.

"I knew she'd stop talking when she tried the food." Jonas grinned at them both.

"It doesn't keep you from talking," Deborah pointed out.

"*Ya*, but I've had years of practice."

"This is amazing. Deborah, do you know how to make this?"

Their conversation then turned to recipes and details about

the wedding, but Deborah couldn't forget the look of longing, the look of loss that had passed over Callie's face. She, too, had once enjoyed the kind of closeness that Esther now knew. Deborah needed to remember to pray that God would bring a special helpmate into Callie's life.

The afternoon went on like that—sometimes filled with melancholy, but more often saturated with laughter.

At one point Deborah had Callie and Melinda all to herself. "What with the murdered girl in the pond and Callie searching for Ira's daughter, we haven't talked about selling quilts for ages."

"Which reminds me—" Callie tucked her hair behind her ear, often a sign that she felt guilty about something—"I haven't had a chance to mention that I might have a new way to sell your quilts."

Melinda stopped fiddling with baby Hannah's *kapp* and looked up eagerly. Deborah glanced over at Esther. Her friends depended on the money brought in from their quilts. She was more than eager to hear new ideas.

So Callie quickly recapped Nancy Jarrell's offer.

"Chicago?" Melinda squeaked. "It's so far, and it's such a big city."

"Yes, but we'd only be going to the museum, and you wouldn't have to go if you didn't want to. I could take the quilts myself."

"We'll need to talk to the bishop first." Deborah reached down and picked up Joshua, who had flung himself at her legs.

"Of course."

"But I see no difference in selling them in a museum or selling them in your store." She hugged Joshua to her, grateful that when there was more need, God always seemed to bring added blessings.

"I was hoping you'd say that. Talk to Bishop Elam and let me know. I'll email Nancy to tell her know you're interested and would like to know more details."

Melinda hugged them both, then hurried off to oversee the games and matchmaking. They had barely started when Deborah noticed Callie slipping her small cell phone back into her purse, a puzzled look on her face.

"Is there a problem?" she asked.

"No. No problem. That was Professor Reimer from Notre Dame." She shook her head and pulled her purse over her shoulder. "He thinks he may have found Ira Bontrager's daughter."

Esther reveled in the feel of Tobias' arms around her. She had thought their time alone might be awkward. It was anything but. Tobias was both gentle and attentive. He made her feel like the beautiful young woman she'd once been. Now lying together in her bedroom, the bedroom of her childhood, it seemed that her life had come full circle.

"Are you asleep yet?" Tobias whispered.

"No. I thought I would be."

He pulled back her hair and kissed the nape of her neck. "Perhaps you're too tired. After a full day of wedding—"

"And an evening in your arms . . ." she teased.

"*Ya.* There's that too." He pulled her closer as the wind outside rattled the shutters of the upstairs window.

"It was a *gut* wedding. A *gut* beginning for us."

Tobias nodded, but didn't interrupt—waited instead for her to find words for the joys and aches that were keeping her awake so late this night.

"I was a little surprised so many of our *freinden* attended."

"Because?"

Now she flipped over, needing to face him in the dark, even if she couldn't see him. "Because not everyone believes in his innocence. Because not everyone understands why . . ." She stuttered, fumbled in the dark with her pain.

"Do you think they wouldn't do the same for their own family? Perhaps you misread others' looks or silences." Tobias' fingers traced her cheek in the dark. "Often folk are silent when they don't know how to express their concern. I think the time you've spent alone might have made it more difficult for you to accept their desire to help."

Esther wanted to argue with him. Wanted to tell him about the time she'd been alone with Leah and had only her family to help her.

But had she been alone?

Those days were blurry now. There'd been Deborah and Melinda, always. Others had come though. Perhaps she'd pushed many away while she'd been hurting.

It could be that there were some who wanted to help Reuben as well, who believed in him, but didn't know how.

She wanted to help Reuben but didn't know how.

So instead she snuggled into Tobias' arms. "*Ya*, maybe you're right."

"Words every man longs to hear."

"Reuben was right as well." Esther yawned, sleep finally winning over the dozens of thoughts flitting through her mind—like birds hopping over an early morning's frosty field. Thoughts of the next three days filled her dreams, when they'd travel to a different relative's home for each meal, collecting wedding presents and even staying overnight.

But by Sunday evening, they'd be back at their place—at Tobias' *grossdaddi*'s home.

At their home.

"And what was he right about, sweet Esther?"

"When he told us not to postpone our marriage." The words were a whisper on her lips, barely uttered before sleep claimed her. Or perhaps she only dreamt them.

Chapter 29

CALLIE TALKED TO GAVIN as she nervously watched out the shop's windows. It was Andrew's day off, and today he was dressed in a gray sweat suit. Not baggy sweats like Callie wore on her day off. No, these sweats outlined his shape, accentuated the fact that he was still in military condition — tip-top military condition. Not that she stared at him or his muscles when he walked in because that would be rude. Besides, she could have a good look when he was on his way out of the shop so as not to embarrass the poor man.

Gavin had stopped by to see if Max would like to go for a run. This had become a regular habit of his at least twice a week, and Max was becoming quite spoiled. As for Callie, she wasn't quite sure what to think about it.

Gavin and Max had just returned from their five-mile jog, and Callie had fought off a temptation earlier to put a chip on Max so she could track them when they ran. Where could you possibly go in Shipshewana that would take you five miles? You'd have to run in circles.

"Explain to me again how you managed to find Bontrager's daughter? I thought she was dead."

"It's pretty complicated, and we're not completely sure Faith is Ira's daughter. For one thing, his daughter's name was Bethany. But either because of the trauma, or because of her age, Faith may have been unable to tell anyone that."

Gavin sat down on a stool she'd pulled out from the kitchen. They were alone in the shop, which wasn't unusual for eight o'clock on a Saturday morning, but the shoppers would start popping in soon.

"I told you Miss Morton referred me to Professor Reimer?"

"Yes. He teaches at Notre Dame."

"Correct, and the Palm Sunday Tornadoes have been a pet project of his. You should see his office. It's like a living memorial to what happened in the central plains that Sunday—with a particular emphasis on Indiana. He has more letters, maps, and information than you can imagine."

"How big is his office?" Gavin asked.

"No bigger than my small work area."

"Then how does he fit it all in?"

"That's part of the project. He's collected material over the years, and the more he accumulates, the more people send to him. Now his graduate students are helping him transfer it all to data files. As they do, he'll place the originals in the university archives or local community centers—"

"Like ours."

"Exactly."

"All right. So you think your professor is knowledgeable, but that doesn't mean the woman who is coming here today is who he thinks she is." Gavin sipped the hot coffee Callie always had ready after his run, smiled when she pushed a fresh bagel his way.

There was something in his smile that picked up her day more than a cup of coffee from Margie's. In fact, having a visit from Andrew was always a highlight of her weeks. What did that mean? Did it mean she should say yes next time he asked her out? If there was a next time?

"Are you suspicious by nature or did they teach you that in the service?"

"Actually I learned it overseas. So how did he make the connection?"

"If you remember, Ira isn't always coherent. He suffers from dementia, so he stumbles back and forth between the present and the past."

"Which doesn't make for the most reliable witness."

"But it might help recall a seemingly unimportant detail, something you or I might have forgotten. Perhaps that's why, after all these years, Ira was convinced his daughter was still alive. Maybe part of his mind knew, but another part had dismissed it."

Gavin frowned visibly. "Dismissed what?"

"That no Amish died in Shipshe that day. Ira and his wife had been down at Rainbow Lake that day for the Palm Sunday church services and celebrations. They'd allowed their daughter, Bethany, to stay with her *aenti* afterwards."

"He said that?"

"In his way. He mentioned rainbows around the lake. I didn't know what that meant, thought he was rambling."

"The area around Shore and Rainbow Lake was practically devastated by twin tornadoes that day."

"So Professor Reimer told me. The night I visited him he asked me to fill out an information form. After I told him Ira suffered from dementia, he had me write down everything that Ira focused on, everything he rambled about. Professor Reimer had a student enter the information in his database which immediately narrowed the incident down to the Rainbow Lake area."

Gavin began pacing in front of her counter, causing Max to raise his head and watch with interest. "Let me see if I have this straight. Ira and—"

"Sharon."

"Sharon went down to Rainbow Lake for the day with their daughter—"

"Bethany." Callie smiled, then took a sip of her own coffee.

"Got it." Gavin gave her a salute. When his playfulness crept in, it always surprised her. Most of the time he was so serious, but then usually she saw him when he was on the job. "Ira, Sharon, and Bethany at the lake. Ira and Sharon decide to head home, but little Bethany wants to stay with her *aenti*. The storm hits, devastating the area, and Bethany is never found."

"She was found, but miles away, among the rubble, among the dead, according to Professor Reimer's information. No one knew who she was. According to his records, she was found next to an Amish man and woman who were dead, and the people who found her assumed they were her parents."

"But they were her aunt and uncle?"

"Apparently."

"Didn't Ira go looking for his family? Wouldn't he have followed the trail and found her?"

"Yeah, he looked for his family. But I think he probably thought they'd already gone home. The Shore Mennonite community south of Shipshe was devastated. Ira didn't realize they'd stayed at the lake. He was looking through the rubble at Shore."

"It wasn't that many miles apart, Callie."

"The tallies vary from what Ira told me. The Internet says there were forty-seven tornadoes and two-hundred and seventy-one people were killed. How many more were made homeless or were injured? All in an eleven-hour period over four hundred and fifty miles."

When Gavin continued to shake his head, she pushed on. "Think of what it was like that night. The chaos and confusion. Ira and Sharon were uninjured, but by the time they're able to return, all that they found was destruction—a scene nothing like what they'd left, and no sign of their child. Sharon apparently went into shock and never completely recovered, though they did eventually have another child—"

"Caleb."

"Yes."

"Then who took Bethany?"

"Someone found her, helped her."

"That's kidnapping." Gavin said, indignation rising in his voice.

"You can't mean that." Callie walked around the counter, intending to unlock the door, but instead she stopped and reached up to straighten the ball cap he'd placed back on his head. "Whoever found Bethany—now Faith—saw only a child in the midst of a horrible natural catastrophe whose parents were dead. From what I can tell after talking with Faith, she had a good life."

"I don't know." Gavin followed her to the front door. "Seems criminal."

"According to Professor Reimer the church districts weren't as close then. By that I mean they didn't communicate as well between one another. Also the Amish communities weren't as integrated with the *Englisch*. There weren't as many phone shacks and, of course, no cell phones. Also they were hesitant to work with the police. Ira and Sharon searched for their child, in the wrong community apparently, but in the end they accepted it as God's will . . ." The silence between them lengthened as they both considered the tragedy. Finally, Callie shrugged. "Maybe we are wrong. Who knows? But Faith is coming to see Ira this morning."

"Wait a minute. How did Reimer get her story to start with? How did he learn that she'd been found as a child?"

"Faith's mother died a few years ago. Apparently she always kept a journal. When Faith was going through her mother's things, reading the journals, she found the full description of that Palm Sunday. Faith had always known her parents weren't her birth parents, but she didn't know the entire story. She went to the bishop in their district then and asked him about it and what she should do with the journals. The bishop put her in touch with Professor Reimer."

"You know, you've given me a headache."

"Go work out some more, Gavin. It'll wipe those wrinkles right off your forehead."

An hour later Callie was feeling the beginnings of her own tension headache. Lydia had come in to work the ten to two shift, and Callie was sitting in front of the *Grossdaddi* House. Faith had arrived at the quilt shop thirty minutes earlier via a driver. She was now waiting beside Callie in the passenger seat, and they were both looking across the parking lot—as if answers might pop out of the pavement.

"Are you sure you're up for this?"

"I didn't come all the way from Goshen to wonder." Just under fifty years old, Faith was round with a little gray hair peeking out from hunder her *kapp*, and she was about the sweetest thing Callie had ever met. Tiny wrinkles feathered out from her blue eyes, and it seemed that Callie saw a resemblance there of the man who had popped up in her garden eleven days ago, but maybe that was what she wanted to see.

They had talked for twenty minutes, long enough for Callie to be sure this wasn't a woman trying to take advantage of Ira. Yes, Gavin had convinced Callie that she needed to be careful, and Callie valued Gavin's opinion.

As if Faith's Amish clothing and humble demeanor weren't convincing enough.

"It's an odd feeling to think of seeing your *dat* after all these years."

"We don't know for sure, Faith. What I mean is, I don't want you to build your hopes up and then—"

"Dear, you needn't worry about that. This had been in *Gotte's* hands for longer than you have been alive. Since I was a wee one and those black funnels fell from the sky." She stared out the car window, at the clouds that had begun to gather. "Even after so many years, it's not something you forget. The particulars maybe, but not the faces—I still remember the terror, the fear, wandering about, and then ..."

She stopped and the most angelic of smiles covered her face. "Then two arms wrapped around me. I never will forget that."

She reached for the door handle. "Let's go inside. Shall we?"

"Yes, but Faith. I haven't told Ira who you are. I just said I was stopping by. I didn't want ... that is, I didn't want to raise his hopes either."

"I understand." Faith reached across, patted Callie's hand where it rested on the seat between them. "You're a *gut freind* to him."

Then she made her way out of the car, and Callie found she had to rush to keep up.

Erin Troyer sat in the front hall, knitting, this time with blue and yellow yarn.

"Baby blanket?"

"Yes. One of the workers here has a *boppli* on the way this month." Erin finished her row, then set her knitting aside. "And who did you bring with you today, Miss Callie?"

"This is Faith from Goshen. We've come to see Ira."

Erin studied them both for a moment, then nodded once. "*Gut.* That's *gut.* Ira was hoping for company today."

"Is he in the barn?" Callie asked.

"No. After the horse episode, doc says he's to stay away from the barn for a week or so. Ira's on the back patio shelling walnuts. Don't believe he's happy about that. Yes, he'll be glad to have some company." Then Erin picked up her knitting and began another row.

Callie led Faith toward the patio. Her own heart was pounding hard enough to set off a monitor alarm. She wondered how Faith was doing. When she glanced over at her though, the expression on Faith's face seemed peaceful enough: focused, lost in thought, perhaps lost in memories of years ago.

As they stepped out into the enclosed patio area, Callie thought she saw the briefest of smiles soften her features.

Ira was sitting in the midst of several women.

He appeared to be muttering to himself, and his expression was frozen in a scowl. Then he glanced up and saw Callie. "Tell me you brought Max today. They're forcing me to sit here with all these hens—shelling black walnuts like I'm old and feeble!"

The women around him shared a tolerant look that told Callie they'd heard it all before. They said good morning, then vacated a few chairs.

"Ira, I brought someone to meet you this morning."

"Hmph." Ira focused on the bowl of walnuts in his lap.

"This is Faith. She's from Goshen."

Ira's hands stilled over the nuts. He glanced up, as if he was going to wave Faith away, but something in the way she stepped forward caused him to pause and look at her more closely.

As he did, he reached for his cane, which was never far from his side. Reached for it and ran his hands along the smoothness of the wood, until he found the symbols at the top, traced the cross, the hammer, and the nail.

Faith watched his fingers, her eyes glued to the cane, to the engraving. She tried to speak, swallowed once, her hand at her throat, and Callie could see that she was having a hard time maintaining her composure.

"Sit here, Faith. I'll find you a glass of water," Callie offered.

There was a pitcher and some glasses on a cart in the corner. When she returned with one, Faith and Ira were still staring at each other. Faith sipped the water, set it down on the patio table, and finally reached for Ira's cane. "May I, please?"

He released it reluctantly.

She ran her hands over the three items, engraved in a row but touching at the corners, forming a ring that circled the top of the cane. Tears pooling in her eyes, she said, "I remember my *dat*—my real *dat*—had one of these. He used to let me hold it as we rode in the buggy."

"I had that specially made by my brother-in-law back in 1940 when I hurt my knee jumping down from a wagon. He died in the twisters, died with so many others, though we were spared here in Shipshe." Ira scooted forward in his chair. "Beth? Child? Come closer." Ira's hands began to shake as he reached for Faith. "Is that you?"

Faith went down on her knees beside his chair, tears falling, burying her face in his hands so that Callie barely heard when she said, "It's been many years since anyone has called me by that name."

There had never been a time when Callie had wished for a talent she didn't have. Oh, she would like to be able to quilt as Deborah and Esther and Melinda did. She'd like to be able to make the perfect square and turn that square into the perfect quilt.

But at that moment, as she watched Faith kneel at her father's side after decades of separation, as the sun poured in through the clouds that had yet to completely cover the sky, as Ira took one shaky, wrinkled hand and placed it over her head, Callie wished with all of her heart that she had the ability to paint.

If she did, if she could, she would have painted that scene.

She would have painted love.

Chapter 30

SAMUEL LOOKED OUT over the clouds that were building on the horizon. Tomorrow's storm would be a big one. Wish that it could wash the earth clean. That it could wash his soul clean.

Such wishes were the dreams of children though.

And Samuel had left all such childish things behind.

As he watched Katie's sisters play in the last of the sun's light, he wondered if the ache in his heart would ever ease. She wasn't coming back. He'd managed to convince her parents that she was on her *rumspringa*. But to what good? He couldn't bring back their daughter.

How many mistakes had he made since the day they'd left?

And why couldn't some things be redone . . .

Samuel walked from the bathroom into the bedroom, but Katie wasn't there. The smell of breakfast came from the kitchen, which surprised him. Where had she found dishes, or food, for that matter? For the last three days, they'd mostly been living off of dry goods and the leftovers that Reuben had been smuggling to them.

Samuel didn't like living like this, on the sly, but tomorrow he'd report for work. Then they could find a proper place to live, and after that they could formally join the community. If they went home now, what would change? Life would continue as it had before, with no hope of their lot improving. They would be trapped under Timothy's strong hand.

No. Better to hide now, for a few more days. He couldn't risk them being seen by someone who had done business with Timothy, someone who might send word back home. Timothy was persuasive. Samuel had watched him change Katie's mind before. What if it happened again? What if it happened now, when they were almost free of the old house and Timothy's old ways? What if he lost her? Samuel wanted to have Katie settled in a new area before her dat learned of their marriage. Otherwise he might convince her to come home.

Now where was that smell coming from? Either he was dreaming or there was kaffi and bacon in the kitchen.

Samuel walked down the hall, his boots clomping against the wood boards of the floor. When he stepped into the room, one of the prettiest sights he'd ever seen met his eyes.

His wife, Katie, standing on a kitchen chair, reaching up onto a top shelf. She wore the green dress that she'd sewn for her winter wardrobe and a freshly pressed white kapp. She had brought two new dresses—the blue she'd married in, and the green she wore this morning. Both looked lovely, and he marveled again at what a beautiful bride she was.

Instead of helping her, he crossed his arms, leaned against the wall, and watched.

She stood on tiptoe and pulled something from the top shelf.

"What did you find there, Katie bug?"

"Samuel, gudemariye." Katie smiled over her shoulder, looking as fresh as the first snowfall of the year.

"Gudemariye to you. Have you been discovering bacon in the cabinets?"

"No, silly. The cabinets are gorgeous though, just like you said." She ran her hand down the front panel.

Jealousy sparked as she complimented the woodwork, which was ridiculous. He'd show her that he could do work just as good.

"I need to be going, if you're done messing around on that chair." The words came out sharper than he intended.

"Oh, all right. I was looking for plates, and I saw something winking down at me from the top shelf."

"We don't have time for that—" His exasperation grew. He'd thought breakfast was ready. They had much to do today. Tomorrow he'd be gone at work. Today was their last full day together.

"Look, it's a key on a string, not plates. Now why do you think someone would store a key on a top shelf?"

She was so like a child sometimes. She pivoted in the chair and held it out like a prize.

"Older folks never do lock the doors. I suppose whoever lived here before kept it up there and forgot about it. Put it back and come down."

"I should give it to Reuben. He probably doesn't know it's here." She settled the string around her neck, looking down to see how long the string was.

"Katie! I said put it back." His voice rising, Samuel stepped forward, and that was when three things happened at once.

The first thing is that the bacon on the stove began to burn.

Then Reuben drove by the window in his horse and buggy. Samuel would wonder later if it had startled her. But he would never learn.

Because the third thing was that Katie took one step backward.

Even though there was no chair for her to step on.

Chapter 31

CALLIE LOCKED AND CLOSED THE SHOP for the day. Detouring to the little kitchen, she returned with a tray of teas, hot water, and a plate of cookies.

"Now tell me all about your visit," she said. "I know you're tired, but I want to hear everything."

Faith swiped at her gray hair and smiled. "Oh, I'm not that tired. I'm still in a bit of shock. To think that I have family, after all these years." She stopped, selected a tea bag, and took her time unwrapping it.

"I didn't mean that the way it sounded," she finally confessed.

"It didn't sound any way."

"I love my *kinner* and my *grandkinner*, but it's a different thing to realize that everyone before you is gone." Looking up from the tea, she met Callie's gaze. "You know what I mean."

"Yes, I do."

"Is that why you found me? Why you wouldn't give up?"

Callie reached down and patted Max. "I'd like to say it was something so honorable, but truthfully I'm a stubborn person. Once I start unraveling a thing, I have a hard time letting it go until I've reached the end of the—"

A knock on the door startled them both, but Max only stretched and padded over to see who it was.

"Must be someone we know or he would have barked," Callie said. "Wait here and rest while I shoo them away."

But when she looked through the pane of glass, she saw that it was Deborah. Rather than shooing, Callie opened the door and threw her arms around her best friend. "How is he? How's Reuben? Did he even agree to see you this time?"

"Yes, for a minute. He's no different. No better. Things don't look *gut*," Deborah admitted.

Callie nodded, then clasped her hand and pulled her back toward the circle of chairs. "There's someone I want you to meet. Faith, this is Deborah Yoder, who I've told you so much about. Deborah, meet my new friend, Faith, from Goshen."

"Pleased to meet you," Deborah murmured.

"Callie has told me a lot about you. Apparently you saved her from complete starvation, not to mention a life of misery and solitude back in Houston."

Deborah smiled as she sank into one of the chairs. "She's prone to exaggeration, if you haven't noticed."

"Guilty—a little. Now tell me, are the children with your sister?" Callie perched on the arm of a chair.

"*Ya*. Joshua is still teething. Adalyn and I were trying to work on a defense with Reuben, but we're not having much luck. It's why I'm out so late. I had Adalyn drop me off here. I told her you'd give me a ride home. You don't mind, do you?"

"Not at all. I'm glad you came by." Callie popped off the chair and turned toward the kitchen. "Let me grab an extra cup so you can have some tea. You're not in a hurry are you?"

"I probably should be, but I'm too tired."

"Then one cup of tea and we'll go. Faith's driver is on her way." Callie returned with the mug and passed it to Deborah. "Faith was about to tell me about reuniting with her father, Mr. Bontrager."

"So it's true? He's your *dat*?"

Faith ran her finger over the rim of her mug. "*Ya*, there's not any doubt about it. He was quite lucid this morning, and we were able to piece together what happened—and then there's the cane. That alone proved it for me." She gave them the brief version of the visit with her father, though several times she stopped midsentence and appeared unable to continue.

Callie didn't doubt that much of the visit was still too precious, too raw to share.

"It's a miracle how the Lord was able to bring you two back together, and I know it's a balm in his life." Deborah sipped her tea, studying Faith as she spoke.

"Well, it isn't only a blessing to him. My parents passed on several years ago, and I've been a widow now for five years. I had no *bruders* or *schweschdern*, because my *mamm* wasn't able to have children. It's part of what makes this such a miraculous thing. Mr. Bontrager, my father, is the last tie to my past."

"And now you have an entire family you didn't know about," Callie said, her voice filled with awe.

"Yes, if they're willing to accept me."

Callie thought she might say more, but she reached for an oatmeal cookie instead and nibbled around the edge.

"It might take time," Deborah suggested.

"*Ya*. You're right. And it's not as if they're rude. Just a bit shocked." Faith set her half-eaten cookie on her plate and looked at them with a smile playing at the corners of her lips. "Time is something I have, and my own family has been very supportive. I'm not alone, remember. I do have four lovely children and twelve *grandkinner*."

"But to have a *bruder* would be a real blessing," Deborah said.

"Yes. I think Caleb is hesitant to accept me, but perhaps the idea of having more family will grow on him. His wife seemed uncertain too."

"Because you're from Goshen maybe?" Callie asked.

"No. Probably it was the shock, and then they're so protective of their *dat*. He's a truly lovely man."

Deborah shook her head. "I owe you an apology. I kept telling Callie to let it go. Kept telling her she'd never figure it out and that it was a waste of her time, but now look. God had a purpose in Mr. Bontrager's stumbling in here."

"I'm stubborn," Callie admitted for the second time.

"*Ya*, you are." Deborah agreed, but instead of smiling a frown creased her forehead.

Callie waited for Deborah to say more. When she didn't, Callie reached forward and gave Max an affectionate scratch behind the ears. "It's no different than you with Reuben's situation though. You won't give up. You're determined to stay with him, and see this through. No matter how bad things look."

When Deborah heard Callie's words, they bounced around in her mind for a while. "No matter how bad things look."

Perhaps it was true. Perhaps Deborah had been too focused on how bad things looked. She suddenly had the oddest feeling that she'd overlooked something obvious.

But what?

It was like when the twins were engaged in some activity they shouldn't be—those pigs for instance, which they were slowly training to like mud. It had become quite the family project, and truthfully it was good for the twins. For all Deborah knew they'd grow up to become prosperous pig farmers.

She had a sixth sense though for when something was amiss.

Jonas called it her mother's instinct.

The house would become unnaturally quiet, and Deborah would know she should go and check on the twins. Often she didn't though. Even after years of experience, even though she knew better, she'd wait and pretend everything was fine—even when her natural warning system was screaming at her to go see what was occupying the boys' attention.

Even though she knew her instinct could be, and should be, trusted, she often ignored it.

She was having just such a moment now.

Her instincts were screaming at her.

But what was she missing?

"I don't know any of the details about the trouble you're going through with your *freind*," Faith said. "But I am sorry to hear he is suffering. From the little I've heard since this morning, people think highly of him."

"*Ya*, Reuben is a *gut* man," Deborah murmured. Deborah and Callie had gone over Reuben's situation together—discussed it from the inside out.

She looked over at her *Englisch* friend, met her quizzical gaze. Callie had shown up on the scene almost as soon as she had, shown up in her Amish dress. She'd been there nearly from the very moment the body had been found.

Perhaps it had been important that they pass over this road together. Just as they'd traveled down the other road earlier this year. That road had also been touched by death, but in the end, it had led to Callie's life here.

Deborah glanced around the shop.

Could the clue she'd been missing lie here?

In the quilt shop?

That made no sense, but the more she considered the idea, the more certain she felt that it did. They'd looked everywhere else. Scoured Reuben's farm, dredged the pond, even advertised in the Amish newspaper *The Budget*.

How could the missing answer be here?

"I suppose I should go," Faith said. "My driver will arrive any minute. We're both staying at a local bed and breakfast so I can see Ira again tomorrow, but then I head back to Goshen in the afternoon. It's *gut* that we don't have church this week. I would hate to miss worship with the children, but I want to spend time with my *dat*."

She stood, pulled her scarf off the back of the chair, and wrapped it around her neck. The wind outside had picked up a bit, rattling the windows, causing Deborah to look toward the front. She saw the "Information Wanted" poster, thought again of the young Amish girl.

The wind reminded Deborah that fall was practically gone and winter nearly upon them.

Max whined once, met her gaze, then dropped his head to his paws.

"Don't forget your coat," Callie said, jumping up and pulling Faith's coat off the rack by the door.

As she held it for Faith to stick her right arm in, Faith turned, shuffling the package of items she'd apparently bought from the store into her left hand. Deborah forgot for a moment about Reuben and the tragedy of the dead girl and Esther and Tobias. She forgot about feeling responsible for others' happiness, and she forgot to concentrate on solving anything. Instead her mind relaxed, unclenched almost, and did what it naturally wanted to do.

It noticed the style and seam of Faith's dress.

The way the seam of the sleeve was cut into the bodice of the dress. The unique style of the plain garment.

Deborah saw what she'd been missing.

A shiver started a slow, cold crawl from the base of her neck and crept out in both directions—toward her hairline and in the direction of her toes.

She felt paralyzed.

Faith tugged on her coat, pulled her *kapp* strings free where they had caught in the collar, then reached down to say good-bye to Max.

Deborah realized Faith was leaving and that she had to stop her. Her mind's eye, though, remained fixated on the cut of the sleeve, wanting to be certain that it exactly matched the sleeve of the girl in the pond.

Deborah heard Callie walk Faith to the door, saw the sweep of headlights as a car pulled into the parking lot, and she finally, finally managed to call out. "Wait. Please don't go yet."

Both women turned back to look at her, surprise marking their features.

Deborah carefully set her cup on the square table, which sat in the middle of the chairs. Then she stood and faced this woman she didn't know. "Your dress, the way the sleeves are cut into the bodice. It's a bit unusual, *ya?*"

The puzzled look on Faith's face fell away, and she smiled — her first relaxed and genuine smile since Deborah had walked into the store. "You have a good eye for sewing. *Ya*, the Amish in Goshen have some strict rules regarding dress, and all of the sleeves must be cut and tucked the same. The bishop thought it would help to set us apart."

"Only Goshen?" Callie said.

"I believe so. At least I haven't noticed it anywhere else. I've been sewing dresses this way all my life, and I don't even think about it anymore." Faith swiped again at her hair, her fingers brushing at the *kapp* pinned to the top of her gray curls. "What made you ask about the dress? It's an interesting style, but I'm not sure it's one you'd care to copy."

"I don't think her interests were in the sewing." Callie stepped toward Deborah, put her hand out, and touched her arm. "Are you okay?"

"I'm fine. You're right though." Deborah chose her words carefully, feeling she was close now and not wanting to scare this woman — her only lead — away. She was keenly aware that Reuben's future might hang in the balance of what occurred in the next few moments inside Callie's shop. "The girl who was found in Reuben's pond, the girl who died here in Shipshewana, was wearing such a dress."

Faith didn't move, didn't blink for the space of several seconds. Her calm blue eyes met Deborah's. In that time, Deborah sensed that Faith was absorbing the full weight of her words, the implications of both what she said and what was to come.

"Callie," Faith said, "I believe we might need another cup of tea, and I need to go and tell my driver that I'll be staying a bit longer."

Chapter 32

AN HOUR LATER, Shane had joined them in the back room and the sky outside had turned completely dark.

"I called your *Englisch* neighbors," Callie reported. "They'll get word to Jonas that you're going to be a little late. Would you like more tea?"

Deborah shook her head and pushed away her mug. "*Danki*, Callie. But if you put any more tea in front of me, I'll float away like Jonas' bobbers when he's fishing."

"All right, ladies. This is the one lead we have, and I think it's worth following." Shane sat with his forearms propped on his knees. He'd rolled up his shirtsleeves thirty minutes ago, and he had the "Information Wanted" poster, crime scene pictures, and witness reports spread out across the table.

The pictures should have bothered Deborah, but they didn't. They confirmed what she suspected. The girl was from Goshen. The dress patterns were identical.

"I wish I could say for certain who she is." Faith shook her head. "There are so many young Amish girls, and I don't see them as often as I did since our district has grown and split into smaller churches."

"But you think she could be the daughter of this Mr. Lapp?"

"I'm fairly sure. There are a lot of Lapps in Goshen, but Timothy Lapp on Old Branch Road ..." Faith's voice faded away as she reached forward and picked up the picture of the girl in the pond. Finally she shook her head and dropped the photo on the table. "He's a *gut* man, and this will break his heart. Timothy Lapp ... well maybe you have men like him here, in Shipshewana. He has not changed at all. He doesn't abide with the idea that *rumspringa* is a part of a child's passage into adulthood."

She took a last sip of her tea, which had long since grown cold, grimaced, and set the mug carefully down on the table, next to the girl's photo. "There are no cars hidden in his barn, and his older children have no cell phones in their belongings that they charge when they go into town. At least if they did, they would never let their *dat* know about it. He follows the old ways."

"We have families like that here too," Deborah said gently. "They want what is best for their children, and they worry that any type of change is bad."

"Exactly. Don't misunderstand me. He loves his family. It's only that he's a bit strict."

A dozen unanswered questions swirled in the air around them, made the room seem close and crowded. Deborah thought Shane would begin questioning Faith then, about whether the father might have killed the girl or at least caused her to flee her home, but instead he sat back and waited.

She'd watched him work for many years now, and his ways always surprised her. She had once thought it was because he was an *Englischer*, but tonight she thought it was because he had the instincts of a panther. Her father had once described watching a big, black cat on a far ridge, stalking its prey, not moving closer until it was sure of its attack. Shane was like that elusive animal.

Faith reached out and turned the photo, so she was looking again at the girl. "When his oldest *dochder* wanted to marry the

259

Eby boy, Timothy agreed, but there was some scuttle about where they would live. This was a little while back—before the marrying season. I'd say four or six weeks ago."

Deborah noticed that though Shane was listening intently to every word that Faith said, occasionally he'd glance up at Callie, as if he were waiting for her to jump in and add something. The two seemed different tonight, as if something had changed between them. Deborah was going to have a talk with Callie about the men in her life. She was tired of guessing!

For her part, Callie was silently following the exchange as if it were one of the Agatha Christie novels she always had on the counter of the shop.

In the back of her mind, Deborah had to wonder if this would help Reuben's case at all. What if it incriminated him further?

But she realized she needed to tamp down that fear.

The important thing at this moment was to find the girl's family, to give them a last bit of peace.

"You know a lot about the family, given that you can't positively identify the girl." Shane spoke quietly, in a matter-of-fact tone.

"*Ya*. I suppose it seems that way." Faith smiled sadly. "But even in Goshen where we have several districts there is a ..."

She looked to Deborah and Callie for help, unable to find the expression she wanted.

"Grapevine?" Callie asked.

"*Ya*. Grapevine of sorts. It's not so much that we gossip, as it is that we share one another's burdens. The word in Goshen was that Timothy's daughter had run away. At first with the boy, but then, a week ago, Samuel Eby came back. He said Katie stayed among the *Englischers*. We all believed she would return in time. Most Amish kids do. No one was really worried, and it hasn't been that long."

Everyone considered her words, even as they looked at the

pictures the crime techs had shot of the body at the pond. Callie didn't reach for any of those though. She reached for a shot Trent had taken—one that did not appear in the *Gazette*. A shot of the girl before the medical examiner had pulled a sheet up and over her face.

The young girl looked almost as if she'd been sleeping, the skin of her face remarkably un-deteriorated—which was part of the evidence the lawyers had used against Reuben, stating the body had only been in the water a short time when Esther had found it.

"Whoever she was, you can tell she was a beautiful young lady." Callie fingered the picture carefully, her voice full of the loss they all felt each time they considered the tragedy of such a young life cut short.

"*Ya*. It's heartbreaking for sure," Faith agreed. "And the cause of death was some sort of blow to the back of her head?"

Instead of answering her question, Shane looked down at his notes, flipped to a new page, and picked up his pen. He sat back in the chair and began drawing circles in the margin of the paper. "Wouldn't Mr. Lapp have seen the notices we put out? The ones that stated we found a girl? We advertised in *The Budget* and all the local papers."

Faith stared across the room a full minute before answering. "It's possible he might have seen them, but then again, their farm is in a remote area. If I remember correctly, they don't come into town often. He's busy running the acreage, with only girls and not wanting to hire out the work when he doesn't have to. The mother has her hands full raising all the girls."

"But wouldn't their bishop have brought it up?" Deborah asked. Her mind was spinning, wondering how it would feel to open a paper and see your child's face staring back at you. Her stomach clenched, and she wished she'd had less of the tea.

"Of course the bishop would have spoken to them, if their

dochder had been missing. But remember, they think the girl is with *freinden*."

Everyone considered the possibilities.

Finally, Shane stood and began gathering up his photos and papers, touching Callie's arm as he scooted by her. "There's one way to know for certain. I'll go down to Goshen tomorrow, show Mr. Lapp the pictures, see if he can identify the girl as his daughter."

"I'll go with you if that would help." Faith stood as well. "It's been a while since I've spoken with the Lapps, but I believe it would be *gut* to have a familiar face there."

"I'll go too," Callie said.

"And so will I," Deborah added.

Shane stopped and gave them his most serious officer-on-duty look. "That's hardly necessary, ladies. I believe I can handle this alone."

"If I know Timothy Lapp, and I do, things might go better if someone he knows is there when you first show up." Faith didn't look as though she would take no for an answer. "The man doesn't have a temper, but he doesn't take kindly to *Englischers*. He's likely to ask you to leave his land and walk away."

"Ask a police officer to leave?" Shane's eyebrows rose.

Faith shrugged. "If he's done nothing wrong—and I'm sure he hasn't—then, *ya*. You'd never have a chance to show him your pictures, because he'd never listen to you in the first place. Timothy Lapp lives very strictly by the law, but as I said, he prefers to keep to himself. He won't abide outsiders. It's part of the reason no one was surprised when the girl ran away."

Before Shane could respond to her reasoning, Deborah began gathering her things.

"I want to be there also," Deborah said. "It matters to me, Shane. This might not help Reuben at all, but I'm sure he'd like to know that the girl's family has peace at least. And I do still believe he's innocent. If he has to suffer for a crime he didn't commit, at least let me be able to tell him I was there and able to ease someone's pain. At least let me be a part of closing this case."

Shane shook his head, even as he continued gathering the papers and photos and picked up the worn leather work bag that held his investigation folders.

Deborah realized she hadn't changed his mind at all. She hadn't really expected to. Of course, she could hire a driver or she could possibly ride along with Faith's driver, but she barely knew the woman.

"I'm the reason Faith is here."

Callie's statement was the one that stopped Shane cold. Deborah wasn't sure if the look on his face was one of exasperation or admiration. She could not figure out the relationship between Shane and Callie. There was something going on between them, some energy in the air like before a big storm, but was it hostility or passion?

"What?" Shane asked.

"I'm the reason she's here. When everyone told me that Ira Bontrager was babbling and I should ignore him, I didn't." Callie walked around the table, took the folder out of his hand, and opened it. She shuffled through the pictures as if they were a deck of cards, not stopping until she came to the one of the girl on the ambulance gurney. The one taken before the medical examiner had covered her face.

"Are you trying to say that I owe you?"

"No." Her voice grew softer now. Max stood and walked between her and Shane. "I'm saying there's something else at work here, and we shouldn't ignore it. I tried to forget Ira's ramblings, tried not to look for Faith, but the thought of her out there not knowing about her *dat* haunted me."

Faith's eyes met Deborah's, and Deborah suddenly realized she did know this woman. She knew her because they shared a friend, and that counted for more than years or distance.

"If I hadn't found Faith ... if she hadn't come here today ... and if Deborah hadn't stopped by before Faith was about to leave ..." Callie looked at the photo one last time, then snapped the folder shut and handed it to Shane, "I would never have told Faith about the intricacies of the case. It never would have occurred to me to tell her. There's a reason we're all involved in this, and we all need to go to Goshen tomorrow."

Shane started to reach out and touch Callie's face, but stopped himself when he realized they weren't alone in the room. Instead he nodded slowly, then stuffed the folder in his bag. "All right, but you're not a part of the investigation. Your role is completely unofficial. You can follow in your own car."

"Fine. I'll drive. Deborah and Faith can ride with me."

"I'll leave at seven." Shane said, as he walked out the door, not bothering to say good-bye.

Deborah rode with Callie as she dropped Faith off at the bed and breakfast. Then Callie turned to take her home.

"Want to explain to me all those looks and touches between you and Shane?"

"We touched?" Callie's voice squeaked, though Deborah couldn't make out her expression in the darkness of the car.

"Nearly, several times. I'm your closest *freind* here in Shipshe—"

"You're my closest friend anywhere."

"And you don't want to talk to me about being *in lieb*?"

A truck passed them, its headlights brightening the interior of their car for a moment, long enough for Deborah to see the confusion on Callie's face.

"I don't think I'm *in lieb*."

Deborah reached over and patted her hand. "But you like him, *ya*?"

"When I'm not angry with him." Callie laughed, but it was uneasy, as if she wasn't sure whether she should laugh or cry.

"I feel that way when I'm pregnant," Deborah admitted. "Never knowing if I'm happy or sad. Jonas says it's because the baby is pushing on my heart, causing my feelings to run together."

"But I'm not pregnant!"

"I think it's the same though." When Callie didn't add anything, Deborah confessed, "I had wondered if you had feelings for Andrew or even Trent."

"That's part of what confuses me." Callie pulled into the Yoder's lane. "Andrew is such a sweetheart. He's very important to me."

"And Trent?"

"At first—yes. But the more I know him, the more I think of him as a charming college kid who hasn't grown up yet."

Callie brought the car to a stop, and Deborah waited for the sound of the engine to die away. "I wouldn't worry about it," she said.

"Because God will show me?"

"Oh, *ya*. He will show you, but I was thinking that time has a way of sorting such things out. And there's no rush."

Deborah reached over with her left arm and hugged her friend tightly. Callie reminded her of her younger *schweschder*, which was really how she thought of her now: family.

Then Deborah stepped out into the night, hurrying up the steps toward Jonas, content in the knowledge that those years of uncertainty were behind them.

Deborah didn't worry about Reuben at all that night. The hug she and Callie had shared before she walked up the front porch steps said it all. Deborah knew tomorrow wouldn't decide Reuben's fate—the Lord had control of that—but she felt certain, down to her very bones, that tomorrow was going to reveal an important piece of the puzzle that had begun when she'd stopped by Reuben's pond to let Esther pick a bouquet of fall flowers.

The next morning dawned so dark, Callie had trouble believing her alarm. She rose anyway, dressed for bad weather, and took Max outside for his morning romp. While he did his patrol of the little side yard, she studied the sky. What she saw didn't look good.

Callie hadn't experienced a really good Indiana rainstorm in November, but she'd heard about them. Temperatures were predicted to drop—not enough to freeze, but enough to make everyone miserable.

Snow she thought she could handle. She'd missed snow when she'd lived in Texas, which was why she'd taken up skiing. As a child, Callie had always fantasized about visiting her Aunt Daisy in the winter, dreamed about romps through snow-covered fields, sled rides, and choosing a Christmas tree from a snow-filled lot. It seemed as if this year she'd have her chance.

Today though, it looked as if the forecast should read: wet and wretched.

Callie went back inside and pulled a sweater on over her cotton blouse, changing her shoes for rain boots. Donning a yellow rain slicker over the entire outfit, she studied herself in the mirror and decided she looked like an ad for Outdoor World.

Max whined once as she headed down the stairs.

"Sorry, boy. This is one day you should be glad I'm leaving you behind."

By the time Callie had picked up Deborah and headed back to Faith's bed and breakfast, the rain was beating a pattern against her windshield. When they pulled in front of the Shipshe police station, Shane blinked his lights once as he pulled out in front of them.

"Does he know where we're going?" Callie asked.

"*Ya*. He called me at the bed and breakfast last night and confirmed directions to Lapp's place."

"Wants to be in the lead," Deborah said with a half smile on her face as she pulled her knitting out of her bag and began working on what looked like a scarf.

To Callie, everything being knitted looked like a scarf. Then, when it was done, it looked remarkable and soft and like something she wanted to learn how to do.

"You look better this morning, Deborah. More ..." Callie glanced at her friend, who was sitting beside her in the front seat, then back at the wet black road. "More at peace I guess."

"I couldn't have said it better. Jonas and I talked a long while after you dropped me off." Deborah's needles were a blur, much like the white lines painted down the middle of the road, which they were speeding past. "He helped me to see that none of this is a surprise to God, and God still does have Reuben's best interests at heart."

"He has a hope and a plan for him?" Callie reached for her travel mug full of coffee and took a big gulp.

"Exactly."

"I'm not following you two very well." Faith leaned forward, sticking her head between the front seats. "Reuben is wanted for the girl's murder, right? No offense, Deborah. I know he's your *freind*."

"No offense taken." Deborah slowed in her knitting to smile at the older woman. "Reuben is wanted for the murder of this girl, because she was found on his place."

"And because he won't testify as to how he knew her. He won't explain how she came to be staying in his house," Callie added.

Faith pulled herself up straighter, and when Callie glanced in the rearview mirror, she could see that her eyes had widened to big blue circles.

"She was staying in Reuben's house?"

"Reuben's abandoned house," Deborah corrected. "Reuben

and his cousin Tobias live in the barn on the property, which they've remodeled. No one has lived in the house since their *grossmammi* and *grossdaddi* moved out."

"Oh. Well, maybe he didn't know then."

"There are other things though, that seem to indicate Reuben had spoken to her." Callie went on to give her the quick version of the grand jury findings, including the fact that Reuben had been in the house. Traces of blood had been found on the bottom of Reuben's shoes, which is how they tied him to the clean-up of the blood splatter.

"Splatter? So did she fall or did someone hit her on the back of the head?"

"That part the crime techs couldn't determine, or they didn't reveal to the grand jury." Callie sighed. "I'm sure they'll bring in experts to debate the point."

Somehow talking about the case this way, explaining the facts as they traveled toward what felt like the conclusion of what started two weeks ago, helped. When Callie was done, she glanced again into the rearview mirror.

"So what do you think now?"

"I think I'd like to meet this Reuben. He sounds even more stubborn than my Adam, and I'll tell you—before he died, he was known as one of the most stubborn plain folks in all of Goshen."

Deborah glanced back at Faith. "I sometimes think we grow men that way here in Indiana."

"Nope," Callie said. "Same thing is going on in Texas. Rick was terribly stubborn, and he most certainly wasn't Amish. Must be a nationwide trait."

They all considered that for a moment, Deborah and Callie exchanging pointed glances as they pulled up behind Shane's car, which was stopped at a red light.

"Speaking of hardheaded," Callie muttered.

Faith sat forward again. "What you first said though, about

God having a hope and a plan for Reuben—and yes, I recognize that Scripture from the book of Jeremiah—"

"It's one of Deborah's favorites. She throws it at me all the time." Callie smiled to soften her words.

"You need some reminding is all." Deborah didn't slow in her knitting.

"But you believe it applies in this case?"

"I do." Deborah set her knitting in her lap. "I'll admit, yesterday I was worried. Reuben seemed more tired than usual, and staying inside, in the jail, has taken its toll on him. But Jonas reminded me that God is doing something special inside of Reuben and that maybe today will be the day of his freedom."

"Deborah, I don't want you to get your hopes too high." Callie reached over and clasped her hand. "We don't know what we'll find in Goshen."

"*Ya.* Jonas said that too."

They drove the rest of the way south on the state road in silence, each considering the possibility of Callie's last words.

Before Callie felt quite ready, she was slowing, turning onto Old Branch Road behind Shane's car. The lane was long and not quite like the type Callie was accustomed to. This looked more like the driveways to the horse farms near northern Houston, and in fact, horse fences lined the rolling pastures to the right and left of the lane. They continued to drive for several minutes as Callie studied the tremendous trees that spotted the fields beyond the fences. Most had dropped their leaves, stripped by the recent winds.

The leaves lay piled on the ground.

Callie wondered what type of trees they were. She hadn't lived in Indiana long enough to be able to recognize all the foliage, but when she glanced over at Deborah, she saw that her friend had stopped knitting and her eyes were focused completely on the scene in front of them.

Now that they'd finally reached the end of the lane, the home looked to Callie like any other Amish farm.

A medium-sized house sat beneath a stand of trees. Behind it, hills unfolded for miles, draped in the morning's rain. Adjacent to the house were the obligatory barn and grain silos. The barn, as usual in this area of the country, was painted gray and was much larger than the house. Callie noticed no electrical lines ran to the house or the barn.

What was different, what she studied as she pulled to a stop behind Shane and cut the engine to her car, were the silos. She'd never seen anything quite like them.

She'd never seen so many.

Chapter 33

SAMUEL STOOD AT THE WINDOW looking out at the two *Englisch* cars, and he knew that today was his day of reckoning.

Somehow he'd known it when he woke before dawn. There'd been a pit viper curled between his work boots, and he'd nearly set his feet down next to it. Even after he'd seen the snake, he'd thought, "Perhaps this is an answered prayer. Perhaps this is an easier way."

Now, watching the two cars pull into the Lapp's drive, he found himself thinking again of the snake and wondering why he had reached for the hoe and killed it.

He had killed ... again.

"We have company, Samuel?" Rachel placed a hand on his shoulder as she peered out the window, out past the rain.

It was all he could do not to flinch at her touch. She still treated him with kindness, but that would end soon.

"*Ya. Englischers.*"

Timothy looked up from reading the Scripture and scowled. The two of them had come in for *kaffi* and a bite to eat after working since five. Even on Sunday the animals had to be taken care of. The rest of this day would be spent studying Scripture and spending time with family.

Across the district, other families would be meeting together to share meals, but not the Lapps.

They'd always lived in isolation, but it had grown worse in the days since Samuel had returned, since he'd told them Katie had gone to the city.

Looking out the window at the man who walked toward the front steps, he knew that now Timothy and Rachel would learn the truth, and he thought to run. His heart began to beat so fast it sounded louder than the knocking of the man's fist against the door.

He thought to escape, but his feet remained rooted to the floor, as if they no longer retained the power to move.

So this was how it would end.

He remembered the snake again, remembered the feel as he'd chopped off its head, as he'd killed it.

Should he run?

He'd been taught ever since he was a young child to be peaceful. He'd lived all his life in a community committed to peace and nonviolence. "If it be possible, as much as lieth in you, live peaceably with all men." Samuel knew the verse well. Until this season of his life, he believed he'd followed it.

What of the rest of the verse from Romans? "Be not overcome of evil, but overcome evil with good." How was he to do that? He didn't understand. Katie had been *gut*. What had happened to her was wrong, and now these people were here, intent on bringing more grief to Timothy and Rachel.

He couldn't allow it.

He'd been responsible for enough harm.

Eyeing Timothy's hunting rifle on the shelf, he steeled his mind against his doubts and vowed to himself that he would find a way to protect this family—even if it meant he must fight.

Chapter 34

DEBORAH HAD THE SENSE OF STEPPING into a quilting pattern.

She was certain she'd seen a quilt top that was pieced together exactly like the scene in front of her. That was the first and most disconcerting thing, rather like stepping into an *Englisch* photograph.

The second thing that made her *naerfich* was the number of grain silos in front of her. She didn't know why it would make her stomach flip and flop, but it seemed so unusual she could only gape through the car window and press her hand to her apron to calm her nerves.

"Did I not mention Mr. Lapp has quite a large place here?" Faith asked, once again leaning forward between them.

"Can't remember that you did," Callie murmured.

"It looks like several farms." Deborah reached down to put her knitting in her bag, never taking her eyes off the sight outside the car window. "It looks like a picture rather than a real thing."

"Timothy's parents died, leaving quite a bit of land, then his *bruder* died, and finally his *onkel*. He kept consolidating, kept thinking he'd have sons. And each time he'd build another grain silo and work longer hours on the extra fields. Each year he'd have another *dochder*."

"He must have a lot of fields." Deborah opened her door.

"He must have a lot of daughters," Callie added.

Five silos. Deborah counted five. Three to the east side of the barn, two to the southwest. The sheer number was surprising enough, but as they followed Shane to the front porch of the house, she caught sight of a type of catwalk between the silos in each group.

It wasn't unusual for silos to have a ladder on the exterior that led to an opening at the top, but she'd never seen a catwalk between two. Perhaps Mr. Lapp had so much work, he had to devise ways to save time. Still, Deborah shivered at the thought of walking so high off the ground, between the silos, on the grated metal walk.

To be sure, it must be safe, but she'd rather never attempt it herself.

By the time they reached the porch, Mr. Lapp had opened the door, but he hadn't stepped outside. Deborah couldn't make out his expression through the screen, but she could see he was a big man. And she could tell he wasn't happy to have visitors.

"Timothy Lapp?"

"*Ya.*"

"My name is Shane Black, and I'm here to speak to you about your daughter Katie."

Deborah had noticed in the past that Shane didn't usually give his official rank when he introduced himself to Amish folk. She'd asked him why when he was investigating the death of Esther's husband, and he'd explained to her that Amish people were wary enough about *Englischers* in general. It wasn't so much that he was worried about intimidating the people he was questioning. It was that he wanted to get as much information as possible—and sometimes if he started out casually, he achieved better results.

She could have told him that in Shipshewana the entire point was moot. Everyone knew who Shane Black was. Everyone certainly recognized his vintage Buick. And she imagined the same was true for most of LaGrange County.

But Deborah didn't bother correcting him. She guessed *Englisch* men preferred to do things their own way as Amish men did. So he proceeded in his customary manner—doling out information a little at a time, so as not to frighten people off immediately.

Mr. Lapp did not look like a man who startled easily. Then Deborah's mind flashed back to the pictures of the girl, of Katie. Was she his daughter? She shivered in spite of herself, and Callie stepped closer.

They were standing on the steps under the roof of the Lapps' porch, but the rain had increased. It continued to splash on them. In the distance, thunder crashed and rolled.

"Timothy, perhaps you should invite them inside. The storm is worsening."

An Amish woman in her late forties hovered in the background. Deborah couldn't make out much more than her white *kapp* and her gentle voice.

Timothy ignored the woman, most certainly his wife, to say, "My *dochder* is in the city. We haven't heard from her in days. I have nothing to say to you on the matter."

"Mr. Lapp, I'm an officer with the LaGrange County—"

Before Shane could finish his sentence, Timothy Lapp had pushed his way through the door. Deborah was right in assessing his size. He was a giant of a man, standing well over six-and-a-half feet tall. He had the body of a man who'd worked more than twenty years on a farm, hard and muscular. He had the expression of the Old Order Amish—closed to those who weren't a known part of their community.

"I told you. My Katie is in the city. Now I'd thank you to leave my land."

Shane had backed up to allow Mr. Lapp to open the door.

When he'd backed up, Deborah, Callie, and Faith had been forced to take one step back as well, placing them squarely in the rain.

Deborah felt the water falling on her, soaking through her overcoat, but she couldn't take her eyes off what was happening in front of her. She wanted to run past these two men, run to the woman who still waited beyond the screen door and comfort her in some way.

Lowering his voice, Shane said, "I have information that is possibly related to Katie Lapp, and I have photos I need you to look at. We can do that at the police station in Goshen, or we can do that here. But we are going to do it."

Mr. Lapp seemed to deflate, like a tire on a bicycle that *kinner* rode in the summer. He peered out into the rain, over at his silos, and then a tremor passed through him.

He finally met Shane's gaze.

"My Katie's in the city." His voice was softer now.

"Then look at the pictures. Tell me it's not her, and we'll be out of your way."

"Not here. In my office. In the barn."

"Do you want the ladies to stay with your wife?" Shane asked.

Timothy's voice fell to a whisper. "No. It would frighten her more."

He turned and spoke to his wife through the screen door. Deborah could just make out the words, even as she saw the brief shadow of another man passing behind the woman.

"We're going to the barn," Mr. Lapp said. "I'll be back in a little while."

"Is everything all right?"

"Yes, of course. You stay inside with the younger ones." Then he pushed his way through their little group, and he trudged off through the rain, oblivious to the fact that it was now falling in sheets.

They walked four abreast—Deborah, Shane, Callie, and Faith.

They walked behind Mr. Lapp, carrying their pictures and their news of death.

Deborah prayed as she sloshed through the stream of water that was already running across this fertile land, carrying away sticks and leaves and tiny pieces of the crops that had been harvested and stored in the silos towering over them—carrying away the last evidence of fall.

She prayed that Shane would use the correct words, that the man in front of her and the woman in the house would find the strength to bear whatever awaited them in the moments ahead, and she prayed for the boy—she could now see it was a boy and not quite a man, though no doubt he was at the end of his *rumspringa*—who circumvented their little group and hurried toward the back of the barn.

Callie blinked twice, hoping her eyes would adjust to the dimness of the barn. She didn't consider herself a city girl, not any longer, and even when she'd lived in Houston, she'd sometimes visited the outlying farms in Normangee. But southern farms were different from Amish farms, and Timothy Lapp's farm was proving a bit different from the four or five Amish farms she regularly visited in Shipshewana.

There were the silos: both odd and numerous.

Then there was the barn. In a word: gigantic.

Callie stepped through the door and stared straight up. Would that be three stories? She'd lived in Shipshewana less than six months, but already she was used to smaller buildings. This reminded her of the Galleria Mall in Houston. Ladders on each side led to a loft that circled the building on three sides. Windows at the top would have let light in on most days, but today she could only see the darkness of the sky and rain pelting against the panes.

Callie might have stood staring, earning a crick in her neck, but Faith nudged her forward, nudged her closer to Deborah and Shane, closer to the event she was no longer sure she had the courage to witness.

They followed Mr. Lapp into his office area, located at the northeast corner of the building. Unlike the rest of the barn, it was the size of most Amish offices, meaning it was small and utilitarian. By the time they all crowded inside, it was obvious there wouldn't be room enough for everyone to sit.

Mr. Lapp stepped to the far side of the work table and nodded at Shane. "Like I told you, my girl's in the city."

Shane held the man's gaze for ten heartbeats, then pulled the folder of photos out of his bag and set it on the table. "Have you heard from Katie since she left, Mr. Lapp?"

The older man flinched at his daughter's name, but didn't reach for the folder. "No. I haven't, but then we don't have a phone here. Don't even have one in the workshop, though our bishop would allow it if I wanted one. I don't."

Shane nodded as if that made sense.

When Lapp didn't add anything else, Shane cleared his throat once and reached for the folder. Reaching out her hand to stop him from opening it, Faith spoke up.

"I don't know that you remember me, Mr. Lapp."

"'Course I do, Faith." He looked up at her, met her gaze. "There's no need to be formal, just because you arrived with *Englischers*."

"*Danki*, Timothy." Faith ran her hand down the front of her dress, wiping at the wet material.

Callie realized anew what a tenuous thread had brought them all together—Mr. Bontrager, Faith, the Lapps. The search for family, and Deborah's ability to notice the smallest details in any pattern, even the pattern of Faith's dress.

"I saw Katie occasionally in town, though it had been a while, what with everyone so busy during the harvest months and her being grown now." Faith waited for Timothy to add something, but he only stared back down at the folder, which remained unopened, sitting on the table. "Did Katie write to you at all, since she's been away?"

He didn't answer, but when he finally raised his eyes, Callie saw the fear there, saw the hope behind the fear, and she found herself praying that they were wrong. She had the irrational urge to grab the folder and the pictures and run out of the barn, run back to her car, and take them away from this place.

Perhaps it would be better if they didn't know.

Before she could act on that urge, Shane reached forward and opened the file. He set the pictures on the table, in front of Mr. Lapp for viewing, placed there like tablets of stone.

Timothy didn't have to answer.

He shut his eyes, and his face lost all color.

He began speaking in German, softly at first, a painful anguished sound.

Deborah rushed around the table. "Sit down, Mr. Lapp. I'm sorry. I'm so sorry. Would you like me to go and get your wife?"

"No. Not yet. Please, no. Give me a minute." His hand trembling, he reached forward, picked up the picture of Katie on the stretcher.

Callie didn't realize he was crying until tears splashed onto the photo.

She didn't realize she was crying until she tasted salt on her lips.

"What happened to her? Can you tell me what happened to her?"

"No, sir. We don't know exactly. Her body was found two weeks ago. There's a trial going on in—"

"That's not possible." Timothy Lapp placed both hands flat on the table, as if to push up, as if to stand. He shook his head and repeated, "That can't have happened."

"What do you mean, sir? This is your daughter, Katie Lapp?"

"*Ya*, that's her." Timothy reached forward, touched one of the photos gingerly, pulled it toward him as if he were pulling a piece of his heart across the table, shredding it as he dragged it across the oak surface. "It's her or it's her twin."

Callie wanted to look away from the agony on his face, but she hung on to his words, was mesmerized by the look of confusion that now played across his features.

"But you say her body was found two weeks ago, and all this time a trial has been going on in the *Englisch* courts?"

"Yes, sir. There's a man, an Amish man, who's been accused of your daughter's murder."

Timothy flinched at the word, but shook his head, and this time he did stand. "Well, it can't be her then. I don't understand how they can look the same, but it can't be her."

"Your daughter is missing?"

"*Ya*, and she left just over two weeks ago. Seventeen days to be exact. I've counted each and every one. Prayed each morning and night that God would see fit to guide her steps back to this home."

"Mr. Lapp, I'm sorry, but if your daughter is missing, and this looks like your daughter, then chances are it is her. We could do a DNA test to confirm."

Timothy pushed the offending picture away, continued shaking his head. "You don't understand. It can't be her. Samuel went down to the phone shack and spoke with her two nights ago."

"You're sure?"

"*Ya*, I am. He came back and told us that she's still in the city. That she's fine."

"Sir, is it possible—"

Shane never had a chance to finish his sentence.

It was cut off by Mrs. Lapp, who rushed into the room, pushed past Callie and Faith, and threw herself at the photos on the table. When she saw the photos of the girl, saw the evidence of what she must have feared every night since her daughter had left, a high-pitched scream escaped from her lips.

Faith had described Rachel Lapp as being in her late forties, energetic, and motherly. But the woman who now clutched the photos to her breast and wailed was no more than a shadow. Tendrils of brown and gray hair had escaped her *kapp* and hung in rivulets down her face. Her dress was soaked and clung to her thin frame, as if she'd been standing in the rain since they'd arrived.

But what struck Callie, what she knew would follow her into her dreams that night and for many nights to come, were the woman's eyes. Dark semicircles rimmed the bottoms, reminding her of the football players she once watched on television. And when Rachel Lapp looked up, when she finally sought her husband's eyes, Callie saw such agony and distress, such complete and naked grief, that she feared the woman's heart was literally breaking in two.

Chapter 35

DEBORAH WAS STILL HOLDING on to Mr. Lapp's arm when Mrs. Lapp hurled herself into the room.

The woman grabbed a photo off the table and began wailing.

Though Deborah had seen death several times, and even been with families when they'd learned of the death of a loved one, she'd never witnessed this type of scene before. She looked to Shane for any indication of what to do, but his eyes were again focused on the doorway.

At that moment a boy came crashing through the office door. Nearly six feet tall, with blond hair, he was wearing suspenders and traditional Amish clothing.

Deborah barely had time to notice those things before he snatched a photo of Katie off the table and began shouting. "Where did you get these? Who are you? Why did you come here? You can't come in here. You can't come in here with your photographs."

"Samuel—" Timothy tried to stand, tried to reach out to the boy, but he froze when his wife crumpled to the floor.

"Rachel? Rachel, are you all right?" Stumbling around the table, Timothy grasped her hand.

But Rachel didn't answer or respond in any way.

"Lay her down. I think she's fainted." Callie rushed the few feet to the woman's side. "Mrs. Lapp, can you hear me?"

"What can I do?" Shane asked.

"Help me lay her back on the floor and find me something to place under her legs." Callie loosened the top pin of Rachel's dress to make sure her airway wasn't restricted. "We need to give her plenty of room."

"She's had a few dizzy spells before," Timothy said, "but nothing like this."

"Does she have low blood sugar?" Callie asked.

"I'm not sure. She just sits down and they pass."

Shane pushed chairs and boxes out of the way to give Callie space to work, then knelt down closer to her and whispered, "Do you know what you're doing?"

"I've had basic CPR, but no more." Callie glanced at Deborah. "I would think you'd know what to do."

"Me? We Amish are usually calm in situations like this. I'm not accustomed to hysteria."

"It's going to be all right, Rachel." Mr. Lapp knelt on the other side of his wife, still grasping her hand as if he could lend her his strength.

"She's breathing fine, Mr. Lapp. Probably the shock caused her blood pressure to drop." Callie had her hand on Rachel's wrist and was counting her heartbeats. "Her pulse is strong. If we could get her some water for when she comes around—"

"I usually bring some with me, but today ..." He looked around in confusion. "We'll have to go back to the house."

"I'll fetch some," Faith said, then turned and rushed from the room.

Deborah knelt beside Callie, who was still monitoring the woman's pulse. "You have your cell phone, don't you, Callie?"

"In the car."

"I have mine." Shane pulled his from his pocket and checked it. "No service. I'll go after yours."

Shane jumped up and headed out of the room.

"Shane." Deborah hurried to meet him at the door. "There was something wrong with that boy."

"What do you mean?"

"I don't know."

They both looked out into the main section of the barn. There was no sign of the boy now.

Deborah reached out and put both hands on Shane's arm and looked into his dark eyes—eyes that had once frightened her as much as the storm and the situation in this room. But she and Shane had been through much together. Her mind flashed back on the night she'd climbed down the trellis outside Callie's bedroom window, the night she thought she'd die. Though she couldn't say why, something told her this moment was every bit as critical.

"I don't know what I mean, but be careful. Watch for him."

Shane nodded once, squeezed her hand, and headed out into the rain, nearly running into Faith as he did.

"I have the water, but the children became frightened when their *mamm* rushed out. I'm going back to the house to stay with them."

"Thank you, Faith." Deborah took the thermos of water from Faith and carried it to Callie, who was still kneeling beside Rachel. Rachel was beginning to stir.

"I have some water here, Mrs. Lapp. Can you take a small sip?" Callie asked.

"My daughter, my *dochder*, my sweet girl." Rachel Lapp was openly weeping again, but her color had improved.

Deborah pulled a handkerchief out of her pocket and placed it gently into her hands.

"She's with the Lord now, Rachel." Timothy swiped at his eyes. "At least we know she's with the Lord. We can stop worrying. Finally we can stop worrying."

"Oh, Timothy." A wail escaped from the woman's throat, and she threw her arms around her husband's neck.

After a few moments, Timothy pulled away from his wife, making space for Deborah and Callie to continue their ministrations.

Deborah met Callie's gaze. When Callie nodded slightly, they both helped her into a seated position.

"Try to stay calm, Mrs. Lapp. You have other *bopplin, ya?*" Deborah kept her voice low, soothing, as she closed her eyes and forced herself to picture the quilt that lay upon her and Jonas' bed. The pattern was blue on white and one of her favorites. It was simple and peaceful.

"*Ya,* I do. I have six children. My Katie was the oldest."

"And we'll miss her terribly. We have missed her since the day she left." Timothy wiped at the tears running down his face. "But now we know, and we believe she is with the Lord. She's resting now, Rachel. It hurts, and we'll miss her, but she's resting."

The two clung to each other, rocking back and forth, Rachel still sobbing and Timothy rubbing her back in small circles, as one would a child.

Callie motioned to Deborah from just outside the door.

"Where's Shane? He should be back by now." Fear mixed with worry in Callie's stomach, brushing up against her insides like a hundred swarming bees. She wondered if this morning would ever end. She wondered when they could all go back to Shipshe, back to what now seemed like a nice, safe life.

"Shane said he was going to fetch your phone to call for an ambulance and more officers." Deborah glanced at the office. "Are you still worried about Rachel?"

Crossing her arms tightly around her middle, Callie peeked back into the office. "A little. Her color is better, but I don't have any real medical training. It bothers me that she's been having dizzy spells and hasn't seen a doctor. What I don't want is another emergency on our hands. This family has been through enough."

"*Ya*, you're right."

Callie uncrossed her arms and began fiddling with the buttons on her raincoat. "Maybe Shane had problems finding my phone or finding service."

"I'm more concerned about the boy," Deborah admitted.

"The boy?"

"Large, blond-haired, stormed into the room and grabbed a picture off the table—"

"That was hardly a boy."

"He was grown, I'll grant you that. Probably eighteen or so, but I could tell by his manners ... he was still a boy. And there was something else about him I didn't like."

"What do you mean? What else?"

"I don't know, Callie. Did you not get a *gut* look at his face?"

"No, I was watching Mr. Lapp, worried he might keel over or grow angry and start chucking things at someone. Then Mrs. Lapp crumpled to the floor, and I forgot all about the kid. Why?"

"Something wasn't right with him. Something—" But before Deborah could finish her thought, they heard a sound Callie had once described to Deborah. A sound Callie had heard when Max was hurt. The sound of a gun going off.

Callie's heart slammed into her rib cage with the echo. Her legs turned to jelly, and she wondered if Mrs. Lapp's condition was contagious.

Deborah grabbed her hand. "Callie, was that a gun? Who—"

"Shane's out there ... and that boy you're so worried about ..." Callie sputtered.

Deborah clasped both of Callie's hands in her own. "Look at me. I'll go and check on Shane, but you need to stay here with Mrs. Lapp."

"What? Why should I stay here?"

"I don't know how to help her. I don't know anything about fainting spells."

"I'm not a doctor. I only sold medicines to doctors. You can stay with her as easily as I can."

"One of us should go and check on Shane. Someone has a gun out there."

"A gun. Listen to yourself, Deborah."

They both turned and stared out the partially open barn door. Rain continued to pour from the sky.

"*Ya*. I'm listening, but maybe Shane needs help." Deborah put both of her hands on Callie's face. "He helped us before. Remember? He risked his life for us. I can't leave him out there for a crazed boy to kill. Now go in and stay with the Lapps. Be sure that Rachel doesn't have another attack."

"No, Deborah. You should stay here. You have children." Callie felt wetness on her face and wondered if the roof had begun to leak, if the heavens were intent on dropping enough water to soak them all, to wash every bit of filth and sin from each one of them.

She wondered if Shane was lying bleeding in the storm that continued to pelt down on them, and once again she felt as if a giant fist were squeezing her heart.

"God will protect me, Callie." Deborah kissed Callie's cheek and shoved her back into the workroom before slamming the door shut.

Callie stared at the couple, still on the floor.

Mr. Lapp had heard the gunshot.

She was sure of it. The way he looked at her and the dread in his eyes confirmed it. But he clung to his wife, and his eyes once again strayed to the pictures still on the table.

Callie walked over to Shane's folder, scooped the pictures up, and placed them inside. Then she closed the folder and placed the Bible that was sitting on Mr. Lapp's desk on top of it.

When she looked back at Timothy, his eyes were shut and his lips were moving, but she couldn't make out what he was saying.

She looked around the office and found a blanket and brought it over to cover Mrs. Lapp, who was lying down again, curled in a ball, as if to ward off any additional tragedy.

Her husband still had his arm wrapped around her.

Mrs. Lapp seemed incoherent as her breathing evened out and her weeping turned into a stream of silent tears.

Another minute passed before Mr. Lapp reached over and put Callie's hand on top of his wife's. "Stay with her. No matter what happens or what you hear, promise me you'll stay with my wife."

"You don't have to go out there. Shane is trained to handle these situations."

"But I know Samuel. I understand better than anyone the burdens that are troubling his heart and clouding his judgment."

Callie tried to swallow past the lump in her throat. "It might be dangerous."

"*Ya*, I know. Life is dangerous at times. My Katie found that out. But I need to talk to the boy." Timothy kissed his wife on the forehead so gently it reminded Callie of the way Ira had placed his hand on top of Faith's head.

It reminded her of Melinda holding Hannah.

Her heart ached with how much tenderness and pain life held.

Timothy Lapp stood, adjusted his suspenders, and muttered as he walked out the door, "One death is enough. Whatever this is—it stops today."

And then he was gone, leaving Callie on the floor with Rachel and her fears.

Chapter 36

DEBORAH RAN FIRST TO THE HOUSE, ran to check on Faith.

"We're fine. What's going on out there?" Five heads popped out from behind Faith, all girls. Best as Deborah could tell, they varied in age from three to twelve—all equally young and vulnerable.

"Can we talk alone?"

"*Ya.*"

Faith convinced the girls to fetch paper and crayons to distract them.

After Deborah explained what had happened and what she'd heard, Faith glanced back into the room where the girls were sitting at the table. "I'll stay with them. You're sure their *mamm*'s all right?"

"She seemed better when I left. Callie's still with her, and Shane was to have called the emergency medical people. I don't know whether he reached Callie's phone though."

"I never heard or saw him." Faith peered past her, through the pouring rain, at the two cars parked between the house and the barn.

It occurred to Deborah there might as well be a giant red X

painted on the top of the automobile, and suddenly she was grateful it was a car and not her buggy hitched to her mare, Cinnamon. At least this way, if the boy started shooting, he'd only hurt a machine.

"Callie's purse is sitting on the front seat. I could run and—"

"No!" Deborah reached out an arm to stop her as Faith stepped forward. "I know I heard a gunshot, but I don't know what direction it came from or who was doing the shooting."

Faith stepped back, sighed, and worried her hand over the front of her dress. "I was hoping that was thunder, but it sounded to me as if it came from the direction of the silos."

"I'm going over there now to make sure Shane wasn't hurt."

"You? Why you? Shouldn't you stay here with me?"

Deborah shook her head. "One of us should go, and you've done enough already—bringing us out here. Stay with the *kinner*. I'll be careful." She hugged her new friend once, then turned and fled back out into the storm.

Deborah spied Shane crouched down behind a feeding trough. His back to the barn, the roof overhang provided a little protection, but she could see even as she ran toward him how thoroughly soaked and miserable he was.

His shirt was plastered to his shoulders, and his hair, which he wore a bit on the long side, stuck to his forehead and neck. Water dripped down his face, but he didn't bother wiping it away. Instead his eyes stayed trained in front of him, barely flicking her direction.

She could also see the gun he had pulled out and rested against the top of the trough.

"Go back inside, Deborah." Shane still didn't bother to look at her, as she crouched beside him. Instead he continued to scan the tops of the buildings surrounding the barn—the house, the silos, the outbuildings, even the trees.

"No."

"I don't have time for this." He briefly turned toward her, his eyes searching hers. "Think of what Jonas would want you to do."

"He'd want me to help that boy."

"That boy is shooting at us."

"Amish use hunting rifles, perhaps fitted with a long-range scope for deer hunting. You'd already be dead if he wanted to hit you, Shane."

Shane shook his head once, sending water droplets in every direction, then he turned back to scanning the buildings. "I realize that, but he's already made several mistakes, and I don't want you—or myself—to be the next one. Now go back inside and stay beneath the roof overhang as you go."

"Why do you think he shot at us?"

"He saw me heading toward the cars. Spooked him I guess. Kids—they react more than they think, which is why I hate calls involving teenagers. Give me anything else, but don't give me a teenager with a weapon."

"If he's guilty of something, why didn't he just run?" Deborah shivered as water splattered down her back and thunder rolled across the skies. "Why fire the weapon and give away that he's still here?"

"Same reason he's shooting at an officer. Same reason he'd lie about talking to a girl who has been dead for two weeks. There is no explaining what a teen backed into a corner will do."

Deborah didn't bother answering that. She didn't have an answer any more than Shane did.

"You're going to catch pneumonia, and Jonas is going to kick my *Englisch* backside all the way into the next county. Now I appreciate the conversation, and thanks for checking on me, but I want you to go inside and get dry—"

At that moment the door to the barn opened once again and Timothy Lapp stepped outside. He didn't pause for the rain, didn't act as if he noticed it.

Instead he walked out into the middle of the clearing, his shoulders bowed as if he were carrying a weight heavier than five sacks of feed. When he reached the middle, he turned back toward the barn area, straightened his shoulders, and cupped his hands around his mouth, making a megaphone of sorts.

"Samuel, I want you to come inside. Come back, son."

Deborah wondered at the use of the last word. It was the last piece of the puzzle that clicked into place for her.

Timothy considered Samuel his son, the boy he'd never had.

The look on the boy's face when he stormed into Timothy's office suddenly made sense—it was the look of agony wrapped in guilt.

It was the look of a child who'd taken away the most precious thing a father has: his *dochder*.

"Samuel killed her." Deborah grabbed Shane's arm, digging her short nails into the skin beneath his shirt.

"Deborah, we've been through this. I don't know what's going on with the boy, but I do know all the evidence points to Reuben's guilt. I don't want to believe it any more than you do."

"No. You don't. And maybe the evidence doesn't prove what you think it does. All you know is that Reuben knew Katie."

"He cleaned up the blood in the house. He hid the rags."

Deborah hesitated, not having heard this part before, then pushed on. "You know that Reuben spoke with her and she stayed in his old house for a few days. You don't know that he killed her. I'm telling you, Reuben couldn't kill anyone."

"Deborah ..." Shane finally wiped at the rain running down his face, careful to hold his gun steady with his other hand.

"Look at Timothy and stop staring at me that way. Timothy knows it too. Samuel did it."

"You haven't seen all our evidence, Deborah."

"And I don't need to."

"Evidence doesn't lie." Though his voice wavered, he continued to scan the barn's rooftop.

"All right. It doesn't lie, but perhaps he's only guilty of something else."

"Don't think I haven't considered that. He could be covering for the boy. Could be covering for someone other than the boy. But as long as the evidence we have points to Reuben, then Reuben stands trial."

"And Samuel?"

"Samuel's coming in as well. Samuel's going to explain what's going on."

Samuel looked down from his perch near the top of the barn. He looked down and thought that he would fall, though not from the height. He'd been walking Timothy's barns and silos for over a year.

No, the reason Samuel was sure he'd slip and fall was because of the scene below him.

When Katie had first died, when he'd first killed her—time to admit to what had happened—he'd thought he could make it up to Timothy and Rachel. He'd come back, created the story of Katie going to the city, even lied about the phone call, because he couldn't bear the pain in their eyes, and then he'd worked harder than he'd ever worked in his life.

Samuel had set out to be the son that Timothy never had.

Looking down at Katie's father now, he knew it would never be enough. The man standing in the middle of the clearing was broken.

Timothy could never forgive him for what had happened.

So how could Samuel end this?

Scanning left, he looked over at the *Englisch* cop and Amish woman. He nearly rolled his eyes. They looked like two ducks in a barrel at the county fair. Shooting them would be easy.

But then he'd have two more deaths to answer for when he faced God, and Samuel knew he would face God—perhaps sooner rather than later.

So what were his options?

The photos of Katie played through his mind, making it hard to think clearly. She hadn't looked like that when he'd carried her to the flowers she'd loved so much, intending to leave her there, but even that last act of love hadn't gone as he'd intended. The blood from her head wound had soaked through the quilt, soaked on to his sleeve and he'd set her down, suddenly frightened by her still form. Then he couldn't force himself to pick her up again.

A big strong man—afraid of a dead girl. Afraid of his wife.

So he'd dragged her on the quilt, dragged her the final distance through the flowers.

And when he'd reached the banks of the pond, it had occurred to him that perhaps she wouldn't rest there, perhaps some wild animals would come and find her. So he'd cried—sat and wept like a little child—before rolling her into the water and praying that at least there she would be safe until someone found her.

She had still looked like his Katie then, floating face down in the early morning sun.

He'd gathered the quilt and run into the woods, hoping Reuben would find the body and think of a way to give her a proper burial. He couldn't stay and do it. If he'd stayed, Reuben would have to hide him or turn him in, and Reuben didn't deserve that type of trouble.

He hid knowing no one would ever suspect Reuben. He was a well-respected man in the Shipshewana community—Samuel had been able to tell that from his short time there. Plus Reuben had never so much as touched Katie. The *Englisch* police would simply meet a dead end and let things be. The responsible thing for Samuel to do was go back to Timothy and Rachel. He had to find a way to make things right for their family.

But nothing had worked out the way it was supposed to.

His hand began to shake on the rifle's stock, and he gripped it more firmly. Wouldn't do to drop it. Not now.

He could make his way down, and he could run.

Samuel knew he could disappear into the *Englisch* world.

But suddenly he was tired, too tired.

"Samuel, whatever happened we can talk about it. Come back inside." Even across the distance between them, Samuel could make out the tears mixing with rain streaming down Timothy's face.

He'd caused this family enough pain.

He shifted the rifle to his back, adjusted the strap, then began to make his way down and toward the ladder of the tallest silo. Once there, he began to climb.

Chapter 37

CALLIE HELPED RACHEL LAPP struggle to a sitting position again.

"I think you should probably stay seated awhile longer, Mrs. Lapp. Deborah and Shane will see to any problem that's outside. And your husband. Don't forget he's out there as well—surely he will know what to do. You need to take care of yourself."

"I've had these dizzy spells for a year now. I suppose I know when they've passed. And you can call me Rachel. When people stumble through the valley of death together, they're on a first-name basis." Rachel adjusted her *kapp* as Callie tucked the blanket around her, then the older woman pulled her legs up under her dress in a more comfortable position.

Though she had to be in her late forties, she looked younger when she crossed her legs, as if she might be ready to plop a story-book or a child in her lap.

"How serious is the dizziness?"

"Not too serious. It always passes after a few moments." Her gaze slipped toward the folder still waiting on the table, the Bible holding it firmly in place. Rachel's eyes shimmered with tears, and her right hand went to her lips.

"Are you okay? Are you feeling light-headed again?"

"No, no. I'm all right. It's my soul that's grieving ... grieving over the loss of my *dochder*." Rachel closed her eyes and began to rock gently.

"So you're sure it was her?" Callie clasped Rachel's other hand. It felt icy cold and she worried anew about the woman's medical condition. Where was Shane with that phone? Where were the emergency medical personnel?

"*Ya*. There's no mistaking your own flesh and blood. It's Katie, though I can't imagine what could have happened." Opening her eyes, Rachel peered at Callie through the tears that slipped past her lashes and down her weathered cheeks. "What town did you say you were from?"

"Shipshewana."

Rachel shook her head. "Can't say as I know anyone in particular from that area. 'Course Timothy might. He does business with folks from all over, but I don't know what Katie would have been doing there. I can't—"

She put her hands down on the floor, pushed, and made an awkward attempt to stand.

"You probably shouldn't be up and about yet."

"But I need to know, and I don't understand." Rachel rocked herself forward onto her hands and knees, managed to grab hold of the table and pull herself up.

"Patients who've fainted should rest for at least one hour." Callie searched her mind to remember what she'd been taught in the CPR class. "Especially if the patient lost consciousness for more than one minute, which you did."

Rachel turned on her with the fury of the rain beating against the barn. "I'm not a patient. I'm a *mamm*, and I'll be finding out what happened to my Katie."

Her voice gained strength as she straightened her dress and wagged a finger in Callie's direction. "I believe the person who knows what happened is out in that storm. Now you can help me go out there, or you can stay in here spouting nonsense."

Callie blinked once, then hurried through the office door to catch up with Rachel before she stepped out into the storm.

She'd begun praying again since moving to Shipshewana, though she couldn't have pinpointed the exact moment it had happened. Perhaps it had been when she'd found herself alone with only Max for company. Or maybe it'd been when she'd discovered the editor's dead body in the newspaper's office. Definitely she was well into the habit by the time she, Deborah, Trent, and Andrew had faced death at the hands of a mafia thug.

Regardless of when she had first turned back toward God, Callie found herself calling on him now.

That he would calm the storm raging outside, that he would ease the pain in this family's hearts, and that he would find a way to bring Reuben home.

Shane pushed Deborah flat against the feeding trough when the boy turned and stared at them. "He saw us. Don't move."

"He has a rifle, *ya*? That's what we heard?" Deborah peeked over the top of the trough, but Shane pushed her head back down before she could see anything through the rain.

"Yes, he's carrying a rifle, and he could have taken out either one of us if he'd had a mind to. Are you happy? What is it about a woman that loves to be right?"

"I don't love to be right, Shane. It's more the pieces of a puzzle coming together, exactly like the pattern of a—"

"Stay here. Don't move unless I manage to draw him to the other side of the silo. If that happens I want you to run to the house and stay inside with Faith and the children until I tell you to come out. Do you understand?"

"Yes, but—"

"Deborah, look at me." Shane put his hand to her shoulder, his face close, and she saw more than the usual intensity in his eyes, she saw the concern and something that approached fear. "You give me a man with a gun and nine times out of ten I can tell you what he's going to do, but a teenager is a different thing altogether. Teens don't know their own minds or emotions yet. They're volatile. You do what I say."

Without waiting for an answer, he began to run along the side of the barn, his pistol held tight to his chest.

Deborah watched him until he turned the corner, until he was out of sight. Timothy still stood in the middle of the yard, calling out to Samuel, though the severity of the storm had increased and it was hard for her to make out what he was saying. But that wasn't what made her completely disregard Shane's instructions.

Looking toward the front of the barn, she saw the door open and saw Callie and Mrs. Lapp step outside.

She watched as Katie's mom hesitated, then ran through the rain to her husband, nearly collapsing in his arms.

Callie followed, standing beside them and glancing occasionally around, as if aware that they were perfect targets for an angry young man with a rifle in his hands.

So Deborah stood and ran toward them as well, but her foot slipped in the mud, and she fell hard against the rain barrel, tearing the corner of her sleeve and opening a small gash in her arm. The bleeding wasn't bad that she could see. She stood again and moved quickly toward the group, using more caution this time.

By the time Deborah reached them, it felt as if the wind had turned and was blowing from the north. She thought she'd been wet up to that point, but now she was soaked and shivering. She fought to stop the tremors as she leaned in and spoke to the little group, telling them what Shane had said—all the while holding her sleeve together with her other hand.

Timothy broke away from his wife. "I'm going after him. Rachel, go inside with the *kinner*."

"I won't. If Samuel had anything to do with this, I'll see it for myself."

Turning, Timothy put both hands on his wife's arms. "I will bring him to you, Rachel. I'll bring him back and he'll explain what happened. You know that Samuel wouldn't have hurt our Katie. He loved her. It's only that he's afraid now. He'll come back inside and explain what happened. I'll bring him to you."

"Do you promise?"

"*Ya*." The one word and Timothy was gone.

Rachel turned toward the house and stumbled. Deborah and Callie both reached out to stop her from falling.

Deborah's eyes locked with Callie's.

"You take her inside and I'll follow Mr. Lapp," Callie said. "The dress would slow you down."

"But—"

"My gosh, Deborah. When did this happen?" Callie moved Deborah's hand, inspecting the gash in her arm.

"It isn't bad. I fell and hit it against—"

"Go inside, Deborah. Faith will clean this and bandage it. Go inside and stay with Faith and Rachel."

Realizing she would slow everyone down trying to hold the sleeve of her dress on, Deborah relented. "All right, but be careful. Samuel headed toward the east silos, and Shane went after him."

Callie paused for a quick hug, and then she rushed to catch up with Shane.

Deborah put her arm around Rachel and helped her toward the porch steps of her home.

Chapter 38

WHEN CALLIE rounded the corner of the barn, she was confronted with three silos.

If she had thought they looked enormous from the road, she really had no idea. From the ground, they towered over her like the redwood trees she'd seen when visiting California.

Attached to the side of each was a metal ladder that climbed straight to the top of the silo where a door was placed to allow access to the interior of the silo. Suspended between each silo hung metal catwalks. While she'd paused to stare, Timothy had caught up with Shane, who'd stopped as well.

"As I came around the corner, I had a visual on the boy headed in that direction, but he disappeared." Shane pointed toward the far side of the silos.

Timothy nodded once and stepped forward, toward the nearest silo. Shane grabbed the big man's arm and pulled him back under the roof overhang of the barn.

"You understand he's armed?" Shane asked.

"I understand Samuel's carrying my new hunting rifle, and I mean to take it back."

"He took a shot at us earlier."

"He's scared."

"Sir, that boy may have killed your daughter."

"He may know something about what happened." Timothy wiped at the water on his face. "But I thought you said the man who killed my daughter was in jail."

Shane stared toward the silos and back again, then glanced at Callie. It was plain he wanted to say more, but there was no time. "I thought he was, but it could be we have the wrong guy."

Timothy seemed to consider that, ran his fingers through his rain-soaked beard, and nodded once. "Fair enough. Only way to find out is to fetch Samuel and take him inside. Can't talk to him outside in the pouring rain."

Shane shifted his pistol from his right hand to his left. "All right. We'll circle the silos completely, then we'll meet at the back. Do not head up unless there's a definite sign of him up there."

"Agreed." Timothy glanced from Callie to Shane. "Whistle once if you see him above ground. I'll take the left silo."

"I'll take the right."

"I'll take the middle one," Callie said.

"No you won't." Both men turned on her as one.

"Wait here, Callie. I don't even know why you came."

"*Ya*, it could be dangerous. Plus those ladders are slippery. I'm used to climbing them, so it's no problem for me."

Timothy headed off to the left.

"I can't believe you're okay with him charging out into the middle of this. He's personally involved and unarmed, but you want me to stay put? It's because I'm a woman, isn't it? Since when did you become a sexist, Shane Black?"

Shane hesitated, pulled Callie close, and ran his hand up and down her arm, leaving a trail of goose bumps in his wake. Kissing her on the forehead, he whispered, "For once, please listen to me."

Then he was gone.

Callie wanted to fume. She wanted to be angry with Shane. She wasn't a china doll that needed protecting. But thinking about the way Shane had looked at her, the way his hand had felt on her arm, and his lips had caressed her skin, Callie couldn't muster any anger. Her forehead still tingled.

Which was ridiculous.

The last thing she needed were romantic notions in her head at a time like this. He'd probably kissed her to distract her. It would be just like him to use unfair tactics.

Callie could walk around a silo as well as anyone.

Glancing left, then right, she dashed forward into the pouring rain. Within two minutes she had run around to the back of the silo. From the front, she'd thought she would be able to see Shane and Timothy, but the silos weren't exactly in a line. For one thing, they weren't the same size.

The middle silo was a bit smaller in circumference but taller. Perhaps it was older. Looking toward the other two silos, she could only see their backs, not their fronts nor the sides where the ladders were located.

She also couldn't see Shane or Timothy at all.

No doubt, if Samuel were here, he would have hidden in the farthest structure. Right?

In fact, if Samuel were here, and if he were guilty of killing Katie, why was he hanging around at all?

Why wasn't he on the run?

Callie had turned to walk to Shane's silo, questions tumbling through her mind, rain soaking through her clothes, when she heard the clamor of boots against metal.

Pivoting around, she saw only the back of her silo.

Timothy had said the ladders were on the side. The side she hadn't seen yet. She ran toward the east, and there was the metal ladder, stretching to the very top. Looking up she could just make out Samuel's figure, more than halfway up the metal ladder of her silo. The hunting rifle was slung over his shoulder, and he seemed completely focused on placing hand over hand, on climbing as quickly as possible.

Why?

What was the point?

What could he possibly do from there?

Then she realized again that her silo was taller. Much taller. Stepping back she studied the layout, pushing the water out of her face as the rain continued to pour from the sky.

The ladder went to the very top of the silo, to the door. But the catwalk that stretched in between this middle silo and the other two was at the two-thirds mark. As she watched, Samuel was approaching it. Would he stop there? Or would he continue up?

From the top, he'd have a perfect perch, a perfect sharpshooter's position.

Callie put two fingers into her mouth to whistle and blew hard, but no sound came out.

She'd had trouble whistling as a child, but finally caught the knack of it somewhere along junior high. Now? Nothing. It wasn't like she'd been practicing, but you'd think she could produce something.

She thought about hollering. Would it alert Samuel though? Would he do something crazy if he heard her?

She thought about running to one of the other silos. But both were too far. She could run there, but by the time she reached them, Samuel would be in place at the top of hers. So instead of running for help she grabbed hold of the metal ladder and began to climb.

What could she do if she caught up with him? Talk to him. That's all. Persuade him to calm down, to hand over his rifle, to climb back down with her. Maybe, just maybe, he would listen to a woman if he was intimidated by and responding aggressively to a man. Maybe.

As she climbed, Callie tried to remember what her handgun

instructor in Texas had said about rifles. She hadn't paid much attention, since she wasn't a hunter. She seemed to recall something about rifles having an effective range of up to a thousand meters, depending on the caliber. Pausing halfway up the ladder, she looked over her shoulder, looked back through the pouring rain toward the silo Timothy was checking out.

Both Timothy and Shane would be easily within range.

When Samuel reached the platform of the silo, he paused to catch his breath. He didn't know why his heart was racing so, but perhaps it was the thought that he was finally going to have to face up to what he had done. After all, he'd backed himself into a corner by climbing to the top of the silo. He'd only thought to put some space between himself and the strangers. He'd panicked, and he'd gone to the one place he didn't think they'd follow. The one place where he was sure he could see everything.

But now what was there left to do?

Give himself up?

Jump?

Admit the terrible thing that had happened?

All the options running through his mind were awful, as awful as the memory of Katie lying on the floor of Reuben's house. Samuel couldn't think of a way to make this situation right. Once again he'd left himself with no options. Or had he?

Could he escape?

Did he even want to escape?

He couldn't imagine living in the *Englisch* world, which was why he hadn't run into the woods and across the fields. It would have been easy enough to lose the *Englischer* who'd arrived in the car. But Samuel had been to Fort Wayne and Indianapolis to take care of errands for Timothy, and both towns had left him feeling crowded and a bit dirty.

Not as dirty as the memory of what happened with Katie though.

Thoughts of Katie made his chest hurt worse than the climb up in the pouring rain. He slung the rifle off his back, checked that the scope was adjusted correctly, and raised it to his shoulder to peer through the lens.

The shot he'd fired into the air had sent everyone scurrying. A scope worked as well as an *Englischer*'s high-powered binoculars. He'd walk around the catwalks, make sure the coast was clear, then decide what to do.

Samuel moved away from the ladder, walked to the front of the silo, and brought the rifle up again to look toward Timothy's farmhouse. Then he heard his father-in-law's voice, calling out to him from the adjacent silo.

"Put the rifle down, Samuel."

Lowering the rifle a fraction, Samuel saw Timothy beginning to cross the catwalk.

"Stay where you are!" Samuel yelled. "Don't come any closer."

He'd picked the center silo because it afforded him a good view of both the barn and the other two silos. The catwalks stretched away from him like spokes on a wheel.

Timothy continued walking slowly, his hand stretched out in front of him.

"I want to talk to you, Samuel, but we can't do it here."

"Drop the rifle, Samuel."

Samuel jerked around and saw the *Englischer* fifty feet away on the other catwalk and closing in. Gripped between both hands, he was holding a pistol.

"Put the rifle down, then push it away with your foot."

Samuel tightened his grip on the rifle, tried to decide if he should try to explain about what had happened in Shipshewana, if they would even believe him at this point, or if it was too late.

Wind tore at his clothes and rain continued to pelt against his skin.

"Samuel, Katie wouldn't want you to do this." The woman's voice came from behind him.

Spinning around, Samuel saw a woman nearly in front of him, so close he could practically touch her. She was petite like Katie. But she was a good ten years older and definitely *Englisch*. What was she doing on his silo? How had she managed to climb up here? Rain soaked her hair, and her clothes revealed a figure that was more like a boy's. Did she know his Katie? How could she?

"Callie! Move away from him!" The *Englischer*'s voice was sharp, like the sound of boots on metal. "Put the rifle down, boy, or I will shoot."

"He's a good man, Samuel. He doesn't want to hurt you." The woman moved toward him, glancing down at the ground nervously as she did. "You've frightened him because you're holding the rifle."

"How can I frighten anyone?" Samuel replied, backing up from the woman, backing up until the edge of the railing pressed against his back.

"He doesn't know what you're going to do. Put the rifle down or hand it to me, and he'll put away his gun."

"No. Then he'll take me to the *Englisch* jail. Don't you see? I can't go there. I'd rather die first."

Salt ran across Samuel's lips, dripped into his mouth, and he realized he was crying. He hadn't allowed himself to cry since the hours he'd spent hiding in the woods behind Reuben's house. Now the tears were building inside of him like the giant storm clouds that pressed down above them. He bit down hard on his lips, clutched the rifle tighter until he felt he must be leaving marks in the stock of Timothy's new Browning A-Bolt.

"Look at me, Samuel. Look at me." Timothy's voice brokered no argument, and against his will, against all of his doubts,

Samuel turned to look at him. "Give me the rifle. You know it's wrong to take what doesn't belong to you."

Samuel looked down at the rifle he gripped, ran his hand along the walnut finish, now slick with rain. They'd talked for months about the hunting season, about the meals they would share this winter. About the small home out back that he and Katie would live in once they'd been married. The home that still hadn't been built. He hadn't been able to force himself to walk past the little clearing.

Both Shane and Timothy were closing in on where he stood, but he could barely focus on them. A sob shook Samuel's body, and suddenly he didn't want to hold the rifle anymore. He tossed it to Timothy, who caught it with one hand.

"That's *gut*. Now come with me. Come inside and explain what happened to my *dochder*."

"What is there to tell, Timothy? She's dead." The confession shot out of him like the lightning that flashed across the sky. "She's dead, and it's my fault. Isn't that enough for you? Must you have every detail?"

Samuel placed his hands on the railing, certain now of his path. With the agility of someone comfortable on the high catwalks of the silos, he did what he must have known he'd climbed the silo to do. Before anyone could move, he climbed over the rail.

"*Ya*, I do want to know the details. You think a father doesn't deserve to know how his oldest died?" Timothy said. "You owe me that and more."

Timothy's words were like a slap to his face.

"Did you love Katie, Samuel?" The woman's voice was soft, soothing, and nearly a statement.

"Why would you ask me that?"

"I can see that Timothy respects you. The way he argued with Shane shows he cares about you as well, or he'd have allowed Shane to come up here after you alone. I'm guessing you must have loved Katie."

"Of course I loved her!" The words hurt more than they should have. Love shouldn't rip at your chest this way, shouldn't tear and shred.

He and Katie had imagined a life together. Why had it ended so suddenly? Tears clouded his vision and he released the railing with one of his hands, wiped at his eyes.

Everyone moved closer at once.

"Stay back! Why don't you all just stay back? Can't you see I deserve this? I didn't protect her like a husband is supposed to. I should have been the one to die."

"You married her?" Timothy asked, his voice a broken thing.

"Yes. Yes, I did. And she died, and it's my fault, and now I'll pay for that, but I won't go to an *Englisch* jail. I won't do that for you or for anyone else."

"But you will come to my house and explain to her *mamm* what happened. You owe her that, Samuel. You're Rachel's son now, and you owe your *mamm* that." Timothy stepped closer, reached out a hand to the boy, waited for him to grasp it.

Samuel froze there, suspended between his jump and his acceptance of Timothy's grace.

"Take my hand." Timothy waited. He didn't move forward, though now he was so close he could have reached out and grabbed Samuel. He didn't flinch as the rain continued to pelt them.

The metal felt slick beneath his grasp, and Samuel knew that all he had to do was let go.

Letting go would solve everything.

There was no doubt in his mind that the fall would kill him, and then he could join Katie. He could be with her at last, and this pain that had been smothering him for weeks would finally be gone.

But his eyes remained focused on Timothy's hand, calloused, weathered, and open.

Slowly, cautiously, and with tears still pouring down his face, Samuel reached forward, and grasped it.

Chapter 39

FORT WAYNE, INDIANA
LATE JANUARY

JUDGE STEARNS' COURTROOM was nearly empty when Callie entered, followed by Deborah, Esther, Tobias, and Reuben. Mr. and Mrs. Lapp sat with Shane, directly behind the defendant.

"I'm surprised Reuben is here," Deborah whispered. "He's barely left the farm in the three months he's been home, has he?"

"No. Reuben's back to his normal self, which means staying on the farm." Esther smiled. "Though since we've moved into his *grossdaddi*'s house, I believe he's eating a bit better. It seems as if Samuel's process has dragged by so slowly. Reuben's initial arraignment happened so quickly, like a whirlwind we were all caught up in."

Callie leaned forward and peered down at him. When she did, Reuben turned her way, caught her staring, and winked. She jumped back and looked over at Esther, who smothered a laugh.

"Takes time to grow used to Reuben's sense of humor."

"I'll say. The man's as big as an oak tree. Didn't know he had a sense of humor."

Deborah shushed everyone as the bailiff ordered them to all rise for the Honorable Judge Stearns, which they did. Callie resisted the urge to peek back down their row at Reuben again, but her mind was on him, wondering.

Reuben had been released and the charges against him had been cleared. When he'd cleaned up the blood he'd found in the house, he hadn't realized Katie had died. It was true that he hadn't told Shane about the chair he'd straightened up or the blood he'd found. And he'd also burned the rag he'd done the cleaning with, but he'd done it thinking one of them had cut themselves in the kitchen, and he'd hoped all would be fine. He had no reason to believe serious harm had come to either of them. It wasn't until he saw Katie's body in the pond that Reuben realized something far more tragic had happened.

Would Samuel have been found sooner with Reuben's help? Possibly. But Shane chose not to press charges against Reuben, which was something else for Callie to think about.

How did Reuben feel sitting on this side of the partition in a courtroom in Fort Wayne?

Did his heart race as he watched the proceedings?

Did his hands still sweat as if his own life were hanging in the balance?

In fact, why had he decided to come at all?

There was so much about the Amish that Callie still didn't understand, but after that terrible day on the silo, she knew she had to be present for Samuel's sentencing. If only in the hopes that the boy's eyes would no longer haunt her dreams. At least once a week, she still heard him cry, "I won't go to an *Englisch* jail," but in her dreams he didn't accept Timothy's hand.

In her dreams, Samuel didn't trudge back to the farmhouse and explain what had happened at Reuben's farm the days after he and Katie had secretly married. No, instead, he always turned and stared once more into her eyes. Then he let go, and fell backward, into the darkness of the storm.

She always rushed forward, but as often happens in dreams,

she moved slowly, as if her feet were stuck in molasses. And it always seemed as if she knew he was going to let go of the metal rail, knew it a second before he did, but she was never able to stop him or warn Shane or Timothy.

Why couldn't she warn them?

Why couldn't she cry out?

Instead the dream repeated the same hopeless cycle. It had all winter long.

Samuel would stare at her. She would hesitate one second too long, then move slowly and try to reach him. But never in time.

And always she would wake, covered in sweat and shaking, Max pressed against her side.

So when Deborah had mentioned that she and Esther and Reuben and Tobias were coming for the sentencing, Callie had asked to tag along. Deborah had tilted her head, pulled Callie's hands across the counter, squeezed them once, and said, "Of course."

She hadn't asked any questions, and that, too, was proof of how deeply their friendship had progressed.

For today, Callie needed to put an end to her nightmares, whatever the outcome of the hearing. Callie realized how selfish such thinking was as the judge's voice broke through the reverie of her thoughts.

Samuel and Adalyn had moved to a podium in front of the judge. Judge Stearns had been asking after Samuel's health, but the boy only answered in one-word replies. Finally, the judge settled down to the matter at hand.

"Samuel, we have kept you in jail until this hearing because your actions convinced me you were a flight risk. According to the paperwork before me, you have pled guilty to obstruction of justice. Has your lawyer explained to you what that means?"

"Yes, ma'am."

"Has anyone coerced you into pleading guilty or promised you anything in order to persuade you to plead guilty?"

"No, ma'am."

"By pleading guilty, this court will determine your sentence, Samuel. And I will be able to choose a sentence in the bottom quarter of the sentencing range. Has your lawyer explained that to you?"

"Yes, ma'am."

Callie could see now that the boy was visibly shaking. Adalyn Landt put a hand on his back to steady him.

"If you were to plead not guilty, you would be subject to a trial by your peers. In that case you might be found not guilty and freed. Or you might be found guilty and receive a sentence anywhere in the range of the sentence guidelines, from the most lenient to the most extreme."

Samuel nodded.

"With a jury trial, you have a right to an appeal. By pleading guilty, you lose that right to an appeal. Whatever I decide will be your sentence and must be carried out. Has that been explained to you by Ms. Landt?"

"Yes, ma'am."

"All right. Now according to my records, you are nineteen years old and have an eighth-grade education with no prior criminal record. Is that correct?"

"Yes, ma'am."

"According to your testimony, which I have before me, and the coroner's testimony, Katherine Lapp Eby died from a blow to the back of the head. You two were staying in the house on Mr. Fisher's farm. Katie had been standing on a kitchen chair to reach for something on a top shelf, and she fell."

Samuel's head dropped, so Callie could see nothing except the back of his neck. She thought again of how he had looked hanging onto the metal railing, of his insistence that he would not go to an *Englisch* prison.

But he had been in prison for the last three months.

Would he stay there?

Was that what he was thinking about now?

Or was he thinking about that final morning with Katie?

"Is that correct, Samuel?"

"Yes, ma'am."

Judge Stearns sat back, took off her glasses, and wiped them with the sleeve of her robe. With her glasses off, she looked to Callie more like a grandmother and less like a judge. She put the glasses back on, crossed her hands, and sat more erect.

"It's important that you understand why the charges for negligent homicide were dropped, Samuel. Even if you had possessed better first-aid skills, in all likelihood you could not have saved her. Many people, especially young people, wouldn't have known how to stop the bleeding of a head wound."

"I should have known." It was the first thing Samuel had said that wasn't a *yes* or a *no*.

"Perhaps, but that you didn't know wasn't a crime. Negligent homicide is a criminal offense committed by someone whose negligence is the direct cause of another person's death. Your negligence did not cause Katie to die, Samuel. Your crime is based on what you *did*, not on what you *failed* to do. Your crime by the laws of this state and according to this court does not involve Katie's death."

Samuel stood straighter now, and it seemed to Callie that it took all of his strength to do so. As if he were, as she watched, shedding the last visages of childhood and putting on the mantle of being a man. One that for Samuel would begin with the burden of grief and guilt and the loss of the dreams he'd shared with a beautiful young woman.

"It is true you did not call for medical assistance when Katie

314

Lapp, then Katie Eby, was injured. If you had done so, her life could possibly have been saved. This is complicated by the fact that you had a phone. Perhaps you forgot you had that phone. Perhaps, being Amish, you didn't understand how to use the 9-1-1 system. We don't know. No one knows, because no one else was there that day." She paused and for the first time Judge Stearns' gaze sought out Katie's parents.

Turning back to Samuel, she continued. "The coroner's report indicates that Katie died very quickly, so in all likelihood a call would not have saved her. However, it was your civic responsibility to try. It was your civic responsibility to place that call." Judge Stearns cleared her voice and looked down at her paperwork before she continued. "However, that is not the crime you are being charged with.

"The crime you're being charged with is obstruction of justice. You attempted to cover up the crime by depositing Katie Eby's body in Mr. Fisher's pond and by not reporting her death to the proper authorities."

Callie couldn't help it. She shifted slightly on the hard oak bench and glanced at Reuben. Not that he would have noticed if she'd stood up, moved over, and grasped both of his hands. His eyes were glued on what was occurring at the front of the room, his jaw clenched so hard that Callie could see the muscle from his eye to his neck jumping.

And then it occurred to her.

It finally all made sense.

She understood the reason he'd spent thirteen days in the Shipshewana Municipal Jail, the reason he'd refused to admit that he'd known the young couple and given them permission to stay in his home, the reason he was gripping the side of the bench so tightly now Callie feared he might break it.

Reuben counted his life lived—she'd heard him tell Tobias before that he was grateful for the years he'd had. They'd all teased him about it, since he was essentially a young man at only thirty-five. But in many ways Reuben felt his choices had taken him down a different road than most.

"We can't turn back and choose a different path." Wasn't that what he'd said to Deborah?

Reuben had finally admitted to Deborah and Tobias that he hadn't known about Katie's death, hadn't understood what had happened or where Samuel had gone. He'd been as surprised as Deborah and Esther when they'd found Katie's body in his pond that day. And he'd made the instantaneous decision to switch paths with the boy. To allow Samuel to live a life that Reuben was willing to forfeit. He'd also admitted to knowing Samuel's mother, Emma, to promising her that he would look after her son—as if he were his own.

But the *Englisch* system didn't allow for that type of mercy.

"Now I'm going to call a twenty-minute recess. I want you to take that time to consult with your lawyer, to think one last time about what you're doing. If when I return, you remain convinced you want to plead guilty, then I'll hand down my sentence. Do you understand?"

Samuel nodded, and when he turned, Callie saw what she hadn't seen when she walked into the courtroom: His hands were bound by handcuffs in front of him. It was a sight that might have scraped her heart even more, except for the light in his eyes. He didn't look at Katie's parents, but instead paused a moment to make eye contact with Reuben.

When he did, it was as if some of Reuben's strength flowed across those old marble floors to the boy. Callie knew that wasn't possible, didn't believe in such things at all, but she saw Samuel pull his shoulders back and a quiet assurance pass over his features.

Then he turned and shuffled from the front podium back to the defendant's table.

Noticing the same thing Callie had, Deborah grabbed Reuben's arm as soon as Judge Stearns exited the courtroom.

"What was that about?" she asked in a voice louder than she intended. She needn't have worried though, the courtroom was suddenly abuzz with talk.

"*Ya*, cousin. Have you been speaking with the boy?" Tobias stood and stretched, cracking his back as he did so.

"Tell them about the letter, Reuben." Esther placed her hand on her stomach, rubbing in a circular fashion.

"Is the baby moving?" Tobias asked.

"No. It's too early for that, but he seems to be making things uncomfortable already. I believe I need to find the girl's room."

"He? Since when is this baby a he?" Callie demanded.

"Since I started having night sickness. *Mamm* says night sickness means a boy. With Leah I had morning sickness, so maybe she's right. Now back to the question, Reuben. What did your letter to Samuel say?"

Reuben stood, touched Esther's back gently, and in the touch, Deborah thought she could sense that much of the tension from earlier had left him.

"I did send a letter to Samuel. As to what was in it . . . well, I said what needed to be said. I'm glad to see the boy received it. Now if you'll excuse me, I'd like to speak a word with Shane before the judge returns."

Deborah noticed that Esther no longer flinched at Shane's name. Instead she looked over to where he sat and a soft smile crossed her lips. Was all the old bitterness gone then? Was that one of the results of this terrible tragedy? Shane had worked hard on the case and had personally seen to Reuben's release the day they had come back from the Lapp farm.

Esther excused herself to find the restrooms, and Deborah reached over and squeezed Callie's hand as they waited. She wanted to go speak with Katie's parents, but now didn't seem like the time. The Lapps sat up front, shoulder to shoulder, heads bowed as if in prayer.

Twenty minutes later, when the bailiff stood to announce the judge, everyone hurried back to their respective seats.

Deborah didn't know what she expected, wasn't familiar enough with *Englisch* ways to have a clear idea of how the judge would rule, though Shane had explained the process to her. One person judging another was so far outside her concept of things. Shane had said it was similar to what their bishops did.

In Deborah's mind it was completely different though.

The bishops were guided by the Scripture.

Was this judge a Christian? Would she rule with compassion?

Nothing Judge Stearns could say in the next few minutes would bring Katie back to her family. What had happened had been a horrible mistake. Taking away more of Samuel's life, more of his freedom, wouldn't change any of what had already happened.

It wouldn't give the Lapps back their daughter. Nothing could replace that loss. And only God could heal their pain.

"I'd like the defendant, Samuel Eby, to please rise and approach the bench."

Samuel was escorted back in front of the small podium that stood in front of the judge, the same place he had been standing through the morning's proceeding. This time, though, his posture was straight, and when he glanced around, it seemed his gaze passed slowly over Callie, Deborah, and Esther. She noticed his left arm was still shaking, but she gave the boy points for mustering as much courage as he did.

"Your lawyer sent me a message via the bailiff that you wish your plea to remain guilty. Is that correct, Samuel?"

"Yes, ma'am."

"I want you to know that this court has received a petition from Timothy and Rachel Lapp asking that your sentence be commuted. However it's not in my authority to do that. As explained before, I must rule within the bottom quadrant of what the law requires."

"Yes, ma'am." Samuel brushed at his eyes with his arm sleeve.

"Then by the power vested in me by the state of Indiana and the upper district court, I, Judge Beverly Stearns, do find the defendant, Samuel Eby, guilty of obstruction of justice. I sentence you to one year in the state prison, with time served to count toward that sentence."

A groan came from the direction of the Lapps, but Judge Stearns pushed on with her sentencing. "I further sentence you to one thousand hours community service and five years' probation." The judge hit her gavel against her podium, the sound echoing through the chambers, slicing off another portion of Samuel's life. Then the woman stood, gathered her things, and exited the room.

When Samuel turned to face them, Deborah expected to see despair, fear, maybe even anger. What she didn't expect to see was quiet acceptance.

Rachel and Timothy rushed forward, trying to reach Samuel, but the guards stopped them.

"Don't worry, son." Timothy spoke around the guards. "It's nine months. You'll be home before next winter."

Reuben didn't say a word, though he, too, was standing. He met Samuel's gaze over the small group of people, and Deborah knew that something passed between them. She knew because Samuel again drew back his shoulders before nodding once and turning to walk out of the courtroom.

Chapter 40

CALLIE PULLED HER COAT tightly around her as the January wind threatened to whip it away. She didn't mind a bit. The feel of the sun on her face, the scent of fresh air, made it all worthwhile. Why was it that a courtroom felt so claustrophobic? It was only a room, but it seemed like so much more.

If you worked there did you become accustomed to it? Did you grow used to watching lives being shredded and weighed, like Jonas' wheat had been in the fall?

Snow piled up along the street. Callie was experiencing her first Indiana winter, both the joys and the loneliness of it. Fort Wayne was large, but not nearly as large as Chicago. In March, she and Deborah would be traveling to the Windy City together for the quilt exhibit. Bishop Elam had approved the venture at the beginning of the year. Callie wondered what Deborah would think of the busy streets and myriad skyscrapers.

She wondered how *she'd* feel — back in a metropolitan area.

The driver Deborah had hired idled at the curb. Callie had offered to drive everyone, but in the end it was decided they'd need a bigger vehicle. Callie presumed the car behind theirs was for the Lapps.

"Quite a serious look on your face. Tell me you're not planning a shopping trip." Shane placed his hand on her back, letting it rest there as they stood on the steps waiting for everyone else in their party to catch up and find their way outside.

"Shane Black, I would not think about shopping at a time like this." Callie tucked her hair behind her ears and found herself wishing Max were with her. She hadn't spent enough time with her dog the last few days. Perhaps she could talk the driver into stopping at the local pet store on the way out of town. It had one of those treat bars for dogs with the biscuits he liked so much.

"Where did you go, Harper?"

"Hmm?" Callie looked up into Shane's dark eyes, thought of warm chocolate, and felt herself melting.

"I lost you for a minute, and you look as if you're still not back." He reached down and tried to tame her hair, which was flying in a thousand directions. "Maybe you *should* go shopping. Buy yourself a hat."

"Maybe you should buy me a hat!" Callie batted his hand away, felt the color rise in her cheeks when he laced his fingers with hers. The last three months she'd shared many late-night phone calls with Shane and more than one cup of coffee with him at Margie's. She didn't know what to think about her relationship with Shane Black. What she did know was she liked the delicious way her heart tripped when he was around. Maybe what Deborah had told her was right. Maybe time would sort things out, and there really wasn't any rush.

"I think I might do that. I know just the place that sells gorgeous hats."

"Oh, really?"

"Yes, really."

"There you two are. We were looking for you inside." Deborah hurried down the steps, holding onto her dress with one hand and her *kapp* with the other.

Callie pulled her hand out of Shane's grasp as she fumbled in her purse for sunglasses, but she didn't take a step away from him. After the scene in the courtroom, she needed the steadiness of him next to her. The thought occurred to her that he was almost as comforting a presence as Max.

Esther, Tobias, and Reuben completed the circle of friends.

"Do you think Samuel will be all right?" Esther asked. "I can't stand the thought of him being locked up through the spring and summer."

"The boy will make it." Reuben's voice was strong and steady, surprising Callie with its confidence. "He can't turn back and choose a different path."

Shane reached into his pocket for his keys. "Katie's parents will be a help to him. They want him to return to their farm when he's released."

"They consider him their son. After being on that farm, we can see how sorely Timothy Lapp needs a young man around the place." Deborah smiled, but it was weak, just like the winter light shining down on them. "More than that though, I think he had become a part of their family long before he and Katie married."

The words hung there between them for a moment: *married, family, son.* And then another breeze skittered the words away, a horn honked somewhere down the street, and Shane looked at his watch.

"I have a few errands to run, maybe even a little shopping to do." He winked at Callie. "Guess I'll be seeing you back in Shipshe."

"Guess so," Tobias said.

They climbed into the van, Callie choosing a seat near the back, and Deborah settling next to her.

"Want to tell me what that was about?"

"What what was about?"

"Shane Black holding your hand and winking at you."

"Was he holding my hand?"

"And winking at you."

"Maybe something was in his eye."

Callie glanced over at her friend and smiled. Esther and Tobias sat in the seat in front of them, heads together, murmuring. Reuben had opted to ride home with Adalyn, which surprised everyone.

"Were you able to contact Samuel's mother?" Callie asked.

"*Ya.* We phoned her as soon as the judge finished. She's upset, but also relieved that his sentence is less than a year."

"Does she wish she'd come? To see Samuel? I can't imagine not being there for my child."

Deborah turned to study her. "She's prayed for him every night and written letters. Traveling would have been difficult and wouldn't have changed the outcome."

When Callie nodded, she continued. "I remember Emma just barely. She was such a sweet thing. Samuel is her only child, which is why she wrote to Reuben. She wanted someone to watch out for him. Reuben is the one person she contacted occasionally over the years."

"Did Reuben and Emma once love each other?"

Deborah ran her hand down the strings of her prayer *kapp.* "Not in the way you're thinking. Emma was older for one thing, but she did help Reuben. Reuben felt he owed Emma a great debt."

"Great enough to sacrifice his life?"

Tobias turned around. "He didn't believe that would be necessary. Reuben always trusted that things would work out. He believed in—"

"*Gotte's wille?*" Callie asked.

"*Ya.*" Esther smiled. "You're learning our language well."

As they drove away from the courthouse, Callie had an odd

323

feeling, like when it's very cold outside and you take a nice big drink of hot tea. You can sometimes feel the warmness travel down your throat and into your stomach. She felt that way now, felt that combination of opposite extremes at the same time.

Looking at the courthouse, she felt such sorrow over Samuel and the loneliness he would face that she wanted to break down and cry—just lean her head on Deborah's shoulder and sob out a good one. And she knew that Deborah would probably reach into her pocket for the clean handkerchief she always kept, pat Callie on the shoulder, and not say a word about it.

The wind rattled the van, reminding her of the coldness of winter, of how harsh some things could be—like Samuel's sentence, and Callie actually shivered.

In light of the suffering she'd witnessed inside the courthouse, some of the things Callie focused on in her day-to-day life seemed somewhat petty: for example, her feud with Mrs. Knepp, which had continued into the cold dreariness of winter.

She'd also spent long winter nights struggling with her feelings about Shane. She had finally come to terms with the fact that just because she was ready to move on with her life after Rick's death didn't mean she was being disloyal. In some ways it meant she was honoring who he had taught her to be.

Thinking about this, Callie felt a warmness despite the physical cold of winter—it was the warmth of true friendship. Looking around the van, remembering Shane's hand on her back, even thinking of Gavin and Trent and Melinda waiting in Shipshe, the warmth Callie was feeling grew and radiated all the way to her fingers and toes.

Their lives weren't perfect, like the squares in Deborah's quilts, but the way they fit together, the way they cared for one another and supported one another, the way they had all come into each other's lives at the exact time when they needed each other ...

Watching out the window as Fort Wayne fell away and the

Indiana countryside slipped into view, Callie realized there was only one explanation for those things. Their lives were stitched together by a divine quilter, and she could trust the pattern would be a good one.

Epilogue

THE EARLY JULY SUN had finally begun to set when Samuel jumped out of the back of the farmer's pickup truck. He waved, settled his hat, and stared at the farmer's taillights as the man continued to drive down the two-lane road.

Then he began to walk.

Two miles. He would be there before dark.

How many times had he replayed this moment in his mind? But even Samuel's imagination hadn't been able to call up the way the sunset colored the western sky or the smell of the corn growing in the fields — nearing its time for picking. Or Reuben's pond turning from light to dark to midnight blue.

Samuel stopped when he reached the edge of the pond, still a fair ways from the house. He stopped at the place where Katie had first seen the old farmhouse. Taking in a deep breath to steady his nerves, he pulled the oft-read letter from his pocket and smoothed it against his pant leg.

The six months after his hearing had almost been a blessing. He could see that now. He hadn't been ready to face Timothy and Rachel — to tell them he couldn't live on the farm where memories of Katie were so strong. And he didn't want to live in the *Englisch* world. His work in the prison shops and good

326

behavior had quickly reduced the nine months remaining on his sentence to six.

Six months to pray, to seek forgiveness, to try to find peace within himself and a way to continue life once he was released.

He looked down at the words he'd long ago memorized.

> When I began courting the only girl I've ever loved, I didn't know how to control my emotions. Always I loved her, but one moment I would be tender, the next angry about some minor thing. Before we could wed, she died from the sickness gripping our district. I wanted to die with her, but *Gotte* didn't choose that path for me. Your *mamm* was my closest friend and helped me through that dark time, so long ago. Some days the ache is still fresh. Many wonder why I haven't married another, but *Gotte* didn't choose that path for me either. At least he hasn't yet.
>
> I don't know by what design *Gotte* brought you and Katie to my house, or why things turned out the way they did. But I do know it isn't our place to question *Gotte's wille*. And so I extend to you *Gotte's* mercy, my forgiveness, a place of work if you ever need it, and always the hand of friendship.
>
> Samuel, you can't turn back and choose a different path. Live the life you've been given.

Samuel folded Reuben's letter, placed it back in his pocket, and began walking the final distance to the farmhouse. In the distance, he could see the woman, Esther, was standing on the porch, her hands resting atop a very large stomach—no doubt her time to have her child was near. The tall man, Reuben's cousin, was unpinning laundry from the line. He looked like a poplar tree, he was so gangly. Reuben stood next to the barn, brushing a horse with sure, steady strokes. A young girl stood beside him, helping.

Pulling in a deep breath, Samuel walked toward his new life.

Acknowledgments

THIS BOOK IS DEDICATED to my father-in-law, George Robert Chapman, better known to our family as Paw. Paw came into my life the same year that my father stepped into the next. I have no doubt that the Lord smiled on me that year and provided in my hour of need. He has been a blessing beyond measure. We have watched him struggle with Alzheimer's the last several years and the character of Ira Bontrager was my way of painting a tribute to Paw. I remain grateful for every day we share. Paw is a veteran, a patriot, and a very dear man.

I would also like to acknowledge the help of all the wonderful people at Zondervan, whom I could not write without, and my agent, Mary Sue Seymour.

Amy Clipston, Beth Wiseman, Shelley Shepard Gray, and Mary Ellis always provide good counsel when I need it.

Rick Acker, a top-notch author and a Deputy Attorney General in the California Department of Justice, helped with legal questions. Any mistakes are my own.

Janet Schrock, President of the Shipshewana Area Historical Society, provided help in regard to the Palm Sunday Tornadoes, which actually did take place on April 11, 1965. I did take some liberties with the details—no Amish people lost lives in the storm but one Amish man was killed in the cleanup operation.

I could not write a book without the support and help of my pre-readers: Donna and Kristy. Thank you for faithfully reading everything I email you and giving me honest feedback. Cindy and Toot continue to correct my errors in regard to equestrian matters.

The friends I have made in Shipshewana are too numerous to name here. You all have been incredibly supportive and good natured about allowing your town to be the site of murder mysteries. Nothing could be further from the truth. Shipshewana is a lovely, friendly town. I can't wait to go back!

Once again, thank you to my family who make it possible for me to write full-time. My husband, children, mother, sister, and in-laws have been incredibly supportive. It's appreciated more than they can know.

And finally . . . *always giving thanks to God the Father for everything, in the name of our Lord Jesus Christ* (Ephesians 5:20, NIV).

Discussion Questions

1. At the end of Chapter Six, Tobias called Esther's attention to the flowers growing at the edge of the field and along the road. He says, "It was *Gotte's wille* that you look up and see the ones by the pond's edge." As Christians, do you believe we're put in the midst of difficult situations for a reason? Or was it chance that Esther happened down to the pond that morning?

2. In Chapter Nine, Deborah's twin boys were once again in trouble. This is a funny scene, but if they were our children we might not be laughing! Children often do make extra work. Did you think Deborah's solution was too harsh or was it fair? There's no doubt she loves the boys, so why does she saddle them with such chores at such a young age?

3. Ira Bontrager is introduced later in Chapter Nine. If you read the acknowledgement page that follows, you'll see that the book is dedicated to my father-in-law, who has Alzheimer's. Ira also suffers from a form of dementia. What was your reaction to this character? Do you have anyone in your life who has suffered from this disease or a similar disease?

4. In Chapter Eleven, we first see Reuben and Adalyn interact. They seem to be complete opposites, but they will have to find common ground in order to work together. Have you ever had to work with someone that you had nothing in common with? Why does God sometimes put us in situations with people who are nothing like us?

5. In Chapter Thirteen we are given another glimpse into Samuel and Katie's past. What is Samuel's biggest mistake so far? Does he really love Katie?

6. At the end of Chapter Sixteen, we learn the emotion Reuben is struggling with the most — regret. How can regret block our path? What does the Bible have to say about our past?

7. In Chapter Twenty-One, Ira tells Callie about the Palm Sunday Tornadoes. Forty-seven tornadoes actually did strike the Midwest on Palm Sunday in 1965, including the town of Shipshewana. What comfort does Scripture give us to help us through such horrific times?

8. In Chapter Twenty-Four, Callie has a dream. What do you think the dream means? Do dreams mean anything? What does the Bible say about dreams, and does it still apply today?

9. We finally have the reunion scene between Faith and Ira in Chapter Twenty-Nine. Do you believe such reunions are actually possible in this life? Or only in the next?

10. This story ends with an emphasis on grace: Katie's father offers Samuel his hand in grace; Deborah doesn't understand why the legal system can't rule by the same grace the bishops would use to guide them; and Samuel pulls from his pocket Reuben's letter, which offers mercy, forgiveness, and friendship. What place does grace have in our lives?

About the Author

VANNETTA CHAPMAN is author of the bestselling novel *A Simple Amish Christmas*. She has published over one hundred articles in Christian family magazines, receiving over two dozen awards from Romance Writers of America chapter groups. In 2012 she was awarded a Carol Award for *Falling to Pieces*. She discovered her love for the Amish while researching her grandfather's birthplace of Albion, Pennsylvania.

Visit Vannetta's website: www.vannettachapman.com
Twitter: @VannettaChapman
Facebook: VannettaChapmanBooks

A Shipshewana Amish Mystery

Falling to Pieces

Vannetta Chapman

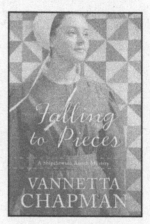

In this first book of a three-book series, author Vannetta Chapman brings a fresh twist to the popular Amish fiction genre. She blends the familiar components consumers love in Amish books—faith, community, simplicity, family—with an innovative who-done-it plot that keeps readers guessing right up to the last stitch in the quilt.

When two women—one Amish, one English—each with different motives, join forces to organize a successful online quilt auction, neither expects nor wants a friendship. As different as night and day, Deborah and Callie are uneasy partners who simply want to make the best of a temporary situation. But a murder, a surprising prime suspect, a stubborn detective, and the town's reaction throw the two women together, and they form an unlikely alliance to solve a mystery and catch a killer.

Set in the well-known Amish community of Shipshewana, *Falling to Pieces* will attract both devoted fans of the rapidly growing Amish fiction genre, as well as those who are captivated by the Amish way of life.

Available in stores and online!

ZONDERVAN®
.com

READ MORE VANNETTA CHAPMAN
IN THESE AMISH COLLECTIONS

ion can be obtained
ng.com
?3
3/15